Stella Duffy was born in L[...] d and has lived back in London since 1986. She has published twelve novels. *The Room of Lost Things* and *State of Happiness* were both longlisted for the Orange Prize, *The Room of Lost Things* won Stonewall Writer of the Year 2008. She has written over forty short stories, including several for BBC Radio 4, and won the 2002 CWA Short Story Dagger for *Martha Grace*. Her eight plays include an adaptation of *Medea* for Steam Industry, *Prime Resident* and *Immaculate Conceit* for the National Youth Theatre. In addition to her writing work she is an actor and theatre director.

Praise for *Theodora*:

'As bold, seductive and passionate as its subject, Theodora is an exuberant performance, a vivid exemplar of how women make history against all the odds'
Jake Arnott

'Stella Duffy's first historical novel will set a benchmark for others to aim for. Magical, moving and inspiring in one, this is easily Duffy's best novel to date – and that's setting the bar pretty high'
Manda Scott, author of the bestselling Boudica series

THEODORA

Actress, Empress, Whore

STELLA DUFFY

virago

VIRAGO

First published in Great Britain in 2010 by Virago Press
Reprinted 2010
This paperback edition published in 2011 by Virago Press

A CIP catalogue record for this book
is available from the British Library.

ISBN 978-1-84408-211-7

Typeset in Bembo by M Rules
Printed and bound in Great Britain by
Clays Ltd, St Ives plc

Virago Press
An imprint of
Little, Brown Book Group
100 Victoria Embankment
London EC4Y 0DY

An Hachette UK Company
www.hachette.co.uk

www.virago.co.uk

For Esther and Jack
with my love

BRITAIN

Atlantic
Ocean

GALLIA

KINGDOM OF
THE FRANKS

R. Rhine

R. Danube

A L P S

Milan

BURGUNDIANS

LIGURIA

Ravenna

ISTRIA

R. Po

TUSCIA

Rimini

Urbino

DALMATIA

R. Tiber

Adriatic Sea

PYRENEES

CORSICA

Rome

Portus

Cuina

APULIA

KINGDOM OF
THE VISIGOTHS

SARDINIA

Naples
Pompeii

LUCANIA

Cordoba

Mediterranean Sea

Cartegena

Carthage

SICILY

Gibraltar

Septem

Hippo

MAURETANIA

NUMIDIA

Justiniana

CARTHAGO

BYZACENA

TRIPOLITANIA

------- Roman Empire before Justinian

LOMBARDS   Peoples

0   200 miles

0   200 km

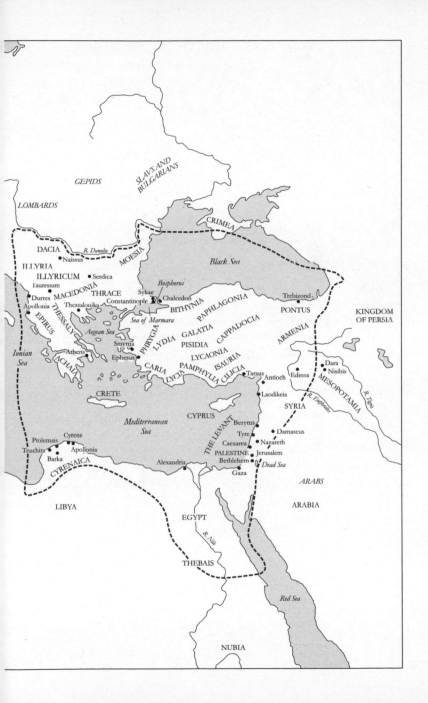

One

'And where is the Pentapolis?'

'Cyrenaica. North Africa.'

'North of . . .?'

'Libya.'

'On what day do we celebrate the feast of our city?'

'May the eleventh.'

'Why?'

'Why?'

'Why do we celebrate that day?'

'It's the day the City was consecrated. Constantine said—'

'Yes, yes. Who has higher status? Consul or General?'

'Status?'

'Consul or General?'

'Ah . . . I . . . General?'

'Are you asking me or telling me?'

'I'm . . .'

'Yes?'

The girl tried to lift her head. She knew if she could only see her older sister, Comito would confirm the answer, but the man was holding her chin tight, his eyes locked on to hers, moving her head was impossible, and she knew too that eventually her teacher would ask a question she could not answer; they'd been going on like this for ten minutes now, sooner or later she would fail and then he would be on top of her and her body would be more his puppet than ever.

'General?'

'No. Down.'

And down she went, to the ground, where he kept her for another twenty minutes as he lectured his troupe on the finer points of military structure. Menander's teaching was thorough, his girls well versed, not only in their routines, but also in the geography, economics and governance of the Empire. Too young to work regularly on the public stages, these girls were worth a great deal as entertainment in private houses; the older ones were highly prized for their conversational abilities as well as their undoubted physical skills. As their eunuch teacher told them, any actress could be taught to dance and sing, to fuck with some skill: those who became truly successful needed intelligence to go with the dance. Other companies might sing prettily and recite their Greek and even Latin poems with flawless accents, his girls could actually converse with the men they entertained. Theodora was not yet old enough to be required to do more than dance and tumble, but – like all the girls in the rehearsal room – she would be one day. Having created chaos in today's class, she'd been singled out for questioning. Menander believed that those who failed in matters of the mind were invariably punished in the body.

Twenty minutes later Theodora was swallowing the sobs, every muscle shivering in pain. Her left leg was ramrod straight behind her, stretched into a back split, her right leg pulled up and across her torso so the foot reached past her left shoulder. Once he'd placed her in this position, Menander bent her forward so her chest and face, leaning on the right leg, were pushed into the ground. At which point their master and teacher laid the full weight of his own body across her narrow back, stretching her frame to its limit, trying – and, as always, failing – to break her will. He wanted Theodora to cry in apology. Eleven years old, and triple that in strength, she gave him nothing but the acceptance of her pain, exactly as she had done for the past six years.

When Theodora's father Acacius died, killed by the body-ripping claws of his own bear, her mother had assumed she would fall back on the faction her family had supported for generations, grateful for their charity. Like every other citizen of the Empire, Theodora's family paid allegiance to either the Blues or the Greens, the two parties that ran so much of Constantinople's life, from local police forces, fire departments and small-time mercenaries, right up to the military and government policy makers. It made sense then, when Acacius died, for Hypatia to form a new partnership with another man of the Greens. Basianus was also an animal-trainer, a good enough man. The bear-keeper's widow thought it wise for the younger man to take on his predecessor's job, both at home and in the Hippodrome. Unfortunately, the Greens' leader was a true businessman, he knew someone else who would pay to take on the chief bear-keeper role, and Hypatia's second husband was denied her dead husband's job. The widow, her three daughters, her new husband and – not to anyone's surprise – the baby on the way were, literally, hungry for support.

Theodora was five, as old as the new century, born in the city of Constantine less than two hundred years since it ceased to be Byzantium and became the holy city of Constantinople, the centre of the new Rome, the sparkling gem in a Christian crown. In the west the Empire was parcelled out among Barbarian kings, some of them not even Christian. In the east there were the constantly disputed Persian borders and Sassanid rulers, none of them Christian. Hers was a century that, so far, felt very much like the one before, not least because the Emperor Anastasius, the frugal old man with

3

mismatched eyes who had banned animal fights in the Hippodrome – much to his people's displeasure – continued in his
opposition to the Council of Chalcedon's decrees concerning
the nature of the Christ. Theodora was too young to know
the intricacies of a schism born at the ecumenical council fifty
years earlier, intricacies spinning out from the interpretation of
a single word to questions of national identity, but even she
had noticed that her parents' friends, and the dancers in their
rehearsal breaks, and the man who preached on the corner
near their house, not to mention the monks who had recently
physically attacked each other for their different beliefs, all
took the matter very seriously indeed. Many people, and more
of the religious, agreed with the prevailing Western orthodoxy
that the Christ was two in one, both fully divine and fully
human; the Emperor Anastasius on the other hand, along with
many key figures of faith in the Eastern branches of the
Church, was confident in his belief that whatever humanity
the Christ had possessed was subsumed by his more vital
divinity. In a city founded by a man obsessed – on his
deathbed at least – by faith, in a religion needing to formalise
its beliefs as it scooped up more and more of the Western
world, the core notion of just how divine the Christ truly was
could not have been more engaging to the population. All
across the City, sailors and soldiers, tradesmen and civil servants, debated the true nature of the Christ as they drank their
wine late into the night. Poor women in shared kitchens considered the safety of the Persian border and the vexed question
of whether Mary was Theotokos – mother of God, or Chris-
tokotos – mother of the Christ. Those scrutinising the market
stalls and buying goods from the shops that lined the porticoes
of the long Mese fretted over the influx of non-Christian
refugees still fleeing Goth kings in the west, and everyone
bemoaned the Emperor's parsimony, his refusal to build them

4

a fine new church. At the age of five, God was everywhere Theodora looked.

In their tiny home meanwhile, with no pennies to pinch and far more pressing concerns than the nature of the Christ or His mother, while the new baby in her belly kicked her awake, Hypatia seethed that the Greens, the faction she and her late husband had been born into, had failed to take care of them. Having been an acrobat herself, her husband having died in abject pain, she'd wanted anything but the stage for her three daughters. Now she lay awake and planned their first public performance.

There is a break in the racing. Hypatia has bribed the tall Vandal couple who usually perform at this point – a slapstick display of tumbling pornography loved by the crowd, those who are watching at least, those not in a hurry to piss or eat or place bets – and she has taken their twenty-minute slot. For a fortnight she has been rehearsing her three daughters. Even Anastasia, just three, has been drilled in steps and gesture. The girls look perfect, white robes down to their bare feet, garlands of fresh flowers on their hair, beetle-dye to redden their lips and cheeks. They walk out into the centre of the Hippodrome. It is early in the programme, there is maybe a third of the capacity crowd of thirty thousand. Ten thousand people, though, could be any number to a child of five. Her back to the carved owl on the southern obelisk, Theodora looks past the Nekra Gate, hoping to see Hagia Sophia, the church she loves because her father loved it, but the bench seats rise too high. Men sit on these seats, men of all ages and rank, men used to the smell and sound of this place. The girls have been to the Hippodrome before of course, to see their father work, to watch from the sidelines, to follow him through the maze of passageways and rooms dug out beneath the wood and sand stage, but they have never sat in the audience itself, and they have not stood here before, in the place of performance. They have not held the crowd before. Unfortunately, they are not holding the crowd now.

Hypatia has rehearsed them in what they must do. Make their way to the centre. Acknowledge the empty Kathisma, where the Emperor would stand were he here – and they are lucky he is not. Turn to each of the four directions: east for Jerusalem, west for Rome, north and south for the furthest reaches of the Empire. Then, the girls having calmed the noisy crowd, forced their silence and attention, Hypatia will make her case to the Greens. The same woman, the same three daughters, the new husband who should be reinstated in the old husband's job. What could be simpler? Except that the girls do not have the crowd's attention, and when she tries to speak for her family, Hypatia's voice does not carry. She opens her mouth but, faltering with nerves and mounting anger, her words emerge as a croak, a gasp, and then nothing. She turns back to the girls, nods that they should take up their supplicant pose again. They do so; the theatrical language is well known to this crowd. Skilled in interpreting chorus gesture, they didn't need to hear the mother's monologue to know the daughters were pleading.

Asking for what? yells one rude voice.

Too young even for you, answers another.

I'd give her a go, says a third: your oldest girl, with the lovely hair.

Take the mother, returns the first voice, at least she'll know what to do, and we all know – the crowd wait, aware the shout is directed at a famed pedagogue in their midst – you're a hopeless teacher.

A roar of laughter, applause for the heckler, even less attention for the four at the centre of the ground. Time passing, the races will start again soon, three little girls in white dresses and wilting flower garlands holding supplicant poses, a pregnant mother begging for her family, no one listening.

And then the middle girl steps out and takes up another pose. One she has seen her father take up time after time, in rehearsal, in training, and on this very ground. The little sister catches on quickly: this is a game they play every day at home; Anastasia is the bear, Theodora the keeper. Comito is shocked, Hypatia furious, as the little sisters begin to play. Theodora raps Anastasia on the back of the head with her knuckles, the 'bear' turns and growls, the rich men in the front seats smile, someone grins, another laughs. The bear lumbers in a confused circle. Theodora mimes a stick, poking it from behind, whispers directions to Anastasia, who – as always – is happy to do as she is told. Laughter, as Theodora will learn to anticipate, picks its way through the crowd, at first faltering, and then catching in an eager fire. When a critical mass of attention is finally reached, Hypatia steps forward again, the girls once more take up their pose – though not before Theodora has demanded a round of applause with a saucy bow – and the mother pleads her family's case. And even so, she is rejected. It is too late. Her dead husband's job has gone to another man. The leader of the Greens is adamant – there is nothing to be done, it is over.

She should have left it there. Hypatia knew the rules, the gesture had been daring enough, brave enough. But something of Theodora's spirit – a spirit Hypatia was always trying to dampen, knowing it was dangerous in any young girl – had infected her. She grabbed Anastasia's hand, pulled all three children right across the arena and stood instead before the Blues. The girls in their same pose. The mother with the same speech. The Greens behind them silent in disbelief, the Blues in front, cat-calling and whistling to their rivals at the audacity of the bear-keeper's woman. The leader of the Blues, knowing exactly what he was doing, acknowledged Hypatia's entreaty, complimented her on her well-trained daughters, the elder one's beauty, the little one's prettiness, the middle girl's – he paused, he too was an orator – the middle girl's passion. Then, not speaking now to the woman and her daughters at all, but addressing himself directly to the callous, uncaring – a pause again before uttering the worst of epithets – 'uncivilised' Greens, he offered aid to the woman and her family. Said there was, of course, with the Blues, always with the Blues, hope for an ambitious man, alms for an honest woman, succour to children in need. He gave her new husband a job. After more than two hundred years with the Greens, champions of the artisan, the merchant, the working man, Theodora's family joined the more conservative Blues. And Theodora learned her first lesson in stagecraft. An actress may be as beautiful as nature, or makeup, will allow, but if the audience don't care, there is no point.

Back beneath the Hippodrome, in a rehearsal room that smelt strongly of horse-racers and charioteers, of caged bears and lions, Menander the dance-master ensured his protégée Theodora knew exactly how much he cared. In the six years since that scene in the Hippodrome, six years under his tutelage, Theodora had often seen her teacher angry, but this morning was worse than most. She knew his head ached from the wine he'd had last night. She'd served the wine and, because she was tired, as were all the girls, and because the night was always easier when Menander slept deeply, she did not water his wine; not much, not after the first few glasses, once he had a taste for it. And so they had a good night's sleep without singing or lectures, or worse, from their teacher and his friends. When the girls had finished work yesterday, Menander had warned them today would be hard, there was a lot to get on with, much ground to cover, and the other girls were grateful for Theodora's actions. Glad she had poured the undiluted wine and given them a quiet night of rest. A quiet night she was paying for now.

Theodora had had a bad day. Arms and legs uncoordinated, her body as stiff and stupid as her feeble mind – Menander's words, but she was always her own worst critic, and Theodora knew her teacher was right. She was among the least skilled of the girls in dancing, with a singing voice more frail than most: that was not news to any of them, but this morning Menander had been a bear with a sore head and Theodora understood bears only too well, she'd known what was coming, tried merely to hold it off as long as she could. Their eunuch master was a respected teacher and a severe taskmaster. For once Theodora had realised that making the others laugh would not work. Sometimes it did – occasionally coaxing an unwilling smile was a way to deflect his disappointment in her small frame, her dark colouring, her sallow skin. Some days she left practice with no scars at all, just the joy of having pleased her mentor, but those days were rare. And not today.

There was a moment, quite early in the rehearsal, four somersaults in, none of them perfect, each one executed more nervously than the last, each one a little more uncertain, a lot more faulty, when she heard his first groan. Then, not long after, she slipped, pushing a leg out of line, and jolted one of the older girls, who knocked the youngest, who fell flat on her perfect face, a frail nine-year-old screaming in pain. That was enough to send him into a rage. Understandable, too. Theodora knew she was not the prettiest – that was her little sister's role, Anastasia was delicate and small and so sweet. Though slightly less sweet now, with swollen lips and her eye cut from the fall. All Theodora's fault. She knew what was coming, let her muscles go slack, and prepared her mind in the twenty seconds it took Menander to limp across the sandy floor and reach her, grab her by her hair, wrench her to him as the other girls stepped back, ducking away from his anger, leaving Theodora to soak up their teacher's fury.

He slapped her first: that was normal. Hit her across the back and buttocks with his stick: that was normal. As was the list of questions, the reminders of their place as dancers, as baby whores to the great and the good. Then, using her hesitation as his excuse, he held her down for fifteen minutes. Twisting her into shape he explained to Theodora, and to the others, what he was doing. Pointing out where her muscles were too tight, her legs too stiff, that she needed to loosen, to let go, to be free in her body and then her energy would flow. She was too proud, he said, her head so high, her back so tight, too fond of making others laugh, never knew when to shut up, when to just work, to let it be about the whole, not just about her. She was too fond of being watched. Given her family background, her stature, her colouring, she was damn lucky to have a job at all. He would teach her to yield, cede, it was his duty to her as teacher and mentor, he would be failing her if he did not, it would only be harder later, when she was in the chorus and the director gave instructions she could not follow because she was too fond of standing out. And, if Menander could not get through that wilful mind, then he would start with muscle and bone. Her flesh would make her learn.

Theodora fought back, resisted him, she fought because the other girls did not. And still Menander forced himself on her, pushing her body into position, laying himself out across her back to keep her still, keep her in place. She could not move beneath his weight; big and strong for a eunuch, Menander had spent his life fighting the constraints of the biology his own parents had sold him into, he would make Theodora overcome her physical limitations too. Eventually she grew silent. It was permissible to fight back once, it was what everyone expected of her. Twice and she would be in real trouble. Three times and she would be out of a job. Theodora readily acknowledged she could be wilful, disobedient, was merely an adequate dancer, with an ordinary voice, good only for acrobatics and comedy, but she had always been responsible and she was also ambitious. She could not afford to lose this job.

One ear ground into the sand and dirt, the other twisted beneath Menander's flat palm, she listened to him training the other girls. Their rehearsal went on; she would have to make up practice in the brief break. This was punishment and lesson. The girls, encouraging each other, were talking to her, their coded messages and shouts, apparently intended for one or the other of them but really for Theodora in the dust beneath their teacher's body. Menander counted out instruction, method, placement, action, talking the girls through one scene and into the next, taking his team through their everyday paces. Theodora had displeased him and so here she was, exactly as he said she would be, as he had threatened, promised, so many times before. He whispered she was not as pretty as the other girls, she needed other skills. He would make sure she knew those skills, that her body knew those skills, that she – as he had himself – would overcome nature's limits.

Theodora's older sister Comito was already being considered for the public stages at the Hippodrome and the Kynegion amphitheatre, she was known for her voice and her beauty. Little Anastasia was so fine and delicate – or she would be once the cold water had taken down the swelling on her lip and the makeup woman had painted her face for the evening. Their friend Chrysomallo would never be as good a dancer as the others, but she had that long, golden hair, and a pretty voice. Helena had done well today too, and the half-dozen others in

11

the company. Everyone had done well but Theodora who, with her lack of skill and her big mouth and her ignorance, had done this to herself. Ending up posed in pain beneath the body of the man she feared and loved. She wanted only to please and daily found herself fighting instead, forced to yield instead.

Later, Theodora lay on her stomach as Comito massaged oil into her sister's aching back and cramped thighs.

'Sometimes I think you do it on purpose.'

'Do what?'

'Annoy Menander. To get his attention.'

'Yes, you're right. A six-foot, fifteen-stone ex-acrobat eunuch lying on top of me, while I eat dirt – that's exactly the kind of attention I crave. Careful!' she shouted as Comito dug into a particularly knotty muscle in her calf. 'It hurts.'

'It's supposed to.'

'Like everything else I have to endure.'

'You're such an actress. You could just work harder and have him sit on you less.'

'I'm sure he'd rather go and sit on his Armenian.'

Both girls laughed then, at the idea of their harsh teacher and his supposedly even tougher boyfriend, the eunuch soldier.

'You know I work hard, but it's different for me. I don't have a beautiful voice like you, and I'm not sweet like Anastasia. If I'm not careful I'm going to end up as one of the swimming whores.'

'You'll never be a swimming whore, you're not pretty enough.'

Comito wasn't being unkind. The girls who wore thin silk robes and danced in the water when part of the Hippodrome was flooded for their shows, were much less dancers than beautiful models for the men to ogle, more lovely once the water rendered their expensive silk costumes practically transparent.

'God, you're right. Can't sing, can't dance, not pretty. I don't fit.'

Comito smiled, digging her thumbs into the knotted muscle, her hands keeping time with her words. 'You don't fit because you don't want to. You wouldn't want to be just pretty, you'd rather stand out, make them laugh.'

'Nothing wrong with comedy.'

'Not at all.'

'It's dull, all that looking lovely and keeping quiet, and there are so many funny things, absurd things.'

'You don't need to point them out every time.'

'I can't help it. Menander hates it when I get laughs, says it distracts from the show.'

'It does – and it's useful. He knows that, every audience needs a break from even the best singer, the loveliest dancers. We're just a sideshow to the main event, when they want a break from the racing: the old men go to piss, the young men place their bets.'

'So you singers are their sideshow and I'm yours?'

'You are when you make your performance about the laughs. It's good, it works. You just need to judge when to speak out and when to stay silent. Menander's only another man, little sister, don't worry so much about what he thinks.'

'I fight him. I argue more than any of you.'

Comito wiped her hands on her rehearsal gown and helped Theodora sit up. 'That's just another way of begging him to see you. None of us is perfect all the time, not even me, but he hardly ever shouts at me, because he knows I don't care. I'll do my best, not his. If you didn't care so much about gaining his praise, you'd get a lot less blame as well.'

Two

An hour later, walking away from the rehearsal space beneath the Hippodrome, Theodora broke away from her sisters. Comito and Anastasia were both keen to hurry home, to grab whatever they could find to eat, have a quick rest and then return, ready for a final rehearsal before the evening's show in a private home overlooking the Sea of Marmara. Theodora told her sisters she wanted a moment to rehearse alone. Anastasia, the tiny and delicate little one, had the appetite of a dock worker – if Theodora didn't care to eat and rest before they were called again, then all the more for her. With too many mouths to feed with their stepbrother and sisters, and too little to feed them on, the household did not do leftovers, and certainly not for girls who upset their teacher and bruised their little sister, accident or not.

Comito knew Theodora was lying, but she also knew that after a day like today, so close to tears with every shout and blow Menander directed at her, Theodora would risk even their mother's wrath to have some time to herself. Comito knew Theodora ached for room to spread her body, and peace in which to think, neither of which was available in their three rooms, a mile and a half from the city centre, in the jumble of half-finished, overcrowded slum houses between the old Constantine Wall and the Golden Gate. It had been a hard day, a hard week, and tonight's private performance was very important to Menander; food was the last thing Theodora

14

cared about right now, and anyway, if she found herself hungry later, there would always be a passing worker she could beg for a share of his bread dole. Theodora might be too smart-mouthed for their teacher, but it was a mouth that could charm and cajole a coin from even the hardest-hearted patrician, hidden behind the curtains of the sedan chair that carried him from one place to another without ever having to touch the polluted ground.

It was the end of a warm spring day, and there was excitement about the coming City festival. The May holiday would mean a day off school for the children and for some workers and slaves. For just as many though, it meant more to do in prep-aration – local police needed to be ready to come between Greens and Blues when the rows broke out, after the young men had spent the day drinking; in the churches and monas-teries priests were gearing up for the long round of extra ceremonies to perform, more masses than usual to bless the great City; Palace staff could expect to work double-length days over the next week as they prepared for the celebratory and thanksgiving processions. Theodora made her way back through the extra-busy crowd. When she was once again near the Hippodrome gates, she stopped to look over the people's heads at the obelisk, silently giving her regular greeting to the owl carved halfway up the ancient stone. She had few clear memories of her father, but cherished one of sitting high on his shoulders, being carried through the crowds, the big man explaining if she ever lost her way she need only look out for the owl. Theodora no longer believed in that safety, but she trusted in the owl anyway. From there she made her way over the City's second hill and down to the narrow streets lining the Golden Horn. It was a less direct route to her destination, but easier this way, in the alleys and lanes, to avoid the excess of

15

people. Even stage girls were not that common a sight in streets paved by men for the feet of men, crowded with partisan lads who cheered their teams, jeered each other, and did far worse to young girls when drink had stirred them enough. Foreign men were also thick on the streets, dressed in the strange clothes and stranger haircuts of Goth and Herule mercenaries, come to Constantinople looking for work and all too often finding wine and argument. Theodora knew exactly how to perform for these men when they spent money on a show; she was less keen on the street performances they sometimes demanded for free.

At the narrowest point of the Golden Horn, where the ferries travelled all day and much of the night across the stretch of water to Sykae, she climbed back up the first hill right to the edge of the Palace wall, sneaking past sentries who were more interested in throwing dice than they were in girlish shadows. Finally she came out into a short lane that led close to the Chalke, the main entrance to the Imperial Palace. It was safe to ignore the beggars and supplicants thronging there, these refugees had far more to worry about than a girl out on the streets alone.

The warm day often meant a cold night ahead for the street-dwellers crowded between the Chalke, the Senate and the Baths, the beggars who supposedly did not exist in this perfect City of the perfect Empire. A chill and potentially illegal night if they could not find an administrator to agree charity, or a penitent sinner hoping to placate the Christ who believed rich men were the camel's impossible hump in a needle's tiny eye. If that didn't work here – practically on the doorstep of Hagia Sophia – then the hungry many could always try further up the Mese, heading towards Constantine's statue, where Christianity was diluted by the nationalities of the market traders, and any number of other gods' blessings could be employed to charm aid from the superstitious. These newcomers to the City – traders fallen on hard times, disabled soldiers damaged in war, young chancers with nothing left to chance – had discovered that it was wise first to make their case at the meeting point of Church and State.

Theodora blessed herself as she passed the cripples and the begging children. She had work, she was learning her skills, she earned her own keep, and some extra to help the family. She knew she was lucky, her mother and stepfather made it very clear – Menander told her so several times daily. There but for the grace of God. She came eventually to a side entrance of Hagia Sophia, the hundred-year-old church that would have been far older but for the riots a century before, riots Theodora understood only as a laugh-line, a final gag, certain to cheer the Hippodrome crowds as they waited for the next race, guaranteed to bring down the Kynegion house, just as the rioters had laid low the Great Church, making way for this new sanctuary. Great enough for her current need.

Theodora stood at the side door, an entrance she'd found by chance several years ago, a door left unlocked more often by accident than intent. She tried the latch, felt her tight shoulders and chest begin to ease as the heavy carved wood opened into the dark of the building and made her way forward; silent, slow, cautious, moving into the heady scent of spent incense and a solid wall of other people's lingering prayer, their pain and desire forced into the marble and the stone by sheer strength of want, entreaties of hope and despair trapped in windows of translucent alabaster. Always, in this building, Theodora felt other people's pain and shook it off to concentrate on her own need; now she climbed on shaking legs, with stiff muscles, to the gallery, the place of women, unlit and quiet.

*

Her father is standing by the animal and even though he is so close to the claws and the teeth, close enough for the child to touch the beast's fur if she reaches out her hand, he takes a step closer still. Holding her tight in his arms now, he lifts her high and swings her on to his shoulders. She can smell his hair; it is the smell of his work, of cages, stables, animals, of this bear. Her father spends his days with the animals, and his hair smells of this bear. The bear is bigger than her father, her father is bigger than the other men working here, in these dark rooms beneath the Hippodrome: he is tall and wide and dark-skinned. Her mother shouts at him in the late evening, tells him to wash himself, he looks like a Barbarian. The little girl has her father's colouring, like him she is strong, he and Theodora are special, they are the same, just the two of them. He holds her tight on his shoulders, she is used to being here, good at balancing, everyone says so already, that she will be a fine acrobat. She would like that, loves to watch the acrobats rehearse, even when their master shouts in anger and screams at them to do it again and again, to be better, better, she loves it, the leaping and jumping and flying. These tumblers can fly on the ground, make a loaded catapult of a wooden floor. She copies them sometimes, at home, when her mother is not watching, or when she is pushing them at their lessons, letters and numbers and more letters – their mother who hates her body for not yet providing a son, who curses her flesh that is so female it produces only girl children, who knows how hard it is to be a girl child and will claim education for her daughters if it is the last thing she does. Education, and ridding them of the stink of the circus. Hard to do when your husband is the chief animal trainer, the only bear-keeper, and famous for it too, but not impossible – other women have climbed a little, and a little is better than nothing. Her girls will read and write, they will speak their Greek better than the street, and, if she has any say in the matter, they will have Latin too. Above all, they will not be actresses. At least then she will be able to find husbands for them, marry them legally, marry them out of the stink of theatre. Meanwhile though, the dark and small Theodora sits proud on Acacius' shoulders, one still-chubby fist gripping his hair, the other waving proudly to her father's assistants who comment on her smile, her loud voice from the tiny frame, her deep-set eyes. She is just five years old, and already she feels the power she has over an audience.

Then something happens. She has been laughing, enjoying the height and the strength she feels up here and, with no warning, the place of safety on her father's shoulders disappears, she thinks he must be playing, this is what it feels like when he throws her in the air, when suddenly there is nothing beneath her, soon he will lift his strong arms and catch her. Soon. But not now. She is thrown up and back and there are no arms catching and she falls smack against the wooden wall behind them, a fistful of her father's hair in her hand. There is screaming, loud, wailing screaming, from her mouth and also from his, and then the screams are coming from all over the building, from all the others, watching in sick horror. And though someone runs to pick her up, and though adult hands try to shield her eyes, and though it is over almost before it has begun, Theodora sees the bear, her father's bear, the bear he loves best of his beasts, she sees the claws drag through his skin as easily as her mother pulls a stick across the Marmara shore, writing their letters in the sand. Her father's skin parts as the wet grains do, falling back, there and then not there, swiftly displaced, but where the sand moves allowing the water to fill the narrow trenches that spell alpha, beta, gamma, her father's flesh is opened and it is his blood that wells up, spilling over. Three minutes later his heart has pumped him dry into the sand and dirt beneath the Hippodrome. There is no tide to wipe him clean and begin again.

*

19

Theodora lay in the gallery of Hagia Sophia, her skin clammy, head aching. She had not meant to fall asleep, certainly had not meant to see again in vivid dream the picture she pushed away when awake. Her dead father, his face twisted in pain, the bear's claws and teeth, the blood running through the creature's fur, running down to the child, blood on Theodora's hands and face. And, in her five-year-old's mind, all that blood was her fault, because she was on his shoulders and she must have distracted him and she had been there beneath the stage with her father when she should have been at home learning how to be a lady with her mother and sisters. Her mother had never said so, never would, but Theodora knew it had crossed her mind too, more than once. She shook her head, trying to dislodge the image, to regain the sense of security she'd felt as soon as she lay on the gallery floor, letting her aching limbs and back sink into the cool stone, as gentle a touch as Comito's oiled hands.

At the thought of her sister, Theodora's body went cold. She looked to the translucent windows and saw that it was dark outside, the only light from the torches lighting the Palace and the lamps the soldiers carried in the street. An owl screaming in the Palace garden told her she was late. She had no idea how long she had slept, no idea how much time had passed, but she knew it was hours rather than minutes. She was late, and she was in trouble.

Three

The first thing Menander did was punch the wall so that he did not punch her face. One bruised dancer was enough. Then, with his bleeding-knuckle hand, he held her chin so tight she thought her jawbone would crack. He wrenched her head up to look directly into her eyes and, without saying a word, promised fierce punishment. Then he pushed her over to the makeup woman, an old actress herself, who had been waiting with the other girls while Theodora was sleeping and missing their final rehearsal, while she was dreaming and missing their last preparations, while she ran through filthy crowded streets, dodging beggars and soldiers alike, hating herself and the dreams, and the stupid hope of a different life that made her weak and scared and, right now, very late.

Comito stood centre stage, her long smooth arms extended from a straight back, a perfectly angled neck. The gold and blue mosaic on the wall behind her made a perfect backdrop, depicting four semi-naked golden girls, one for each season, with the smiling, joyous Christ above them, holding the year together. The audience had left their plundered food some time ago. Plates and empty glasses were quickly cleared by silent servants, new wines poured while they waited for the dance master to present his girls. Then, finally, after the brief delay, with Theodora shoved into place, Menander was ready. He knew some of the audience, men he'd befriended over many years working with acting and dancing troupes. He would never be invited to sit among them, but they were men who valued his services, respected him as a eunuch if not as a man, understood he offered a good evening's entertainment, well worth the fee. Their host's family was originally from Illyricum, his grandfather's money made long ago, trading goods in return for the safe passage of Imperial armies, an inherited fortune their patron now spent in night after lavish night on entertainment, fantasy made true, the want of nothing. This particular businessman was known for his generosity, and not one of his friends had turned down his invitation. Menander's work was famed; the guests were delighted to accept their wealthy friend's gift of a private viewing. They would offer favours later in turn – a safe ship's passage here, a voice in the Senate there, this new Christian Rome thriving on the give and take of friendly men as readily as the old one had ever done.

The girl at the centre of the dais was speaking, her voice elegant, low, perfectly modulated. Despite her youth she had the strength to be heard from the orchestra to the farthest height of the Hippodrome benches; in this room she was holding back all the amplification and none of the passion. The men dragged their gaze from the graceful folds of fine cloth barely skimming her shoulders, breasts, hips, thighs and forced themselves, out of politeness, to watch her blue eyes, to study her lightly tinted lips, follow the gentle sweep of her soft blonde hair as she recounted the story of Penelope. They knew exactly what was coming; of all the scenes this troupe told, the Penelope story was one of their favourites – the waiting wife patiently sitting out long cold years with only her women to keep her company. Comito spoke well, sang even better and was applauded after her opening oration. The night had turned cold, but there were plenty of deep, soft cushions, the room was both warmly heated and well ventilated, so that even with the copious quantities of wine, no one was ready to sleep, not yet.

The audience were happy, his girls knew their parts. Menander had drilled them day after day for this, now he could relax. Comito's speech became song, became one dance and then another. The men were entranced. Even Theodora wasn't spoiling anything at the moment: keeping her place in line, she waited for the climactic moment and then took centre stage to tumble and leap with no care for her bones or her muscles, with abandon and joy in the ever-increasing space between floor and ceiling, both holding her steady. Helena picked up amused laughter with her comedy song, not the belly laughs Menander might have hoped for, but if her timing left a little to be desired, none of the other girls had her perfectly formed breasts, and he knew his audience well enough to understand that by this stage in the evening the gentlemen preferred comely to comedy. Golden-haired Chrysomallo and the pretty Claudia were perfect angels on either side of the dais-turned-stage, having held their positions for over forty minutes without once wavering. And delicate little Anastasia, playing Penelope's dreamed child, leaned elegantly into her eldest sister, their voices blending in sibling harmony. A last song, the whole group as one, a final dance with a few acrobatic flourishes from Theodora, then their bow, and the end of the night, and his payment in gold coin. Nothing could go wrong. Until it did.

Anastasia, being the smallest of the girls, was positioned right at the front of the group, and was therefore easy to reach when one of the audience members, over-zealous in his approval, brimming with food and wine and the thought of what was yet to come, reached out a strong arm to pull the girl to him, the better to enjoy her charms, to see her more clearly through eyes reddened with wine. In response Anastasia did the one thing

23

their mother had trained her three daughters to do as long as they could remember. So many possibilities of harm, both at work and in the City, Hypatia had drilled the girls: if grabbed, bite, scream, kick – all three at once, if possible. Anastasia bit. She sank her teeth into the fat hand that held her and she did so with force and anger. The man roared, his companions laughed at first and then, when they saw that the sharp little teeth had drawn blood, there was a silence. A yawning, fearful silence from the performers on the makeshift stage, and a growing, furious rage from the bitten man, backed up by the anger of his friends.

Theodora stepped into the gaping breach between stage and seat. With a leap and a loud cry that Menander would have beaten her for there and then if he had not been stuck at the back of the room, she ran to the dining table, jumping over the laps of the few men who were still seated, to pick up a knife that had fallen to the floor and been unnoticed by a servant who would later be punished for the mistake. Then, before the audience could see what she was holding and become even more agitated, Theodora rounded on the horrified Anastasia, her mouth wide with the cry all three girls had heard every day of their lives. The call of the bear-keeper, lion-trainer, animal-master. The fierce shouts and sharp yells, descending to the low-pitched whistle and cajoling whisper with which their father, and now their stepfather, entertained the crowds who came to see him put the great creatures through their paces. Comito caught on immediately and, pulling Helena tightly by the hand and forcing her to join in, began to play a patrician gentleman, fat with good living, disappointed in his wife, life and career – a character fairly close to many of the men before them – and happy to enjoy a session of animal-baiting as release. It only took a few words for Anastasia to realise her role – it had, after all, been one of the first games she had ever played, one of the few, shadowy memories she still kept of the father who'd been part of her first starring role. She roared, she snapped her dangerous teeth, she advanced on Theodora, who ducked beneath her little sister's outstretched arms and clawed fingers, to come up behind her and hit the girl-as-bear lightly on the top of her head with the knife handle. Anastasia took on the bear's bewildered look of pain and sorrow and their audience relaxed a little: seeing the girl punished with the knife handle, even if only in jest, accorded with their sense of propriety. Sensing the happier mood, Anastasia advanced, Theodora parried, back and forth, all the while offering asides to the relaxing audience. She commented on the excessive girth of the patrician Comito was now playing – funnier still because everyone knew the audience had spent half the night ogling Comito's tall, lean and very fine body, and they all knew Theodora was really mocking the barrel shape of their evening's host, with a perfect alliterative rhyme about the 'lard-loaded lech'. While acrobatically fighting off the bear's advances, her twists and turns applauded by the other girls in order to encourage applause from the real audience, she stage-whispered a lewd story about Chrysomallo and Claudia, describing over her shoulder, under her arm, and once, bent double, through her legs, the series of shocking pictures that had been running through their pretty but empty golden heads as they surveyed the room all night. Both girls stayed stock-still in their statue poses, one white with fear that she, with no skill in anything but dance and still-mime, would also be called on to improvise and help ease the tension, the other embarrassed by Theodora's Hippodrome-coarse language, suffused with a deep pink blush that clashed horribly with her perfect golden hair.

By the time the game was over the audience were crying with laughter, the bite had been tended by an obsequious servant, and Menander's girls were toasted in still more wine, Theodora above all. As Comito, the elder of the two mimes, and several of the older dancers were led away for the rest of their evening's work, Theodora was grabbed up and hugged by the man with the bitten finger. He called out to Menander at the back of the room. 'This one, I'll take her. She has fire.'

The dance master walked slowly to the man's side, speaking quietly but firmly, in Latin rather than Greek, making his point with the language of the law. 'I apologise, she is not yet mature sir, she cannot work further tonight. Besides,' he added, taking Theodora firmly from the gentleman and sinking his thumb and forefinger into the fold of her collarbone, pinching hard, 'it is her fault we were late beginning our performance. She is to be punished.' He sighed, looked into the gentleman's face for understanding of servants and students and women – even if he, as a eunuch, knew only the tribulations of two – and the men laughed together at all the burdens life had imposed on them.

Menander was true to his word. While they waited for the older girls to finish the night's entertainment, in the private bedrooms the host had prepared, he kept Theodora beside him, striking her every now and then with his cane, stinging blows to her back and buttocks while he sang a lullaby to the younger girls curled up on couches around the room. He lectured her about the placing of her head when she'd whispered two of her funnier asides, pointing out that if her chin had been slightly lower then even the gentlemen furthest distant would have heard her better and she wouldn't have had to speak in such an obvious stage whisper, explaining in full detail exactly why the laughs she did get were not quite good enough, that her timing was just a little out, that her instinct was nothing and training was all. And Theodora, who at eleven was not yet old enough to go on the public stage alone, who had to wait another hour at least while Comito, in a private bedroom, earned extra coin for herself as well as their master, heard Menander's words and felt the stinging blows as praise. Which they were.

While Theodora was feeling the bite of Menander's cane, and Comito and the older girls were entertaining senators and City merchants in private rooms, some of the other guests were already making their way home. Several travelled together, talking about Comito's amazing voice or Anastasia's pretty face, and then, in lowered tones, one mentioned Theodora, another raised an eyebrow, a third whistled quietly. It was one thing to acknowledge a fine singer, quite another to comment, no matter what was going on in the private bedrooms behind them, on how very forward the small dark girl was, how at ease she seemed on stage, in her body, in her flesh. These men prided themselves on their cosmopolitan nature and broad minds, they made a skilled audience, and it was obvious they were watching a child on the cusp of blossoming into a fine comic actor. In addition though, to her clear intelligence, Theodora also had something almost primal about her, something that glowed on stage – very carnal, very old Rome, definitely not quite the new Christian. The sooner her family married her off, the better – that one was clearly wilder than was good for her, or for any man who might be tempted.

Most of those leaving early were happily married men who preferred the charms of their wives to those of dancing girls, one or two were committed Christians – as was every citizen, no doubt – but these few took the religious injunctions against adultery and lasciviousness more seriously than others. Justinian was leaving for neither reason. He simply wanted to get back to his desk. There was work to do.

Justinian had come to the City as Flavius Petrus Sabbatius, a twelve-year-old boy, sent from Illyricum to live with his uncle Justin, who himself had travelled as a boy from their Slav village, had risen steadily through the ranks, and was now Chief of the Excubitors, the Palace guards. He renamed the boy for himself and brought him to live in an extended family that included another nephew, Justinian's cousin Germanus. Germanus had followed their uncle into the military, but Justinian had always preferred the intricacies of strategy and historical battles to the truth of blood on the field. His work in the Palace, in the study, creation and implementation of law, gave him access to the libraries and the records dating back to the City's founding that were stored in locked vaults beneath the Hippodrome. Justinian believed his uncle knew enough about the military for any man; if Justin was to rise even higher than his present rank – and it certainly seemed possible – he needed to know about everything else as well. Justinian was far too interested in his work aiding his uncle's ambitions to waste a night with a dancing whore.

He had certainly enjoyed the evening, the food was excellent, the wine even better – what little of it he took, never one to indulge his appetites – and the dinner companions proved themselves not only wise but useful. The host, a fellow Slav whose family had done very well for themselves both at home and in the City, had promised that several of the other guests would be good contacts for Justin, and he had been true to his word, making introductions that Justinian was keen to follow up on later. Unlike most of the other guests though, once those contacts had been made, Justinian was as keen to sit at his desk as he was to dine, to read a treatise on the new Egyptian tax proposals as to read a young girl's face, to study by lamplight and to sleep in curtained dark as to pay for a dancer by the hour.

His ambition, for power, for office – both for his uncle and, maybe, eventually for himself – was born of a desire for change. Justinian was not impressed with Emperor Anastasius' strategy of safety and thrift: it kept the coffers full and the military well fed, strong enough to defend the borders – but it was not exciting, it was not what Justinian expected of an Emperor of the new Rome. Nor, as a Western Roman, did he approve of the August's anti-Chalcedonian leanings. This Emperor was good enough for now, but there would be better times to come, and Justinian wanted to be at the centre of them. Not that he shared these thoughts with anyone other than his uncle, but the boy who had travelled halfway across the Empire at just twelve years old admitted in private that his true aim was to help realise a glorious new Rome. Wider and stronger and fully one. One state, one Church, one leader. It was a big idea, and Justinian – lacking the battle scars or the charisma of other equally ardent men, of his cousin Germanus, even – set out to do what he could, in the way that suited him best. He went back to history and studied strategy instead of force.

Justinian enjoyed his life, working with his books and papers, advising his uncle, and if his few friends sometimes mocked him because he didn't want to pay for a different actress every second night, or because he was overly temperate with his wine, he didn't mind. Let them think he was boring, he already knew that seeming dull was a better cover for ambition than any backtracking his cousins could manage when they were hungover and apologising the morning after for abusing the Emperor or rudely mocking the Patriarch. There was only one other person Justinian discussed his hopes with, and the brilliant Narses could hardly be considered competition. A eunuch might rise high in the court – with no children to build his own dynasty on, he would always be considered safer than a whole man – but no matter how well he did, or how loved he might be, he could never become Emperor.

Justinian walked out into the spring evening. The night smelt of wood smoke and, this close to the harbour, the mussels the fishermen had earlier boiled up for supper before their own night's entertainment with other young women, whose stage would only ever be the street and the harbour bars. He turned away from the crumbling stones on the waterside, walking steeply uphill, picking his way through the people still out despite the late hour, soldiers and beggars and a few drunk young men; he felt safe from their often violent and always lewd late-night behaviour more because he was a fellow Blue than whatever sanctity his patrician's cloak supposedly offered.

Before going into the house, down the long passageway that opened out from a very ordinary street into the spacious and beautiful courtyard of his uncle's home, he peered up through the low cloud, hoping to check the stars. Several astronomers had suggested they would see a new comet soon; if they were correct, there were plenty of people, from the fully ignorant to the best educated, willing to believe that the comet was a sign in itself. One of those believers was the Emperor Anastasius; the first sighting would be a good time for Justin to propose some of the new ideas they'd been discussing for the military. Justinian and his uncle both believed in the value of military might, the City needed a fine army, it was the present core of the great Empire after all, an Empire that was rising in the east even as it was, unfortunately, fading in the west. But the clouds were too dense for him to see clearly, and whatever comet might be on its way would not be revealed tonight, so Justinian, his duty done, went inside.

Within ten minutes he was settled at his desk, a glass of well-diluted wine close by, the evening still clear in his mind. That girl who'd saved the little one's skin with the bear story, she was very clever. It had been a joy to see such a child – she couldn't have been more than ten or eleven – put her native intelligence to such good use. And of course, clever was even more enjoyable – though his very proper aunt Euphemia would certainly not approve – when it could turn somersaults and make a dozen men laugh aloud at the same time. Justinian unrolled a sheet of paper, and took up his pen, surprised – and a little shy – to find himself imagining all those young women again, cavorting before him. Two hours later the management of Egyptian grain levies was fully occupying his thoughts, the dancers forgotten.

Four

The City's feast day began with services in the dozens of churches all across the metropolis, long processions into the street, priests holding relics high above the people. Blues and Greens held back their jibes as a splinter of the True Cross or a fragment of cloth from the True Shroud passed by, a moment later their animosities cried all the louder for the solemnity before. As light fell fast to let the night begin, flower garlands were carefully removed from statues of saints and holy men, taken down to one of the harbours and thrown on to the water, Christian offerings given to pagan water deities by sailors keen to appease all the gods of the past and present, just in case, no matter what their priests' more Christian injunctions might be.

Comito used the day off for extra singing rehearsals, Anastasia chose to stay close to home, closer to the second family Hypatia and Basianus were making with the new step-babies and happy to act little mother. Theodora hurried out of the apartment long before Hypatia could demand she help with the younger ones or Basianus insist she help him clear out the stinking cages of his stinking beasts. She said the smell of their captivity revolted her, but it was also true that the stench of the pens was forever tied to the smell of her father's draining blood. The only creature Theodora now had any time for was the owl she fell asleep to, screeching in the night, or in her dreams, clawing out of the stone of the Hippodrome obelisk and away to the full moon rising over Chalcedon, across the Bosphorus. She had a strong, fit body, trained to climb towers of acrobats, and equally useful on a feast day to climb the great aqueduct for a better view of the procession below. Today she had a perfect view of the lauded Juliana Anicia, carried through the streets in her sedan chair.

What those on the street couldn't see, their eyes averted either from politeness or awe, was the bald patch right on top of the famously pious lady's head, neither her hairpiece nor her lace scarf thick enough to hide it from Theodora's gimlet gaze. Nor did the public have Theodora's vantage point to count the many coins the much-praised princess had in her purse, and how few her servant handed out. Juliana of the Anicii was renowned for her building works and Theodora supposed she was keeping her coins for grander schemes. As a child of the City, Theodora had often been tempted by the scaffolding for one of Juliana's new churches; like any other citizen she took pride in the building works of her town as the city spread further back, well beyond Constantine's original walls, right out to Blachernae in the west. Unlike the protected princess in her sedan chair, she also saw the damaged ex-soldiers and refugees begging for food and drink, despite the rich men at their private performances laughing about how well the City was doing, and what good fortune it was to be born now, with the Empire once again on the rise.

'Good. Enough. You may go.'

At Menander's quiet command the girls of his team let out a collective sigh and slowly lowered Comito to the ground, from where they had been holding her, high above their heads. They'd kept the pose, as demanded, for over half the time it took the hourglass sands to run through. Every one of them was aching and sweating, and the younger ones, less accustomed to the constant pain of their work, especially after the rare relief of their time off yesterday, were crying.

'Not you, Theodora.'

Comito reached for Anastasia, pulled her close and wiped away the tears before Menander could see the little sister and punish her for weakness. She looked at Theodora. 'What did you do?'

'Nothing. I was perfect. I've been perfect all day.' She shook her head. 'Damn him, he probably just wants a back to smack.' She was whispering just loudly enough for the other girls to hear. 'Wrinkled old eunuch, he doesn't have anything else to beat.'

The other girls were picking up their robes, rubbing down their cramped muscles, laughing at Theodora's gall in the face of what was surely yet another beating from their master.

Comito and Anastasia waited by the door until Menander turned from the wardrobe mistress and shouted at them too, 'You girls – fuck off! Your sister's clever enough to mock me when she thinks I'm not listening, you think she's so stupid she can't get home by herself? A mouth that big won't frighten away any Huns in the Mese? Piss off now, before I make you stay and repeat the routine. I saw those tears Ana, you could do with some extra training.'

Comito shrugged an apology at Theodora and, putting her arm around Anastasia, pulled the younger girl away.

What Theodora should have done next was quite plain. Asked to stay after rehearsal, certain to be punished for yet another infraction of Menander's infamous company rules, or for a more specific weakness in action or line, she should have knelt before the teacher, kissed his foot, begged forgiveness and then meekly taken whatever punishment he handed out. Any one of the other girls knew the routine, all of them would have followed the form, knowing that the sooner they begged forgiveness, the sooner Menander would let it go, hand out the

34

beating or the extra practice, and she could then go home, eat and rest before another long day's rehearsal and the show booked for the next evening. But not Theodora. She stood, left hand on her hip, lifting her right foot back and behind her head with the help of her right hand. When she had her foot in what she believed to be the perfect position, she took her right hand away, and reaching out with both arms, addressed Menander.

'Great teacher, revered eunuch.' She slowly lowered the right leg, bringing the left up into the mirror position before continuing. 'What now? What terrible sin have I committed?' She lowered the left leg even more slowly, delicately lifting her short skirt, parting her legs and, agonisingly slowly, lowered herself to the floor in perfect splits. 'What – could I – possibly – have done wrong – now?'

Menander stared at her. Then he sat down and waited five minutes, ten, fifteen, until he was sure she must be in excruciating pain, though only the finest beads of sweat on her brow told him he was right. Theodora had learned all his lessons well, and the one in which she had most skill was in hiding everything but her art.

Eventually he relented. 'The left foot is sickled, the little toe sticks out and spoils the whole leg line. The first finger on your right hand is just out of joint with the others, your left eyebrow is slightly higher than the other, it mars the symmetry of your face.'

Theodora let out a groaning laugh and shook her head. 'Mother of God, I just can't please you, can I?'

'You could try shutting up for a moment.'

But she wasn't listening. 'I've been so damn good today. I worked hard all week, all month, you know I did. Even you weren't shouting at me quite so much.'

'Then I was mistaken, your mouth is still too wide.'

'I've been working harder than ever before.'

'You need to. You're not as perfect as you think.'

Theodora looked at him and then smiled, raising herself, even slower this time, directly from the splits without bending either leg. 'Or perhaps you're not as good a teacher?'

'Maybe. That's why I asked you to stay.'

Theodora was not expecting this, she'd been waiting for a blow, a slap, for her teacher to bound across the room and pull her from the floor. This little private performance had been intended as a way of placating him before the violence began, of distracting him from what was bound to come. His admission of less than perfect teaching sent her immediately off balance, she began to wobble, her muscles demonstrating the uncertainty that her mind could not contain, and then Menander was there, at her side, as he always had been, holding her into place, halfway above the ground, halfway to standing, pummelling her muscles, moulding bone and flesh into perfect position as he had done for almost every day of the past six years, since she'd first come to his class a frightened five-year-old, her father just dead and any older man a comfort. In the pain of this touch, this teaching, she knew his care. She tried to stand fully but he would not let her.

'Stay. You listen better in pose anyway, it's the only time I can be sure you're fully concentrating.'

Theodora stopped moving, allowed Menander to shift a finger ever so slightly, straighten her head by the merest angle, slap in her tiny stomach, flick a sharp finger at the eyebrow he insisted was out of place.

'The City company leader has asked for you.'

'I'm not twelve yet.'

'Shut up.'

Stunned, she did.

'He saw you at that dinner, when you made Anastasia the

36

bear. Elena, his comedy actress, is leaving, she's decided to keep the child she is too damn full with already. He needs a comedian who can dance a little.'

'I dance more than a little.'

'On a good day. It doesn't matter. For whatever reason, he liked what you did.'

'I'm too young.'

Menander nodded. 'I said that. He likes your spirit, he was impressed by your behaviour the other night. I told him he'd be a damn sight less than impressed once he started working with you, but it's his choice. It'll be good for you, you need a higher standard.'

'You are the highest standard. Everyone knows that.'

'I don't mean me. I mean those you work alongside.'

Theodora began to turn her head, lower her hand, the better to make her point, 'But I don't want—'

Menander simply whispered, 'Don't. You. Dare.'

She shifted immediately into position, trying one more time 'It's just that—'

'Dear God, do I have to gag you, girl?'

He allowed her the barest shake of her head before continuing, all the while poking and prodding her into more difficult poses. 'It's really not up to you, is it? There's money, quite a lot more. Your mother will agree, as will Basianus. You know they've been wanting to take Comito on, he approved of her showing at that dinner as well. He'll take the two of you at once. Seems I gave you both a wonderful audition opportunity.'

'You knew he was there?'

'Of course I knew, it's my job to know who comes to these things. To show you lot off.' He saw she was about to speak again and pre-empted her. 'Anastasia stays with me for the moment. She's too young for them, and we don't yet know what she can do, not really. We know what they'd like to do with one as pretty as she is, but not yet – even a eunuch understands it's too soon for that. So, there is no argument.' He waited. 'You may rest. Sit.'

Theodora sank to the ground. She had always known this would come, but it was unusual for it to come so soon. The girls who joined the Hippodrome and Kynegion companies, as dancers and performers, also went in as whores. It was part of the job. The tears were just behind her eyes and she was praying Menander would release her before they fell, but he knew, and waited, standing over her, saying nothing, until her body could hold the flow no longer, and they came, a thin stream of bitter salt water, Theodora hating herself for showing weakness in front of him, hating him for forcing her here and, more than anything, hating him for sending her away. When the ground was wet with her crying he knelt beside her, yanked a handful of her hair at the back of her head so he could stare into her face, trying to see, as he always did with this girl, what was real and what for show. He felt uncomfortable when he saw real pain.

'You can stop now, the tears won't help, and they mar what little looks you have. I've agreed the terms of your contract with their leader. This is done. I do not let you go lightly, girl. It will not be an easy transition of course, but you and I know there is nothing your body cannot bear, no punishment it cannot take. I've trained you well. And we also know you need a bigger stage. There are hard things that will come of this, and there will be good. What have I always told you?'

Theodora intoned his mantra as she had been trained: 'Enjoy the good, bear the bad.'

'Exactly. That is all there is to do. Go now, tell Comito I will see her early in the morning, she should come before breakfast. Tomorrow night will be your last show for me. Go home.'

Menander waited until she was almost at the door before he called after her. 'Theodora, what have you forgotten?'

She came back, every step a resistance, and knelt before him to kiss his foot. As she did so, he grabbed her shoulders, pulled her up and embraced her, whispering, 'I know you child, you crave attention, and you will take punishment and pain over praise because it feels bigger. It is my hope that a larger stage will teach you the pleasure of praise. You will hurt too much otherwise. You must learn there is more to feeling than pain.'

Theodora looked up at him, all tears gone, furious. 'You could have taken longer to agree.'

Menander shrugged. 'They offered a good price to get you this young.'

She stepped back and then spat at him, 'I'll be richer than you, eunuch.'

When she reached the door he called after her, in a perfect hidden whisper, so it seemed to come at her from the walls of the room, 'Yes you will, actress.'

And they both laughed, understanding each other only too well.

Five

A week later, Theodora met Sophia for the first time. Of course she knew of the dwarf's reputation, had seen her on stage plenty of times – four foot nothing of controlled energy combined with an unstoppable charm and a mouth that, on occasion, could make even a Vandal blush – if, as Sophia said with a grin, winking at a young man in the front row, she was using it well enough.

For more than a decade, Sophia-the-half-size had been one of the company's biggest attractions. Unusually for a dwarf she was perfectly proportioned, just extra small – in every way but her cunt, as one of the front row lads once heckled. And then promptly shut up when, in response, she showed him her perfectly formed, and brightly tattooed, arse. Sophia had no qualms about trading on her size. While the oddly shaped attractions of other companies eventually tired of being constantly paraded less for their skills than for their bodies, Sophia saw her difference as a blessing. Unlike the other girls, she did not have to sing or act or tumble to earn her salary, she could simply stand on stage and earn applause being herself. Essentially lazy, she was happy to do as little as possible: if people paid her merely for being small, she was fine about taking their coin. The fact that such a glorious voice emanated from her tiny frame and that she had a talent for learning lines that even the old-school actors admired, just added to her status.

Sophia made sure never to work too hard or try too much – only consenting to perform her most successful routines when houses were down or they needed a sharp opening to a new piece that was, as yet, lacking the indefinable something that would make it a regular crowd-pleaser. While the writers kept on trying to hone the perfect sketch, Sophia would, often as not, take their piece of basic smile-and-nod material and, with a raised eyebrow, a particular pause, skilfully placed, turn it into belly-laugh comedy. The audience had long ago grown out of the classic Greek works everyone knew they were supposed to appreciate, if not enjoy – this public wanted their performance in street Greek and would take the likes of Euripides and Sophocles only with sweeteners of sex or comedy or song. Sophia could deliver all three, and her renowned one-woman-as-twelve-maenads scene was always guaranteed to draw a huge crowd, no matter how many times it had been seen before. If only for the joy of watching the tiny woman rip off her own head a dozen times.

Face of a girl, voice of an angel – and coin collection of a madam. While she openly admitted getting away with as little as possible on stage, Sophia worked very hard behind the scenes. Having turned the requisite tricks early on in her career, working her way through stage manager, dance master, touring writers, important patrons, each bedding advancing her status and reputation a little more, Sophia quickly decided the constant jokes about easy access blow jobs and the little girl requests weren't for her, no matter how much money was offered. She then set about finding out what else she could do that would give her plenty of time to appear on stage, which she still far preferred, and also pay the little, or the lot, extra she wanted to earn. By sixteen Sophia knew she was more interested in talking about sex in theatrical asides than actually doing the deed – for money; she always enjoyed it in private – and took to selling her company sisters instead. As a madam she had all the skills of the men who usually sold the stage-girls – good with

41

money, great at haggling, dangerously reckless of her own and others' bodies when called on to fight – but she had the further advantage of having done the job herself. Sophia knew what her girls liked, understood that playing to type applied to whoring as much as it did to acting. Consequently she was able to pair the girls, and some of the young men of the company, with the kind of paying guests each one could best pleasure by also enjoying herself.

Sophia and Theodora should not have got on. They occupied too much of the same ground. Both loud, smart-mouthed and quick-witted, both the kind of women that the men in their audience feared and wanted in equal measure, if only to tame. As actresses there should not have been room for two of the same: confronted with a younger woman who might feasibly steal her place in the audience's heart, Sophia would usually have given the new girl a very hard time, had seen off lesser rivals plenty of times in the past, and was ready to do so with this one too – but that Theodora came prepared.

She made sure to get to the rehearsal room before the other performers. The company members would know she was joining them, today was not the day to make a late entrance. She sat carefully on one of the bench seats, leaning back against the wall and tucked her legs beneath her in a twisted position only a girl with her years of training could possibly achieve. She then made sure the folds of her pale blue gown fell open at exactly the right point, perfectly revealing henna-tinted toenails. She lifted her hands to her hair and pulled it back behind her ears, checking that the dark curls – curls made by hand, not nature – were not obscuring her fake pearl earrings. Finally she pulled a bracelet from her leather bag, and pushed the coiling silver snake above the elbow to sit proud against her acrobat's bicep. She took a deep breath, and waited.

Slowly the room filled. Comito was there, aware of Theodora's preparations and worried that it might all backfire horribly. Several other singers and dancers arrived, each surprised to see the young woman in the corner, sitting there so very familiar and yet so wrong. There were a few nervous giggles. Then, as Sophia's raucous yell was heard from upstairs, shouting for water, wine, bread with honey, anything to help her start this fucking new day, dear God, how she hated morning – the room became silent.

Sophia-the-half-size walked into the room in mid-rant and stopped still. She stared at Theodora, glared at the young woman who was wearing her own trademark pale blue dress, famous silver snake armlet, and a version of the long pearl earrings she herself always wore – not genuine though, Sophia could see that at twenty paces. Which would be enough to rip them off the sallow bitch, she supposed, once she'd found out what the fuck was going on.

'Good morning, Lady.' Theodora began, leaving just enough pause before 'lady' to make everyone in the room wonder how quickly the fight would start.

'Yes?'

'Well, not good, exactly,' and now she stretched her legs out from beneath her body, just managing to hide the wince as the blood flowed painfully back into her limbs. 'I had a little trouble with the toenails, they're not as neatly coloured as I'd have liked, I couldn't quite keep a perfect edge on the henna. I suppose it's easier for you? Being so much closer to your own feet?'

Sophia blinked, opened her mouth to let out a stunned half-laugh, took in Theodora's poorly made curls that even now were beginning to fall lank and straight again, and then, planting her hands firmly on her low-slung hips, asked, 'So who's the smart-mouthed bitch?'

Theodora, still leaning against the wall, looked Sophia up

and down, and answered, 'You are, of course. But I thought, perhaps, it was time you had an apprentice.'

'Are you suggesting I'm of an age to have an apprentice?'

Theodora waited, lowered her face just a little, and then looked up again through half-shaded lashes. 'I'm saying, Miss Sophia, that you must have skills – and tricks – you would like to pass on.'

'Two or three.'

'And a half?'

There was a pause, a stifled groan from one of the actors who had to rehearse a scene this morning with Sophia and knew she'd be hell to work with if she was in a bad mood, and then Sophia flung her head back in pleasure, her dark – natural – curls bouncing up and down with the bellows of her laughter. 'Dear God, I do like a cheeky cunt.'

'So, Madam . . .' Theodora said, rising from the bench and at the same time sinking immediately to her knees, so that at no point did she raise herself above Sophia's height, 'I have heard.'

At this, the room erupted in the nervous laughter it had been stifling for twenty minutes, causing the stage manager to run down the dangerous wooden staircase, shouting that they were all late, everyone would be fined if they weren't careful, and for fuck's sake, noting Theodora now standing at her full height beside her new mentor, had half-size-Sophia suddenly grown in her night off? And if she had, why in the name of the sainted Helena couldn't she have grown a little prettier at the same time? Upstairs now. Please. God, are there no hard-working actors in the world any more, must he turn to pagans and Barbarians to fill the stage?

When both Sophia and Theodora rounded on the man and told him to bite his balls, with no care for the consequent fines, the dwarf and the acrobat knew each had made a new friend.

Six

When Theodora told Menander she was too young for the main company, she was not referring to their acting roles. She had no problem imagining herself accepting the applause of a grateful crowd who, released from the shackles of their old and boring actresses, would frantically welcome her advent on their stage. She meant that she was too young to start working as a whore.

The company master Cosmas agreed and left her alone for the first few months, drilling her instead in their famous routines, finding out where she needed more rehearsal, where her skills came in useful on stage. By her twelfth birthday though, Theodora was deemed ready. She had, as Cosmas said to his colleagues, seen plenty of bed-work while in Menander's company, it was not as if she didn't know what was coming. Or, he lowered his voice, as if she wasn't ready for it: she could do with something to sap her wilder energies. It was common knowledge among the other girls – and therefore among their bosses – that Theodora had not yet had her first period, but the precociousness that had been noted when she was in Menander's troupe was even clearer now she was strutting the main stage, taking absolute control of the five-minute interlude slot she'd been given, where she played up the comedy with two other dancers and far outshone her more technically adept older colleagues. She had plenty of energy, too much most of the time; in Cosmas' opinion it was better to put that energy to work, than to allow it to run wild on stage.

Theodora took her concerns to Sophia.

'It's not that I don't want to . . . I mean, I don't know if I do or not, right? Some people enjoy it?'

'Most people enjoy it Theodora, once they've had some practice, and some just enjoy it more than others.'

'But don't you think I'm too young?'

'You didn't bleed yet, so yes, theoretically, you're young. But there are girls bleeding younger than you, and eunuch boys younger than you, they are also working.'

'I don't think I want to do it.'

Sophia shook her head, remembering the horror of her own first time, the performance it had turned into, the ghastly spectacle of a huge man deflowering a tiny dwarf virgin, the pain and the blood, but more the humiliation, as the man who had paid for her chose to share his moment of triumph with half a dozen of his friends. It should have put her off for life, it certainly put her off a certain type of man, the all too many who saw her as a freak, an act to be indulged rather than enjoyed. She had, though, found some men could, with the right coaxing, be kinder, more careful, and there she could help Theodora. 'I'll take care of it.'

'You'll tell him I can't do it?' Theodora was grinning in relief.

Sophia looked up at her new friend. 'No girl, I won't say that. You don't have any choice.'

'Then what?'

'I'll take care of it. I can't make it wonderful, but maybe I can make it less frightening for you. Yes? Trust me?'

Sophia did not need to explain the act itself to a girl brought up beneath the Hippodrome, who had played among the animal cages since she was a toddler, nor did she need to coach her in

46

skills of either temptation or coquettishness: both had been learned in Menander's dance classes for years. Instead she told her about dealing with the customer, encouraging him to talk to waste time, then to play him with her body before he played with hers, and finally how to speed him to his release so the act itself was concluded faster. She explained about the use of herbs and wine to ease any pain and further told Theodora to listen to her own body, to use her acrobatic and dancer's skills of relaxation, of ease in the physicality, most of all to see the thing itself as a show. A private show, a more revealing show than usual, but a show nonetheless. She taught Theodora to see her body in the act as that of a performer, not her real self. It was the old prostitute's trick of dissociation, and no less useful for being so ancient.

And then, when she thought Theodora had learned all she could from mere talk, she set her up with her first paying customer. The son of a senator, who already – at nearly sixteen – knew he preferred the company of boys to girls, eunuchs to women, soldiers to anyone else, but whose father had declared it was time that he too got on with the deed.

It was not good sex, for either of the parties, but it was not bad either. It was perfunctory, and a little messy, and it was done. And when it was done, Theodora accepted Sophia as her pimp, as most of the other girls in the company had done. Cosmas had no problem with this, he took his cut after all, knew Sophia was probably better than he would be at matching girl to client, at keeping them all happy, and a happy actress was both a good performer and a better earner off-stage. He certainly didn't want to give reluctant girls to his clients, his men liked cheerful girls.

'This is the new Rome after all – we're good Christians, not Barbarians who would force unwilling girls to fuck.'

And his friends raised their wine glasses in agreement.

*

Soon after Theodora's backstage debut, Anastasia took her place as Comito's stool-bearer and cloak-holder, and Theodora graduated to bigger roles. Comito had quickly become a favourite and the public didn't care who stood behind their new songbird beauty, just as long as no one interrupted the perfect view. The comet-like streak of her hair that matched her name, the height and majesty in such a young woman, in addition to her lovely voice – within a very short time Comito had earned both fame and, for an actress, was even starting to amass a certain amount of fortune, not least because she had a mastery of the old songs the audience knew and loved, as well as a knack for choosing the best of the new ones regularly offered her. On the several occasions she was invited to give private performances in the homes of respectable matrons – having graduated from the private dinners that quickly became private brothels – Comito behaved with impeccable grace and tactful discretion. The fact that on the public stage she refrained from singing the old pagan songs, even in the Kynegion, despite the building itself being ringed round with pre-Christian statues, and that she kept her body fully covered, albeit in the most translucent of costly silk, meant she was now at least on nodding terms with patrician society. Even in Constantinople, the stage and the circus kept their old function as a vent for the wilder excesses of the masses. That those masses loved Comito could have made her dangerous, but Comito knew her place, was grateful for it. She was no threat to society – a singer and actress, she didn't even speak her own words – the upper echelons were safe with her. The same could not be said of Theodora.

From the moment she was first allowed on the main stage as a fully fledged public performer rather than as Comito's assistant or just a comedic interlude, Theodora was totally at ease. The people did not fall in love with her immediately, years of watching her father, as well as other actors and singers, had taught her they would not – she knew she would have to make them want her, and so she wooed them, won them without their even noticing it. While Theodora allowed the audience to think she was earning their applause and working for their appreciation, she was actually forcing them to come to her. From her first monologue, she never once changed her manner, she simply convinced the audience – offering her routines in the same style over and over again – that she was hilarious. She had been studying this crowd all her life, she believed she knew exactly what they wanted, and she would make them learn it, earn it.

Gradually, once the public started to smile as soon as they caught sight of her waiting off stage, or parrying a mock blow from an outraged classical actor whose line she'd stomped over with a joke of her own, once she could be certain that her mere presence guaranteed a relaxed anticipation in the audience – they knew Theodora would be on time, on cue, could be heard, always hit her mark – she began to play up to them, give them exactly what they expected and just a little more. A nod of the head that included a secret wink for the first two rows only. A single line, perfectly enunciated, ideally when the piece was at its bawdiest, while sticking word for word to the writer's actual script, would be delivered in just the right tone and timbre to recall immediately one of the City's most famously arrogant matrons, a patrician lady renowned for her virginal piety, even after two marriages.

As she grew older, her audience watching her turn from girl to young woman, Theodora learned to use the tricks of adulthood as well. One week there was a wave to a non-existent character just off-stage, allowing her gown to slip off her shoulder, revealing a hint of swelling breast and nothing more. The following week there was the barest possibility of a nipple, almost revealed. The week after that she turned, just as she lifted her hand to wave, and berated an old man in the front row for daring to sit so close when he knew what was coming – and then, as the audience applauded her telling him off, she let the robe fall away anyway.

Theodora had trained her body to accomplish astonishing acrobatic feats; now she took her audience by the hand and, knowing she did not have Comito's voice, Anastasia's grace, she made them leap and jump and dance to her whim. She taught the crowd to assume she would be good even before she started. Having done so, she made them love her.

Eventually, all three of Hypatia's daughters from her first marriage were living the life she'd hoped to spare them. The two older girls learned to cope with the disparity between their fame on stage, and that other fame backstage, fame on their backs, but as members of the main company they were at least working at a higher level, earning well. Courtesy of their own fan base and Sophia's management skills, Comito quickly had several wealthy patricians who vied for her favours and the income from their attention was enough to take care of herself and contribute to the family, especially once she was a few years older and living in the small villa on the third hill, where a grateful patron kept her, a comfortable walk from the Hippodrome in a quiet street, carefully placed to avoid too much of the raucous Mese crowd. Less reserved than Comito and far less delicate than Anastasia, once she'd been introduced to the process, Theodora had no qualms about fucking a wealthy man for an evening if the family purse demanded it, but her friendship with Sophia ensured that the men were of a higher class than most who paid for theatre girls, and better looking too. She had always seen her body as a tool of work. Theodora found that as long as she maintained the split between her body and her spirit, she could enjoy whoring for Sophia and, not surprisingly given her other physical skills, that she was good at it as well. But no matter how much money she made from the men, Theodora's main focus, and all her real energy, was reserved for her time on stage. She loved her work, loved her audiences, and in a very few years she was their star.

Theodora stood alone, waiting. The audience were restless, eager. They were, she knew, giggling in anticipation of the belly laughs to come. These people were here specifically because they expected Theodora to make them laugh – she had trained them well in the past five years, her hungry public were now ready to enjoy themselves before she'd even made her entrance. Forty minutes earlier, Comito had opened the show with a song the whole crowd knew, a song made successful by another actress more than a generation earlier, but even the old men had to agree, Comito sang it better. Anastasia was ready to help with the fast change into her second costume, and then Comito hurried back on with the dancers to perform their chorus number, a chanted rendition of an old speech by Euripides. This crowd were not much interested in traditional theatre, they liked song and dance, adored bawdy comedy, but they would sit through an artistic number they understood to be good for them, as long as the Golden Voice was singing and there were barely dressed dancers to watch.

Comito left the stage to a generous round of applause, and then the dancers were joined by three young acrobats, bringing on an even higher energy, readying and enticing the crowd. With each layer of soft silk removed from a dancer's body by a leaping tumbler, with every scarf pulled away and thrown to the ground, there was another whoop, another cry of pleasure. From the Green section of the audience came a yell of feigned ecstasy, taken up and amplified by a dozen or more of the Blues

51

opposite, always keen to stress that Theodora was rightfully theirs. The echoing call was a crowd-sized impersonation of Theodora's most successful character, the one they had all come to see, a character she was about to disappoint them by not performing. Theodora had a new showpiece to offer, a further edge over which to push her already bold reputation. As Menander had always said, the girl was nothing if not daring. And, as Theodora now understood, if she was not daring, she would be nothing. The audience loved her, and would keep doing so as long as she kept feeding them what they wanted. She was about to feed them something they didn't even know they wanted.

Semi-naked dancers, tumbling acrobats, covered the centre of the stage. The crowd could tell they were being primed for something, but were not certain what that something was. Various whispers had gone out, secrets told to the right gossips, several members of the audience alerted that there'd be something different in this show, their excitement filtering through to those who knew nothing yet, but felt the frisson immediately on arriving. A new performer perhaps, or a new piece. This crowd loved their singers and dancers, adored Theodora's comedy sketches, her soft-porn mime shows. Like any crowd they enjoyed both the comfort of sitting back to watch old pieces they knew to be good, and also the nervous anticipation of the new – that knife edge where, no matter how well written and well rehearsed, a new piece might fall flat on its face in front of a full crowd. For the regular theatre-goers, an on-stage disaster could be almost as much fun as triumph.

The drumming intensified. Theodora was locked into a private space of her own – performing her private ritual as she always did before walking out to the crowd, lightly slapping her body all over, arms, legs, feet, torso, head, face, striking her skin, her flesh, snapping her mind into awareness, total concentration. She took a deep breath, held and then relaxed her shoulders, lifted her chin. Then, at her signal, the dancers parted, the acrobats threw their last tumble and, focusing directly ahead, Theodora walked out between them, centre stage.

She was not wearing the costume the audience were hoping for and there were a few groans, a murmur of disappointment; one of the Greens called out 'Shame!' Others who knew, or thought they did, shushed them and whispered to wait, just wait. Theodora smiled and with a tiny move that shimmered through her body – hip-wiggle, shoulder-lift, breast-push – she shrugged off her outer gown to reveal a short, old-fashioned Greek dress more appropriate for the classical repertoire than for her usual material. As the cloak fell to the ground, she slowly lowered herself to follow it, speaking so quietly she forced the crowd to hush, and as they did so they realised that she was giving one of the old, famous speeches. Theodora was Leda, lying in bed on her wedding night, waiting for her Spartan king to attend her. The crowd listened, uncertain. Theodora was acting. Nicely, prettily, quite well, no one could fault her enunciation, her vocal technique, but this wasn't what they wanted from their Theodora. They were a crowd of eager men, they wanted what they were used to. She kept on. An old speech, one most of the crowd had grown up hearing, had seen performed by several famous actresses from the old days, it was traditional acting, the real thing. Theodora continued until there was an attentive, if slightly sulky, silence. And then, having forced them to wait, made them listen, she generously gave her people what they wanted.

One by one the dancers returned. Now they were dressed as the handmaidens of Leda. Regular theatre-goers had seen this scene dozens of times. As the dancers mimed brushing their mistress's hair, readying Leda for her husband, the audience were confused: more straight acting, more traditional theatre. But when Theodora lay back on the cushions the dancers had piled high behind her, the short robe she was wearing fell apart, revealing that she was almost naked beneath. The crowd let out a gasp that became a sigh of collective relief and obvious enthusiasm and the show proper – the show they had been hoping for – began. Each of the dancers reached into the cleavage of her own, equally brief, classical dress, pulled out a small gilt bag and began sprinkling grain over Theodora's torso and legs. Several young men on the front benches offered to come and help.

When her lower body was covered in little mounds of grain, she called off-stage, 'Come husband, come master, come King!' One of the oldest actors in the company waddled on, looking even fatter and more lecherous than usual, and a laugh ran through the crowd. This was more like it, the much-loved Petrus of Galatia as Spartan King. The moment his plump and wrinkled fingers touched the edge of Theodora's spread cloak, the dancers, now reformed as Chorus, began to whisper the arrival of the god, Zeus himself, and then the actor sat back, opening his own robe and allowing half a dozen geese to jump out on to the stage. The geese, having been starved for a day prior to the show, began, quite naturally, to peck at the trail of grain laid across Theodora's body. Chorus and old actor stepped back and with each peck Theodora screamed Zeus! and oh god! and more, please more! writhing and undulating on the stage. The audience were delighted – the elegant and ferocious god-as-swan of myth reduced to six fat geese, the virginal Leda a rapacious tart, and the Chorus intoning the many names of the great god Zeus exactly as they would have done in a serious theatrical production while Theodora provided a counterpoint of wriggling orgasmic squeals. Ten minutes later she left the stage after the third round of raucous applause, pausing as she went to allow half a dozen of her most eager fans to prostrate themselves, granting them one by one the great privilege of kissing the soft arch of Theodora's daintily proffered left foot.

Much later that evening, to the continued applause of her delighted co-workers, sweet wine and honey-grilled figs protecting her hard-worked vocal cords, Theodora adopted the voice and pained expression of one of the City's most notoriously hard-line bishops, intoning in his strong Thracian accent, 'The girl's a slut, it's true, but it's the old gods she mocks, not the Christ. I'll say this much for her – she's no pagan.'

Seven

Theodora, seventeen years old, toast of the Kynegion, beloved comic of the theatres, star of the Hippodrome, was not prepared for the pain she felt when her little sister Anastasia died. She and Comito clung to each other sobbing, holding their dazed mother between them. They stood the requisite distance behind the men at the funeral, praying to the Christ and His mother for succour, for understanding. Praying too, silently, to the other god, the one they had learned of from that impossibly ancient woman, Hypatia's grandmother who'd lived with them when they were very little girls. Theodora's earliest memories were of her grandmother's frail body hunched over the fire, mixing herbs for teas and poultices for their father's animal scratches, offering remedies in her strong Syrian accent, and whispering of the seasons and the moon and her own family's prayers from a time before the Christ was King: the prayers which still permeated everyday life in the City, which popped up unannounced in the thoughts and wishes of the people; prayers to the now-defunct gods whose statues remained above the town walkways, whose chants and charms filtered down through the drunken songs of old men and the whispers of even older women, praying for help and hope and understanding, from wherever it might come.

Anastasia had never risen as high in the ranks as Comito or Theodora, though some of her sisters' gloss had rubbed off on her. None of Hypatia's three older girls had to take on the worst of the work: that was left to the lesser-skilled dancers and the poorer singers of the chorus. They still, though, traded in their own flesh. It was part of the job, as were the unplanned pregnancies that came with the work. Generally the actresses, well aware of their bodies as both on- and off-stage tools of the trade, dealt with the problem early enough; they were lucky that the wardrobe mistress was also highly skilled in herbal medicines, she knew her girls and usually knew what to do for them. Occasionally though, there were mistakes. Comito realised too late that her bleeding was missing and, though the old women tried every method they knew, the little thing stuck fast and grew faster. Eventually she gave birth to a girl, taking two months off work, fed the child backstage, and carried on. It was not unusual and, wonderfully, Comito found she even began to enjoy the company of her daughter as Indaro grew older.

Theodora's child was also the result of a failed abortion. Theodora was fourteen when she gave birth to Ana, not that plenty of other more respectable women weren't mothers by that age, but there were far too many years ahead in which to work and earn to waste time bringing up a child or spending good cash on a nurse. Unlike Comito, Theodora was no natural mother, she took the child home and left her there. Hypatia and Basianus were already reliant on the income from their most successful daughter to take care of the young step-family; Theodora thought it was time they did her a favour in return. Though she was careful to caution Basianus that if she ever heard he'd used the whip on Ana the way he had done with her, she'd make sure he paid – and it would cost him more than his livelihood. Basianus, bitter at his lack of success in the job his wife had begged for him, was all too aware that Theodora held far more influence in the Hippodrome than he did, and so, if he was not a kind foster father to her child, he was at least a careful one.

Things were much harder for Anastasia. As Theodora said, their little sister was simply too sweet. Too sweet to work half a dozen men a week and take their money willingly, using it to further herself, to lift herself out of the brothel that was their backstage life and into a nice little apartment with a sea view and just one or two regular suitors. Instead she'd fallen in love with a pallid Lycian boy from the stables, keeping them both poor by turning down offers so often that in the end the offers ceased to come and she and the stable boy lived on what little they could earn from legitimate work. Even then she'd been too sweet to say no to sex at her fertile time, too gentle – or too damn coy, Theodora thought – to push the horse-boy away, to offer something else instead, anything else instead, to make sure her womb stayed empty. Later still, Anastasia had been too soft to deal with the pregnancy immediately, no matter that both Comito and Theodora assured her the herbs would be easy, the three days of discomfort now so much simpler than an invasive abortion later. When the belly finally began to show, despite her wearing tighter bindings and eating still less food, Anastasia, now unable to work on stage, agreed something must be done.

They took her to the Cappadocian surgeon, paying well over the odds for the privilege of even entering his home, but catching sight of his knife and the skewer, Anastasia ran crying from the room. The man demanded half his fee anyway, offering to take a blow job from the famous Theodora if they didn't think he was worth the coin. She threw the money in his face with her spittle. Finally, Anastasia had been too gentle and far too tired when, after four days of labour, her own mother had begged her to allow them to kill the baby, the one that was ripping apart her daughter's too-small frame. Anastasia died and the baby boy did too. Theodora cursed the baby as she'd heard the old street whores do, damning him to Hades and to hell and the netherworld, all three in one furious ecumenical breath. When damning the dead baby made no difference to her tears, she turned, as she always did, back to work. To the succour of applause, the balm of the crowd, the drunken embraces of her friends backstage.

Late in the evening, two days after the funeral, their hysterical audience that afternoon none the wiser, no sign of grief on either sister's face or in her performance, Theodora sat with Comito and their friends, Anastasia was remembered and remembered until the dead young woman in the ground had her own monument of words. Each of the dancers and actresses knew it could so easily have been any one of them. Sophia knew for certain it would have been her, but for every abortion, every procured miscarriage, every single termination of all her own pregnancies. No small number in a woman sold into the theatre and its concomitant whoring by her disappointed parents at the age of four. That Sophia had proved good at theatre work was pure luck. That she had learned early what dangers there were for her in sex and procreation was down to watching another dwarf performer racked in vain by the full-size child she'd birthed backstage. Dead with the cord round its neck and the mother never able to work again either. Experiences that made Sophia keener always to pimp than to whore. That night she gave in to Theodora's demands for a job, gave in even though she had said half a dozen times it would have been better for the actress to go home and sleep away the last two days of abandon and pain. Theodora was having none of it and finally Sophia relented.

'But only one tonight, yes?'

'One, two, half a dozen, I don't care. Just give me their money.' Theodora was more drunk than Sophia had seen her before, and yet not a single word was slurred. 'I want to work this pain out of my body. I don't care how I do it and I don't care how many. But I can't sleep, and I can't lie alone.'

'Lie with me.'

Theodora smiled. 'Little One, I'd take you any day . . .'

'I wasn't offering sex.'

'Why not?'

'I only make love to women who are awake,' Sophia replied.

'I'm not sleeping.'

'Yes you are. Grief is like sleep.'

'Not enough like sleep.'

'You'll wake from it, but it takes time.'

'I haven't got time,' Theodora answered, shaking her head. 'I need to feel better now. So if you won't fuck me into oblivion, bring me some men who will. And make sure they have full purses.'

She'd spoken louder then, louder than she'd intended, too many years of theatrical training making their presence felt, and two soldiers leaning against a bench on the far wall looked up.

One nudged the other and they stood up together, the first saying, 'We'll take her.'

The second added, 'If you can take two men of the Greens?'

Theodora turned from Sophia, very slowly, and carefully looked them both up and down. Neither older than twenty-five, they had country accents. One was short and round, his hairline receding already, the other a reedy half-man, half-boy, still trying to encourage whiskers with a daily face-scraping shave. She sighed, and then, as elegantly as she had ever per-formed a gesture on stage, she reached out a hand to each man's groin, weighing them up for a moment, before she spoke in her most elegant classical Greek accent: 'How about I pierce both my nipples? You could fuck one each and then I might feel something.' Then, both hands still holding tight to the terrified soldiers, she walked backwards pulling them out of the bar to Sophia's rented room two houses away, calling over their shoulders as she went, 'Collect their money in twenty minutes Little One, this won't take long.'

Sophia shook her head and picked up her bag to follow Theodora and make sure she was safe; several of their friends raised drinks to toast their stage star. Most of the patrons in this theatre bar were used to these scenes, but one was horrified. He didn't enjoy theatre at the best of times, had only come along today because his friend had asked him, and now he'd seen the woman Theodora – who he thought had been perfectly adequate on stage, certainly overrated given her fame – offering her body for money.

The friend he spoke to, an ardent fan of Theodora's stage work, and one who'd been hoping for just such an opportunity this evening, wasn't really listening, as he gathered his cloak to follow his lust. 'Procopius, mate, stop being a cunt and give us a few coins, will you?'

'You can't be serious. Didn't you just hear her? Asking for further orifices to better be pleasured?'

'To be fair, it was a joke, she was only saying those blokes had small dicks. And we know you do too, so don't let your jealousy make you rude. Give us your purse and I'll go and help the girl out. Clearly she's had a hard day, after that pair she'll need someone she can actually feel.'

With that, he grabbed his friend's purse from the table, leaving just enough to pay their drinks bill, and ran out calling for Sophia, wondering how much it cost to get between the legs of the fêted star, the fated whore.

Too few hours had passed when Theodora wrenched herself awake, mildly surprised she'd ended up in her own bed. She reached for a cup of wine, but before she'd even brought it to her lips, her stomach had changed her mind for her, and she threw it down, not caring about the sticky mess it made of the floor; instead she drank water straight from the jug. She tried to walk to her door, gave up, sank back down on the bed, head aching and body bruised from men she'd taken the night before. She listened to the sounds from the street, children yelling and men shouting, Greens and Blues vying with louder and nastier insults. Today was a race day, they were starting early. Two narrow alleys away women were shopping in the cheapest market, in courtyards behind broken-down tenements grandmothers were already preparing meals for families, lucky children were in school, and those less fortunate were working or training as she had been not so long ago. Down at the wharves fishermen were unloading the early morning's catch, ferries crossed the Golden Horn, while at the various City gates strangers piled in as they did every day, citizens of the Empire from so far away they had never heard a word of Greek in their lives, Goth and Vandal and Herule mercenaries hoping the newly anointed Emperor Justin might find a use for their skills where the old August had been content to keep his armies small and the treasury full.

Life everywhere continued. Theodora understood this, though her dreaming in the drunken night had been so violent, so charged with blood, she could not but feel a little surprised to wake and find the City so alive. She tried to stand again and this time it was a little easier. Her head clearer, she took a cloth and began to wash the night from her body.

Looking at the bruises on her thighs, licking the swollen lip where one man had kissed her too forcefully, and then later, much later, another had bitten her, she sighed. Menander was right, she never knew when to stop. The night of excess had not lessened her grief, she had not honestly thought it could, but she had hoped for a few hours' release from the vision of her little sister, still covered in her own and the baby's blood, dead on the bedroom floor of her mother's apartment. And there had been some small respite, in the moment between drunken sleep and dream, the brief moment when exhaustion and wine claimed her mind, before her dreaming let in the ghastly picture of her dead and bloody father and her dead and bloody sister, and then others too, bodies she did not recognise, among some she did, the first man she'd fucked for money, the last she'd taken in the night, friends of theirs from the company and total strangers she knew only as people who sometimes went to the same shops in the Mese. All dead, all bloody. The Hippodrome ground full of them, body after body, piled upon each other, benches layered with death, the smell of blood and pain and above it all, the rasping, throat-burning cries from thousands of wailing mothers, circling the City like hungry gulls.

Washed and dressed, her face unpainted, she left her own little flat and turned out into the street. To the left was her mother's apartment, where she knew the older woman would be having a hard day, Theodora's daughter Ana and the three little step-siblings didn't understand why Hypatia kept crying, Basianus didn't much care, just wanted them all to shut up so he could have a little peace at home, there was certainly no peace in his work. Several narrow streets away was Comito's much more elegant home, where Theodora would be welcomed, if not by Comito who hated to miss her rehearsals, then by her sister's new maid, who had too little to do with only Indaro to watch and was always looking for someone to look after. The last thing Theodora wanted now was to be looked after: any gesture of kindness would have her in tears again, and her face hurt too much for more tears. Her eyelids and cheeks were dry from the salt and her jaw ached from being wedged open with wailing. Beyond Comito's elegant little apartment in the quiet back street was her real world. The crowds around the Bull Square and the Mese, Greens and Blues charging into the Hippodrome, a whole city crammed between the Theodosian Wall and the lighthouse on the far side of the Imperial Palace gardens. Actors and dancers hurrying late to rehearsal or performance, men strolling in and out of the Baths of Zeuxippus, Blue and Green youths trying to foment rebellion, recreate the riots they had so enjoyed a few years earlier, market traders screaming their great deals, builders hard at work on yet another wing of this new church or that, fishermen, sailors, soldiers, beggars, priests, nuns, whores, citizens and barbarians. It was her only world and she was sick of it.

Eight

Two days later Theodora met Hecebolus. He was, even to a woman jaded with men, quite lovely. He was tall, with fine dark features and light eyes; his dark skin was usual for a traveller, a trader, less common in a man who was about to be given a political posting. Theodora slept with Hecebolus for pleasure. She had intended to make him pay, it just didn't work out that way.

'You're not what I expected from a whore.'

Theodora looked down at the man beneath her, 'You're not much like the average government lackey, either.'

'No?'

'No. And most of my tricks tend to be less . . .'

'Good looking? Good in bed? Good?'

He was smiling up at her, tired and comfortable after the pleasant endurance of their past two hours together.

She laughed out loud at his arrogance and then nodded, agreeing that this man, who'd waited after her show, offered to buy her a drink, extended that offer to a good meal, and then took her back to his pleasant rooms overlooking the Golden Horn, was definitely a cut above most of the men she took to bed for money. But still, she did mean to take him for money. She stretched herself out along his body, her much smaller frame easily fitting inside his and, skin to skin, lips to mouth, whispered what she thought was a fair price, given how much they'd both enjoyed themselves.

Hecebolus was still smiling as he sighed, wrapped one big arm tight round her shoulders and with the other across her hips held her close and said, 'No.'

'What?' Theodora was not used to being refused her fee. It had happened once or twice, but as a good citizen, she had not only the weight of her fame, but also the power of the City behind her – the City that officially decried her second profession, but also taxed her earnings both on-stage and off.

'Sorry, I don't pay.'

'You should have said that first.'

'You should have asked for payment first.'

'I usually do,' said Theodora.

'And why didn't you this time? Because you were happy? Enjoying the body of a man who enjoys yours? Eating a pleasant dinner and drinking good wine in the company of a man who has travelled and seen something of the world and met plenty of women in his time . . .'

'Hardly a recommendation.'

'For either of us.' Hecebolus was still holding Theodora close though she was trying to move away now, pushing against his body, digging her toes into his shins, her fingers on his torso, sharp nails threatening to spoil his skin at any moment. 'But still, it is not usual for me to see someone on stage and know the moment I see her – the moment I saw you – that I wanted you.'

Theodora did not stop pushing, he did not stop holding her to him.

'It is, though, usual for me. I am used to men wanting me.'

'Not used to me wanting you. Not used to me wanting you as a lover, not a whore.'

'Don't be silly, we've had a nice evening, that's all.'

'We can have more.'

'We've both drunk too much.'

'We can do this sober.'

'I don't fuck sober.'

'Maybe you'd like to give it a try.'

'And maybe you'd like to pay my way.'

'I don't pay my lovers.'

'I don't have lovers.'

'You do now.'

For so many reasons, and for none in particular, Hecebolus was different. He was smart and bright and ambitious – all good things and all very much the kind of thing she saw day in, day out among the young men of Constantinople. Unlike the men she usually met, he really did want to spend time with her, he liked to talk almost as much as he liked to have sex. He wasn't frightened of her – her passion for work, food, drink or, now, for grief did not scare him off. Theodora could not talk easily to her family about their loss, she had never been especially close to Hypatia, and in their pain the two women became even more distant; Comito dealt with her tears by concentrating even more on her singing. Hecebolus happened to be in the right place at the right time for Theodora's grief. He had never known Anastasia and so it was easier to talk to him about her. It was easier for Theodora to make a story of her loss. Eventually, she even let Hecebolus see her cry. Just once, but it was enough. And because he held her, and listened, and did not offer solutions or try to make it all right, or tell her she would get over the pain, because he simply allowed her to cry, Theodora chose to trust him. Trust him enough to leave with him.

Not a good enough reason for Sophia.

'Dear God and whatever goddesses there might ever have been, don't be such a stupid tart. You're heartbroken about

Anastasia, you're in lust with that great oaf – and that's all it is, lust – that new piece we put in the second half of the show doesn't do as well as the geese, the company's in a bit of a slow period . . . but none of those things are a reason to leave.' She paused here, drew herself up to her full height and then came back down again, a small woman making an important point and, even in the moment of doing so, knowing she would make her point more clearly without performing. She grounded herself, took up her full height and no more. 'Please, we're your family, this is your home, don't go with him.'

'He listens to me.'

'I listen to you.'

'You lecture me.'

'Because you're being stupid. It won't work.'

'Why not?'

'You're running away.'

'What's wrong with that?'

'It can't last.'

'What can?'

The offer was just too good. To come away, be his partner, his consort – not, Sophia emphasised, not his wife – to join him in his new job, just confirmed. Hecebolus was to be Governor of the Pentapolis, the Five Cities at the tip of Africa, the point where the Empire gave way to desert and an unknown world. They would travel to serve the Emperor. It would be a relief to go with him and leave Anastasia's death and Comito's increasingly cold ambition and her mother's unbearable sadness and the constant barb that was her non-existent relationship with her own daughter, to get away from all those people who, in the street, in the theatre, in the market, knew too much about her. Hecebolus' offer – made in the heady throes of lust, and then repeated, soberly, more than once – to make her his mistress, the concubine of the new Governor, was her perfect escape route. They would be based in Apollonia, the chief of the Five Cities, he would take up his new job, together they would experience a new life. In some ways, in many ways, Hecebolus was offering a far more prestigious position than the one she now occupied as Hippodrome star, albeit a position with no safety net, as Comito pointed out and Sophia repeated, shaking her head. But Theodora was not listening. Even without her grief she had been restless: with it, she was positively hungry to get away.

It was all change at the Imperial Palace – with the new Emperor Justin and his nephew Justinian advising him, the Blues were once again in the ascendant and, from the opposing side of the religious divide to his predecessor, Justin was clamping down hard on those who opposed the rulings of the Council of Chalcedon. He had already deposed Severus, the Patriarch of Antioch, and now he needed a good man out in Africa where the Copts and the anti-Chalcedonians and any number of growing sects were increasingly at odds with the Church of Rome and Constantinople. This would be a great opportunity for Hecebolus to show his skills in diplomacy, both with the religious rebels and with those he would now rule – and, more importantly, tax – on behalf of the August. It was late spring, fishermen said the seas were generous just now, sailors looked at the stars and commented on their favourable position: if ever there was a time to move on, this was it. A sea-path in soft weather would give them time to get to know each other better as they began a new life together.

Hecebolus had been kind in his compassion for Theodora's loss. He really seemed to mean it when he asked her to join him, to be his lady both on the voyage south and when he took up his posting as Governor. She could not be his wife, of course, the world had not changed so much that all the old pro-prieties could be ignored, and on the outskirts of the Empire even less so. Through an alliance with Hecebolus though, Theodora had another chance to gain fortune. The Governor-to-be was full of talk about what could be done with tax revenue and crop gains, some to pass on, some to siphon off and invest – especially as part of a new regime and, even for an ex-actress, a rise in fortune would mean some rise in status.

Theodora had gone as far as she could as the people's darling. She was eighteen, the mother of one living child; if she was lucky her physical skills would last another ten years at most, not more – not at the rate she'd been working. Her audience was no more fickle than any other, and no less. She understood that money and position, in that order, were what she needed in the next stage of her life and with this posting Hecebolus had the means to offer both. Theodora had always been drawn to doing anything she'd been warned against. Hecebolus' offer was, in many ways, a challenge, a dare. She packed her bags.

In the theatre there were drunken protestations of friendship forever from her colleagues and five encores from the crowd, disbelieving but finally persuaded – by Theodora throwing her actor's cloak into the crowd – that this was indeed her last show. And then it was done, the makeup removed, the costumes hung up. The geese were pensioned off and, once out of Theodora's hearing or the reach of her furious fists, auctioned for supper. They fetched a good price at market, the added incentive of where they'd been feasting made them worth double the going rate.

At home Hypatia grumbled that God had taken one daughter and now this damn son of Tyre was taking another, that she was left with Ana to care for and that her life could not stand more change. But, as the pragmatist she was, Hypatia eventually turned to hope. That Theodora would do well. That her skills would come in useful as the consort of a new Governor: no one could silence a crowd the way she could, no one command either a servant or a lord with such passion in her slow, low voice, fire in her eyes. If she was to lose Theodora – and both knew she was least close to Theodora of all her children – then Hypatia would do her best with Ana instead. Fortunately, and contrary to what most might have expected from her reputation, Theodora had saved a good deal of her income over the years. Unlike Comito she had never seen herself settling for one or two men, and had always assumed she'd need the cash once her body was no longer good currency. As long as Hypatia spent the money wisely, and with three other children to raise there was no suggestion she wouldn't, there was a chance Ana would never have to go on stage. Kissing her daughter goodbye, Theodora bit her tongue before she could say how fortunate that was, the quiet child simply had no spark. Lucky indeed that her mother's skill had already earned her, at four years old, a dowry worth trading. For her part, Ana barely looked up from the dolls she was dressing in scraps of cloth. While she knew Theodora was her birth mother, Hypatia was the woman she turned to for nurture and care. Perhaps if she had ever seen her mother on the stage she might have felt the public's love for the star; as it was, she already knew her own looks and her temperament to be a disappointment and a mother many miles across the sea was at least a mother she could pretend was kind and soft.

Comito had no qualms about encouraging Theodora to follow her heart, and her groin. Theodora was leaving for love, lust and fortune, while the older sister was committed to her glittering singing career – a career that would benefit from being out of her little sister's shadow. And though Theodora was sad to leave behind her beloved Hagia Sophia, the gallery she still crept to in secret, even more so since her heightened fame, the church would always be there to welcome her home, high on the first hill of the City. She had no doubt she would come home in the end. Right now, she was simply hungry to get away, into Hecebolus' life and their new world.

There was one farewell that did not come easy. Theodora had not had a friend before Sophia: she'd had her sisters and her colleagues, but she and Sophia were different. Theodora was used to being adored, in Sophia she had a friend she adored in return. Unfortunately, the Theodora who was not only in love but also prepared to leave the City and the stage for it was a woman Sophia did not recognise. Sophia tried to reason with her, to dissuade her, and spent the last three days that Theodora was in the City arguing with her, ranting that whatever magic Hecebolus had in his fat cock and his heavy purse could not possibly be equal to the world her friend was giving up. Their goodbye was difficult and drunken and loud, surrounded by a large group of actors and dancers who left the stage after that last show and immediately set to partying in Theodora's honour, with her name on their lips and her money behind the bar.

Theodora had hoped to spend a quiet night, or even a few hours alone with her friend. 'We could go somewhere else, just the two of us, for a meal?' she suggested.

But Sophia, sitting proud on the shoulders of a tattooed Herulian wrestler, his body as wide as hers was tall, motioned her stallion of a man to turn away, shouting over her shoulder as she went, 'Don't be stupid Theo, this is your party. Have a good time, dance, sing, enjoy yourself. Fuck it, who knows when you'll have any fun again? It's dry in Africa, sweetheart, dull and dry as Juliana Anicia's cunt. You make the most of tonight, you'll regret it if you don't.'

'I'll regret it if I don't spend some time with you, Little One, please,' Theodora pleaded, even as Sophia was carried ten, fifteen, twenty feet away.

Then Sophia turned her man fully now, wrapped herself around his shoulders to lean into the centre of the room, and whispered, with all the force of a comedian in command of her usual audience of thirty thousand baying spectators, 'My name is Sophia. My friends call me Little One. And my friends . . .' she paused, looked round the room, waited until she was sure everyone was listening: 'My friends live in the City.'

Saying goodbye to Menander was even harder. The teacher wouldn't speak to her after class, he had no time, nor would he let her make an appointment to see him later, saying he was too busy with his new young dancers. So Theodora simply turned up on his doorstep. She had never before been to her teacher's home. The servant she announced herself to said he doubted very much his master would receive her, but she sent him into the dark of the house anyway, and when he came back smiling, telling her he'd been right in the first place, that Menander was seeing no one, she fought to stop him slamming the door in her face.

Eventually Menander himself came to the door, hit the servant over the head for making such a fuss and proceeded to shut Theodora out himself.

She stepped forward and put her foot between the door and the ledge.

'You think I won't close the door on your foot?'

'And waste all those years of teaching by crippling me?'

Menander rubbed his face, sighing. Theodora was surprised to see how tired he looked. 'Theodora, you're the one who is leaving the theatre, I hardly think you can accuse me of wasting your skill. Now if you don't mind, I have another rehearsal in an hour, I'd like to rest.'

Theodora put out her hand, reaching for her teacher. 'I want to say goodbye.' As Menander stepped back, into the darkness of his hallway, she was shouting to him, trying to make him talk to her, 'Please, Menander. I want to thank you.'

The older man left his hand on the door, still ready to close it in her face, and stepped forward into the light, just a little. 'You did your job, I did mine. I continue to do mine, you are leaving yours.'

'Leaving my job yes, but why does everyone have to behave as if I'm leaving all of you?'

'Because you are.'

And then he did close the door and the tears she cried were hotter than any his cane had ever brought.

Nine

Theodora had travelled by sea before, to the few important houses on the eastern side of the Bosphorus, to the old city of Chrysopolis, and to half a dozen of the prettiest country estates in Bithynia, which she loved, but these had been brief voyages, up or down the narrow strait, only occasionally venturing into the more open waters of the Sea of Marmara, the lighthouse beneath the Imperial Palace proving that home was always in reach. More often than not she'd also been travelling with at least one of her sisters, as well as other company members who felt more like family than her own daughter. She had never before sailed on and on, until the coastline she loved became a thin silver line, and, finally, disappeared entirely. Nor had she travelled as anything other than a worker, using the vessel to get from one venue to another, one private show to another gilded whorehouse to a third back-room bedroom. She had never before journeyed to an unknown end.

Now, for those weeks it took to get to the North African shore, Hecebolus was her true destination. Mediterranean crossings, even in perfect spring weather, were notorious for the storms that sprang up unannounced, and the equally stalling calms in which ships sat eddying gently, going nowhere for days at a time, while boredom-dulled sailors sang the same songs hour after hour. Meanwhile, the light on deck was bright and warm, the nights were star-filled and, once Hecebolus closed her lips with his own, Theodora stopped crying for the people she might never see again. For the first week at least, the Governor-to-be was far more interested in learning about the woman by his side than he was in mastering the finer points of the tax laws of Cyrenaica.

The ship's captain snarled at his men every time one of them mentioned the tart from the stage by her more usual name, Theodora-from-the-Brothel. Hecebolus, or his Imperial masters, in paying for this entire journey, had also paid for the entire crew. If the new Governor of the Pentapolis chose to spend the first days of his commission in the arms of that woman, then they were not to judge. And Mistress was as good a name as any if his men needed to address her, though he'd prefer they did not; women were always a distraction, and Theodora was more siren than most. His fierce injunctions to be polite and to acknowledge the woman only in her new role did not, however, stop the captain blessing himself every time he passed her on board, nor did it stop him from offering libations to the sea gods at any opportunity. He asked the Christ's blessing on the vessel too, of course, but he was a sailor, he'd sailed plenty of seas, including the one in Galilee. It was all very well to assume the Christ had walked on that particular body of water, the Mediterranean was a very different matter, and with a whore on board – no matter what her current job title or how he'd ordered his men to treat her – he wasn't prepared to take chances, so he enlisted both Neptune and Peter the Fisherman in caring for the safety of his ship.

Not that Theodora minded: as Hecebolus' mistress she occupied one of the finest cabins on board, and she had her own assistant to take care of any other needs. Chrysomallo had come with her from the theatre. Her friend was very pretty, but that was about all that could be said for her acting and dancing skills, and with no abilities other than her looks and an adequate voice, she had jumped at the chance to leave the company before she was fired anyway. There would be plenty more staff for the Governor's concubine to take charge of in their residence in Apollonia, but for now one ex-colleague-as-maid, all to herself, and one adequately sized cabin, in which she entertained only Hecebolus, was more than enough for Theodora.

She filled her time with entertaining her lover and ignored the tiny waves of panic whenever she remembered that, for the first time in thirteen years, she had no idea what came next. There were private suppers for the lovers, private rituals performed within the four sloping walls of the cabin or, late at night, on deck, with kind under-lighting provided by the moon's reflection on a swaying sea. The ship stopped off in several ports along the way, with goods for the captain to pick up and drop off: his cut from the sales and the taxman was a sizeable chunk of his income. Mostly the time on board was one of easy loving and easy laughter for the new couple, and this ease made both Hecebolus and his new mistress kind to their fellow travellers.

Theodora may well have been the whore of her legend, but the sailors found her willingness to pass the time of day with them – especially when their captain wasn't looking – extremely refreshing. And when the captain was about, her ability to talk to everyone, from lowest cabin boy to her own new master, in the same elegant tone was also impressive. Every now and then, though notably when Hecebolus was otherwise engaged, she gave the seamen a tantalising glimpse of her former life in rather less refined tones, provoking pack laughter and the sailors' increasingly devoted appreciation. No matter what her new title might be once they arrived in the Five Cities, she was certainly no lady, and they liked her all the better for it.

Theodora was definitely in lust, suspected she might even be in love – though she wasn't sure she knew that state well enough to judge – and, once she allowed herself to relax into the lack of routine, she found it was possible to actually enjoy doing nothing other than waiting for another day to pass in the warmth of the growing sun. It was only when they were passing the southernmost Cycladic islands that she started to look behind as well as forward. At Sifnos they stopped to pick up silver for trade and various trinkets to adorn Theodora's fine neck and arms, and at Milos Hecebolus went ashore with several sailors, ostensibly to catch a fresh goat for their supper – which they did – but more specifically to climb one steep hill after another to a hidden temple, there to sacrifice the one goat they did not bring back to eat, offering thanks to local gods, as well as the Christ, for a safe first half of the journey and obeisance for more of the same on the second leg. Slowly Theodora began to acknowledge how much she was leaving behind.

They rounded the long, flat face of Crete and she stood, late one night, on the prow of the ship, alone but for a watchman high above her, crying into the salt water below. Theodora didn't understand these tears, they were not from physical exhaustion or hunger or anger at an uninterested crowd, this was a sadness that could not be quelled with wine or dancing, the kind of feeling she usually let seep into the church floor and away from her body, from her understanding. Theodora was missing the City. She shook her head, angry at giving in to such a pathetic emotion when so much lay ahead, angry and feeling it regardless. Far off on the Cretan hills she could just make out tiny sparks of light from farmers' home fires, from herders grazing goats, keeping their night fire warm until the morning, drinking wine in the dark and wild sage tea with the dawn. She would not want their lives, she had never possessed the simple acceptance all farmers must have in facing the elements, but she knew, too, that once away from Crete and out into the really open sea, she would be facing a new world in earnest.

At first she thought the sound came from the island, a slow plaintive flute, perhaps, the long-held note of a young farmer bored with the night and his sleeping animals. Then she heard the same note again, and again, and realised it came from far closer than the dark mass of land. She followed the call back, quietly making her way towards the stern, and there, small as her fist, perched on a pile of carefully folded and stacked sails, was the tiny Skops owl, the one the sailors called the invisible minstrel, heard often in the night and rarely seen. She sat ten steps from the bird and waited. She held her breath, willing it to stay. It let out three more long cries, then, in moonlight turned milky by the thin clouds, she watched it turn its fine head towards her, give out one more low call, and simply lift off from its perch, arcing slowly above the boat and away, back to land.

Many days later, on the last leg of their journey, Crete far behind them and only Africa ahead, Theodora – with Hecebolus' permission, acknowledging he was her new troupe-master now – danced for the ship's company while Chrysomallo sang. Neither woman was exhibiting her best skills, Theodora was fully dressed and, with her mouth open to let out the semi-pure notes, Chrysomallo could not offer the finest pose of her perfect face, but the sailors were entertained. Theodora and Chrysomallo were delighted with their applause. The captain led a toast to the women and Hecebolus was praised by all the men for his choice of lady as he grinned and bowed and held his Theodora tight with one arm round her waist, smacking his free hand on his thigh in loud applause.

*

An hour later he was smacking that same hand across Theodora's back and legs. Like Menander, he knew exactly where to hit so the bruises would not show in public. Theodora and Hecebolus had engaged in play-fighting for sex, more than once, but this was not fun and the third time Hecebolus lifted his hand against her, Theodora backed away.

'Stop. I don't like it.'

'I don't like you flirting with the entire fucking ship's company.'

'It was a show.'

'It was showing off, and I know you well enough to know you weren't acting when you sucked up their praise. You loved every minute of it.'

'Of course I did, you stupid bastard. I like praise. Who doesn't?'

'A lady should not enjoy the praise of a bunch of sweaty, dirty working men.'

Theodora stared at him then, 'I'm sorry?'

'A lady should not—'

'But I am not a lady,' she stopped him. 'I could act like one. I could be reserved, constantly aware of my status. I could believe myself to be better than those men simply by virtue of being born to a rich father, but then you would never have met me, I would not be here now. You would have found some other theatre trollop to come with you on this great new adventure. You chose me – I was no different then.'

'We will arrive in a day or so. It is important to start as we mean to go on, I have to make a good impression in Apollonia.'

'Hecebolus,' she said, softening her voice. She looked at this angry, worried young man, the second son of a successful dye merchant, trying to make his own path, away from his family's demands and constraints, 'There is nothing I don't know about making a good impression.'

'They will talk.'

'Who?'

'The crew.'

'Yes,' she nodded, explaining. 'And they'll say I was kind, pleasant. They'll say that although I didn't take off my clothes or sing dirty songs, I gave them an hour of fun. It will be busy, hard work for them when we arrive, they need to let off steam first. Their captain said as much himself, he was grateful. He wasn't just being polite when he toasted me, I know when men are being polite. He meant it.'

Her lover rubbed his eyes, torn between jealousy and understanding. He tried another tack. 'Fine, but that's done. I need you to behave like a lady now.'

'You mean act like a lady?'

'If that's the best you can do.'

'Oh, I can do far more than that,' she answered, her own anger rising again as he failed to accept her compassion, to pick up on her conciliatory tone, 'I could actually be a lady. A real one, elevated in social status as well as pretence, but I'd have to marry a gentleman for that to happen.' She waited, a half-pause to see if he understood her. His anger was still too high in his face though, and she chose to speak with still more clarity just to be sure. 'And a gentleman would have to ask me.'

They stared at each other then. She knew he could not ask her to marry him, his father would never forgive him if he did and anyway, the law and too much that lay back in the City made it impossible. Hecebolus was a product and a property of the Empire. Other actresses might do well, in time, with their own money and their own fame, but Theodora had been so well known, it was too soon. She understood that his father would die eventually, Hecebolus knew that her fame would fade, faster for being away from the City, that anything might happen one day: with time in Africa and a chance for her to

81

gain a different status away from the stage, new choices might yet be made. In time. One day. Not now.

In the dark that was nearly morning, and for much of the following day and night, they made love that was nearly anger. Passion with a biting edge, literally, of frustrated hope and muttered disappointment. Neither could change their place in their world, neither wanted to accept that this journey, almost complete, to a new continent and a new life might not make the difference both hoped for. And so they fucked the dark into light through another day and, as the setting sun turned the new world a deep red, they arrived in Africa, each knowing the other a little better, and not necessarily happier to be wiser.

Ten

After a full night and most of a day given to their bodies, the landing was a disappointing return to the real world. When they disembarked in the port of Apollonia, the centre from which the new Governor would rule the Five Cities, the harbour waters were choppy, the moorings littered with rotting vegetable matter and packing materials from the last ship in dock, and the Governor's retinue that arrived to greet them stood in a slovenly mass of bodies that gradually morphed into a few soldiers, an ageing household master and someone who announced himself as Hecebolus' new treasurer but who, given his lack of beard and the uncertain timbre of his voice, would have been better used playing Theodora's understudy.

The messy welcoming party led them along a pitted road that had long lost its Roman elegance, to a house that was little bigger than the tenement where Theodora was raised. True, she and Hecebolus didn't have to share it with four other families, nor was their water supply from a single well at the far end of the street, but they did need to make space for the servants his status demanded, and the various clerks he would have to employ under his own roof. Overcrowding was a minor problem, compared to the architecture of the place. Theodora had always thrilled to space and light. She adored the openness of the Kynegion stage, the high gallery of Hagia Sophia, had performed in hundreds of private homes where the views from balconies and terraces conformed to the revered Constantinopolitan law that no one home should block the sea view of another. Even in poverty, Theodora had understood that much suffering could be alleviated by light and space, and if she couldn't have that at home or in the crowded streets of her home town, she had always been able to find it on the Marmara shore, in the expansive arc of an aqueduct, or high on one of the City's hills. There was virtually no natural light in her new home. The Governor's dwelling was sensibly made of thick walls, designed to keep out the brutal North African summer heat; it had high narrow windows too, to make it harder for the fine gritty sand to flow in, though flow it did. Even if their home had been staffed by the most accomplished servants, it would have been impossible to keep the place truly clean at this time of year, when the building was daily assailed by a sand so fine and constant it became a solid dust in the air, in the eyes, the throat – and their home was not staffed by the most accomplished servants.

As a star in her own right, Theodora had grown accustomed to good service. In Apollonia though, she was no star, she wasn't even Hecebolus' wife. At best she was considered his companion, an assistant perhaps, but not the mistress of the new home, and certainly not someone with the right to order incompetent and insolent servants. It was a mess in which Hecebolus was meant to entertain bishops, play Governor, demand taxes from recalcitrant overlords, all the while carrying out any number of reforms that were bound to alienate the local populace. The residence needed to look like a mini-palace and Theodora, once she overcame her initial disappointment, had plenty of suggestions for ways to achieve this. She was furious that her renovation plans needed to be turned into requests for finances, and her orders to the higher-ranking staff had to go through Hecebolus' clerk. In Constantinople she had known her place, it was flung in her face by every arrogant patrician wife who caught her husband staring too openly at Theodora's breasts or was said to applaud too heartily from his private front bench, but she had also been able to carve out a comfortable life from the little she was permitted. She could not marry or legally own property in the City, but she could rent and she could hire a maid who would call her mistress to her face, no matter what she called her in private. In Apollonia it soon became clear that the only time Theodora was called mistress was to differentiate her new job description from the more respected title of wife.

'They hate me.'

Theodora was lying in Hecebolus' bed, her narrow frame draped across his much larger torso, her legs twisted into his.

'Why do you care?'

'So you agree they do hate me?'

He sighed, his chest rising and falling heavily with the effort of going over this once again. Four months into the job and his concubine's paranoia was rather less interesting to him than grain yields and tax thresholds and how best to maintain order in the overcrowded Ptolemais ward that looked ready to erupt into street fighting any day.

'I didn't say that. I said, why do you care?'

'I don't want them to hate me.'

There was a whining note to her voice that Hecebolus was tiring of, especially first thing in the morning.

'They're just servants.'

'Is it wrong to want them to respect me?'

'My darling girl, for a woman of the stage, you know fuck-all about human nature.'

The last thing Hecebolus wanted was yet another complaining mistress, he'd already left one of those behind in his home town of Tyre, dropped when she started nagging about children and family, and another in Constantinople, deserted when it became clear that he might actually capture the famed Theodora for himself. It had never occurred to him that a girl from the bowels of the Hippodrome would find anything to complain about out here. And there was no chance he'd find an even bearable replacement in Africa. Hecebolus knew the further reaches of the Empire and wasn't much impressed by what they had to offer in the way of tarts. He needed to get Theodora past this, he wanted his smart-mouthed little acrobat back, his passionate woman – not this grumpy, disappointed girl.

'Look, this lot, they're servants in the arse-end of the Empire and the best job they can find is to clean up after you. Of course they're going to behave like cunts. We're here to rule them and they hate that too. We come from the City and like any other small-town plebs, they hate that. We don't think much of their housing and we've stated very clearly their furnishing is crap, and whoever the artist was who did that vile mosaic in the dining room should be roasted slowly over a spit of his own making. It would at least make a better meal than the swill we've been offered so far.' She laughed and he went on, 'You and I appreciate theatre—'

'They have a theatre,' Theodora interrupted him.

'Yes, and they're so insanely religious that most of them won't go and the ones who do are treated to some third-rate tour of a show written when my grandfather was a child. We've had our pick of good music and fine storytelling in Constantinople; these dogs like cheap wine and flat doughy bread, and falling pissed on their faces counts as entertainment out here.'

'I don't mind their bread, it's good for soaking up what little gravy they serve with the meat.'

'Fair enough, and we've both been known to drink more than our fair share of cheap wine as well . . .'

'Only once we've finished the good stuff.'

'Of course. The point is, they'd hate us whoever we were. If you were as chaste as the Virgin they'd hate you for speaking better formal Greek than they'll ever possess . . .'

'And Latin.'

'Just.'

'I could stumble through a court paper if I had to.'

'I'm sure you could, though God knows why you'd want to.'

'To help you?'

He ruffled her hair, a gesture he didn't care that she loathed. 'You take care of the house, I'll look after the court papers.'

She smiled. Having heard Hecebolus' own stilted court Latin she was sure she'd be able to use the language of state far better than he: perhaps not in the perfectly phrased and parsed terms necessary, but certainly with far more skill in oration. It wouldn't do, though, to let him know she thought so.

'The problem is, girl, they think we're snobs, and we think they're peasants.'

'They are peasants.'

'And we're probably snobs too.'

Theodora shook her head. 'Not me. You might be, with your fancy degree.'

'Bollocks, you actors are the worst snobs of all, you watch your audiences and judge them from your first day backstage.'

She had to admit he was right. 'Maybe, but I didn't have years studying in Berytus . . .'

'All the better to understand their small provincial minds.'

'They call me your concubine.'

'You are.'

'And your whore.'

'Oh no, that would require payment, we're far too civilised for that.'

'Aren't we just?' She pressed her body harder against his.

87

'I really should get to work . . .'

'Are you sure?' Her voice was more insistent as his body acceded, then she leaned back to smile at him. 'I do have a price, of course.'

He grinned. 'Whore.'

'Cock.' She smiled back.

'Go ahead.'

She nodded, beginning to move her body very slowly in rhythm with his.

'So, this price?' He groaned as he spoke, the deputy forgotten, his papers ignored.

'Fire the rudest of them.'

'Which is that?'

'The household clerk.'

'He's the most skilled of the lot.'

'And the nastiest. I'll find someone better.'

'It's a high price.'

'I'm a good whore.'

She could feel his mouth stretch into a smile as she stroked his face with her spare hand.

'Ah fuck it,' he laughed, 'Done.'

'Good.'

Eleven

The fiercer excesses of summer, and then the autumn equinox passed, the ferocious winds that screamed through the narrow streets faded to a low hum, a breeze that on a good day – very good day – might almost be called gentle. The Jews were preparing to celebrate their harvest festival, those who still spoke to the old gods in private honoured Cerelia as quietly as they could, and Theodora relaxed into the comfortable warmth of the dark North African evenings, aware that back in the City a sharp chill would already be invading from the north.

Following just a little more verbal, and much more physical persuasion, the arrogant clerk was fired and Theodora persuaded Hecebolus to employ a young eunuch to run the household. With Chrysomallo, the three of them made a good team. Ambitious himself, Armeneus had no interest in Theodora's reputation beyond the famous people she knew and might one day help him meet. Two years younger than his new mistress, but far less worldly, he saw her as a tutor and a step on a ladder. For her part, Theodora was probably the first woman Armeneus had met who didn't mock him for his castrated status, who understood that somewhere between man and woman could be a place of value, of understanding. She didn't care if he wanted to use her; if anything, she appreciated his honesty – it was nice to have someone around who understood the way of the world and wasn't afraid to acknowledge it.

*

The three of them set to making the Governor's dwelling less like a barracks and more like a home. Theodora taught the cook new recipes, both those that were simple but well loved from the City and others from her lover's Levantine homeland, so similar to the recipes she remembered Hypatia's grandmother making. She had not been interested in learning them as a child – Theodora realised very early on she wasn't interested in housewifery – but now she racked her memory and, true to the teaching Menander had beaten into her, the recipes arrived at the forefront of her mind, like a clean scene from a just-learned script, added to performance in half an hour or less. Armeneus trawled the markets for new fabrics – not the delicious silks Theodora really wanted, the Governor's purse did not stretch to that, but there was fine cotton from Egypt, vibrant dyes from Mauretania to the west and Libya to the south. Theodora and Chrysomallo combined their theatrical skills so that within a few months the house had at least a semblance of elegance. Like any set, the image lasted only as long as the light was soft, the cracks and joins all too obvious in bright light. Fortunately, partial illumination was all the local windows afforded.

Theodora created the ideal setting for her new relationship and, for a time, both lovers played their parts well. In the end, that was their problem. The role of Governor and the role of his beloved – the woman who runs a fine home and takes care of her high-achieving man, the successful concubine who plays the part of wife so well she practically is his wife – this was the best Theodora could hope for. She had always known she could never marry Hecebolus, she could only ever act the part. Eventually even the star of the Kynegion and Hippodrome became bored with just the one role. Eventually even Hecebolus from the Levant became bored with just the one woman.

This did not happen immediately.

What happened first was that Hecebolus was called on to entertain a bishop. As far as he was concerned, it was utterly inappropriate to have any woman at table with a bishop, let alone his mistress.

Theodora did not see it that way. 'Hecebolus, I'm good with clergy.'

Chrysomallo, darning Hecebolus' only good cloak, smiled to herself where she sat in the one well-lit corner of the sitting room, passing her needle through fine linen, joining broken threads.

'No,' Hecebolus said. 'You're good with shagging clergy and making them think it's fine because in some way they're redeeming you, so they don't have to feel utterly damned the morning after.'

'Oh, I told you that?' Theodora asked, hearing the coda of one of her own stories repeated back to her.

Chrysomallo raised an eyebrow. Theodora had always had a big mouth.

'You did. With actions. Thank you.'

'You're welcome.'

The lovers nodded to each other, each with the pleasant memory as a brief distraction, then Hecebolus went on, 'But even if you hadn't, I'd know it to be true, hypocrites the lot of them, wasting all this time and money deciding the true nature of the Christ when it's beyond them to know anyway, sinful as they are.'

'Sinful as we all are, we can still discuss divinity, surely?' Theodora answered back. 'Wasn't that one of the main points in the break from the Jews? The break from their priests?'

Hecebolus looked at her, shaking his head. 'For a tart, you really are very naive sometimes.'

'How so?'

91

'Back there in the City, you all see the faith as such a simple thing, this or that, heresy or truth, one nature or two, belief or not.'

'I never said I was a believer.'

'No, and I've seen you light candles and offer incense to any number of midnight deities that I suspect have very little to do with the Mother of God . . .'

'Oh that's all superstition, ideas from my mother, my grandmother, it doesn't mean anything, every actor does it.'

'I'm not asking, I don't care. I've never had any real faith myself, not beyond the daily, weekly observance. I'm a clerk turned soldier turned petty Governor, and the only reason I ever did any of that was because my father insisted on giving the business solely to my brother and he didn't want to share it with me.' Hecebolus smiled. 'Do you have any idea how long it takes for the Imperial Purple to rinse from the fingers of a child who has no business near the dye vats?' She shook her head. 'My father tanned my hide that day, but I lay in bed for the next fortnight examining my purple hands as if they might have the spark of Empire in them . . .' He shook his head. 'I had hoped this posting might be a stepping-stone, but already it's clear they're just using me, as they always have – our leaders, our betters. I'm never going to rise as high as I once wanted, it's obvious here. These past months have been a hard lesson, but I've taken it in. You're just going to have to accept it too.'

'Accept what? That all this wind is wearing down your ambition? Or is it just the fucking that's making you too tired to bother? Because it would be easy to sort that.'

Hecebolus was hurt then, that she didn't seem to understand how much it cost him to admit he wouldn't go much further. 'I know my truths. You're the one who needs to learn. You are who you are, Theodora. That won't change.'

'I've made this home, I've taught your cook, employed the right staff . . .'

She began to protest and he shook his head. 'Those things are pleasant, that's all. I don't care about any of that. Well no, I do, I like that the walls have better hangings on them, I'm delighted the food is palatable now, I think whoever the artist is that you got to cover over those horrible old mosaics with the new fresco is a genius. But those are trappings, what matters is you and me. And I don't have any problem admitting the truth of who we are, who you are. You are the smartest woman I know, will ever know. But Theodora, you know as well as I do, it doesn't matter how bright you are: unless you are my wife, you cannot sit at table with the Bishop.'

She knew she was speaking the impossible and said it anyway. 'So make me your wife.'

'I would if I could change the law.'

'Really?'

He shrugged in reply, his second-best cloak falling in great folds about his shoulders and Theodora noticed for the first time how tired he looked, how his hair seemed to have greyed since their arrival. They both knew that neither meant exactly what they said. Theodora still hoped to do better than Hecebolus, Hecebolus was still sure he could do better than her, there was still a bishop coming for dinner, and Chrysomallo sat sewing silently in the corner.

The meal progressed smoothly at first. The fish was fresh, the bread baked to a City rather than local recipe, the meats perfectly tender, the wine watered just enough to hide its immature acidity but not so much that the guests did not relax. Relaxation led to chat, chat led to discussion, and discussion – invariably, inevitably – led to the nature of the Christ.

The chief of the First Regiment started it, nodding across

the table at the Bishop and asking, 'Tell me, Bishop, now I've eaten everything on my plate, would you say the meal and I were still two, or are we now one?'

Several of the men around the table grinned: like most soldiers they enjoyed a little clergy-baiting. Hecebolus was less pleased. While he was as interested as the next noncommittal Christian in the subject of the Christ's divinity, he knew the Bishop to be staunchly anti-Chalcedonian, as were most of the North African faithful, believing the Christ was purely divine. He also knew that these Macedonian and Thracian soldiers were more likely to support the Council of Chalcedon belief espoused by the new Emperor Justin – equally certain that the Christ was of two natures, divine and human. He had no wish to offend the Bishop, but nor did he want to antagonise the military with whom he had to work every day.

'I really don't think we need to discuss divinity yet—'

He was interrupted by the Bishop, who knew a challenge when he heard one and was more than happy to take it. 'Given, sir,' he replied, addressing himself to the thread-veined Thracian captain opposite but making sure he had everyone's clear attention, 'how little you have eaten and how very much more drunk, I'd say the question is rather whether or not you have, indeed, committed some sin yourself, in drowning the food before it even had a chance to become one with your own nature?'

While there was laughter at the captain's expense, there was an even louder retort from a grain exporter at the other end of the table that the Bishop's reply was no more than a classic case of clergy dodging the real subject and concentrating on minor matters, 'As your lot always will when there's any chance of a confrontation.'

At which point the Bishop slammed his cup down on the table, spilling barely watered wine on his own plate and soaking half a loaf of uneaten bread.

'Oi! Bishop!' shouted a second military man, waiting for everyone else to quieten so his words would be better heard. 'There's no need to go wasting good wine, or good bread for that matter, first time I've had real bread in months.'

'I didn't . . . I'm not . . .' The Bishop tried to mop up the mess in front of him, ashamed to be accused of wastefulness in anger.

The soldier continued, 'We're all grown men, we're perfectly capable of remembering Him with our own bread and wine, however many natures we believe in, you don't have to go mixing good bread and better wine to a soggy paste to prove your point.'

The Bishop spluttered, the military applauded each other, the exporter began arguing with the merchant trader about which made more sense, the Greek translations of the latest one-nature texts, or the Syriac originals, and Hecebolus watched the first dinner he had hosted as Governor of the Pentapolis begin its descent from an elegant soirée to the North African equivalent of a drunken brawl, the kind he could see any Saturday night in the City's own harbours.

Armeneus came into the room. Leaning close to his master's ear so the warring guests would not hear, he whispered, 'The Mistress would like a word, sir.'

'Not now, bitch, can't you see there's more to concern me here?'

While Hecebolus was keen to ape the Imperial Palace in as many areas as possible, his provincial upbringing showed in his distaste for the eunuch, whom he privately considered an abomination. Usually he was able to keep his dislike in check, but the passion in the room was too close to boiling point for him to be careful of Armeneus' feelings. The Bishop was ready to storm out, the army captains appeared to have turned on each other now they'd had their fill of attacking the prelate, and far from using the meal to broker better deals, the merchant captain and the exporter were halfway through a long-winded argument about the best of the hidden passages on the silk route.

Armeneus looked at the men ranged before him and sighed in disgust; clearly their intact balls didn't ensure any greater ability to behave well in company. 'Sir, the Mistress understands the difficulty.' It was already in his mouth to add that the whole street understood the problem, they'd been listening to it at full pitch for the past hour, but he remembered his own elegance and swallowed the jibe, whispering in a low and careful voice, 'She and Chrysomallo have a suggestion.'

Theodora would entertain the men. In the corridor outside the dining room she hissed to Hecebolus that anything was better than what was developing on the other side of the door. He had to agree. Chrysomallo would sing, Armeneus had a small harp and could add a tune or two, Theodora would dance. She'd make it up as she went along. If the guests would shut up and pay attention she might even give them one of her more famous scenes. At that, Hecebolus glared at her and Armeneus paid still closer attention. Theodora told them both to run away, she'd done with the geese. She meant one of the big speeches, Helen or Cassandra or Clytemnestra.

'Though the way that lot are carrying on, if you don't let me get in there and calm things down soon, I might as well give them Agave and set them to tearing each other apart.'

Hecebolus knew she was right. At the very least her appearance would be a distraction, and Chrysomallo had a perfectly adequate voice to go with her pretty face and beautiful hair. He agreed. Then Theodora added that she did have a price.

'Of course you do, once a whore always a whore.'

Armeneus sucked in his breath, Chrysomallo gasped and Theodora stepped back in shock. Hecebolus shook his head. 'Oh, don't be so fucking delicate. I'm not saying it in front of that lot in there, but we know where we come from, let's not be coy about it.'

Theodora said nothing, simply gathered up her cloak and turned away from her lover.

'Theo! Come back. Look, I'm sorry. All right? Sorry.'

She stopped, but did not turn around.

Hecebolus sighed. 'Theotokos spare me! All right. What is it? What's your price?'

Theodora turned slowly, raised her head to look at him square in the eyes, staring down the man well over a foot taller than her. She spoke quietly so he had to come closer and stoop to hear. She wanted Hecebolus to introduce her to the Bishop before he left the house.

'He won't want to talk to you.'

'I know he probably won't, but you didn't expect him to get into a fight with the captain either, did you? Maybe he has other surprises as well. Maybe he likes to talk divinity with actresses. Bishops often do, in my experience. I am not asking that you force him to speak with me, merely that you request he consider the matter. I'll distract your vile guests whatever his answer, just give him the chance to say no. To say yes.'

The sound of a copper platter clattering to the ground in the next room made up his mind. Hecebolus shook his head and gave in.

Chrysomallo began singing with no introduction. From a dark corner of the room, quietly at first, came the opening chant that called the audience to attention, bringing latecomers to their seats, silencing – a little – the vendors selling cold drinks and spiced foods. It was a tune many men at the table had heard in the theatres of the City, and for those who didn't know what they were hearing, it was clear from the repetitive notes on a rising scale that something was about to happen.

The Bishop, listening to the soft, light voice coming from an unseen woman in the dark corner, couldn't help whispering to his neighbour, 'Music. A perfect example of the divine emanating from, but not one with, the human.'

The army captain across the table from him slurred, 'You're comparing a singer to the Christ?'

'No, I'm offering you a small analogy to simplify an enormously complex matter, in the hope it will help your dull head understand. Obviously I needn't have bothered.'

The captain growled but held his tongue. He loved the theatre, and if their host had something to offer that was more entertaining than arguing with the old priest, he'd happily shut up and give himself over to the entertainment. He was bored with the fight now anyway.

Chrysomallo's song became a call, the guests arranged themselves better around the table in order to look towards the sound and then Armeneus arrived in the doorway, playing the small painted harp he held in one hand, alternately picking and strumming with the other. Theodora, veiled, followed him into the room and, at a clap from Hecebolus, the three waiting servants ran and lit a dozen candles, placing them in a half-circle to light their master's mistress.

She began with a speech of Niobe. Plaintive, heartfelt, yet also soothing. It was just what the men needed. Their glasses were refilled, the dented platter quietly removed, small plates of stuffed dates, sugared almonds and honeyed figs laid out for them to pick at as they watched. From Niobe, Theodora segued into Antigone for a little more passionate agonising, using the speech to soak up the anger that had been raised and transform it into something more manageable. She flung off her veil just before the last stanza of the speech and several of the theatre-goers in the room gasped. There had been plenty of rumours about Hecebolus' concubine, that she was a dancer or an actress, that she'd been known in the City, but none of the suspicions had been confirmed until now. Not any actress – the actress. The merchant captain whispered to the exporter that perhaps now was the time to consider leaving grain in the harbour and not shipping it out and the two men giggled to each other. Theodora, trained to listen as well as to speak, replied in perfect classic Greek to contrast with the men's rough accents, that it would take more than the puny grains of an African exporter to tempt her geese out of retirement, her birds had been fattened on much juicier stuff. She did so without skipping a beat and without departing an iota from the rhythm of her speech, returning immediately to Antigone in chains, and the merchant captain, laughing, raised his glass in surrender and salute.

More singing, more music, another short speech from the classics, followed by a modern piece from one of the Kynegion's youngest writers – the most barbed comments on the clergy softened in the telling by Theodora smiling sweetly at the Bishop and offering an apologetic curtsy when she finished the piece berating the religious for spending too much time discussing the poverty of nature in relation to man and too little dealing with the nature of real men's poverty. The two women concluded with an old Lebanese dance in honour of their host, Armeneus playing the tune and, once he'd heard the first few notes, Hecebolus' countryman, the spice exporter, singing along in a good bass-baritone. The evening was over. The guests left the house, shaking hands and patting Hecebolus on the back, both as a man of the people, always a useful thing in Africa, but also as a man of the wider world, able to bring a touch of City elegance into this cultural backwater.

His evening saved and his reputation enhanced, Hecebolus did not go back on his promise. He had a quiet word with the Bishop at the door, and an appointment was made for the two ladies to visit the older man in his office the next day. Theodora went to bed very happy. She had the glow of performance on her still, the Bishop had not immediately refused her request as any of his peers would have done in the City, and she had proved herself useful to Hecebolus. Not a wife, but something like a wife. It was a lot better than fighting him. Their love-making was sweeter too, not as passionate as one of their after-fight fucks perhaps, but soft and careful, layered with kindness. Theodora lay in the darkened room, her hand on Hecebolus' broad chest, her fingers rising and falling as he slept, hoping she wouldn't become too accustomed to such pleasures. She'd seen far too many other women fall from grace through their dependence on what had once been kind.

Twelve

The Bishop was not unkind, but he was honest. He received the two women in his office, two lower-ranking members of his clergy in attendance. He offered them only water. He praised their performance, while reminding them that their talents would be better used in praise of the Christ, than in a theatre. Then, clearly believing his obligation met, he nodded to the women and told them he had business to attend to, wishing them well in the Pentapolis. If they cared to kneel he would give them his blessing before they left. Chrysomallo knelt, Theodora stayed in her seat.

'I'd like to speak about redemption Father, if we may? And what lies beyond?'

'Beyond redemption? What are you talking about?' The Bishop glared from beneath heavy brows, last night's wine still staining his teeth.

Chrysomallo winced at his tone. 'Theo, come on.'

Theodora continued sweetly, 'As you see, my friend does not have a passion to understand the Church – but I do, and I would ask a little more of your time?'

The Bishop squinted at Theodora and sighed, he would have refused to meet any of her kind back in the City; it was merely that they were so far from the centre – and, admittedly, he'd enjoyed her performance last night – that had convinced him to allow the Governor's request. He went back to his desk, motioned for one of the young priests to refill his cup with watered wine, then he leaned forward, looking Theodora up and down. Her face seemed to match her words and it was true there were many women whom the Church revered for their passionate interest in matters of faith, the sainted Helena for one. Striking face, small wiry body, voice held soft and low for now – but he'd heard the stories, this was not just any actress, this was Theodora.

'No, I'm sorry, you are too well known. And even now . . .' The Bishop hesitated, wondering how to put it politely in front of the young priests hanging on every word, and realising he could not: 'You are the Governor's concubine, yes?'

Theodora nodded. 'I would be his wife if the law were different.'

Chrysomallo groaned and went back to her seat.

The Bishop frowned. 'It is not your place to make law.'

'The laws of God and man are often united and becoming more so.'

'You flatter me. Perhaps the clergy in the City have influence in the Imperial Palace. Out here we can only hope to have influence with the people.'

'The people are the Empire.'

'So the phrase goes, but there is a hierarchy for good reason: just as man is subject to the Church, and woman subject to man, so we keep our ordained positions. Your position now would be bettered not by argument, but by penitence.'

'But there is much to engage in. Your conversation last night, for example, on the divinity of the Christ . . .'

At this, one of the young priests let out an involuntary gasp: the idea of an ex-whore daring to bring this up was too much for him to keep quiet.

'The nature of the Christ is not a question for any woman. You would be better to remember that this region does not take kindly to women acting out of their true domain.' The Bishop had had enough.

Chrysomallo jabbed Theodora from beneath her long thin cloak, and Theodora realised she'd gone as far as she could. They curtsied and turned to leave the room, Chrysomallo pinching the skin on the back of Theodora's hand all the while to shut her up. By the time they reached the door the Bishop was already sitting back at his desk and working through a pile of papers.

He spoke aloud, as if he were not addressing Theodora, but speaking to the paper beneath his hand, 'Find yourself a teacher, girl. Nothing is impossible in the Christ.'

It was not the conversation Theodora had been hoping for, but it was better than nothing. She had finally met a bishop, as herself and not as some whore brought in secretly to satisfy his silent lust. She had talked to him, however briefly, and he had not dismissed her outright. It was a start.

The women left the cool of the Bishop's house for the noise and crush of the Apollonian street. Theodora longed for a sharp breeze from the sea, bouncing off the Constantinopolitan hills, Chrysomallo for a market where every shopping expedition didn't come complete with a barrage of new sensations. They moved on, edging around the stalls, picking up bracelets, putting them down when Theodora asked the price and was told, yet again, a figure beyond the allowance Hecebolus gave her. The constraints of being kept had come as an uncomfortable shock to both of them, as did being followed everywhere by one of Hecebolus' servants. Both women had walked freely, if not appropriately, about Constantinople, but here they had to behave as the female members of any good household should. Everyone in the Pentapolis now knew Theodora was not Hecebolus' wife; for his sake, though, as well as for her own, she had to behave as if she were, and that meant not even going to the market without a man to accompany them. Yossef, who followed them now, came from the kind of poor but pious family that would truly rather have starved than risk offending the priest, and resented having to spend any time in Theodora's company, let alone walking the two sluts through his home town.

The women made their way down streets burned with shafts of brilliant afternoon light, walking with their heads close; the noisy market was in many ways an easier place to chat than Hecebolus' quiet house, both of them too sure they were being spied on there.

'I still don't get what we were doing back there?' Chrysomallo asked.

'Giving a skinny old man an excuse to look at your lovely face.'

'Other than that.'

'I was talking to the Bishop about the possibility of raising my status some day.'

'We're actresses. We can't marry, we can't gain status, it's not news, Theodora.' Chrysomallo raised her hands at the futility of the matter, and three hopeful beggars looked up from their place on the ground, thinking she was preparing to throw them a coin.

'Now look what you've done.'

'Sorry, soldiers.' Chrysomallo apologised to the men, clearly ex-military from the wounds they were sporting, amputated legs and scarred faces, but she gave them only apology, no coin.

Theodora stopped by a spice stall and spoke quietly into air thick with heat and noise and the bittersweet scent of the ground sumac she asked the trader to weigh out. 'Who says I can't marry Hecebolus?'

'He's asked you?'

'Of course not. But assuming he wanted to, why can't he ask me to marry him?'

'Because the law says you can't marry.'

'Good,' Theodora paid for the spice and handed her purchase to Yossef, walking on before he could complain that the cook didn't like these City spices she kept forcing on them. 'And who makes the law?'

'The Emperor?'

'Well done. And who advises the Emperor?'

'God?'

Theodora groaned, 'Oh for fuck's sake, other than God.' Then she thought again. 'Although yes, like God, in a way, I suppose.'

'See? I'm not as stupid as you think.'

'You have no idea how stupid I think you are, Chrysomallo.'

They turned away from the main market street, heading up the narrower causeway to the Governor's dark mansion, and Theodora explained. The law insisted that once a woman had been an actress, and by implication a courtesan, it was impossible for her to marry. The Church said only a sinless woman could marry, but as Theodora pointed out, there were plenty of divorced women who married again, and widows, so merely having had sex wasn't the problem – the problem was the sin. She had no intention of taking herself off to a convent in the traditional manner of a repentant actress: living out here in Africa was bad enough, but Theodora did think it might be possible, one day, to find an amenable priest or, even better, a bishop, to take her case to a higher court. Someone with power or influence, and ideally both, who – assuming an ex-actress could find a man who wanted to make an honest wife of her – believed a woman might redeem herself enough for marriage. Theodora herself could marry in those circumstances. Further, if she could be married to Hecebolus then, some time later, she could also be divorced from Hecebolus and find herself someone who would rise further than merely

105

Governor of this hellish dustbowl, someone who might matter back in the City.

'I thought you were happy with Hecebolus?' Chrysomallo interrupted.

'I am, more or less. But it won't last, I know he'll tire of me, he did with his other mistresses. If I were married to him, I'd be in a better position later.'

Theodora believed she could, as so many other women had done, rise through marriage and divorce and remarriage. All she had to do was find a priest to agree with her.

'Out here, away from the centre, the priests at least admit they sometimes have different ideas, discuss their doubts. Where better to look for one who'll make me respectable?'

'And how do you persuade him of your good intentions?'

Theodora grinned. 'My repentance could be real, if Hecebolus is keen enough on marriage.'

'And if it's not?'

'I'll act, it's what I'm good at.'

'What if he's not convinced by the act, this mythical priest you have yet to find?'

They were at the door of the Governor's house. Yossef pushed past them into the dark passageway, it was a relief to be out of the harsh light, and Theodora threw off her scarf, her cloak, shook out the folds of her dress, pulled her friend close and whispered, 'In that case sweetie, I'll just have to get on my knees. It's what I'm good at.'

Their laughter rang out into the street and a preaching beggar on the corner opposite picked up his rant again, condemning the sinful nature of Eve, temptress of man and snake alike. Chrysomallo slammed the door on his noise.

For several months following, things were quiet, but quiet did not necessarily mean easy. Theodora settled into a routine of playing Hecebolus' partner, sometimes entertaining his guests with the most innocent of her theatrical repertoire, and meeting with the Bishop on occasion – he had, after all, recommended she find herself a teacher, and when she said he was the best in the city, he couldn't disagree. She began, too, to explore Apollonia and the other cities of the Pentapolis, revising her opinion of the area a little. Yes, it was warm out here, certainly this was nothing like the winter she was used to and was surprised to find she missed, but with the rain greenery began to blossom along the coast and Theodora began taking long walks along the shoreline, stopping off at the small ports and large churches that looked out to sea, with only Armeneus to accompany her, or Yossef, following a grumpy five paces behind. She did not acknowledge it as she walked – even if she had, there was no solution – but always she was looking north, away from Africa and Hecebolus, away from her new life to her old home, the home she had left to start a new life, a new life that had stalled all too soon. Hecebolus would rise no higher than this, no bishop would consider changing church law for a woman like her, Hecebolus was not going to marry her – and she'd be a terrible wife even if he did. Despite her high hopes of a few months earlier, nothing was changing in the Governor's house. Nothing Theodora had noticed, anyway.

Thirteen

The break with Hecebolus, when it came, was as sudden as it was shocking. Chrysomallo told Theodora she was Hecebolus' lover.

'Yeah, right, because you've got so much time between screwing the captain and flirting with that fat merchant Hecebolus keeps asking here for dinner. Christ, I swear, if I have to perform Cassandra for the bloated arse one more time, I'm going to jump off the wall myself.'

'No, really, Theo,' Chrysomallo paused, shook her head: 'We're lovers. We decided I should be the one to tell you. He thought you'd deal with it better, coming from me.'

'You decided?'

'Hecebolus and I.'

'Go on.'

Chrysomallo had the grace to stutter, just a very little, 'He thought it would be better, if I told you. He – well, we – we both know how proud you are.'

Theodora frowned. The other woman's words were jagged blades in sugar syrup, sharp yet so gently coated. Chrysomallo was looking particularly pretty today. Pretty, golden, soft.

'How proud am I, my friend?'

'Well, not proud . . .'

'Have I nothing of which to be proud?'

'Yes, of course you do.' Chrysomallo countered. 'You could go home now . . .'

'Home? Yes, that would make it easier for you.'

'No. I just mean . . . back in the City . . . they'd love to have you back. On stage. You have so much to be proud of. You have so many options open to you.'

'And you just have the one – tagging along on the dregs of my life?'

'He knew you'd be hurt.'

'He knew?'

Theodora hated sounding stupid, a child in the Chorus reduced to learning by rote, but the shock was making her dense. She took a deep breath, as she had been trained to do, ribs separating and spreading, the kind of breath a truly great performer reserves for an entrance, or a death scene. A breath meant for holding back tears, floodgates, fury, horror before the unleashing. The kind of breath that allowed her friend to continue, Chrysomallo too intent on delivering her lines to pay any attention to their shared theatre experience, to Theodora's stance, readying herself to spring.

'I did too, of course.'

'Did what?'

'Realise you'd be hurt.'

'Perceptive of you.'

'But you and I, we've shared all sorts between us, food, lodgings . . . men.'

'Women.'

'God, yes, women!' Chrysomallo smiled now, nodding, relieved, this was more like it. She and Theodora laughing over their conquests, pleased with whatever they'd gained or learned or stolen between them, happy to share. None of it taken too seriously, none of it mattering too much. Now Chrysomallo could explain about the affair she'd been having for the past two months – her friend out of the house too often, Hecebolus just a man, any man, bored with his work and looking for company

109

and finding it between Chrysomallo's sheets, her arms, her legs. The point of this moment being to get her friend on side. She had promised Hecebolus she could do this, make Theodora understand.

'We've certainly shared all sorts of things, people, you and me, so . . . I mean, I know it's a bit of a shock, but really, he needs a lot of attention. Then there's your visits to the Bishop, and God knows, Theo, you've told me often enough what appetites Hecebolus has, and all those walks you keep going off on – wandering up and down the coastline for hours at a time, the view's fine once, but . . .' Chrysomallo was wittering. Blindly unaware of the effect her words were having on her friend.

'Women. Fucking, whoring, thieving women. Woman.'

'Oh, come on, Theo . . .'

'My name is Theodora.' Theodora spoke slowly and calmly, with a deliberation that would have terrified a barbarian who spoke no Greek, let alone someone who knew her intimately.

Chrysomallo stepped back, a little closer to the door, all underestimation gone once she heard the rage in Theodora's tone.

'I brought you here. I gave you the chance of Africa, of advancement, of the world.'

'I'm sorry, Theo . . .'

'Fuck off, slut.'

There were plenty of words the two women might use to each other. Plenty of words used by women in the theatre companies they'd left behind. Whore and tart and hooker among them. Variations on actress and prostitute were a daily occurrence; what none of the women could bear to be called was slut. An actress worked for money, as did a whore, both were work, careers even. A slut, however, gave it away for free, which was simply stupid, and no one wanted to be accused of being stupid, not even Chrysomallo. She threw herself at Theodora. She was weaker than her friend, but she did have the advantage of height. Theodora was beyond surprise, she was so horrified by her friend's betrayal, but she certainly hadn't expected Chrysomallo to attack her. She went over flat on her back, her aggressor's fingers and nails digging into her upper arms.

She wasn't down for long. Twisting one leg up beneath her while pinning Chrysomallo's legs with the other, she gained enough purchase to shove the taller, heavier woman off, prising the fingers from her arms, quite intentionally ripping several of Chrysomallo's famed long nails in the process. Seeing the blood rise from the nail-beds and Chrysomallo's horror and pain simply caused her to smile. Stupid pretty girls, their vanity meant they never could win in a physical contest. A naturally lovely girl like Chrysomallo was only ever reliant on good looks and, right now, at least five of those elements of good looks were scattered on the floor at their feet.

Chrysomallo was sobbing in pain, Theodora ranting in fury. Hecebolus and Armeneus came running, as did half a dozen members of staff, but Armeneus slammed the door in their faces before the rest of them could crowd into the room.

'What the hell is going on?'

The Governor did not raise his voice; if anything, he sounded more concerned than angry. He looked only to Chrysomallo, and in that look Theodora understood that she had lost him.

'Your new lover was just explaining the reversal of my fortunes. She broke a nail or two in the process. You know how girls are – breaking a nail all too often seems the end of the world.'

Chrysomallo ran to Hecebolus and he held the sobbing blonde softly, far more carefully than he'd ever held Theodora.

She pushed Armeneus aside, glared at Yossef and the other servants hovering behind the door, and walked as calmly as she could to her own room. Only once the door was shut did she open her mouth and, ripping her hands through her hair, rocking in fury, fall to her knees and let out just one, long, silent roar of pain.

Eventually, her breath regained, her head clear, Theodora readied herself for the usual evening meal with Hecebolus and Chrysomallo, not easy when she'd been crying in rage for twenty minutes. She called on her training to contain her passion, and then, with rhythmic breathing to steady her shaking hands, applied all the skill she had learned from the old actresses working as makeup artists. By the time she was called to the dining room, Theodora was as lovely as ever Hecebolus had seen her. She had also packed a single bag, gathered everything she would need for a quick flight, including the money she'd been carefully holding back from the housekeeping purse for the past six months, aware that she never knew when she might need to leave, though never expecting it to be so soon. She took a candle to light her entrance, both utterly ready and not at all.

Chrysomallo had not made the same effort with her appearance, and sat at the table looking as bedraggled as she had an hour earlier. They ate figs and dates preserved in wine, small pigeons stuffed with herbs and almonds. Armeneus, knowing the room was a powder keg and keen to keep the staff at bay, waited on them himself, retreating to the dark of the far corner to wait and listen.

He did not have to wait long.

Chrysomallo began, wiping the pigeon grease from her hands. 'Theodora, Hecebolus and I think . . .'

'We think you should stay.' The Governor finished her

sentence. 'We can carry on as we have been. I don't want you to leave.'

'How kind.' Theodora's voice was quiet, interested. 'And how would this work? You'd screw us on alternate nights? Or maybe we'll draw lots?'

Hecebolus sighed, 'Don't be difficult, Theodora, I've become very fond of Chrysomallo—'

'Fond?' Theodora interrupted him, looking at her friend. 'Dear God, I'd have thought you might hope for more than "fond", Chrys – hungry, desperate, can't spend a night without? Weren't they the phrases you used on me, Hecebolus? Back in the City when you promised me a whole new world?'

'I gave you that, but it seems you weren't satisfied. Chrysomallo tells me you want more.'

Theodora shook her head at her friend. 'Oh, but you're good, girl.' Chrysomallo shrugged, she wasn't prepared to be cowed now. Theodora turned back to the Governor. 'Yes, I do – I did – want more from you. A chance to raise my status, to truly change my life. As I'm sure the songbird has been telling you, it's what I've talked about with the Bishop, one of the things he and I discussed. And just as you paid to raise your status.'

'Paid? What? Who?'

'Whoever you paid to get this job. The "usual civil servant bribe", isn't that what you called it?' Hecebolus growled, but said nothing. 'I was hoping for a little of the same myself. Perfectly ready to pay with my body, pay with my charm. Pay, even, with love. Clearly I've been as foolish as I always thought the blonde here was. I trusted you.'

Armeneus refilled their wine cups, served tender strips of marinated, slow-roasted goat. Hecebolus ate and drank for a while in silence, then he wiped his hands and shook his head.

'As if I don't have enough to concern me with this dog of a

113

colony. Look, Theodora, you're upset, I thought our news would come better from Chrysomallo. I was wrong, I apologise. But really, I'm sure we can make this work out, I'll be considerate of both of you, I understand there are accommodations to be made.'

'Not least with the Church? One man, two mistresses?'

'My faith is none of your business.' Hecebolus spat back, and then tempered his voice, placating, keen for his plan to work, for the women to be friends again. Theodora would be useful later, both for his needs and Chrysomallo's. As he tried to explain, 'I'm sure we can get over this. After all, Chrysomallo will need you when the child comes . . .'

'Hecebolus!' Chrysomallo finally spoke up, but it was too late.

'Oh.' Theodora understood it all.

'I thought you'd . . .?' Hecebolus pushed back his chair, sending it slamming to the floor as Chrysomallo shook her head. 'For God's sake, you sort it out.' He walked out of the room.

Theodora spoke first. 'You have put on weight.'

'I'm sorry. I didn't mean to . . . it just happened.'

'Yes, apparently that's how it works. With other women.'

'It did to you.'

'Did. Not since Ana ripped me apart, and not with Hecebolus, not even though I knew he might have liked it – wanting something to prove him the man since this job turned out so much less than he'd hoped. Well done, you've given him proof. What better way to make sure he stays yours?'

'That wasn't why. Really.'

'No,' Theodora sighed, 'I'm sure it wasn't. You always were hopeless at maths and the moon, weren't you?'

Chrysomallo nodded, tears falling down her face into the

uneaten goat on her plate, Armeneus wondering which of the staff would enjoy the salty leftovers for their supper. 'I wanted to ask you . . . I'm not ready, I don't really want it . . . but it's too late now.'

'No it's not too late. I can get the herbs, if you'd like,' Theodora offered, smiling, knowing what the reply would be, and continued without waiting for it when she saw the horror on Chrysomallo's face. 'You mean too late because you do want it, you and he both want it?' Her old friend nodded and Theodora went on, 'He'll leave you, you know. He'll find a good Christian wife one day, some frigid patrician bitch if he's really lucky, and he will leave you and your bastard.'

'Yes.'

'So start readying yourself. Pretty won't take care of you then. Save whatever you can, keep back clothes and any gold you can lay your hands on without him noticing. Get him to rent an apartment for you, tell him it's better the child doesn't grow up too close to him. That way at least you'll have some furniture when the wife makes him kick you out. As she will, as she should, I would, and so would you.' Chrysomallo nodded again. 'And whatever you do,' Theodora was up now, moving away from the table, heading for the door, 'for God's sake, don't give birth to a girl. He might try and help a son, set him up in business somehow, use his family's contacts. A girl will just remind him of where he found you, where he found both of us.'

'But Theodora,' Chrysomallo was wailing now, 'I love him.'

'Yes, you probably do. I thought I did too. Goodbye Chrys.'

Armeneus followed Theodora to her room. He had another bag packed for her, with food, wine, and a few small gold and silver pieces he'd taken from the kitchens earlier in the day when he too realised where this was heading. He also had a

115

warm cloak, not as lovely as her fine cotton one, but far more useful for travelling. She kissed him goodbye, thanked him for his friendship. He promised to come and find her in the City; she promised to get there before he did.

Theodora went first to the Bishop. She did not expect much, but it was worth a try, worth giving the old man an opportunity to show charity. Her expectations were right. There was nothing he could do. Surely Theodora understood? In a way, part of the problem was that she had changed her life at all. As a common whore he would have been able to help her, find her a place in a convent of repentance, a life of penance and two plain meals a day. As a mistress, she was neither whore nor wife, and as such, the Church could not help her. Theodora suggested that even if the Church could not, the Bishop was an individual man, there might be something he could do, but the priest had already returned to his papers. He offered her his blessing and, having knelt for it, Theodora left the room. When he heard his servant close the outer door of the house on the young woman the Bishop sighed. He really was sorry, tied as he was by his vows and, worse, by the politics of his position, there was truly nothing he could do, nothing he was prepared to do.

From Church to bar, Theodora's life had all too often followed the same route. She made her way down into the centre of the town, through narrow alleyways, pitch dark now except for the occasional wall lit from an opened door, a slammed gate. Few heads turned when she walked into the bar: not that plenty would not have been interested to see the Governor's concubine in a public tavern, but that it was so late in the evening, everyone was already sunk deep in their drink, or asleep on benches lining the walls. She bought a jug of watered wine and a dry cake, took up a place in the corner of the room. She ate and drank quietly.

Three men who had been gambling shared out their coins and rose from a corner table. One of them looked across at her. 'Are you looking for business, girl?'

His question was neither rude nor cruel, it was simply the obvious one to ask of a lone woman in the room. There were only two reasons for a woman to be in a bar – serving was one, trade the other.

Theodora seriously considered his proposal. Three drunken gamblers, at least one of them had to have a full pocket, she could have them all and they'd be asleep in an hour, their purses free for the taking.

'Not tonight. Thank you, gentlemen.'

'You sure, love?' asked the least sober of the three.

'Yes,' she smiled, surprised that she was telling the truth. 'But thanks for asking. And sleep well.'

As the night turned to very early morning more men came and went, she accepted cups of wine from two, and a chunk of corn bread from a third, but that was all. She asked several sailors about routes back to the City, and listened for almost an hour as a grain trader told her about Alexandria, the Nile, and the coast road to the Holy Land. Eventually, she could put it off no longer. The barman was closing up, it was time to leave.

Fourteen

Walking out into the quiet street felt almost like old times, although tonight she was walking alone, and for that she was grateful: the few hours left of darkness belonged to silence, not to someone on her skin, in her mind. It had been too much, the betrayal by Chrysomallo, the fight with Hecebolus, her expected and yet still painful rejection by the Bishop.

She stood in the cool night. The sky was clear and the constellations marked, reminding her how far she was from home. Sophia had been right, she was a fool. Hecebolus was not her friend and he never could be. Theodora had lived as an adult woman since she was twelve years old, but on this occasion she'd behaved like a girl, allowing herself to fall in love with a man who was never going to do for her what she did for him. Certainly he'd been a good lover, for quite a while, longer than many. So maybe she wasn't an utter fool, there were always things to learn; as Menander had drummed into them often enough, even a dire performance had lessons, and quite often they were things that could not be learned from a perfect show. She'd learned how to take care of a household, not a skill she could imagine herself using again any time soon, but a skill nonetheless. She'd enjoyed her conversations with the Bishop, realising that she could hold her own, if not in strict theology, at least in her ability to discuss the ideas. She might have gone to the old man virtually unschooled, but she proved a quick student, and had showed herself she was of

118

value – though not enough for the fearful priest, and, more disappointingly, not enough for her own friend either. She walked on, away from the centre of the city, steering clear of the Governor's house, heading south and east of the port, to a small promontory that jutted away from the harbour. Theodora had nowhere to be, and so she went where she had always gone when there was nowhere else to go. She went to church.

Just beyond the main walls of the city, Roman walls built on Greek walls built on however many unknown empires before, Theodora turned a corner and stood before the Church of St Anthony. It had been remade after the earthquake a century before, though like most of the municipal buildings, was constructed as much from the stones of Greek temples as from the broken-down remains of the earthquake rubble. In her time in Apollonia she had attended services as part of Hecebolus' retinue, never processing alongside him of course, and of all the churches they'd been to this was the only one Theodora found welcoming. Perhaps it was the proximity to the sea, or the mix of old stone and newer marble that suggested a faith from the past, as well as one reaching into the future, suggesting that continuity might be possible, no matter how lost she felt right now. It was the only building she'd truly felt at ease in and the one she was drawn to in the dark.

She let herself in through the big wooden doors, turned immediately to her left and felt her way upstairs to the gallery, the wooden and stone interior walls deeply perfumed from years of incense. She found a place by the window where the cloud-reflected moon offered a soft light, and she sat down, and cried. Tears of frustration and hurt and anger, of bitterness and self-hatred. Tears of jealousy that though she did not want a child now, had not much wanted her own daughter in the past, she

119

knew she had not only lost a useful bargaining tool with men like Hecebolus, she had also lost a possible future.

After a while, Theodora took off her cloak, spread it on the floor as both mattress and blanket. She lay on her side, her head on her bag, pulled the cloak up and settled down. She'd slept on plenty of floors in her time, and the cloak Armeneus had given her was warm and soft. The bag, however, was decidedly lumpy. She sat up again, opened it, and carefully pulled out the offending articles. One was the wrist-wide, ornately decorated candlestick she had stolen from Hecebolus' room when she was gathering her own things that afternoon, knowing she'd need to be ready when the storm broke. This piece, a gift from his father, would fetch a good price at the market, and she would need money for her journey to come, wherever she ended up going. It had been a risk taking it, not least because Hecebolus often counted out his personal goods, reminding himself, stuck out here in the Pentapolis, of the wealth from which he'd come, of his own failing ambition. Theodora had walked away from the house terrified that its weight would make her bag too heavy, that Chrysomallo would notice her well-trained friend was carrying something even she had trouble with, but Chrysomallo only had eyes for Hecebolus, and he for her. And so Theodora left with the richest piece that Hecebolus' none-too-generous father had ever given him. She placed it down now, in the light from the window, and enjoyed the weight and solidity, the work of a good silversmith in every curve. There was no point trying to sell it here, something as well crafted as this would need a big city trader to appreciate its worth: it would come with her to Alexandria. She had to go somewhere, it would be easier to get home from there. If she was going home. One step at a time. Picking an initial destination would do for now.

Then she turned her attention to the other item that was

keeping her awake. She held it in her hand for a long time, until it became warm from her own blood. She could not quite believe she had done it, risked both being caught, and the sin of stealing from the Church. She reasoned that it was not exactly the Church from which she stole, it was the Bishop, and while he was certainly a representative, he was not the whole body, the greater mass. The old man had taken so long in finding the perfect teaching that gave him the right to cast her out, to the extent of leaving her alone in his study and going down to his library for another scroll of dry parchment, that he had left her alone in the very room he most guarded. He had always been quite particular about where he allowed Theodora to sit in his study, if he left her there at all. Even after he began to trust her, the Bishop always made her sit or kneel within an arm's reach of the door, against the far wall. He said it was more proper that way, a clergyman and a young woman, and she certainly understood that his servants would have agreed, that they thought it was utterly improper her being there at all, and that he had been bending rules even to speak to her. Today, though, she knew he was going to turn her out, and if it took him all night to find the correct doctrinal reason to do so, then he would find it. When she went to his desk it was really just to see what he had there. A good quill, a spare one, might be worth something in the market; a few coins were justifiable, anything that would mean she didn't have to sell her body just yet. The old man would appreciate that, surely? Thieving instead of prostitution – the sin of stealing came just after that of adultery, it must be slightly less sinful?

The fist-sized piece Theodora now held had been a surprise, and not one she wasted time getting used to. Even in the early evening gloom of the Bishop's study, with just two candles lit, she recognised the stone that was set in ebony, carved into a relief bust of the Virgin, decorated around the edge with gold leaf. The Bishop had always seemed more of a ruby or garnet man, the few silks he had in his room tending towards rose and red; maybe he was dreaming of purple, but Theodora loved emerald green. It was the colour of her sea on a clear spring day, the trees lining the hills of the City and, according to all too many besotted men, her own eyes. And now she loved the emerald beneath her hand. She had considered prising the stone from its wooden setting, but that would take too long, and anyway, damaging it would be a form of desecration, so she took the whole piece. Along with the Bishop's reluctantly offered blessing, she left his house with the icon stuffed right down in the bottom of her bag.

The offending items removed, Theodora lay down again, pulling the cloak close. She fell asleep to the sound of the waves beating against the rocks as they had always done, and – far in the distance, perhaps from one of the groves originally planted by the Greeks – the clear plaintive call of the little Skops owl. If she tried hard enough, the owl sounded like one of the all-night merchants who dealt in fresh bread and warm drinks in the market behind the Hagia Sophia, she might be sleeping in the gallery she had loved since childhood, the sea outside might be her sea, the stars, those she had known all her life.

It did not feel like a dream. It felt real, and calm, comfortable. In feeling that comfort, Theodora realised she had not felt this easy since leaving the City. Even in the dream, she understood she was homesick, understood this was home. She stood up, the cloak on the floor behind her still warm from her heavy sleep, and came to stand at the edge of the gallery. The church had grown. The building she now stood in was wide, and illuminated with a light that was both bright and yet somehow soft, flooding the building. High above her floated a golden dome, forming the roof of the church, and it was from beneath this dome that light streamed, pouring in from windows all around the gallery, and from others, higher still, from a dome that appeared to open itself to the heavens rather than close them off, all this light no matter that when she turned to the narrow window beside her she could see nothing but dark outside. She was standing at one end of the gallery, looking across the enormous distance, equal widths from north to south and east to west. She looked down, feeling the floor cold on the soles of her feet, a smooth circle of deep green marble, the colour of the sea outside, the colour of the Sea of Marmara viewed from the top of the lighthouse on a hazy summer's day. Even as a child, with all the careless bravery youth had given her, Theodora had not dared to climb the full height of the lighthouse, but now, standing on this spot, she knew she was right, she knew this particular piece of marble had been chosen solely for its pure colour, for its exact likeness to the sea she loved. She belonged here. She had chosen to be here.

Slowly, waiting in the gallery above the centre of the huge church, Theodora became aware there was something else, someone else, with her. At least, she did not feel so alone, and she turned her gaze from the mosaic and painted walls all around, from the perfect, suspended dome above, to what lay beneath, to the floor of the main body of the building, where – though she knew this could not be, and these were not real, these written words, and she was dreaming still – she saw in letters each as long and wide as a grown man, the words *Mary is the Star of Bethlehem*, and when she had read the letters, they shifted and swirled, silk colours in a cold dye bath, mutating into the star itself, a four-pointed star with compass markings. The clearest of the markings pointing north, showing home.

In the dream she returned to her cloak and her bag, reluctantly leaving the green marble spot where she'd stood so comfortably, Theodora felt both rested and wide awake, but as soon as she lay down she did sleep again, loosely holding the emerald Virgin in one hand, the candlestick close by, reading the words inlaid in the swirling marble floor, and seeing the north-pointing star.

In the morning, Theodora woke long before the warden came to open the church. She lay for a moment recalling her dream, and her new world, and then she stood up, pulled on her cloak and shouldered the heavy bag that now contained all she possessed. She'd been here before, at five when her father died, at seven when she was sent to Menander's school for the first time, ready to run away by lunchtime, ready to give her life for her mentor by the time evening came. Theodora had had all too many firsts, and each one felt like this. Terrifying and heart-wrenching and often exhilarating.

There was the first time she walked out alone on the Kynegion stage, a solo performer, sure she would vomit with nerves, and then she did vomit with nerves and went on anyway, the smell of sick on her breath with every note she sang out. The first time she screwed a man for money, throwing up again then too, despite Sophia's care, but careful to hide the scent and hide the pallor and hide everything but the appearance of willing and warm and ready: all too often the price of a virgin reduced when the virgin cried or pissed herself or otherwise showed how scared she was, how little she'd enjoyed the experience. Well trained, Theodora knew better than to lower her market value. Time after time when she didn't feel like it and she didn't want to – perform or fuck or greet or charm or act or dance or smile – time after time when, no matter how she felt, she rose from her bed and washed and put on her makeup and combed her hair and dressed for the part and stepped out on to the stage that was theatre or bed or family or stranger or – as it had been here in Apollonia – the Governor's mansion. New stage, new Theodora mask, same old strength required.

Theodora was nineteen years old, sick to death of carrying on, and she carried on.

Fifteen

Theodora had arrived in Africa by ship. Come the spring there would be any number of grain and spice traders heading north, to the Dardanelles at least, if not all the way into the Golden Horn. As it was, the bars of Apollonia and Cyrene were full of stranded sailors trading stories of this vicious storm and that just-formed sand bar, new dangers brought about by changes in currents or weather or even God's will, the men of the waves more than happy to blame wicked weather on wicked heresies. Most ships were in whatever dry docks their owners could find or afford for the winter, and no captain was going anywhere unless he absolutely had to – and certainly not with a woman on board. Women were danger at the best of times, with dozens of signs from fish belly-up in the harbour to carnelian-red morning skies, and any woman, let alone a well-known whore, was far too great a risk to take. Almost as risky as remaining in Apollonia was for Theodora.

Hecebolus would find his candlestick missing this morning, the Bishop might already have realised the emerald carving was gone. She covered her hair and as much of her face as she could with her scarf, pulled her cloak tight, and made for the main coast road, heading east, away from the Five Cities, towards Alexandria. According to the men in last night's bar, even in the best of circumstances it would take her twenty days to cover the five hundred miles to the famed city. Time to get going.

*

The young men who allowed her to share the benefit of their horse and cart were of similar age to Theodora, but they seemed younger, by many years. The elder brother was in his early twenties, the younger maybe eighteen. Back in the City they would have been well through their apprenticeships by now, or have given over five years of their young lives to the real army if they were poor boys, the army of civil servants if not. Theodora could have been their middle sister. She felt as old as their mother. They offered her a lift as a potential lover.

It wasn't that she didn't notice the effect she had on the young men, but she was tired, and keen to lie back, just take it in for herself. Since their arrival, she had seen everything through Hecebolus' eyes: his fears, his concerns, his needs. For the first two hours of the ride with the young brothers she was happy to sit in the stumbling cart beside the sick beast that was too costly to destroy, their only he-goat, the skinny brute breathing heavily, its bony frame loaded on to the low-slung cart. Theodora could see the animal was dull with illness and allowed herself to be sniffed and snorted at, her hand slowly licked. The bear-keeper's daughter settled herself, easy in the company of a quiet creature. The North African sun, still warm by City standards, even in its winter incarnation, shone down, Theodora relaxed, closed her eyes, slept a little.

Just before the small town where the animal healer lived, the cart slowed, turned off the main road. Theodora stirred, opened her eyes to watch the young men nudging each other, and she sighed. The boys had been kind and generously left her alone this long. The elder had given her a wrap of flat bread filled with a meat she was too hungry to question, the younger had kept her supplied with barely watered rough wine. But the sun was halfway to the zenith, their stop just beyond the next hill, and the farm boys required their fare.

The brothers had been whispering to each other for a good ten minutes, gearing up for a fight, a skirmish at least. One to hold her down, while the other persuaded her it was a good idea. They had not expected a woman who knew what she was doing, who was now, in front of their eyes, climbing down from the cart, carefully placing her bag to the side, requesting that one or other – actually, no the older one, you, Phillip is it? – lay down his cloak, the better fabric of the two, that they might be comfortable while they got on with it. The brothers had not expected Theodora would be ready for them, that she would demand the younger turned his back while the other went to work, and that he would then be ready for her after: it wasn't that she minded lads, really, but she didn't want to waste time while he got it up, they all had a busy day ahead. The brothers were not ready for someone who knew what to do with them. As well, there was a sweet charm, Theodora could not deny it, in the dimple of the younger one, in the shocked – and horrified, and excited – raised eyebrows of the elder. The two young men had no experience that would lead them to expect her compliance or pleasure in sex, that was not their understanding of women. Which was why, thirty-five minutes later, they found themselves sharing their lunch with Theodora in the shade of a very few trees, why they finished their wine with her, giving her the bulk of it.

They later enjoyed a brief nap, Theodora layered between the brothers in a warm clasp under the gentle sun. And then more sex, of course, the brothers had not become monks simply because they'd met a woman who knew what she wanted as well as they did, but it was not all giving on her part, nor all taking on theirs. It was new, though, and the boys were better educated for it. They were grateful too, so much so that, instead of leaving Theodora in a marketplace where she might be obvious to anyone Hecebolus had sent after her, they took her right into the port, a good two miles from town, saving her the walk and making it more probable she'd find someone else useful for her journey.

'Thank you for the lift.'

The younger brother jumped from the front of the cart, and helped her down.

'You're welcome, really, that was . . . it was . . .' he shook his head, knowing his words were irrelevant, the single dimple in his left check pulling his grin into a side-smile that was just a tiny bit more attractive than his older brother's. Young Simeon knew that Theodora understood exactly what he was thanking her for. He'd yelled it loudly enough, along with an assortment of invocations to the Virgin, just an hour earlier. Theodora curtsied low and deep, the two boys applauded her, Phillip jumped back up on to the cart beside his young brother and they drove off. They were good-looking lads. Theodora sighed, picked up her bag, and walked into the tavern glad to have a nice image in her mind as she faced whatever else the day would bring.

Another ride with another man who wanted her body as payment, three days of the same with a group of young monks, and then again with an older man, this one wealthy enough to be travelling on horseback. The sex and the journey, the journey and sex. Then she walked alone for a blissful five days, watching the sky and the stars and very little else except her feet passing beneath her and the road shifting from one dusty rock to another. She ate little, which was no hardship, Theodora had been starving herself for shows since she was a girl, and drank less wine than she had since she was a child, which became a hardship as the days progressed and the road moved further inland, became still more monotonous without the company of her beloved sea. The loneliness was broken briefly when she crossed into Egypt proper and spent three days with a young family who were happy for her company, not least because she kept their seven-year-old occupied, the mother minding twins and the father carrying their broken little boy in a sling on his back. The child had fallen from a tree and his leg, though expertly set by the woman's mother, was not healing well. From the child's fever it seemed clear it was not healing at all.

The family, nominal Christians, as had been all of Theodora's fellow travellers so far, licentious monks included, were nonetheless taking the child to the oracle at Siwa. They suggested Theodora come with them; she had already taught the daughter to juggle and was now on to cartwheels, along with a few dance steps, they were grateful for anything to keep their over-bright girl occupied. Theodora was tempted to stay with them, less conspicuous in a family, and seriously considered their offer for a few minutes. But the oracle was a long way off and heading south would add more than a week to the journey time to Alexandria. Besides, she didn't want her fortune told any more than she needed someone else to direct her. Theodora knew she was going straight back to Constantinople, as soon as possible. The traders she'd met earlier in the week assured her the seas would be safe in less than a month if she were lucky, but no more than eight weeks otherwise. It had been a long winter on the water, but all the signs were of an early turn into a kind spring. The family went south and Theodora walked on alone, the wailing of the little girl who had lost her new friend loud in her heart for at least half a day.

Sixteen

A sea breeze, elegant civic buildings with beautiful carving in stunningly varied shades of marble, a glorious obelisk, all the more perfect for never having been moved, Alexandria felt like a real city. Turning down narrow streets into darker alleyways, through twisting lanes and out again into a large central square, always following the sound of the crowd, Theodora came to a massive market overflowing with goods from across the southern and eastern reaches of Africa. She saw the utterly foreign interspersed with the achingly familiar, clothing and dry goods, fresh ingredients and cooked foods, silks and patterns and spices brought from the north, from the City, from home. She heard the hard-working cries of beggars and traders, seamen and merchants, all underscored by the babble of dozens of different languages, from the local Coptic and the not-so-distant Syriac, to the guttural Slav and Goth grunts she'd known well as a child. Everywhere too, there were the constant calls of furious street preachers, telling stories of exile from Syria, from Palestine, from the City itself, anti-Chalcedonian faithful, persecuted by the Emperor Justin, finding some safety here in Egypt. Even the August couldn't enforce his doctrines this far, not while Timothy lived and ruled as Patriarch of Alexandria. A pope to his people, a living saint to those who loved him, Timothy presided over the Church in Egypt and was nominally the Emperor's bishop, but he had enormous influence over the population who both loved him and agreed with his understanding of the faith, and though Constantinople had massive wealth, it lacked a steady supply of grain, the one staple that kept its people content and its status as capital. The Emperor Justin, a little fonder of circuses than Anastasius had been, was still required to keep his people happy by giving them their daily bread, it was his duty and their expectation – and the grain for that bread came from Egypt. He could not, therefore, afford to anger the keeper of the bread basket any more than his predecessors. He followed his religious inclinations everywhere else but, for now, he left Egypt alone.

Theodora, exhausted, drawn, but making an effort to hide her tiredness and to smile sweetly, pulled back her hair, stood straight and walked from almost four weeks on the road into the welcome heat of hundreds of people shouting and arguing, eating and drinking, cursing and laughing and, above all, trading. She stood at the edge of Alexandria's central market, the huge library down one main street, the famous medical school just behind, breathing in the scent of a dozen perfumes and the smell of foreign foods and the stink of strangers as lonely as herself. She stood in the heart of this most commercial of cities and her joy at being back in a mess of people was almost overwhelming.

Ten feet in front of her an Egyptian pickpocket swept by a beautifully dressed young Nubian man, cutting a purse from the black man's waist belt without either of them dropping their pace. To her left she watched as a Visigoth prostitute gave a gurning old man a blow job under a trader's table and five minutes later she saw the whore hand over not quite half the coin to her pimp, the bald man waiting impatiently between the stalls. Theodora noted with approval that the whore spat after her boss as he stalked away. She watched one woman smack another woman's child across the face for cheek and then saw the child come running back for a hug and kiss from the harried child-minder who didn't know which child she truly loved from one day to the next, those of her own blood or the brood of other mothers' brats she cared for, each child tied by a tight string to another, seven of them pulling in different directions like puppies in a sack, on their way to the river.

All this she saw in the two minutes it took her to gather her courage and her story and then, with one deep breath, she squared her shoulders, pinching her cheeks and biting her lips to bring up the colour, opened her green eyes wide and, checking her precious bag was well hidden beneath her cloak, plunged in herself.

Theodora introduced herself to various traders, asking for somewhere to stay, a reputable house. She said she was travelling, a pilgrim, from the City, looking for a room in a clean house; she played with her purse as she asked, so the merchants knew she was able to pay, and she also carefully dropped the names of several well-respected Blues from the City. It was important, if her plan was to work, that she get in with the right people as quickly as possible. She spoke clearly and elegantly with her finest stage Greek accent, giving every impression of being a true lady fallen on slightly difficult times. There were plenty of hard times about – earthquakes, religious divisions, young men, and the not so young, gone off to war in Italy and never returned. It was unusual, but not unheard of, for a woman of breeding to find herself lost, without family to fall back on. Theodora let it be known she was looking for support in Alexandria and had the money to pay for it, but that she planned on heading back to the City as quickly as possible, where any amount of recompense might be available from a wealthy, aged and ailing great-uncle – and she his only surviving relative.

Theodora was just the right age to pick up the kind of man who'd enjoy a well-trained companion and pay for her passage in return, all the while hoping to cheat her when he got hold of her uncle's money. Her story was good, she knew an old man who fitted the bill exactly, and several of the merchants she spoke to thought they might know the street, the uncle, the family villa of which she spoke so eloquently. It did the trick. She was given addresses for three different rooming houses, accepted the kind offers of introduction, promised to look up the helpful gentlemen once she was settled into her new room. Then she walked on, making sure they watched her perfect bearing, the elegance of her could-be patrician pace, and the half-smile as she turned to wave goodbye, a smile that promised rather more intimacy than her assumed accent usually did.

A day later she had her new home. The room was sparse, and far too dark for Theodora's liking, in a small and cramped house, but her landlady Ireni was a quiet woman who cooked well, charged the minimum for room and board, and asked no questions. None at all. Theodora knew enough of the Blues of Constantinople to prove her faction credentials. Ireni's first husband had been a shipping worker, they'd been based in Antioch initially, and when he died she'd gone with an Antioch local to Gaza. Her second husband had been a Green. He'd also been a drunken, aggressive bastard, which meant Ireni was more than happy to take in anyone from the other side, her own family of Blues having warned, before they disowned her, exactly what lay ahead. Even when she returned widowed, reluctantly admitting they'd been right, they still refused to see her. Ireni knew what it was to be alone in the world, said she wanted to help any young women who came to her door, and Theodora certainly needed help. Though while she believed Ireni's tale of the philandering husband, she wasn't quite as convinced by the detailed story about his untimely death down a well in a back square in Gaza, nor did she understand why Ireni's two sons, apparently overcome by grief at their stepfather's death, had felt the need to rush off to join the military in Italy after the funeral, leaving their mother to pack up and come back to Alexandria all alone. Two women, twenty years apart, neither telling her full story, one able to offer a room and sanctuary, the other with money to pay. It was good enough.

Getting a passage back to the City was a lot harder to arrange. The sailors were just as skilled at haggling as she was, and all of their prices were beyond her purse, unless she sold the candle-stick, which she was not yet ready to do. The richer gentlemen she met, in her hope that she'd be taken on as a sailing companion, were keen to spend a night or two in her company but not quite as accommodating as she'd hoped. There were no offers of a paid fare.

Theodora came tired and dispirited into Ireni's house on her fourth night in Alexandria. It was Saturday and her landlady was preparing her Sabbath evening.

'Will you join me?'

Theodora looked at the bread and the wine laid out on the narrow table. There was a small chunk of roast goat to one side, half a dozen home-grown herbs as a salad on the other, dressed with a thin drizzle of oil and the juice of a late lemon Ireni had pulled from her tree that afternoon.

'There was cheese earlier, but I had to eat it. I was too hungry.'

The Egyptian shook her head at her inability to deny herself, rubbed a fat-fingered hand over her round belly and grinned. 'Anyway, at your age, still looking, you don't want to get too fat, do you? We widows are lucky in that, no men to judge our girth. Take my advice, girl, you might not think it now, but a husband will come in handy one of these long nights.'

Despite her irritation at the tone, Theodora thanked her

hostess as prettily as she had ever thanked one of Menander's wealthy patrons, adding that Ireni was quite right about needing to keep her figure in check, then she sat at the table with its small meal and was glad to do so.

One jug of wine became another, then a third when the second jug cancelled out Ireni's concern for her housewifely budget. The blessing loaf was followed by plain flatbread, the women chatted little as they ate and the candle burned low in its holder, an official bronze grain-measure one of Ireni's sons had apparently acquired in Antioch and which the older woman kept even though she had never needed to weigh out the precise measure of grain accorded to soldiers – 'always useful to have something you can sell in an emergency, and it works well enough' – and though it was practically spring now and Ireni certainly had enough flesh on her bones to keep her warm, she even added a precious log to the failing fire.

'Right then, enough of men and waste.'

'Really? Oh, yes, of course.' Theodora nodded, accepting Ireni was ruler in this house, and stood up to go to her bed.

'Sit down, I didn't mean we have to stop talking, would I burn a good log if I did?'

Theodora sat back, relieved. 'I think I'd have to cry myself to sleep if I went to bed now, this is the best night I've had in months.'

Ireni took the wine jug and carefully poured the dregs in equal measures into both their cups, then she asked, 'What do you know of faith, girl?'

'I go to church.'

'We all do that.'

'No, no,' Theodora interrupted her, eager to make her point, 'I love church. My church, back home. I used to sleep there, it's a nice place, it's good, safe.'

136

Ireni nodded, she'd been in some safe churches herself, some unsafe ones too, and it wasn't what she was talking about anyway. She looked at the girl opposite, who was so young that what Ireni had to offer might make all the difference.

'I said faith, not church. What do you make of faith?'

'Ah, well, I don't . . . you do?'

Theodora might look tired, was certainly a little drunk, but like the consummate performer she'd been trained to be, she could summon sobriety at will. She'd been looking forward to the easy sleep of wine, but there was a change in Ireni's tone and – as well as needing to keep the landlady happy, Theodora was keen to negotiate a cheaper rate for a second week – she was interested. There weren't many twice-widowed matrons keen to talk about faith before bed; those who did so tended to be on their way to a nunnery, while Ireni had been telling Theodora only half an hour ago that she hugely enjoyed a good shag and wondered where the hell she was going to get a third spouse to take her on before it was too late and her arse was as big as her belly.

Ireni explained, 'There's a monastery, out in the desert.'

Theodora nodded, the desert beyond Alexandria was famous for its ascetics, the sand and rock-dwellers who took the injunctions to fast on various days to heart and soul, turned forty days into forty months, years. 'There are hundreds, aren't there?'

'Not quite, but yes, there are a good many.'

Theodora grinned. 'So how do fasting nuns fit with you wanting a new bloke? Can't quite see you giving up the husband-hunt and heading for a cave.'

'It fits with you wanting to get home.'

Theodora was fully sober now. 'Oh.'

'You don't seem to be doing all that well on your own, do you? Chatting up businessmen, trying to cadge a lift on any old sailor's ship . . .'

'Thanks.'

'No point my lying.'

'I suppose not.'

'So try my way.'

'A desert retreat?'

'Yes.'

'For . . .?'

'Fallen women. And men. Anyone, really.'

'Right.'

'Anyone ready to repent.'

'But I don't want to spend the next forty years fasting in the desert, Ireni, I want to get home.'

'You said.'

'So how do those two things join up? You think if I go to a nunnery I'll find such peace I'll give up on the City?'

'It's not unheard of, but no, that wasn't what I was thinking. The Alexandrian Patriarch has recently agreed to send a small community of ascetic women back to the City, via Antioch, possibly Sinai, ideally starting new communities in each of the places. But the ultimate aim is to set up a new community of women, in Constantinople.'

'Right.'

'Fare fully paid, room and board taken care of.'

'Bedroll and fasting bread, you mean.'

'Probably, but if the roads are good and the new settlements easy, you'd be back in the City before winter.'

'Next winter?'

'Child, the way you're going, you could be stuck in my house a year, or worse, have to go back where you've just come from.'

Theodora looked up sharply.

'It doesn't take a genius to tell you're running away from something. This would be a way to hide for a while, get yourself together before you go home. I know you think you're so damn strong, but it wouldn't hurt to take some time, peace and quiet. You might even like it. I've been on the odd fast myself, great for the figure, and the spirit too, sometimes.'

Theodora wasn't thinking about her soul, she was wondering who else might have worked out where she'd come from. Thinking how right Ireni was: it was so much harder to get home than she'd expected. And, beneath those more pressing thoughts the underlying one she'd become more aware of in the time since she'd left the Pentapolis – how very tired she was of using her body as her work.

'They'd be after true penitents, of course?'

Ireni agreed.

'I'd certainly have plenty of sin to offer up.'

'I wouldn't expect any less, not with that stage career behind you.'

Theodora held up her hands, of course Ireni knew who she was, she'd been an idiot to hope otherwise. And if Ireni knew, then too many others would as well, those she'd been talking to in bars and pubs in the past few days, trying to arrange her return. She couldn't trust that Hecebolus would leave her alone; this was a way back to the City, and in safety until she got there. She'd take the chance. 'What do I do?'

'You need to meet with Timothy.'

'The Patriarch?'

Ireni smiled, it was good to see that even Theodora-from-the-Brothel could be a little unnerved. 'Yes. Him.'

'And how do I do that?'

'Leave it to me.'

They tidied the little room then, washed their plates and cups, two women moving gently around each other in the small, unevenly lit space.

Before she went to her narrow bed, Theodora asked, 'Ireni,

how can you get me in touch with the Patriarch? How do you even know about this idea for a penitents' community?'

'Timothy's brother Arsenio. Lovely man, but a tedious priest, none of the charisma of his elder brother, dreadful sermons – no wonder he never made much of a success of the job. He works in the Patriarch's office.'

'You know the Patriarch's brother?'

'Arsenio's happily married, unfortunately, but he does like to chat in bed. And he does like to help.'

Seventeen

Theodora sat alone in the open courtyard at the centre of a high, narrow house built around a central fountain. The bench seat she had carefully chosen over an hour ago was lit from above, and soft light, transported down to the courtyard by mirrors and water, dappled perfectly across her face and shoulders. She would move again in a moment, repositioning herself as the sun moved. The penitential symbols of her plain black dress and makeup-free face were all very well, but they wouldn't work if the Patriarch couldn't see her. Six months was a long time to give up, but if Ireni was even half right, she'd be home by the end, arriving with a forgiven past, and it would be worthwhile. All she had to do was make her penitence look real.

A door opened, but it was not the door she was waiting for, it was the door she had come through herself: someone else was arriving to beg the indulgence of the Patriarch. Unfortunately for Theodora, the new arrival was a young man. Knowing the hierarchy of the Church and its priests, she glared at the interloper, her chances of seeing Timothy before nightfall were slimmer now there was a man waiting too. She leaned against the wall, closed her eyes to shut him out and determined to stay there at least until the sun had gone. This was her third day waiting.

Her companion did not take Theodora's attitude for the clear rejection that it was, but began talking to her, telling her his story and, though he was just another dusty pilgrim like all the others she'd met in this waiting area, Theodora listened. She needed to look willing, it was best to start as she meant to go on. Besides, she'd had no luck yet, maybe if she was nice to him he'd put in a good word for her when he was called in to meet Timothy.

He was Stephen, a would-be artist from Italy, he had finished his seven-year apprenticeship in mosaic at home in Ravenna and had made the pilgrimage, in part to see the sites of the Holy Land, but also to see the work of others in his craft, their different styles, maybe pick up secrets his teachers had not been able to show him. He was heading home now, full of ideas, great challenges, keen to do everything differently. Theodora wanted to tell him that different wasn't always better, and as an artist he needed to learn that sooner than most, but his enthusiasm for his subject, for his journey and his studies on the way, didn't leave her any space to interrupt. He had come today hoping to receive a blessing from the Patriarch for his return, less because he was a man of strong faith, more because he'd heard Timothy had several precious mosaics in the building and hoped to be allowed to see them. By the time he finished telling the story of his journey another hour had passed and the young man had tired of waiting. He stood, pulling a well-worn cloak of thick Galician wool round his shoulders. He knew he would not see the Patriarch today, and so he would not see him at all – he had too far to travel and there were always other mosaics.

'I don't mean to be rude,' he said, 'but why are you here? You're the actress, aren't you?'

Theodora nodded, surprised the Italian recognised her.

'I saw you once, when I was in the City. You were wonderful. I went back to my room and sketched you from memory.'

'Really? What was I performing?'

The young man shrugged. 'Truly, I have no idea. I hadn't

seen much theatre, a friend I met travelling told me I should go, as part of my education, so I did. I enjoyed it, I suppose, but not so much for the stories.'

'For what, then?'

He dipped his head, suddenly shy, and mumbled, 'I liked watching you. There was a spark. It's what I try to put in my work – the spark. It's hard to capture, doesn't often come.'

'No, it doesn't.'

He looked at her directly now. 'And you have it. So why would you want to give it up? That is why you're here, isn't it? Why any actress would be here? As a penitent?'

'I think I'm finished with that now.'

The young man frowned, peering at her through the last light. 'I don't think so.'

'I'm sorry?'

'It would be wrong. You should not give up.'

'You know nothing of me. I'm off to the desert, if they'll have me, and I'll be glad to be left alone.'

'I don't think they'll ever leave you alone, will they?'

'I've given plenty.'

He nodded, agreeing, 'Of course, but there's always more. Well,' he stopped, aware of the impropriety of sitting alone in the dark with this woman, this girl, probably several years younger than he was, but so much more a woman than he was a man. He was glad she could not see him blushing. 'I should go. If I can't see him today then I've missed the chance, I have a place on a ship leaving in the morning. It's been nice to talk to you.'

He filled his worn pilgrim's flask with fresh water from the fountain, bowed, and walked back out to the busy street, leaving her alone with the sound of the repeating water and the monks chanting beyond the thick wall.

*

'Theodora? I'm sorry, you've been waiting all day, haven't you?'

She'd been asleep for an hour, was dizzy with wrenching herself from it, and aching with the bite of the stone she'd fallen asleep on. The man who spoke had a dozen just-lit candles behind, glowing from each of the sconces in the courtyard wall. Their warm light was shining through his prominent ears, illuminating nothing more than the crest of his bald pate and the sad few hairs remaining, hairs he didn't even have the City nous to shave away. He leaned over her and she could see that his cloak was stained with ink; his hands too, she noticed as he extended them to her, shockingly touching her himself, were not only inked but nail-bitten as well. But his voice was perfect. The Patriarch spoke her name again and Theodora was on her feet and then her knees. He gave her the blessing and helped her up, asked about her journey and her route, about the young craftsman who'd been and gone that afternoon, and then about her new choice, the reason his brother's friend Ireni had sent her here. And though he was speaking so quietly she had to strain to listen, and though his accent seemed stronger the more he talked, Theodora heard every word as if it were a sermon and she his convert. They walked through dark corridors and long, low-lit chambers as far as the door to his office where he handed her over to one of the nuns who kept the other side of the house. She knelt and accepted another blessing before he closed the door on them. She was his convert.

The nun showed her to a tiny room. The bed – three boards, an old mattress, and a single blanket – was clearly designed for penitents. As was the morning wake-up call, well before dawn, time enough to rise, wash, dress in silence, and be waiting in the Patriarch's own chapel ten minutes later. Timothy himself would not arrive to say the mass until dawn, but it was thought useful for the penitents to have time to reflect before the Patriarch arrived. The service would follow, then more prayer and finally, a basic breakfast. Her guide suggested drinking plenty of water before sleep, and very little on rising: that way she would be less likely to faint in chapel – the Patriarch hated a fuss of any kind – nor would she feel the need to be excused for a moment. Which anyway, would not be allowed.

Theodora shrugged. She too found it irritating when members of the audience left their seats for a piss just at the moment when the actors required all attention on them, it was perfectly fair that the Patriarch of Alexandria also demanded his audience's full attention. As for the water, she had trained under Menander. Theodora had performed while both aching from dehydration and with a bladder about to burst, and never once disgraced herself. She might be a little out of practice, but she didn't think it would take long to get back into the pattern of ignoring her body's needs. She started to say as much to the older woman and was stopped before she'd finished the word 'when'.

'We do not care about your life before now. It is irrelevant.'

'I was just—'

The nun held up her hand. 'We do not care.'

Each word was spoken with quiet deliberation. Menander would have emphasised each one with a whack of his cane, Hecebolus with a jabbing finger in her collarbone, or a kiss. Fine, she'd act the perfect student, ready, willing and ever yielding, put on the show they clearly wanted this one more time if she had to. Eyes on the prize of getting home, paid and cared for, without having to fuck or feign love in return, Theodora offered her meekest smile and curtsied her acquiescence.

'Of course not.'

'Good,' the nun replied. 'And a word of advice. Don't think that you and your work are not known here. The Patriarch and his fellow teachers understand well what they are about, they have seen – and uncovered – more false promises than you have

ever made, more false yielding as well. You'd do well to practise giving in, you might even come to mean it in time.'

She closed the door to Theodora's tiny room, taking the
candle with her and leaving pitch darkness behind. Theodora
spat out a silent oath to the receding back of the skinny old
bitch and lay down on the hard mattress, wondering what the
fuck she'd let herself in for.

She didn't have long to wait. Five hours later she was up and
dressed in the same plain black cotton dress Ireni had given her
to arrive in, on her knees and offering up her sins. As she was
seven hours later. And eight. And nine. There was a brief, and
equally silent, break for thin soup and solid bread, then more
prayer, more lectures. Lectures from the woman who'd showed
her to her room last night, from other penitents who'd been
this way and were now considered saved enough to share their
stories, and one very long speech from the Patriarch's brother
Arsenio, the priest Ireni had considered kind but boring. She
wasn't wrong. Theodora passed the time wondering how it was
that, with two brothers, equally physically unattractive, one
could have such charisma and the other be this dullard of a
man. She figured his mother must have been sleeping around,
and then wondered if perhaps it wasn't the Patriarch who was
the family bastard, that somewhere out there was a beautiful
man with a beautiful voice and it was the mother who had the
dog-ugly face. It wasn't the best use of her time when she was
meant to be considering her own sins, but she passed an enjoyable half-hour remembering all the good-looking men she had
known, imagining them in the throes of orgasm crying out in
the Patriarch's beautiful voice.

Another break and another bowl of soup, still more silence,
then a further hour on her knees. Theodora began questioning her sanity, wondering how she could possibly have thought

146

that this might be an easier way home than screwing her way across the sea. She was well used to physical privation, but boredom was an entirely different matter. And then, out of the long grey day, the Patriarch himself came into the room and began talking to them, touching one on the shoulder as he passed, taking another's outstretched hand, asking this one and that how they were, bestowing blessings as he went. She watched the short, ungainly middle-aged man work the room. Theodora had seen great charm at work before, in senators, leading actors, extraordinary musicians. Her mother maintained the girls' father had some of this quality, certainly with his animals, if not always with people, an ability to make them pay attention, not by any action or word in particular, merely because he expected it. She had never before seen this power in a man so seemingly ordinary and yet, from his manner, and from the way she was surprised to find herself feeling, not ordinary at all.

She tried to work it out. They sat in a room of a hundred or more, roughly lit by high windows that gave the tiniest glimpse of sky outside, all black-robed penitents, and in he came, wandering among them, this richly garbed patriarch. So there was costume. There was also status, of course, their roof was his, their food and drink were his, they stayed in the house on his sufferance – it was already clear that everyone here had their own reasons for turning away from the world, it made perfect sense that no one should want to upset the man who held the keys. And then there were those, Theodora assumed, who truly did believe, who were not just running away from love or loss or bankruptcy or any of the other usual cares of the world, who sincerely believed that Timothy, with his famed sermons and his intellectual grasp of divine truths, as well as his beliefs in direct contrast with so many other Church leaders, was closer to God than anyone else on the earth. Even those he didn't speak to, when he stood some distance from them, still seemed moved by his presence.

As he came closer she found that she was again, as yesterday, straining to hear his voice, hungry for his words, and hungrier that he might see her. Used to being adored, to hearing her name chanted by thousands, Theodora wanted Timothy to see her, Timothy to speak to her. She sat straighter as he approached, raised her chin, ensuring the planes of her angled face were as clear as she would like, as Menander would have liked, making the most of this sparse light. She parted her lips just a little, breathed in to be ready to answer whatever he asked, knowing that a ready breath always made the speaker sound more sure, more engaged. She sat with her hands plainly open in her lap. Waiting. The Patriarch walked straight by. Theodora gasped silently, sitting first in her bitter disappointment, then a hot anger, then regret. Five minutes later she shook her head and laughed at herself, silently congratulating the ungainly red-robed man as he walked away and out of the room, leaving them all desperate for more. Timothy was very good.

After another week of the same she was starting to lose patience. No one had said a word about sending her on to Antioch, there was no sign that this house was anything other than a silent prison. She'd been good, quieter than she'd thought humanly possible, and though she'd come very close once or twice, she hadn't yet spat in Livia's face, the thin old nun from the night of her arrival, who seemed to have been appointed her personal invigilator and managed to pick on Theodora's every action from morning to night.

At the end of the eighth evening, in the one hour allotted for the privilege of conversation, she made her way to the table where Livia sat with three other, equally thin, older women.

'Livia, may I speak with you alone?'

It was one of the other women who answered, 'There is no privacy for penitents. That is one of the privileges you have given up.'

Theodora curtsied. 'Of course.'

She then very deliberately turned her back on the first speaker and addressed Livia alone. Speaking in front of the group but leaving them in no doubt to whom she was speaking. She should probably have tried to get the other women on side, but they were annoying her too much, she wanted them to know she could grab status back too, whether or not they would allow her to use it.

'Livia, when I came here I understood it was to become part of a group of penitents who were to travel on to Antioch.'

The hands of the women sewing stilled a little, the tables nearby became quieter than they already were.

Theodora waited. And waited. More status games. Fine, she was well skilled at this, she could wait longer than these dry old bitches.

Eventually Livia's needle stopped its rhythmic picking of threads and she looked up from the cloth she held in her dark-veined hands. 'I don't believe there are any plans to send you there.' Livia stressed the word you, and one of the other women sitting at the table tittered – until Livia silenced her with a glare. 'No, I do not believe Antioch is part of the plan for you. Perhaps the Patriarch will tell you later today.'

'The Patriarch hasn't said a word to me since I arrived, he's completely ignored me, he walks right by me every night.'

'Then perhaps this night will be different,' Livia raised her eyes from her sewing and looked directly at Theodora. 'Or not.'

It was such a little phrase, and lightly spoken. But it was far too much for Theodora, who released her iron grip on her composure and, kicking herself even as she did it yet still not able to stop herself, leaned down and hissed into the older woman's face, 'Fine, then I'm out of here. I've spent over a week in the company of you dried-up old cunts and not one of you has deigned to offer me the time of day, the Patriarch hasn't given me a second glance. I can get back to the City without you, I don't need your arsing charity.'

Livia went back to her calm stitching. 'You can't leave.'

'Look, I was just using you to get home. I figured I could travel on your charity instead of always on my own back. But it doesn't matter, I'll get home by myself. I know you all believe, and have been touched by God or the Patriarch as God's messenger or whatever it is you think he is, but that's not why I'm here. I'm wasting your time and mine and I might as well go back to my original plan – at least it won't be as dull as this.'

'You can't leave.'

'This isn't a prison, I can do what I want.'

Livia continued to sew. 'That's true, but the Governor of the Pentapolis sent his men to find you, they came to the house two nights ago. They're here, in Alexandria, and they know you are here too. As a true penitent you have sanctuary in this house: if you leave, you do not.' A bell began to sound in the distance, precursor of the final toll that indicated the great silence until the next morning. 'So, Theodora, you might want to rethink your stance on why you're here. If you are not a true penitent then we have no reason to keep you. You might be prepared to lie in order to get somewhere; we have nowhere else we want to go – and no need, therefore, to lie on your behalf.'

The last bell sounded and Livia slowly walked away, followed by her fellow nuns and the other penitents, each one as quiet and calm as if they had just spent their usual hour in gentle handiwork and had not been listening, enthralled. The part of

Theodora that wasn't horrified by what she'd just heard was impressed, they were as good a chorus as any she'd seen on the City stage. The other part of her felt sick. Hecebolus had sent his men more than twenty days' journey to find her. Even if she gave back the candlestick, he could still charge her with theft, she'd have nothing with which to buy herself out of prison, and no one here in Egypt to care. Suddenly, boring looked very attractive.

Eighteen

It was three in the morning when Timothy called for her. Theodora had only been asleep a short while herself; the Patriarch had apparently not slept at all. His desk was covered in paperwork, several fresh candles had recently been lit, and he was hard at work making notes when she was shown into his office. She entered the room and immediately knelt as Livia had indicated, miming the instruction rather than break the rule of silence, even for the Patriarch in the middle of the night. Theodora knelt for almost forty minutes in the centre of the room before Timothy looked up.

He leaned forward over his desk, spilling a few papers on the floor as he did so and stared, frowning. 'Don't your knees hurt?'

She looked up, uncertain whether or not to speak. If this were Menander asking she'd expect him to slap her for not answering immediately, and then perhaps beat her as well, for countermanding the earlier order of silence. She said nothing.

Timothy spoke louder. 'Your knees – do they hurt? Isn't it uncomfortable there, kneeling?'

'A little, Father.'

'Would you like to sit?'

'I have been told that would be inappropriate, Father. As is . . . this.'

'What?'

'The silence?'

He checked the level on an hour-candle close by. 'Oh yes. Livia's a stickler for the rule, isn't she?'

'She is very . . . certain.'

The Patriarch smiled and indicated the chair near his desk. She sat, doing her best to hide the physical relief of getting up from the mosaic floor, sharp dents in her knees and calves from the tile edges.

The odd-looking man watched her rise and walk to the chair, then sit carefully. 'Most people complain of the austerities here, at least initially. I suppose, in your training, you encountered similar physical hardships?'

'I was taught by a man who made Livia's penalties seem like promises.'

'Really?'

Theodora shrugged openly now. 'I'm not saying I wouldn't like to sleep longer, to eat more, that silence isn't a hardship at times, but I'm used to subduing the needs of my own body.'

'In order to provide for the needs of others?'

It was a sharp question, and the candlelight, bright and warm on Theodora but leaving the Patriarch in shade, was working all in his favour. For a moment it occurred to Theodora he might have been asking for her body, he would not be the first high-ranking clergyman to do so. Then she realised he was asking for confession. She felt oddly shy as she wondered how to answer him. There was no good reason for the man to unnerve her in this way, there was nothing she found attractive about him physically, and yet, again, there was something that made her hesitate.

Timothy was not used to waiting, and certainly not used to waiting for a woman. 'I asked a question.'

'I have subdued my body for the needs of others, as a performer and for money.'

'And for your own pleasure?' He was leaning forward now,

the candles behind him back-lighting his pate, cutting frown lines deeper into his wide forehead.

Theodora didn't want to lie, nor did she think it would help: this man was her only chance of safety, she had nothing to lose now. 'Yes, I have had a great deal of pleasure from my own body and that of very many others.'

He sat back. 'Good. I'd hate you not to understand what it is we're asking you to give up.'

He began to speak. About how they'd known who she was almost from the first day she was with them, that it took the perceptive Livia no time at all to see through Theodora's dissembling protest of penitence, and how – contrary, he was sure, to Theodora's expectations – it was also Livia who had spoken for her, Livia who insisted there was a truly penitent heart beneath the pride, that Theodora was clearly a soul begging to be saved, she just didn't know it yet.

'You have treated Livia and the others here as yet another audience, but my community are well trained and eager to share their learning with you. They don't want to see you walk through the motions of salvation. What would be the point?'

Theodora tried to explain, to say as elegantly as she could the truth that the community were her passage back to the City, just as Hecebolus had been her passage to Africa. That all she craved now was a return to her old life, if only she could do so in safety.

'You were happy in the City?'

'I have been.'

'And you have been unhappy.'

'No one is happy always.'

'Livia is.'

Theodora couldn't help herself. 'I'm not sure Livia and I have the same understanding of happiness.'

'Possibly not. What is it to you? Happiness?'

154

'Where can I start? Good food, good wine. Laughter. Applause.'

'When the laughter and the applause and the food and drink are gone, what then?'

'Then I'm just as pleased with what is always there, the company of my friends. People who love me, people I love.'

'And when there is nothing to stand between you and your soul? When you are silent and alone?'

Theodora shook her head. 'I'm sorry, Father, you can't catch me like that. Then I'm happiest. All my life I have run away to silent churches and high trees and the hills that are hardest to climb. The Stylites up on those narrow pillars have always seemed especially blessed to me, far above the mess of daily life. Both the riches of the City and the riches of silence have given me enormous pleasure, though I am happy to admit, I do enjoy both.'

'And you don't feel that this desire to hurry back to the City means giving up the possibility of one for the other? You may have experienced the peace of an hour or so alone Theodora, but have you tried days? Weeks? Have you considered months?'

'I have considered many paths for my life, Father. Unfortunately I have actually had the opportunity to choose very few.'

The older man nodded. 'I'm glad you can see that. It's also true that what I'm about to offer may not seem like much of a choice either. As you know, you have sanctuary with us now, if you leave the house, you will not. However, our community in the desert, with our brother Severus, is also part of this house.'

'Severus? Of Antioch?'

'He was Patriarch there, yes.'

'And he was deposed by Justin, just before I left the City. You want to send me, for sanctuary, into the desert, to join a man the Emperor himself removed from his job?'

'Severus and his community are in a place of safety, where he is able to continue his work. Yes, you could also have sanctuary there. We would like you to go. To choose to go.'

'To choose where I have no choice?'

Timothy shook his head. 'There is always choice. You can choose to go to the desert and follow the rule, but only in action, not in your heart. You can choose to stay on bended knee until your bones break, but keep your spirit closed to change. You can always choose to keep something back, Theodora. I expect you always have?'

She nodded, feeling uncomfortably that not only did he understand her strategies, but also that she wanted him to.

'So now you can choose to do it differently,' Timothy continued. 'To really give yourself. I don't say it will be easy – even for one who wants peace, a single night alone in the desert can be terribly long. I don't say you can make the offer of giving yourself just once and be done with it, either. The true giving of the self must be offered with every new moment. To come to yourself, Theodora? Your true self? That is most certainly a choice.'

She knew what he was saying, Menander preached the same to his students: the transcendence of pain in pure submission to the body, to the dance, to the moment. And she knew that on the occasions when she had risen above, when she had truly chosen to give in to the work, the audience, the theatre, those were the times when she had experienced utter – fleeting – bliss. She understood that in the desert, in a community of ascetics, giving over the suffering of her body and mind to the primacy of spirit, she might find a similar joy. It was tempting. That, and freedom from the men who must even now be waiting at the gate for her, but she did have questions.

'How long will it take?'

The Patriarch laughed. 'Who knows the days of the Lord?'

'All right, but if, after I have truly given myself to your rule . . .'

'Not my rule, Severus leads that community. When he was exiled from Antioch, lost his position, it seemed the safest place to be. An ex-Patriarch is never a favourite with the Imperial Palace. So yes, after you have truly given yourself to Severus' rule, however long that takes . . .?'

'If I still want to return to the City?'

'When that day comes, then it will be your choice to leave and you may do so freely, as an absolved penitent. You will go with my blessing.'

She chose to accept his offer. And, after she had admitted the theft, followed his direction that she should ask Livia to return the stolen candlestick to Hecebolus' men. It would not stop them coming after her if she later renounced her desert pilgrimage, but it would mark the start of making amends. As Timothy said, once he and Severus declared her absolved, then Hecebolus would have no reason to charge her with any crime. Theodora wasn't convinced that simply following the actions of penitence was the same as the spirit of penitence, and Timothy explained his belief that action was the beginning of spirit, that a rule followed faithfully could, eventually, lead to faith. Theodora asked, wouldn't he have preferred faith in the first place? The Patriarch smiled, explaining that he always looked for faith in his followers: some were sure they had it and he could see no sign, others were adamant they did not and yet he felt it shone from them. He was sure of her potential. Theodora was used to hearing her body, her voice and her performance criticised on every level. She was used, as well, to hearing tens of thousands roar with laughter and approval at her on-stage style. And, with Hecebolus, she had grown used to hearing herself praised as a woman, a lover, a partner. She had never before heard herself compared favourably to the faithful, it sounded blasphemous to her, and yet – in the Patriarch's wide smile, in his silly sticking-out ears, and in the certainty that came with the rich depth of his beautiful voice – it seemed almost possible he could be right.

Two days later Theodora accepted an even coarser shift in place of her black cotton robe, offered thanks for the begging bowl she was handed, and took up the small bundle she was allowed to keep – her own cloak, a stretch of cloth to serve as shade, blanket and bag, and joined the group of penitents who would walk before day broke, in less than an hour, into the desert heat. They drank water and ate dry bread, left the house with the Patriarch's blessing behind them. Theodora walked with the others, in silence, leaving it all behind.

Almost all. There was still an emerald, the size of a newborn's fist, prised from its ebony setting in the few moments she'd had alone to wash and now strapped beneath her left breast. It was not entirely comfortable but Theodora did not need comfort. The Patriarch could place his faith in her potential, and she hoped he was right, would be happy for him to be correct about her soul. Meanwhile, though, she was tired and hungry and thirsty before she'd even walked into the sand, but she definitely wasn't stupid.

Nineteen

Within two days of their journey inland the travellers were in an entirely different landscape. As they walked alongside a thin river, away from the slightly more temperate coast, other than a narrow course of green lining the water, the land ahead of them quickly changed from the fertile fields that fed every corner of the Empire to a harsher, hotter, hard-baked earth. Two days later when they turned away from the river as well, the earth receded beneath a covering of stone and sand. Strategically placed so that even fetching water was a two-hour task, Severus' camp sat beneath an ancient mountain, ridges smoothed from years of sand-scouring wind, caves dotted across its sheer surface, massive boulders that had fallen in earthquakes scattered around the site. The mountain was right on the edge of the desert proper, all the travellers could see for miles was sand and stone turned deep red in the low sun, muting to a dark amber as the temperature plummeted and the desert sky light-show took over. They were not quite the stars of home, but they were dazzlingly clear, and Theodora could follow them north if she wanted. Meanwhile, and with no moon yet risen, they gave a welcome pale light as she accepted a cup of hot water and a chunk of desert bread from Severus who, as always, served the newcomers, taking a moment to study each in turn. After they had eaten and drunk, Severus sent each of the new community members to a different place around the camp. Some went to caves low in the mountain, others to the shelter of the very few trees in the area, a couple to the ragged single-person tents dotted about the site. Theodora was allocated a large, irregular boulder as her own place; it would provide shade in the heat of the day, warmth from its heated rock during the cold night. That boulder was to be her home for the next year.

The first three months were the hardest, getting used to the harsh climate, and to the community of people, becoming accustomed to the lack of privacy and the simultaneous loneliness. There was always someone around, it was never really possible to be fully alone, yet these many people, sometimes a hundred or more, did not become friends either. The community was one of nodding acquaintances, who sometimes heard each other's most desperate secrets in the group meetings Severus guided, yet each was on a solo journey to the spirit, and there was no desire, or time, for anything as distracting as friendship. Slowly Theodora came to feel part of the loose group and, in the morning and evening talks with Severus, when they gathered to hear the teacher, she began to understand something of the faith the others professed so passionately.

Theodora's conversion was no glorious epiphany but a slow erosion of her cynicism. The inner sceptic that had stood her in such good stead as a child in the theatre, working backstage, was gradually washed away, not by an astonishing vision or even by the constant desert wind of burning days and freezing nights, but by Severus' humour and wisdom when he taught, explaining the serious and the utterly irrational, bringing the esoteric into the everyday, speaking in many languages and not just the Greek of the Church or the Latin of state, using whatever words he could find to make sense to his disparate group. As the teacher explained his personal understanding of the divine, Theodora slowly realised she too had an understanding of the

160

Christ, a spark of faith she had not noticed — or allowed — before now. It was not as passionate as their leader's, not as eloquent as that of some of the other believers, and certainly not as deep-seated as that of the real ascetics who occasionally joined them, coming back to the community after a year or more alone in the wilderness beyond their mountain — but what was, in effect, her conversion, felt all the more real for having shown itself through thought and discussion rather than a blinding revelation. Not that revelations were not also possible.

Nine months after her arrival, Theodora was sent high up to the other side of the mountain, to a small cave, with her blanket, a water supply, and ten days' food allowance, and left to get on with it, as the Christ had done, for forty days and forty nights. She had been schooled in what to expect, what she would probably experience, how to ration her food and water, but no amount of discussion could really explain what it was to be so truly alone.

On the first night she simply cried, and the second, and the third. By the fourth day she began to realise who and what she was crying for. She kept seeing, feeling, the image of a little girl. Eventually, paying more attention to the phantasm that hunger, thirst and solitude conjured up, really looking at what she saw in her mind instead of simply dismissing it as a mirage, she saw the light brown eyes, the straight brown hair, the stolid, stoic acceptance, and realised the little girl was her daughter Ana. The child she had thought of less than a dozen times since she left the City, the child she had probably thought of less than a dozen times even when she was living two miles from her. According to a letter that arrived when Theodora was still with Hecebolus, Ana was now with Comito, cared for along with Indaro by a child-minder, now that Theodora's older sister was doing so well in her work. Ana would be five, helping the dancers in the chorus, ready maybe to start learning a few lines, little songs if it turned out she had a good enough voice, had developed any stage presence at all. Theodora prayed the girl might have a good voice if that was the case. Singers became whores later than dancers, sometimes not at all. She wished more singing and less dancing on the child she had only just remembered was her daughter, she wished freedom from the theatre for her entirely.

By the end of the first ten days Theodora had seen or created – she was not sure which, and it didn't matter to her experience – visions of all the relatives she knew to be dead as well as several who were certainly alive, and, more strangely, the spirit of the bear that had killed her father. The bear made her cry more than any of them, in its sorrow at the one untamed action that changed the course of all their lives. The next day, the eleventh, she stayed in her cave as she had been told, only going outside when the light finally left the wide sky, to see the rations that had been left for her. She ate a very little bread and took almost an hour to slowly sip a cup of water, and then spent one of the easiest evenings of her life. The visions receded with food and drink, leaving only a sense of peace at having laid a few ghosts to rest, as well as acknowledging in spirit – if not in flesh – the presence of others not ghostly at all.

The second quarter was harder. Told to meditate on her own transgressions and, with the lesser rations permitted for the second quarter, the images came thick and fast. Cheating Anastasia of a handful of coins when they were performing together. Biting just a bit too hard on the cock of a man who liked it mean, but maybe not that mean. Spitting a curse after Menander's name. The dozens, hundreds of times she had fucked not for love, or need, but for the joy of money, and often for the stolen coin of thieving men themselves. In the cave, Theodora cried in pain at her own sins and denied her cramping stomach bread for a fourth day in a late-offered but sincere penance. When she woke on the morning of the sixth day, the fifth having passed in a self-induced daze, she forced water down her swollen throat, forced herself to eat, a tiny mouthful at a time, bringing herself back to full awareness. It had been made very plain to her that while she might want to punish herself with death, only God was able to grant that solace – it was her duty to stay sensible to everything she discovered about herself in this tiny cave, in the space that was now her whole world.

In the third ten days a new shift took place. She began to see where she was, studied the walls of the mountain cave and saw the small marks, indentations, countless signals other penitents had left in the past, marking out time or sins or life for themselves, or those to come. She studied the cave for three days, and when she was finished with the walls inside she turned her gaze outward, to the sand and the rock. Looking into the heart of Egypt she saw Isis and Osiris, Anubis, saw the fish-goddess, the ram-god, saw them all lined up, one on top of the other, as she had every day of her childhood, on the obelisk in the Hippodrome, listening to her great-grandmother's fairy stories of the Roman gods, the Hebrew prophets, all so different to the one divinity that was their Christ. Yet now they seemed to belong. They were of the sand and rock of her cave and, just as they had done when she dreamed as a little girl, they came down from their places on the obelisk and sat with her. Isis whispered of making the ideal man from the best pieces, breathing her life into him and carrying his child as she did so, her own brother's child. Anubis talked of an earlier time, whispering in his cracked jackal's voice of the weight of her heart,

163

insisting there was more to spill, that Theodora could lighten the load still more. Kebechet the snake came offering clear water, life water.

Seeing the snake woman, feeling the cool of the water she was offering, really feeling it running over her skin, through her hair, into her eyes and nose and mouth, Theodora remembered to drink for the first time all day. In her fasting stupor she reached for the cup and then pulled back her hand in slow motion as she woke to see an owl, the owl from the obelisk, swoop down and drag away the snake that lay within striking distance, the one that would have had its fangs in her hand had she touched the cup. Drugged on her body's own sources and lack of nourishment, Theodora watched her hand grasp the cup, sipped her water and acknowledged the bird that had just saved her life. It had not failed her yet. It would lead her home. This land, this sand, was getting far in, she was happy here, would stay as long as they let her, but even so, she knew it was not home.

Awake and sensible enough to order her thoughts, Theodora meditated, as she had been instructed, on the visions that had come to her in the fast. She concentrated on Isis, on the goddess's reconstruction of her broken brother-husband Osiris, and then thought of her own men, father and stepfather, Menander and Hecebolus, lovers and teachers, and often both, and often nothing but pain.

She recalled Severus' lesson on love, the half-sermon, half-prayer he had given, speaking in Syriac as often as any other language, proudly using whatever words were most appropriate to express universal truths, refusing to stick to the Latin the Roman west loved, the Greek the Church preferred, choosing instead to use whichever languages his followers understood to make his point clearer to them. His constant insistence that the only true partnership was between man's humanity and God's divinity, that anything else was ephemeral. Later that night, only the second evening she had been in the desert, and still unsure of the strange people around her, the wild men, the ragged women, those who came late at night to the fire, arriving like wary animals, spacing themselves far from each other and yet as close as they could to Severus, Theodora had raised her voice into the starlit night, asking her question, letting the words fall out in an uneven trickle.

'But there can be love . . . between people?'

It was the first time she had spoken since she arrived, other than to give her name, and the first time she had heard a question asked aloud. She didn't know if she was transgressing some hidden rule, but she did know she wanted an answer.

Severus had one; he was speaking in Greek now. 'There can be a kind of love between people, but it cannot be what you have thought was love until now. You cannot be ruled or taken over by love – when you are, it is intoxication, not love. You are human and therefore you love to be intoxicated. We, very many of us, have loved intoxication.' Several of the older men sitting in the evening dark laughed with him. 'The only true love is for the Christ. In that love you must give everything, break down your spirit until it is only willing, only ceding, only giving. You, and all too many of the others here –' He turned then and looked to one young man close behind him, waiting until the young man lifted his eyes and nodded – 'have given too much of yourselves to each other and not enough to God. You cannot ever give enough to God, put a limit on your idea of enough – you must give it all. Then, if you are fortunate, perhaps God will keep you free of human love. Allowing you more time for His love.'

Theodora pushed her luck. 'But what if God intends you to love another person?'

Severus smiled through the darkness, his stained teeth

165

shining in the firelight. 'I believe it does happen.' Again she heard the disparate chuckles from others in the darkness. 'If He intends you for an ordinary life, then so be it. Until then, there is time to give all.'

Then Severus began to chant all the words for love, all the words Theodora knew, Greek, Latin, Syriac, Aramaic, Hebrew, Coptic, and many other words she did not know for sure but understood from the effect they had on the others that they, too, must mean love. He kept repeating until he found a rhythm and something like a tune and then, slowly, quietly, others began to join. There was no leader and no followers, just the hundred or more of them, sitting on the cold sand and singing into the dark, changing with the people but not changed by any one of them, it was the work of many and the rule of none. Eventually the sounds became a chant, then song, then – for some, for others, finally for Theodora – a dance. It went on for almost an hour, stopping as quickly as it had begun when Severus announced the silence was upon them. Each one immediately retrieved his or her blanket or robe and made their way to their own little hillock or tent or cave where they slept. Theodora felt herself walking close to Severus as she made her own way back and the old man reached out a hand. He did not touch her, not quite, but she felt his blessing and fell asleep smiling. It was insane, living here, among these crazy mystics, these terrifying holy people and, Theodora realised, it was funny. It made her happy.

Now in her cave, recalling that early night in the desert, recalling the holy man's words, Isis had a new message for her. Theodora waited, sipping the water she knew she had to keep drinking – no matter that she did not want it, no matter that the more she denied herself, the greater the clarity of the visions and voices. Severus' voice receded, the whisper of the wind outside the cave grew still until all she could hear was the shushing of her own blood through her veins, in and out of her slow-beating heart. She heard Isis say that that the emerald was hers to keep. Theodora was not yet used to trusting the voices thrown up by days of solitude and fasting, she didn't know if it was real or merely her own desire to hold on to the stone that made her believe what she heard, but she chose to believe the voice, and was pleased with her choice.

Twenty

Theodora slept well that night, her stomach full from the small chunk of bread she had taken three hours to eat, her veins flowing well with rehydrated blood. She woke happy too, the deep green of the emerald catching morning light when she went outside to give thanks for the beginning of her fourth ten-day period. Grateful and already just a little sad that she would have to leave the bliss of this solitude, return to the community.

For three days she followed a simple pattern, drinking little, eating less, and sleeping most of the time. Timothy and Severus both came back to her in the dream, their sermons making more sense here, far from anyone else's interpretations. In particular she felt she finally understood why they rejected the accepted Chalcedonian orthodoxy of the City and of Rome. Here, in the desert, it made perfect sense that the Christ should be man, yes, but also, and more importantly, purely divine. It made sense too, as Severus maintained, that it suited the Patriarchs of Rome and Constantinople to believe in a dual-natured Christ: believing Him both human and divine allowed them to walk their own tightrope between the humanity of the Empire and the divinity of the Church. They had need of a dual Christ just as their Church that preached His poverty had need of the Empire's coin. Here, in the desert, there was no need for church or temple and no need for the funds to build them. No need then, to force the Christ into two natures.

Menander's teachings too, and her father's, also made appearances in her visions, with injunctions to hold her leg line, to curtsy nicely for the Senator, and never to go near an eating giraffe. In her sleep she heard the tunes her mother's mother had sung to hide the sound of Hypatia's birthing cries when Anastasia was born. Her grandmother's songs were in Hebrew mixed with a little Aramaic, words that Theodora seemed to understand in the sleep-trance of her cave. She was just seven when the old woman died and she lost the closest thing she felt to a maternal connection; Hypatia had been far too busy trying to keep her family together to give much attention to the minor matter of mothering. Not that the old lady had been gentle either, but she had sung well and occasionally, when she was in a good mood, Theodora had found her way to the grandmother's lap and rested there.

She used the quiet days of this last week to reaffirm her commitment both to her newly acknowledged faith, and to the branch of that faith espoused by her teachers. As in the desert below, there was no blinding light that persuaded her of the true path, it was instead the confirmation of a gradual conversion that had been growing in her for the past nine months. Timothy and Severus' teachings made sense to her, and Theodora of the Hippodrome, of the brothel, could never have achieved so much if she had not been practical as well as wild. She acknowledged she was their disciple in belief as well as deed.

Theodora had been warned that while there would be pleasant times in the forty-day fast, the greatest pain was likely to come out of her moments of ease. As a well-trained performer she chose to enjoy these quiet days: if suffering was inevitable, then she would rest through the easy moments while she had them. Just as there were always wonderful audiences, for whom she could do no wrong, so too there were always dreadful shows, when sure-fire gags were mistimed, perfect choruses lost their place, and the liquid gold in even the finest singer's throat was replaced by an ugly frog. She would not negate warmth and ease merely because unhappiness would inevitably follow.

On the thirty-fifth day Theodora woke with a searing pain that wrenched its way up from her deepest gut, through her stomach, and had her vomiting bile within an hour, and every hour following. There was a brief respite in the middle of the night when she forced herself to drink water in burning sips, knowing that the cramping pains had not yet left, that it would be worse if she were truly dehydrated. Theodora understood cramp and muscle spasm, understood how much her body, every body, relied on water. She gave in to the pain and it filled her up.

In lucid moments she realised that the pain was quite specific, in her lower abdomen, not entirely dissimilar to giving birth, something she might perhaps ride through – if there had been a rope to hang on to she would have reached for it, allowed herself to be pulled up and out of the sea of suffering, but there was no rope, and then the lucid moments became less, and the pain took in her whole flesh, her bones, her marrow. At times she felt as if it came not from inside out, but from the outside in, her skin was burning, her hair strands of fine glass with which to whip her face and neck and shoulders. She listened to herself bellowing on a surge of agony, and then subsiding again to a whimper. She had heard those noises before, heard herself make those noises before.

Had heard them the first time Menander had truly beaten her, after she'd fallen under his spell, after she loved him, and that had been so much more painful than all the other times he'd hit her before she realised she also wanted him to hold her. The pathetic whimper from her own mouth that proved she would rather be hit by Menander than have him ignore her, that his attention was her drug, and if she could not attain it with her skill, she would reach for it in any other way possible. She had heard this suffering from another mouth too, the ghostly whimper of the first man who had raped her, begging forgiveness afterwards, pushing her away and pulling her to him at the same time. These were the moans of her mother over her father's coffin and the moans of her mother in her stepfather's bed and the moans of both sisters over their dead sister's body. They were Chrysomallo's tears when Theodora confronted her friend, and they were Theodora's tears when Sophia turned away. They were her own baby's screams when she was given over to anyone who'd take the brat off Theodora's hands and allow her to get back to work, the tears of a little girl who understood she could not hold her mother's interest for more than a few minutes at a time. There was a job to do, a fee to earn, rent and servants and families to pay for, work to be done, always so much work to be done – almost as much work as it would have been to hold eye contact with her own child for a moment longer.

Thirty-nine days into her fast, in bone-cracking pain, Theodora stared through desert-dry eyes at the convulsions of her narrow frame and, in a moment of pure revelation, understood that her own pain was no different to the pain she had caused others. Nor was it any different to pain others had caused her. It was all one. All pain was one pain, all suffering was one suffering, and she was in the middle of it all, right now. She smiled in wonder at the understanding that joined each single sorrow into one vast agony. She smiled too, trying to bow her head in gratitude to the people and events that had led her here, in thankfulness to Severus and to Timothy. She could not bow, her body was held too stiff by her cramped muscles, but the intention was there. And even in all this suffering, there was relief that she had finally experienced this revelation so close to the time they would come for her. For the past thirty-eight days her unacknowledged fear had been that she alone, of all those who followed Severus, was too wicked to experience the truths she had been assured would eventually come. Then, the worst of that particular spasm over, she looked down again at her body and saw she lay in a pool of her own thin blood, and that the pool was spreading rapidly, so rapidly, out and away from her, liquid life pouring away. And then the world was black and she thought no more.

Later, when it was over, when they had found her and brought her back to the community, when those skilled in medicine had worked on her, Severus explained what had happened. One of those he allowed to tend her was a Persian doctor, no matter that the Sassanid was not a believer, no matter either that the Church still disapproved of surgery, or that the man admitted he had only a little skill with the knife anyway. Severus felt a heavy duty of care to the young woman: he had sent her out to the cave, had allowed her into their method of the fast. Of course he had lost followers before – when people found him, they were often at the lowest point of their lives. He could never guarantee every one would make it, either physically or spiritually, but he wanted them to, he prayed they would. He gave permission for the doctor to work with several of the women and left them to it. Left them to his prayer.

Now he leaned over her in the low bed and explained in stilted Greek what the doctor had told him in Persian.

'You will have no more children, the damage was too great.'

'He is sure?'

'We are none of us God, no one can ever be sure. But the doctor insists that in removing the growth too much damage was done for another child to grow.'

'He did remove it, though?'

172

'He did what he could.'

'I see.'

'No, you assume,' he answered, understanding she was already thinking ahead. 'You cannot know what else will come from this.'

'I watched my grandmother with a growth. She took a long time to die.'

Severus looked up at the livid sky above the tent where they had kept Theodora for the past two weeks; there would be a storm soon. 'What do you know, Theodora, right now?'

She answered, hearing the lesson in his voice, hearing, too, his warning; she might have been tired and unwell, and the older man a living saint, but she also knew to beware his anger. 'I know I am here, and I am alive, Father.'

He nodded. 'Better.'

'And I know that you have said I will not –' she corrected herself before he could – 'may not have more children.'

'Good. You have a daughter already?'

'In the City.'

'Then perhaps you can be a kinder mother to your grand-children. If you choose.'

Theodora smiled and shook her head. 'I have not had much luck with the choices I've made until this point.'

'You know more now.'

Theodora thought about what she had learned of herself in the cave. 'I know myself better.'

'What else do any of us have? The Christ showed us His divinity so that we could realise the necessity of understanding ourselves as men and reaching for the divine.'

Theodora lifted herself on the bed, the pain in her lower abdomen making her wince, and was more surprised when Severus reached a hand to help her. It was the first time he had touched her since she arrived in the community. She flinched away and then laughed at herself, forcing her arm to relax under the touch of his rough fingers. His touch was a blessing, but it was something else as well, she couldn't quite work it out, reaching through the fog of exhaustion and pain for the answer, and then she understood. 'Oh. Grandmother to my daughter's children. In the City. I can't stay here?'

Severus kept his hand lightly on her arm. 'You didn't come here intending to stay, did you?'

'The reasons I came have changed.'

'Of course. The reasons I stay, or the causes I travel for, they also change from one day, one moment to the next. What matters is I trust my actions are guided by God's will rather than my own. You must get well first, but then we want you to go to Antioch and, eventually, back to the City. There is work you can do for the Church there, as well as for your fellow believers.'

'The Church doesn't care what I think. If they won't listen to you and Timothy how can I make a difference?'

'You've had your visions, Theodora, and so have I. You have a great deal to do with your life, work that Timothy and I hoped you would be fit for, after your time here. You will leave us in a far better state to complete that work.'

'For now,' he added, answering her unspoken question, 'you know all that you need to.'

He stood to leave, his calloused hand scraping across the sunburnt skin of her arm, a gesture somewhere between blessing and the simple touch of a friend who is concerned for another's health and well-being. She felt his hand on her arm long after he had gone. He motioned to one of the women to come and sit with her, and just before he walked out again into the blinding sun he spoke, quietly, so the approaching woman wouldn't hear: 'The emerald, they took it when you were ill, for safekeeping. I have it now. But it is yours.'

*

Three months later, when she was well enough to travel, Theodora knelt for his blessing before leaving with a small group who were also being sent on, and Severus gave her the stone. It was warm from his hand and it stayed warm as she walked away.

Twenty-One

Theodora was spared another mammoth land journey by Timothy's kind provision of a ship to transport his own faithful from Alexandria to Antioch. Some of the half-dozen with her were disappointed, they had been looking forward to the traditional route across the Nile Delta, following the coastline north to Syria through Palestine, stopping off at the sacred sites of the Christ and His disciples' lives. But there was no complaint; years in the desert had taught them the value of immediate acquiescence, though it was true one of the younger women cried herself to sleep at the thought of not seeing the site of the resurrection. Theodora was surprised to find her own pace quicken and her heart rise as the morning of their fourth day walking north revealed buildings on the horizon, early light picking out the library of Alexandria, the medical school, the law school beyond. The newly purified Theodora was no keener on sin than the rest of her group, and so she was surprised, and a little concerned, to realise it was joy rather than fear she felt as they entered the city walls.

Each of the travellers was granted a few moments alone with Timothy and she asked him about it then.

'Theodora, I live in this city and often travel to others, the Christ journeyed to Jerusalem, even Severus leaves the desert sometimes. As a faithful minority, we need to keep our cause in the forefront of public discussion. It is easier to do that in a metropolis than in the wilderness.'

'I'm not saying it's easy, the ascetic life, but it was . . .'

'Simpler?'

'Clearer, there was more focus. I didn't think I'd feel excited to be here. But I do. I mean . . . it's so . . .' Theodora was struggling with words that failed to flow, to come at all.

Timothy smiled at her, kneeling before him. 'Severus and his people didn't bring you back from near-death to become a different woman. We wanted you because we knew you would do well for us, because we need who you are. Theodora, you have great things ahead of you.'

A presumably barren ex-dancer, who'd slept with far too many men, not all of them for money, but not many for free, who had found a new life as an anti-Chalcedonian believer at a time when there were even more attacks on that group than before, and who now couldn't make up her mind if she was hungry for the City or terrified of that hunger, didn't seem to have a lot going for her in terms of greatness as far as she could see. Even those who accepted her new-found faith would still find it a little hard to accept this ex-prostitute as the envoy of a living saint.

Theodora shook her head. 'How do you know that? I certainly don't.'

Then he explained about the project they had in mind, how a skilled actress, more valuable because of her past than in spite of it, was perfect for their plan. The group he was sending to Antioch were to found a new community, Theodora was not to stay with them. She would be met by a dancer, a young woman who had been working for them for some time. The woman, Macedonia, had set up a number of contacts, both in Antioch and Constantinople, people sympathetic to their cause, some of them in the highest echelons. Theodora would spend time with this young woman, learning her work – sometimes actually taking care of their fellow faithful, other times finding information for them, using her skills to create and maintain contacts; and she would then be more useful to the cause once they sent her back to the City. Antioch would be less of a shock than Constantinople, but more like home than Alexandria. It was the perfect staging post. And Macedonia would train her well.

'You already have many of the skills we need, you know how to talk to strangers, have been trained in charming their confidence.'

Theodora didn't like the sound of this. 'Yes, but that was for a very different reasons – wasn't it?'

'Macedonia will explain your mission further when you are in her care.'

Theodora stared at the priest. 'A mission? Is that what you call it these days?'

Timothy was calm, his beautiful voice still resonant, still charming, but everything about him was changed in Theodora's eyes. He spoke softly. 'We are not asking you to sleep with men for us, Theodora.'

'To spy on them, then? To use my skills, gain their trust, lie to them?'

'We believe there may come a time when it will be useful for us to have people, in both Antioch and Constantinople, who are faithful. What we will ask them to do then, I cannot say, it will depend on what comes. Macedonia has been able to help many of our number who have been persecuted. She has also found people who are with us, but need to keep quiet about their sympathies. Since Justin came to power, since his nephew Justinian took charge of the army, we have suffered further. We have our traditional paths for dialogue within the Church, of course, but we have also been looking for new ways to influence those in the City. We think you may be one of those ways. You can be influential, Theodora.'

'And that's not using me?'

'We are all used in the service of God.'

'So why don't you send me directly back to the City?'

'We believe it will be better to take time with this.'

'To see if you can trust me, you mean?'

Timothy did not respond. He stood up, their interview obviously over. 'Macedonia will meet you when the group arrive in Antioch. We will be very grateful.'

He was already walking away from where she sat, her mind reeling, her heart hurting. 'I thought you cared for my soul?' she said.

Timothy turned back, he was quite still, very serious. 'I do, but the care I have for the future of the Church is far greater. You can see that, can't you?'

'That you are being expedient? Yes, I can see that. I've been taught by men like you before. I didn't always trust them as much as I have trusted you.'

'You can continue to trust me. Trust that I will always put the faith first, that is my job. Right now, Severus and I believe you can be useful to us; in truth, we do not yet know exactly how. Your soul is your own affair, the Church is mine, and that is far more important than anything either you or I might want for our own lives. I understand you have been through a great deal in the desert.'

'I have come to believe. Slowly. It was not an overnight revelation, something passing, a vision, an epiphany brought on by the fast. It is real to me.'

'Good. I am glad to hear it. And that belief must now find its root in real life, in the everyday. Not everyone is suited to live a life apart, not everyone is meant to. Some of us must remain in the world, make our changes from within . . .'

179

'Get our hands dirty?'

'Yes. If necessary.'

He shook his head then, as if he really had no more choice than she did, and she thought perhaps she heard a suggestion of regret in his beautifully modulated tones. Then he walked away leaving Theodora on her knees, disappointed and hopeful and clinging to the possibility that her old world might yet feel new with the addition of faith.

The next morning they left for Antioch, the ancient and vibrant Syrian city on the Orontes River, its citizens first brought to the Christ by Peter himself. The community faithful prayed as the ship took them into their new life, hoping to gain inspiration to help them in their next task. Their fellow travellers lounged about the decks: merchants and salesmen, a handful of newly qualified students, young men from the Alexandria medical and law school, returning to their own towns to practise their new skills. Theodora sat alone in the prow and looked ahead. She had spent a year in the desert and discovered a great deal about herself, things she wanted to maintain, allow to grow. Yet now she was being sent back to work – if not in the flesh, then at least in the idea of her old world. To act, to perform, to be directed by men who were telling her to wait for their order and then carry it out, whatever it was, whenever it came. She knew she loved Timothy and Severus. She hoped she could trust them too.

The last few days at sea were hard work, a lack of wind right at the end of the journey held them still for several days, the Levantine coast behind them and the mountains of Syria just visible on the horizon haze ahead, then there'd been a brutal offshore storm that sprang up out of nowhere and had the majority of the faithful reaching for their amulets and good-luck charms, crying out to the Christ to bring them home safely. Slowly the storm calmed, a rainbow in the north-east was seen to be a sign of all good things to come, and the captain led them into dock only four days off target and – he checked, though he didn't tell his passengers – with just a quarter of a barrel of fresh water left in supplies. Theodora held back on deck, waiting to see if her contact would be there. From above the heads of the others waiting on the dock, a woman nodded, just enough for her to notice. Theodora walked down and, with legs still shaky from the journey, introduced herself to the woman who was to become her friend.

The Spartan's conquering – Macedonia would say marauding – influence on her family's home country, the land she'd been named for, was obvious in her light blue eyes, her fair hair, her long strong bones. She was tall, at least a head above Theodora, and her long hair was pulled up higher on her head. She wore heavily patterned old clothes, robes left by her mother, dresses her grandmothers had worn thirty years earlier, cloth and cloaks passed down from old women she had befriended. Although she was just a few years older than Theodora, Macedonia's dress, combined with a self-certain manner, gave her an air of authority unusual in a woman not born to the patrician. While she did not have Theodora's sharp tongue, she was perfectly capable of standing her ground and making sure she was heard, and not merely from the constant jingling of the four dozen gold and silver bracelets she wore on each arm, fine fortunes brought back from Hindustan by her father and his brothers who had worked the spice routes, given to her as a girl and never removed, so that now her wrists had grown too wide to take them off and the slightest movement set her ringing. She had given birth to two children, but neither lived beyond three weeks and, with no husband, her matronly potential was undercut by the kind of vigour that a family would have

181

drained from any other poor woman. Macedonia was attractive, passionate, obvious, open, well known, and well loved in Antioch – everything that Theodora would have thought it better for a spy not to be. Her hostess explained, however, that it was simple to hide her true status behind a mask of exposing all – secrets led to exposure, not the other way round.

Macedonia's home was deep in the centre of the city, on one of the few streets that had escaped damage in the earthquakes of the past century: it had old-fashioned houses spinning off from long alleys, where rooms looked out on to tall narrow court-yards or back down into the street, and the stone steps and cobbles were so ancient that they had been worn soft by the tread of years. Theodora had grown up in streets like this, she felt easy in Macedonia's two old rooms and, despite the peace she'd left behind, she was excited to be living in a big city for the first time in many months, a city she did not know with a woman she didn't know either. She was closer to home than she had been in years and glad to be here.

It took less than a fortnight for the women to become lovers. For Theodora, it was a natural progression. Back on the ship that brought them here, she could not have imagined the pos-sibility of enjoying another's body, it seemed too remote from her intensely spiritual experiences in the desert. In Macedonia's bed, in the middle of the night, it seemed completely natural.

In the morning, her dark-skinned body stretched against Macedonia's softer, paler flesh, she asked what happened next.

'What do you mean?'

'Well, here we are together . . .'

Macedonia smiled. 'You're being very coy all of a sudden.'

'You're my first lover since I found God.'

'The Christ found you years ago, you just weren't paying attention.'

182

'The fact remains, we're not the ideal couple.'

Macedonia frowned. 'I'm not sure what the ideally faithful look like. The Christ told His followers to leave their families and follow Him. I follow the Patriarch Timothy and I trust he knows what he's doing. You feel the same about both Timothy and Severus, and they sent you to me.'

'To become your lover?'

'To be my partner in this work.'

'And what work is that?'

'Other than making me happy?'

'Other than that. I'm used to making people happy, and I don't really think Timothy sent me here to just lie in your bed.'

Macedonia reached an arm around Theodora and pulled the smaller woman on top of her, 'No, very single-minded these priests. Still, we've a few hours before we need to do anything too demanding, why don't I take some time to explain my work to you more fully?'

Theodora smiled. 'Why don't you?'

Twenty-Two

Despite her fears of a return to the world, Theodora quickly became fond of Antioch. It was an astonishing place, seemingly capable of combining prayer and play in equal measure, ideal for the transition from the desert to the City. She found it was perfectly normal to spend an evening eating and drinking and laughing in a bar, and then see the same people the next day in a prayer meeting, everyone earnestly debating, agonising over the smallest discrepancies in understanding or translation of the sacred texts, especially in this city of so many languages. The world still functioned in Latin in the old Rome in the West, as did much of the Church, while in the new Rome of Constantinople, Greek belonged to the people and their faith, with an uncomfortable Latin for the state. Antioch was entirely different. To the citizens of this third city of the Empire, business was far less important than faith. Here the subtleties of the Greek preferred by the poetically inclined, those who liked their religion spirited as well as spiritual, rubbed alongside the Syriac, Aramaic and Coptic of the earliest Christians, spoken by faithful who were demanding faith in their own languages, and were also beginning to whisper that they might want their own nations for those languages too. In Antioch, the religious engaged with the mind as well as the spirit, while it quickly became apparent that the city also engaged wholeheartedly with the flesh.

*

Macedonia's work was a combination of many things, not all of them entirely legal, more often than not involving some kind of spying or information-gathering, and occasionally veering toward the dangerous, though so far she had always emerged safe from her efforts. The few who really knew her work claimed she got away with her meddling because her Blue-leader grandfather had known too many important people in Constantinople for it to be possible to bring her down; others said that the protection of the Alexandrian Patriarch left her inviolate, others still that she was shielded by certain connections in the current Palace hierarchy itself. She admitted to Theodora that she took commissions from both Timothy and the Blues, maintaining what balance she could, and used her spare time for her own endeavours. The big boys could make their plans and schemes around the problems of Church and state; her choice was to ensure the people on the ground were taken care of as well.

The task Macedonia hoped Theodora would help her with first was in aid of one such ordinary person. Phebe and Macedonia had once been friends, but several years earlier, when Macedonia became Timothy's acolyte, Phebe followed another leader, Marcus Orontes, a preacher utterly opposed to Timothy's beliefs. Orontes had grown up in Sykae, across the water from the central City where Theodora had plied her childhood trade. He left the City as a very young man, and travelled to Antioch, where he not only made his name as a preacher, advocating a faith that was unusually pro-Chalcedonian for that area, but he also so despised the City and all it stood for – the corruption of Rome, as he called it – that he had even taken the name of Antioch's river, the Orontes, as his own name. Unlike Theodora, he had apparently cut off his past entirely. Macedonia had heard that Orontes was now preparing to publicly cast Phebe out of his group and, knowing his methods, she was ready to rescue her when he did, not least because what Phebe had learned while part of his group might prove helpful to Timothy's plans in the area.

Theodora agreed to help because it was what Timothy had asked of her and because Macedonia needed another to make the scheme work, but when the plan was explained, her stomach lurched with sick uncertainty.

'Of course I can do what you ask . . . I could always do that, I just . . .'

'Don't think it matches your image of a good Christian woman?'

They were in bed together, going over the strategy again.

'No. Yes . . .' Theodora answered, 'I'm not stupid, I can be as realistic as the next homeless, stateless believer.' They both smiled then and Theodora continued, 'I'd just hoped this kind of work was behind me. Assumed it was.'

'Understandable, but it is another of your skills, isn't it? We have been taught to be true to those talents, to use what we're good at, not pretend to be other than we are.'

'And doing so in the service of the Christ makes it all right?'

'I believe it does.'

'There are plenty of the religious who would disagree with you.'

'Of course, but I don't serve them, I serve the Patriarch. And myself.'

'And which of those two do we serve today?'

'Both. Hopefully.'

Her lover's simple belief in the value of pragmatic action was persuasive to Theodora, who had been well trained in the practicalities of poverty, but it didn't stop her being nervous as they approached Orontes' huge home, the base for his followers. Macedonia's plan was far removed from Theodora's recent experiences in the desert, and while there was certainly going to be a performance of a sort, failure here would be much more dangerous than the sting of Menander's cane.

'We should have left earlier.' Theodora was disheartened by the throng of people already in the courtyard when they arrived at the house. 'We'll never get up front.'

Orontes would be speaking soon and there was a clear sense of anticipation among his followers.

'Yes we will, work with me.'

Theodora watched Macedonia, quickly caught on, and the two women shape-shifted their way through the tight crowd, moving from virgin to whore, working whichever form suited the person nearest. Macedonia pushed slightly too close to a young man who, of course, stepped back where he hungered to step forward, while Theodora smiled shyly at an older woman who had no choice but to let the eager young acolyte past. Within five minutes Theodora and Macedonia were standing in the second row of the courtyard that now held about two hundred people, looking at Phebe, wrapped in a coarse woollen blanket and rocking in fear in the centre of the space.

Marcus Orontes started innocuously enough. As with so many of these new leaders, their small sects dotted all across Syria and the Levant, his text was mainly that of the Jews, as he cited first Ezekiel and then Daniel, with a little Lamentations thrown in for good measure. Then he increased the tension and pitch of his oration, reminding his audience that they stood here, so close to the birthplace of the Christ, and that they, not the dangerously misguided Nestorians or Arians or anti-Chalcedonians, were following the Church's true path. Theodora had to hand it to him, the man was a very good speaker, and he was far prettier than Timothy. He waited until the crowd's murmuring agreement died down, then left the raised dais at the side of the courtyard

187

and began circling Phebe. Eventually, his voice soft and low, he began to speak.

'Each of us is part of a proud tradition of steadfast faith that follows in the footsteps of those who brought the Church to Antioch – Peter the evangelist, Paul, Barnabas the faithful. Yet there is one among us, who has worshipped with us, has adored the Christ with us, who has chosen to leave our community, turning her back on us.'

He paused and the crowd gratifyingly filled the silence with something between an 'ooh' and an 'oh'.

'One who wishes to leave the sanctuary of community and arrogantly strike out on her own.'

He continued for almost a full hour. On and on about the group's sanctity as a unit, each individual as part of the whole, about Phebe's betrayal of them all. Just at the point when he might have sounded cruel, he neatly managed a little self-deprecation, apologising to the group, and further, to the wider city and Christian whole even, for not noticing sooner what a viper he had allowed into their community, for being taken in himself by her cunning, her female graces. He likened himself to Adam, to Samson and then, in what Theodora thought was the kind of narrative leap that would have been booed off stage at the Kynegion but seemed to be going down very well with the Antioch crowd, to John the Baptist, betrayed by Salome. And every time he berated himself, his people confirmed his position as their leader, their head, their teacher. He certainly knew how to work them.

All the while Orontes was lecturing, Macedonia had been quietly working her way around the edge of the inner crowd, and she was now positioned directly in front of the shaking woman. Just as Macedonia had predicted, Orontes now upped his pace, his circling became faster, his rhetoric more fevered, with insults shouted directly at Phebe. The crowd were shuffling closer, starting to join in; Orontes heard their engage-ment and simplified his speech so they could become his chorus. In just a few minutes their responses had shifted from a staggered, individual, murmured agreement to a communal chant – evict the whore, evict the whore. No matter that Orontes had started his oration by explaining she was leaving them: this crowd were determined to expel her first.

Macedonia nodded to Theodora across the tight circle. Then there was a call from the centre of the courtyard, an ululating cry seemingly set up by the woman around whom so much was happening but actually coming from Macedonia's closed mouth. It set off all the others and the circle immediately began to buckle in on itself. Orontes slipped backwards, joining his wealthy guests on the safer raised dais at the side, leaving Phebe to the anger of the crowd. In the mess of bodies, Macedonia pulled the confused Phebe away, passing her first to one strate-gically placed contact, then a second, and then dragging her out of a back entrance, sliding beneath the kicking feet and the angry hands that were clawing in the centre of the courtyard, hungry to grab the traitor. Theodora slipped forward to cover herself with the blanket and take Phebe's place. There was yelling and shouting, pushing from the outer edges, people fighting to get closer to the centre, to the spot where Theodora now crouched and finally, above it all, she heard a whistle from Macedonia, brief and sharp.

Theodora waited, one, two, three long breaths, and then, grabbing at the booted foot that was aimed at her face, she stood, knocking her aggressor flat, and threw down the blanket, sending the crowd back several inches in surprise. This was not the woman they had come to attack. Climbing on the shoul-ders of the closest man she could find, an elder statesman of Orontes' church, who was so shocked to be touched by a woman for the first time in years, let alone scaled by one, that he stood silent in fear – and not a little pleasure – as Theodora, one foot on his shoulder, the other on his head, called across the horrified crowd, 'Marcus Orontes, your mistress is gone. The show is over.'

She then ran across the crowd, lightly stepping from head to shoulder to head, to the main entrance. Years ago she had crossed half the Kynegion audience in the same way, back then the applause had been tumultuous, and Menander's fury palpable. Now the crowd were momentarily silent in shock, but Orontes' anger was just as fierce, screaming at his men to grab her, his perfectly elegant tones cracking with rage. Theodora was at the entrance to the courtyard, ready to leap from the last shoulder to the ground, when she was pulled down by several of the young men in the crowd, suddenly brought to their senses by the rage of their leader. It was only the fact that they started arguing over what to do that limited her pain to a fierce slap across the back of the head and a few flailing kicks to her back. One of the young men then pulled his fist back aiming a punch and Theodora brought up her own foot in a blow to his groin. He doubled over, howling in silent agony, as two guards arrived from the outer door and, grabbing an arm each, hustled her into one of the long corridors of the main house, away from the baying mob.

She could hear Orontes' voice fading as she was pushed up stairs and through long low rooms. The elder guard was all for throwing her out on the street there and then, leaving her to the anger of their fellow faithful, but the younger insisted Orontes would want to speak to her, find out what was going on.

Theodora spoke quietly, wincing a little where the blow to her head had made her bite the inside of her cheek, pointing out she was no prisoner.

'No, of course not,' replied the younger man, with a smile that was not quite as charming as his leader's, 'but I don't imagine it's entirely safe for you to leave, not just yet. And perhaps you would like a cool drink? You must be tired after all that exertion?'

Theodora nodded, 'I would, thank you.'

She was led to the wide, bright chamber where Orontes greeted his most favoured guests. Exactly where she wanted to be.

Twenty-Three

'Theodora, what a pleasure. I saw you perform once, years ago.'

'How nice.'

'We were both young.'

'No doubt.'

'We'd heard rumours you were in town.'

'A man of your influence, you'd have been notified the moment I came ashore, surely?'

Marcus Orontes smiled, 'Well, it didn't take long. I gather you underwent a conversion in the desert?'

'I have turned my face more clearly to the Christ, yes.'

'And more clearly away from man? You're living with the dancer, Macedonia?'

'I have a place in her house.'

'And in her bed, no?'

Theodora smiled and said nothing. Enjoyable though it might be to engage in verbal sparring with a skilled partner, she really didn't have time. She was in his house, with guards hovering twenty feet away and a crowd of followers furious that they hadn't seen their promised spectacle this afternoon. Theodora wasn't here to fight with Orontes or his people.

He preached, she listened. He mocked, she smiled. She smiled, he liked it. He flirted, she parried. He dismissed the guards, and told them to wait just outside, she found a cushion and a soft cloth to lay over it. She poured his wine, he drank it. She laughed with instead of at him, he liked it even more. She leaned back, her breasts elevated, her legs stretched, her arms wide, he sat and stared, waiting. He kissed, she kissed back. He led her through a door behind a curtain into a bedroom.

'I don't doubt you came here planning to seduce me, Theodora.'

'You're entirely correct,' she answered, stepping up naked to his bed, her stomach flipping and hands shaking as she did so.

It wasn't the thought of sex with a stranger, this stranger, that was unnerving her, or that by most standards this was hardly the behaviour of a new convert, no matter how well she accepted Macedonia's belief in a pragmatic life for the greater sake of the faithful – it was the fine line between doing this for Macedonia, for Timothy, for the cause, and doing it for herself. The fear that her body, that old betrayer, might slip away from the very new mooring that was her faith. Theodora had enjoyed feeling her body and spirit as one since the coming together in the desert, and was not keen to embrace again the pain of dissociation, no matter how useful it might be right now. And so, by force of will, she held her spirit present, in her body, as she stepped naked to the man. It was harder to do than letting her mind, letting her spirit fly away, but it was more true, and the converted Theodora would now have herself be more true, whatever she was doing.

Not that Marcus Orontes noticed: he was still talking about himself.

'I'm not sure what you're doing here, but you won't persuade me to take her back.'

'That's not why I'm here.'

'My people hated that Greek bitch. Phebe was a foreigner to them, so Western, they don't like foreigners here.'

'No one likes foreigners, Marcus, that's the way of the world.'

'Very true. Fortunate that we're both from the City, then.'
'Isn't it?'

It was three in the morning before Marcus Orontes was sated, later still before he was sleeping. When he finally gave in to the demands of his exhausted body, it was the sleep of an unworried man who knows his home is protected, his life well arranged, and that a lovely young woman is lying beside him. He knows this because he is sleeping on his front, one arm pulled tight around her neck, and a dead-weight leg slumped over both of hers, caring more to keep her safely beside him than to sleep comfortably.

Fortunately Theodora had been in this position more times than she cared to count. She slipped her legs out from under his prone form, one tiny movement after another, each one barely noticeable, so that she was always moving while always seeming still. He stirred, once, but did not wake. With her legs free, the weight of his arm was even stronger across her neck, pushing into her windpipe. She forced herself to breathe carefully, keeping her heartbeat steady and light. Infinitely slowly, she levered herself up on to the balls of her feet: her legs and full torso were now off the bed, the only parts of her touching the smooth sheet were her toes and the weight of her head where his arm pushed down on her neck. Reaching behind her, she bunched up the cushion she'd used as pillow, with her free hand gently and slowly tickled his ear, all the while hissing a tiny sibilant mosquito buzz. She continued until the minute movement and noise registered in his consciousness, felt the moment he woke just long enough to swat the non-existent creature. As he lifted his arm she pushed off from her toes into a side-twisting somersault, landing silently on the floor by the edge of the bed, at the same time pushing the cushion into place for the return of his arm. Even as she immediately moved away towards the door, she kept up the rhythmic sounds of her own breathing, increasing her volume the further she was from the bed. Her heart was racing but there was no trace of it in her breath.

Grabbing her robe, she carefully pulled back a hanging on the far wall, opening a narrow door behind it. She stood between both rooms and waited until her eyes adjusted to the total darkness of the small, windowless antechamber and she could clearly discern two lots of breathing. One was a small child, his breath the snuffling repetition of a little one who has fallen asleep crying for his mother, the other was very close, older, and drunk. Theodora headed for the child; feeling the low bed cutting into her shins, she bent and reached out her arms to the boy. Her robe was partly around her, her skin was warm, she hoped that, for a few moments at least, the two-year-old would imagine she was his mother, that she wouldn't further upset him, not least because a screaming baby did not feature in Macedonia's plotting for the success of their mission.

Three minutes later the child was strapped to her back, pulled close with a combination of her own robe and his light blanket, the two cloths twisted round her body, locking him tightly to her back as she'd seen the Nubian women wrap their babies in the Alexandria market. Then the little boy simply settled comfortably against her, with no protest, nothing to disturb the night nurse. Crossing the small room to the opposite door that opened into the main hallway, she gently pulled back the bolt. The guards were stationed outside Orontes' door, twenty paces to her right. The standing guard kept on with his broken snore, the rhythmic clicking of the dice assured her his seated companion was no more alert. She rounded the corner and broke into a silent run, bare feet hardly touching the stone, the way Menander had trained the dancers from their very first class: 'We don't want to know you exist until the moment you arrive, so shut up and do it again. Better.'

Then she climbed through the window at the end of the

195

hallway, let herself down to run along a high wall, finally jumping to the neighbouring garden, where, despite Macedonia's
reassurance, Phebe was now frantic. The little boy's strong neck
was arching back, his mouth ready to howl, and then Theodora
had unwrapped him, a gift of flesh and blood, warm child to
fear-cold mother, and the boy's unhappy mouth was stoppered
with his mother's breast, Phebe shaking with tears and hysterical relief, Macedonia both proud and worried. Theodora herself
was quiet and drained, and without even taking time to whisper
a greeting, immediately headed back the way she'd come.

This time she made no pretence of hiding from the guards. Her
robe barely covering her front and none of her back, she saun-
tered along the corridor, coming to stand very still in front of
the dice-thrower.

'Morning, men.'

Her breasts were head-height, her smile wide. His friend still
dozing against the wall, the young man blushed and demanded
to know how she'd left the room without them noticing.

Theodora shrugged, letting the robe drop a little further. 'I
hate to piss in front of a man I've just serviced, especially one as
pretty as your boss. So I went through the brat's room, his nurse
stinks of wine and the child of his own dirt. Someone ought to
sort them out. If you'll excuse me, I'm heading back to the
preacher's bed, I'm sure Marcus Orontes has plenty of prayer to
share with me yet.'

She went in, leaving two very frightened men at the door,
both wide awake.

Theodora was on her knees before Orontes when the nurse came
in, screaming that the child was gone. It was good timing and not
at all accidental. Orontes looked down, Theodora looked up, and
they understood each other perfectly. He issued all the appropriate

orders, shouting at the nurse and the men at his door, but, Theodora thought, his performance lacked a little urgency.

She was strapping on her sandals when he dragged her up from the floor, one hand round her throat.

'You've taken my son?'

Theodora kept her voice quiet and low. 'Your mistress's son, Orontes. I don't think he is yours, strictly speaking. And neither is she any more, didn't you throw her out?'

'He has lived in my home since he was a baby.'

'Perhaps he wanted a change, you know what little boys are like.'

'You think he left by himself?'

She twisted, reaching one hand up to his face, her fingers stroking his cheek, her voice a whisper, 'I have no idea what the child did or did not do last night.' His hold on her neck was still tight and she pulled her hand back a little from his cheek, spread her fingers wide and held them, sharp-nailed, just a breath from his eyes. Her voice still a whisper, she continued, 'But if you don't let me go now, I will put out your eyes. Our Greek classics are littered with blind characters, I understand the people are meant to value their words more highly, purely because they cannot see – will you be a blind teacher, Marcus?'

He let her go then, but not before he had kicked out at her, catching her deep in the belly with his full foot, ripping at the new scar tissue in her gut.

Theodora was winded and fell to her knees. Orontes leaned down to her, pulling back her hair: 'I won't forget this, I won't forget you.'

Theodora used every theatre trick she knew to get back her breath and replied, 'Neither will I, I assure you. But you've got what you wanted, surely? Phebe and her bastard are gone, you are free to continue your work, unencumbered.'

'My work matters.'

197

'I know you think it does. I know you think your faith justifies any behaviour.'

'I have done nothing wrong, you are the thief here.'

'Well, nothing unless I tell your people a little of what happened in your bed last night. Between us? I don't suppose that even this city with its amazing ability to party until dawn and then pray all day would quite understand the allure of fucking Theodora-from-the-Brothel.'

'But you're converted, you're faithful now. Redeemed.'

'True, but I will tell them otherwise if I have to. And I'll add to the story in the telling. That young man out there, the one who fumbled with his dice all night outside your door, haven't you noticed how he looks at you? I'm sure some of your people have. I don't think it would take much to persuade them you are more to him than a teacher.'

'They won't listen to your gossip.'

'Really? Are you sure?' She waited for her threat to sink in, felt his hold on her hair loosen just a little. 'You continue on your path, Orontes, I'll take mine. You didn't really want to keep that child, did you?'

He shook his head. 'Not much, no. But I do not like to be tricked.'

'Who does? Take it with good grace and be quiet about it. The less people know about what happened here, the sooner you will forget.'

'I'll never forget.'

'Well, more fool you. You can waste a very long time looking back.'

Theodora left then, while Marcus Orontes was briefly calm, not at all sure he would stay that way for long.

Safely in Macedonia's house, Phebe and her child already shipped out of the city, Theodora told her night's story, unburdening her physical and emotional discomfort as she gave her body to Macedonia's care, first to warm water and then to soothing oils.

When eventually they made their way to bed, Macedonia admitted she was impressed. 'You're even stronger than they'd told me.'

'They?'

'Timothy's people.'

'I thought I was done whoring.'

'Is it whoring to save a woman and child from someone like that?'

'The cause was good, yes,' said Theodora, 'but a cock in your mouth, for reasons other than love? My dear, that is always whoring.'

'Would you rather have taken care of the hysterical mother?'

'Nothing a slap across the face wouldn't fix. Couldn't see you turning a side somersault to get off his bed, though.'

'Really? I haven't lost all my skill.'

'No, but you have a few years on me, you're not quite so delicate on your feet. And you're tall, tall girls lack agility . . .'

Their teasing became kissing, and the kissing became passion, and the passion was not whoring.

Twenty-Four

For the first few weeks after they rescued Phebe and her son, Theodora and Macedonia had to contend with verbal attacks in the market and, once, an actual physical assault from one of Marcus Orontes' followers – the physical assault didn't stand up to Macedonia's strength or Theodora's agility, but it was disturbing enough. Orontes though, realising outright hostility didn't look good while trying to recruit new faithful to his Church, eventually called his people off, insisting they were all happier without Phebe and her brat.

There followed several missions like the first, some under Macedonia's direction, others specifically for the Patriarch. Once they were asked by Timothy to help free a misguided son from an overbearing sect, another time Macedonia decided that one of the town's pimps had gone too far and it was time his whores, led by herself and Theodora, took revenge. On several occasions they wined and dined visiting traders, passing back information gleaned across comfortable couches and groaning tables to either the Patriarch's people in Alexandria or Macedonia's contacts among the Blues in the City. Despite her initial reservations, Theodora came to relish these games, they were a form of the playing she'd always enjoyed, but now when she went home it was to Macedonia who had become her friend as well as her lover. There was still a little necessary whoring sometimes to get one or other of them out of a tricky situation, but Theodora was happy. Working for Timothy, doing his bidding with Macedonia to guide her, she almost forgot that her bosses intended that she return to Constantinople eventually. Timothy and Macedonia did not.

'You need to leave.'

Theodora stretched in the bed, leaned up to look out of the window, over the tiled roofs to where stalls were still laid out, their sun-bleached canopies dozens of shades of warm red and ochre in the afternoon light. 'There's plenty of time, the market won't be clear for another hour or more, and I hate pushing through the crowd.'

'You need to leave Antioch.'

Theodora was suddenly cold, her voice low. 'Why?'

'The Patriarch has new work for you.'

'What work?'

'He wouldn't tell me, not specifically, but it's important.'

'I don't want to go.'

'He knows that.'

Theodora pulled away when Macedonia reached for her.

'You knew he had plans for you.'

'I thought these were his plans. Here, with you.'

'The Patriarch's not stupid, Theodora. You and I? He knows we've become closer than he intended.'

'So he's sending me away to punish us?'

Macedonia shrugged. 'I don't expect he cares, his concern is always for the Church. We are irrelevant to him.'

'So why does he want to send me away?'

'He's not sending you away, he's sending you to work for him.'

'Where?' Theodora asked even though she knew there was only one answer.

'The City.'

*

201

The Emperor Justin was becoming more aggressive in his behaviour towards their fellow believers, those who maintained the primacy of the Christ's divinity over His humanity; the refugees from the City told angrier stories about the treatment meted out from the officials at the Chalke, entrance to the Palace, and Timothy needed someone working for him from inside. They were sending her home with a letter of introduction to the Palace officials who really ran the Empire. It was a simple enough thing, and it was everything. The people Macedonia maintained contact with, on Timothy's behalf, were very different to Theodora's circle. Many of them had known her work – as an entertainer, Theodora from the Hippodrome had had no equal, but she would never have been welcome inside the Chalke gates before. Now the Patriarch was sending her back to get into the hidden centre of their world, she would need to go home as the newly penitent Theodora.

There were a few days to prepare and then it was time to leave. The ship was sailing on an early tide, they spent their last hours together awake and in bed.

'You will need to be on your best behaviour, all the time.'

'This isn't one of my best behaviours?'

Macedonia curled down and held Theodora, 'It's one of your finest skills, but they need to believe that you are totally changed when you go home.'

'I am. I had no faith before: now I do. That's all the change I need.'

'I know the importance of faith as well as you, and I know, too, that in a place like the City, appearance matters as much, if not more. We have someone who will give you work, and a place to stay.'

'I can stay with Comito. I might have been a few years away, but I doubt very much they'll turn me down at the actors' entrance to the Kynegion.'

Macedonia sat up, her voice very clear in the still room that was slowly gaining light as the sun began to rise over the mountains. 'Theodora, you are part of Timothy's plan to get close to the man who may become Emperor.'

'Justin has other family who could succeed him as well as this nephew.'

'Perhaps, but Justinian is his favourite. Many people believe he paved the way for Justin's own accession, the Emperor owes him. The Patriarch wants you to build influence with Justinian, but the Palace won't let you near unless you approach him as a changed woman.'

Theodora laughed, without humour, 'Timothy doesn't want you and me to make love in this bed, but he has no qualms about pimping me to Justinian.'

Macedonia shook her head. 'By all accounts the Emperor's nephew works day and night at his studies, the man barely goes to bed, and certainly not for sex.'

'Maybe he takes a eunuch?'

'Not that we've heard. All the Patriarch asks for now is that you try to make him like you, engage him. From what our people tell us, Justinian is interested in the world – you've travelled, you're good at charming people, once Timothy arranges the introduction, your job will be to find a way to get close to him.'

'Yes, but he's sending me, not some other woman, and we all know how best I get close.'

'Maybe this is a test for you.'

'What? To see if I can keep from ravishing some lumpen Slav who's only come to prominence because of his mother's brother? Even I can probably hold off there.'

'I agree it doesn't sound like much of a test, but just in case, you have to give the appearance of being a new Theodora.'

'I am. I keep telling you, I know I didn't have some blinding-light conversion, there was no angel, no miracle, I simply came to an understanding that made sense to me. That doesn't mean it isn't real.'

'No, and we know that those blinding-light conversions are more to do with hysteria than anything else, like Orontes' crazed followers. Unfortunately they are also what most people find easier to believe in. So of course I believe in your faith. You, though, are going to have to show it when you go home. Not just believing quietly, but finding a way to make it plain.'

'You want me to act out my faith?' asked Theodora, 'Perform it?'

'Yes, if you have to. Hopefully it won't need to be quite so obvious, but you are going to need to behave differently, at least a little. And that means you can visit your sister, but not the theatre and definitely not your old friends. It will be safer for you to stay away from them until you've established yourself with Justinian.'

'Great,' Theodora said, knowing how well that would go down with her old colleagues.

The two women kissed then, slowly.

'I won't forget you.' Theodora said quietly.

'No, but you will be late if we don't go now.'

Days later, the coastline of Bithynia shimmered finally in the heat of the opposite shore, and then disappeared into the night. Theodora didn't want to go down to the tiny cabin she shared with the other single women. Her fellow travellers might be content to get a glimpse of the City once the lookout had shouted his sightings of Chalcedon to the east and then Constantinople to the north-west, but she intended to catch the first light on the hills and churches herself. She was markedly different to her travelling companions anyway, the only one of them going home. Everyone else was travelling to the City as a trader or adventurer or pilgrim, some visiting for the first time, others returning to buy or sell, there for the deals only, the market in cloth or spice or – in the case of at least one of the older men, she was sure – in flesh.

There was a pilgrim family in their group, all the way from Moesia, and while the older man barely acknowledged the parents, he happily left his private cabin to spend hours on deck playing with their two little girls, building their trust in card games and dice where there was no common language between them. Theodora, meanwhile, made a note to herself to check where the old man went when he left the ship. Everyone in the City knew about the trade in child slaves, the stories of girls bought for a pair of shoes and then contracted until their four-teenth year. In their training sessions Menander had merely to threaten to call in the slavers for the girls to bend deeper, leap higher, spin faster. Dancing girls and nine-year-old acrobats and even teenage whoring were normal in their craft, but theatre girls were paid, in good coin too, and that made all the difference. Her people despised the likes of this man, his money made from forced flesh. She'd keep an eye on him, and if she still had friends in the City, they'd know what to do. Or they would once she found a way, against Macedonia's instructions, to contact them. Whether or not her past friends would welcome her was a different matter altogether.

The leaving felt a very long time ago now, the turnaround on stage could be brutal, Theodora had no idea who she still knew back in the City, maybe all her colleagues had left in the three years she'd been away. She'd only had four days in Antioch to prepare for her departure, but had grabbed a moment to write to Comito, sending the letter on an earlier ship with the news that she was coming home. The sisters had communicated sparingly over the years, but there was enough gossip in the Antioch market for Theodora to know that Comito was singing even more successfully, which meant their family was safe, Ana looked after. Theodora was to return a changed woman, but any repentant ex-actress would hurry to see her family. She wasn't expecting a fatted calf any more than she was expecting a warm welcome from the likes of Sophia or Menander, or any of the other friends who thought she'd been a fool to run off with Hecebolus. Now, as she returned alone and practically penniless, it would certainly look as if they had been right. But had she not met Hecebolus, she would never have been in Alexandria, or the desert, which had quietly turned her life around, just as working with Macedonia had given her a reason to return to the City – even if she didn't yet know what that reason was. And now here she was, actually coming home. It was too much to think about, too much to worry about. There were other people's plans she must follow and that was enough for this night that was almost day.

An owl screamed, the shore must be closer than she'd thought, a hazy line began to divide the forests of Bithynia from the sky, it was morning. There, on the distant eastern shore, were the old buildings of Chalcedon. Soon she would be able to count the hills of the City, maybe even make out the outline of her church, her Hagia Sophia. Theodora shifted her gaze to the still-dark west and waited. She didn't know she had been so hungry for this view, hadn't allowed herself to think about it. Now, waiting for home to emerge from the dark, she knew she was starving, and had been for a long time.

The first thing she saw, vague at this distance, was the wall. Not Constantine's wall, falling down when she left and no doubt even more so now, but the new wall, the one her mother still called the outer wall, that really marked the edge

206

of home. For an hour or more their small ship had been veering west in its northern course across the Sea of Marmara. Slowly the hills took shape as the sun rose from the opposite shore and they were lit with sharp sunshine. Then the inner wall. Then, and Theodora wasn't sure this could be true, didn't know if it was possible, at this angle, there and then gone, she saw the very tip of the Hippodrome with her own obelisk pointing above, the one her father had used to explain the Empire, the distant countries they were part of. It was an imagining, she knew; Menander, and even more so Sophia, would have mocked her for the sentimentality. Theodora had been picturing them more often during the journey. The City could be harsh, she probably would have heard if something had happened to her people, but she couldn't be sure. She couldn't be sure of anything. The land was rushing closer now, clearer, and then they could see the port and then a small hand slipped into hers.

'Why are you crying?'

Theodora shook her head, she would rather not have the little girl see her like this; she had no idea what they had to face in the City, she didn't want her to see weakness as a possibility.

'I'm not unhappy, Mariam,' she answered. 'It's just that I never thought I'd see this again.'

Mariam, who was all of six years old, nodded, knowing. In the long pilgrimage that had begun just days after her third birthday, she had seen her parents in paroxysms of helpless laughter, waves of ecstatic grief, swallowed up by the bliss of blind revelation or a torpor of spiritual exhaustion. It was perfectly normal to her that an adult should exhibit one emotion yet insist they were experiencing another.

An hour later the deck was full, everyone looking for landmarks and signs, the two pilgrim girls certain that the swell they saw further up the Bosphorus must be the whale Porphyry. Theodora didn't have the heart to tell them that in an entire childhood in the City she'd only seen the famed whale twice herself: what did it matter if the girls thought a wave was a whale? They'd see more shocking sights than that in the weeks to come. Sailors pushed gawping passengers out of the way as they climbed ladders and lowered sails, shouting and swearing and sweating as they did so, and finally a local boy caught the heavy hemp rope and was tying the ship into dock and the gangplank was lowered and Theodora picked up her bag, ran a hand beneath her left breast to check the emerald was in place and, joining the long queue of passengers, made her way down on to dry land. Homeland. And even as she did so, she looked around her and made a note to watch the old trader as he watched the pilgrim family.

She had intended to make her way first to Hagia Sophia to give thanks for her safe arrival, and then to the address Macedonia had given her, a street in the main industrial quarter. She would get her bearings, introduce herself to the people who were to give her work and lodging, and she could also wash before heading back uphill to find her family and friends – Macedonia had warned her to take her time, but she hadn't accounted for the surge of longing Theodora felt when the City wall came into view. Unfortunately for her sensible plans, Leon, Sophia's uncle, the chief scene painter for the theatre, was waiting at the dock for a shipment of Persian pigment that was a whole week late already and had only now come in on the ship ahead of Theodora's. She considered walking right past him, wondered if she might be able to make it to the end of the harbour and then up one of the narrow streets towards the Mese without being seen, but Leon was in full oratorical flow, and even as her head urged her to hurry away, her steps slowed, her eyes turned back. After all this time, Theodora couldn't bring herself to miss the spectacle of Leon in mid-tantrum, shouting at the ship's captain who had handed over his delivery with any number of dents and marks on the wooden box, and screaming, too, at his own assistant, who was being too slow and too clumsy with the box in question.

'You lying, arsing thief. Captain? Captain of a fucking row-boat, more like. I pay you good money and for that I get this? I tell you sailor, if a single spot of that insanely expensive lapis has been knocked off and leaked into anything else, that's it, not a damned cent. You think my bosses won't notice just because you're colour blind? Marcellus you stupid little bugger – and I use the word advisedly – lift it carefully, this sea-cunt has fucked me about enough, must my own staff exhibit the same brute stupidity? No, I don't know about full payment, how about a further third now and then the final instalment when I get back to my workshop and check out just how seriously you've screwed up my supplies? Marcellus! If I have to tell you one more time . . .' And then his eyes locked with the woman star-ing, smiling, tears running down her face. 'Dear God, sweet Mary Theotokos, Theo-fucking-dora. What are you doing here? Why didn't you tell us you were coming home? We'd have had the boys out. And the girls. The whole troupe on the dock. Come here, you dark-skinned bitch, have you spent these years just lying in that ghastly African sun? Come here and give Uncle Leon a big fat whorey kiss and prove to me you're not the virgin fucking nun of rumour!'

Theodora laughed aloud, discarded Macedonia's sensible plans, and ran to Leon's strong arms, into the smell of him – stage paint, the last meal he'd eaten crumbled still in his heavy, unfashionable beard, and whatever perfume lingered on his skin from the boy he'd had the night before. Quite possibly the unhappy Marcellus who now tagged along with both the dented pigment box and Theodora's bag. Leon hurried her away, the captain shouting pointlessly for his full payment, Marcellus stumbling behind, and Theodora giving herself over to her people, to the City, to home.

Twenty-Five

Leon took her first to Comito's new apartment; it was on his way to the theatre workshop, and now that he had escaped without paying the full delivery price he was perfectly happy to send Marcellus ahead with the precious cargo and sit in on the family reunion. Theodora let Leon lead her uphill, soaking in the City as they walked. The smell caught her first, the mix of wild herbs and cooking spices, of tens of thousands of people crammed into such a small area, hundreds of them thronging the narrow streets. Beneath the foodstuffs and the bodies there was smoke from cooking fires, the bitter tang of burning metal from the copper and silversmiths' workshops, and above that hung precious incense from the dozens of churches and shrines, each individual perfume stirred into the whole by the constant sea breeze from three directions at once – it was the unmistakable smell of home and it made Theodora want to cry, it was so full of a past she no longer lived.

Leon recognised Theodora's aching nostalgia. 'It's like this whenever I come home from working in other cities, all those years with the touring companies. I know it and I don't. You'll get used to it.'

Theodora shook her head. 'It feels like all my years every time I breathe.'

He nodded. 'It will pass.'

'I'm not sure I want it to.'

She didn't add that while they stood here, in the moment

211

before she saw her sister, her mother, her daughter, there was still the chance that her father might walk down the hill towards them, that Anastasia might be alive, and the big man would pick up all three girls in one massive hug, their mother laughing and telling him it was no way to behave. This was the way the City always smelt, always looked, she could stand here and be four years old and it might yet be easy.

They stopped halfway up the hill. Comito's first-floor apartment had a wide balcony, and even from the street itself there was a good view of the Sea of Marmara. A maid showed them to the central courtyard where Hypatia was fitting a new dress for one of Comito's private recitals later in the week. The maid coughed an announcement and then the family reunion was a spin of amber silk, mother and daughters crying and laughing with pleasure at the sight and sound of each other, while Ana stood shyly behind Indaro, both girls amazed at the whoops emanating from the usually serious Comito.

While the maid and children ran to fetch drinks and food, Comito made it clear she expected Theodora to live with them and take up where she left off – with two growing girls in the house it would be good to have Theodora earning again, and there would always be a job for her with the company. Theodora knew it for a kind lie, her fans had loved her but, like every star attraction, she was only as good as her last show, and that show had been many other star performers ago. She thanked Comito for her generosity and neither sister needed to say they knew things had changed.

She was relieved when Comito had to leave for rehearsal, taking the girls with her. After just half an hour she felt strained in Ana's company, wanting to find a way to be a mother to this child, the quiet little girl who knew her more as a distant sibling than anything approaching a mother, but with no idea where to begin. The sisters parted with kisses and promises and Theodora was glad to see that Comito knew her well enough to demand only that she let them know where she was if she didn't come back that night. If Theodora had somewhere else to stay, then Comito trusted she'd find out about it soon enough. But beyond the vital sibling reunion, with the theatre fifteen minutes' fast walk away, there was no time to hear Theodora's stories, not with a grumpy director and a jealous chorus waiting. Everyone understood that Comito was never late, she cared too much about her reputation for that. Theodora was thankful, too, that her daughter and niece went to the theatre with Comito. She'd made promises to herself about Ana back in the desert, and she hoped to keep them, to be a better mother some day – she was relieved it didn't have to be today.

Leon was not so easily dismissed. 'Absolutely not. The only way to get back into the City is to dive in.' He had the grace to lower his voice a little when he added, 'Anyway, you know you'll regret it if you stay here playing happy families, your mother hasn't got any cheerier with the passing years my love, and her husband is as much of an oaf as he ever was. If you're not careful she'll invite you back to hers to sit around the fire with their tiresome brood and his stinking feet.'

The image of her stepfather made up Theodora's mind, and Leon was her perfect excuse. The explanation that she needed to visit the theatre to ask about potential work didn't fool Hypatia, but she was glad to see her daughter had at least developed the kindness to pretend she had errands to run. The women kissed, Theodora saddened by the stoop in her mother's shoulders, the grey in her hair – the three children with Basianus showing in every line on the older woman's face. Hypatia didn't tell her daughter she'd been missed, though it was true, and Theodora didn't expect to hear it.

213

She splashed cold water over her face and body, then re-bound the emerald safely to her breast, before grabbing a dress from Comito's room and hurrying out of the house with Leon, up and over the crest of the hill, down to the Mese and the Constantine Forum and the streets winding round the Hippodrome, running into the centre as if she were fifteen again and the night was full of parties and shows and lovers and only she was needed to bring every space alive.

It was just supposed to be a meal and a few drinks, the local spiced meats and fresh bread she'd been missing for years, sweet honey cake, and whatever wine was on offer. No more, no less. Theodora had her letter to deliver, it was only meant to be a quick catch-up with each other and the City and anyone they happened to find in one of the actors' bars. That was seven hours earlier. Leon did not make it back to his workshop to check his precious pigments. Theodora did not hand over her letter and move on with the next stage of her life. She drank more and more wine until she simply passed out, not ten yards from the steps of her beloved Hagia Sophia. Leon thought she was uttering a prayer of thanksgiving when she collapsed, very elegantly, into a small heap, though she might just have been asking for help to fall easily. No idea what else to do with her, he sent the skulking, besotted Marcellus to fetch Sophia and tell her he needed help getting a friend back home.

When Sophia arrived, roused from her bed after a long day's rehearsal, she was not pleased. At least not until she looked closer at who was lying on the step. Then she burst out laughing, slapping her uncle around the chest, which was the highest she could reach.

'You bastard, didn't you think I'd want to come and help you poison the tart? Three years gone, and lost all her drinking skills along with her bastard boyfriend.'

She spat and then, exhibiting the strength she was rightly famed for, took hold of the legs, while her uncle more carefully lifted Theodora's shoulders and lolling head, and they carried her home between them.

Sophia was covering her half-dressed friend with a blanket when Theodora finally woke enough to realise where she was. 'Hello, dwarf.'

'Hello, whore.' Sophia passed her a cup of water and Theodora drank it down in one mouthful. Dropping back against the pillow, she patted the mattress and the small woman stretched out beside her old friend. 'Are you coming back to work?' Sophia asked.

'I don't think so. There's something . . . I have a letter to deliver, I've been sent . . .'

Theodora broke off, not certain how much she was allowed to reveal.

'Well, you've probably lost it now anyway.' Sophia lifted her shoulders, shrugging against Theodora's breast, and both women were glad to feel each other's skin.

'Probably.'

Theodora was floating back to sleep when Sophia asked, 'Was it very hard? Being away?'

Theodora was surprised by the tears that came to her eyes. 'It was hard. But it wasn't all bad. It was good for me in the desert.'

'That sounds like hard work.'

'It was. Good hard work.'

'And Antioch?'

'The shock of being back in the City was big enough as it is – is big enough. If I hadn't been in Antioch first, I could never have survived a night back here.'

'So really, the only bad part of the past three years was with him? Hecebolus?'

Theodora smiled. 'Yes, Little One. You were right, I was wrong. Happy now?'

Sophia nodded. 'I am. Thank you.'

'But Alexandria and the desert and Antioch, they all made me who I am now. And none of that would have happened if I hadn't gone away with Hecebolus.'

'What? So you're grateful to him?'

'Oh no. I definitely wouldn't say that.'

'And are you happy to be home?'

'I'm happy to be here, Sophia.'

They slept, and it was ordinary to be together.

Theodora woke in a cold sweat of clarity. It was already late in the day, the ship had docked the afternoon before, she was meant to have delivered her letter immediately, she had not. While she didn't know the full contents of the letter, nor to whom it was ultimately addressed – she'd been told to take it to a minor official who would then pass her on to someone more senior – she did know that she had failed already in this new life, before it had even begun. She howled in anger and exhaustion, threw herself off the bed, cursing herself, her stupidity, and the City. Cursing and loving the City.

Sophia moaned at her noise, 'What are you doing?'

'I have this letter to deliver.'

'Who to?'

'Don't know.'

'What about?'

'Don't know.'

'Oh good. And why?'

'Because I was told to.'

Sophia's eyes were wide open now. 'Who did the telling?'

'A dancer called Macedonia working on behalf of the Patriarch of Alexandria.' Theodora took a deep breath and rattled it out, knowing Sophia would pounce on any pauses: 'I've been working for the Patriarch. I was with his people in Alexandria, and in the desert, I was out there for almost a year, after Hecebolus, before Antioch. I had a . . .' She held out her hand to silence Sophia's ready interruption: 'No, listen, you need to hear this. I had a conversion.'

'What?'

'Something. I don't know what.'

'An epiphany?'

'Nothing as dramatic.'

'No lightning bolts?'

'No.'

'Shame.'

'Not really. I came to an understanding. You asked, last night, was it hard? Yes it was, it was incredibly hard to come to an awareness of my faith, of who I have been, what I have been, and who I want to be. Of where I am now. They helped me, I learned from them. I am . . . I'm with them.'

'You're a Christian?'

'We're all Christians.'

'Jacob the Jew's not. Those Sassanid fire-eaters, they're certainly not.'

'You were baptised, Sophia.'

'So were you. That doesn't have to mean faithful.'

'No.'

'But you are now?'

'Yes.'

'And what next?'

'Now I deliver the letter. At the Chalke.'

'New friends in high places?'

'I truly have no idea. I take the letter and wait for it to be passed on to whoever's supposed to get it, and then they'll tell me what to do next.'

'And do you always do exactly as these new friends demand?'

Theodora shook her head. 'Obviously not. Nearly three years away and I can still let down my mentor in the first five minutes. I can just see Menander's face if I'd done the same to him. Damn, I can feel the print of his boot as well, I think.'

Theodora was rubbing her back as she spoke, tying on her sandals, but she felt the change in Sophia, the pause, and she knew what it meant. She didn't look up.

'When?'

'Two weeks ago.'

This time it was a kick to the stomach.

'Two weeks? I'd have seen him if I had come back sooner?'

'He wouldn't see anyone. It was eating him up, the disease. He was thin and tired and he wanted to go.'

'Why didn't Comito tell me? I spent an hour with her yesterday. I'd have gone to the grave. You should have told me.'

'I just did,' Sophia shook her head. 'And your sister's become a bit of a star in your absence. She's certainly good, but she plays it up. We're her past, us theatricals, she doesn't like to talk about the old days.'

'She must care.'

'Yes, but you don't get many invitations to sing in the Palace while you're mourning your old eunuch dance teacher. This Emperor Justin's very hot on form – for a farmer's boy, with an ex-concubine for a wife.'

Theodora said that was probably exactly why he cared about outer show, and they agreed Comito's life was different now and that Menander had been the best of bastards and Theodora cried that she had missed the chance to say goodbye and Sophia reminded her exactly what their old teacher would have said to the idea of Theodora's new mentor, to her conversion. They kissed each other and Sophia said she didn't understand about the faith, not at all, but she expected there would be plenty

218

more she wouldn't understand about Theodora yet, and Theodora agreed there was a lot she didn't understand herself, but she was glad to be home, and Sophia said they both shared in that.

Back on the street, Theodora was hit again by the City. She recognised market traders from her childhood, heard the bird cries of her youth, felt her mouth water with familiar scents from open doorways, down dark corridors – all of it was known, and none of it felt like home. She had been walking these streets in her head the whole time she was away, but now she was back and she was still homesick. She had left assuming that those staying behind would be here, holding the City still for her return: now she realised she had left the City, and the City had also left her. Just as tears began to stab her eyes, she rounded a corner and saw the Church of Hagia Sophia. The doors were thrown wide and she went in. Ignoring the angry glare from the church sentry, she turned away and up the stairs to the women's gallery. Two old women stood together, shoulders hunched against the years; one glanced at Theodora, the other continued in her prayers, a young woman in a hurry was no concern of theirs. Theodora followed the gallery round to the far corner, to her place, to the mosaic she knew, the wood she remembered, the carved stone she followed by fingertip touch. The scents of the church – candle grease, incense and warm sea air – caught inside for a hundred years, settled on her skin. Her breathing slowed, the tears retracted their threat, the priest droned on, men rocking in prayer below, old women above swaying on tired legs.

Theodora lay on the cool stone floor, and instead of demanding the City come to her she gave herself to it – whatever was to come, it could wait another few minutes. She stayed until she heard people arriving for the evening service; the streets would be clearer as the faithful came in for prayer or went home for food, the queue of beggars and law-office supplicants and refugees at the Chalke Gate would be lessening too. It was time.

She walked the short distance from the church to the Chalke, the carving and stonework becoming more ornate with every step. She arrived at the gate, the main entrance to the complex of government and Imperial Palace offices from which the Empire was run. A bored official, tidying away his day's files, sat behind an even more bored guard. Eventually the official looked up from his nearly packed satchel, and did a double take as he realised who she was.

'Theodora? Welcome home, girl. We missed you over at the theatre.'

Theodora allowed her mouth to form the gracious smile she would have given a fan in the old days, and then stopped as the guard added, 'But not as much as the geese did,' and both men creased up in laughter.

Once he'd had a good laugh, the official shushed his comrade and offered more kindly, 'Heard you were back in town.'

'Already? I only arrived . . .'

'You know how it is. A ship docks, the sailors talk, one of the passengers has a pretty face . . .'

'Or a nice arse,' the guard added with a wink. Theodora did not smile back and he shrugged as if he were used to being rejected.

The official explained. 'Look, we've shut up shop for the night now, not all of us want to work as hard as the boss. Pop back in the morning, I'll let you come to the front of the queue. You always were my favourite.'

Theodora smiled again, less patiently this time. She reached into her robe and pulled out the letter. The parchment was wrinkled, the ink smudged, but the seal on the scroll was intact and clear. She gave it to the official. 'I appreciate your offer, but I was told to bring this to the Chalke the minute I arrived.'

'Yeah, and you got in yesterday,' the guard muttered, still sulking from her refusal to wink back.

'Nothing escapes you, does it, big guy?' Theodora smiled openly now. 'So you'll see this is the seal of the Patriarch of Alexandria. And yes, I am a day late, and no doubt I'll get a bollocking for it, but perhaps not quite as ferocious as the bollocking you'll get if you don't get this letter to the Simeon of Galatia it's addressed to.'

The official was confused. 'Look, I'm sorry, but why would the Galatian, who's only one rank higher than me, be getting a letter from the Patriarch? Are you sure this isn't some kind of joke?'

She leaned in closer. 'Have a feel – that's just the outer parchment, there's another letter inside. For someone a bit more important than this Simeon, perhaps?'

The official jumped into action. 'I'll be right back.' He stopped, turned to Theodora, 'Don't want to be rude, love, but you might want to . . . I don't know, comb your hair or something? If they ask you in . . .'

Theodora smiled and chose to take the insult as the kindness it was meant. 'Thanks, old man. Good thought.'

Twenty-Six

Whatever Theodora had agreed to back in Antioch, following the young slave through a maze of alternating dark passages and brilliantly lit courtyards where the setting sun refracted into hundreds of tiny searchlights from the mosaic gold and glass in every wall, she felt less mistress of her own destiny than ever before. After a long ten-minute walk, they came to a series of colonnaded patios and one final corridor, busy even this late in the evening. The slave knocked on a door, opened without waiting for an answer, and ushered her into the room, leaving Theodora temporarily blinded as her eyes accustomed to the darkness inside.

Narses nodded his shaved head from his chair by the window, dismissing the slave without words. While she waited for him to speak, as was proper in this place, and knowing it made her look nervous but preferring sight to stature, Theodora began to blink fast in the way she'd been taught as a child, to accommodate the difference between the sunlit stage and the pit below, the blinking forcing her retina to adjust more quickly until she was able to see the man before her. She had been raised in Menander's harsh school, and knew better, as her teacher had often said, than 'to judge a man by his bollocks' – or lack of them – but even so, Narses looked nothing like the traditional joke of a City eunuch, running to fat with age, soft and girlish, lisping for comic effect. Despite his age – and she could only guess that he was somewhere between forty and fifty – he had a wiry strength that was obvious even as he sat entirely still.

She stood for a minute, then five, then ten. Neither moved. The high tide threw spray against the wall below and Theodora realised she had walked almost the length of the Hippodrome and must now be in one of the offices perched above the rocks, where the Bosphorus joined the Sea of Marmara.

Eventually Narses sighed, 'This is a very dull game.'

'I didn't know we were playing,' Theodora answered.

'Liar.'

'My apologies. I don't know what game we are playing, so it's hard to judge whether it is truly dull or not.'

'Macedonia didn't tell you?'

'Macedonia gave me the letter for Simeon of Galatia, I knew it contained another, I have no idea what either say.'

'You didn't look?'

'You didn't see the Patriarch's seal?'

'Wax is easily come by.'

'I would not cheat my mentor.' Theodora's voice was quiet but certain.

'No, but you would turn up at the Chalke Gate, a day later than expected, reeking of stale alcohol and looking as if you spent the night in a brothel, instead of directly delivering the letter as was expected?'

Theodora held up her hands, offering no excuse where there was none. 'Mea culpa.'

'Indeed.'

The light outside was nearly gone. Narses leaned forward and lit the candles on the table in front of him. Now she could see his face more clearly – dark skin as might be expected from his accent – a finely shaped head that showed itself better for being hairless, thin eunuch's brows, and even darker eyes that gave nothing away. She hoped there might be a sense of humour somewhere, the lines at the corner of his eyes looked as if he must laugh, occasionally.

His next question contained no humour, though. 'Is that just City Latin, or do you have more?'

'I have a little more.' Narses looked irritated, so she added, 'I can converse if I have to. The basics, obviously, it's hardly a language for the comedy theatre.'

Narses allowed the beginning of a smile. He didn't disagree, but he wasn't ready to let Theodora know that. 'And?'

'And I learn fast, I always have. I can learn more if that is meant.'

'Meant? You think this is a matter of destiny?'

Theodora paused. If she said yes, there was every chance he would interpret her answer as heresy. If she said no, it might sound as if she was rejecting whatever she'd been sent here to do. She spoke carefully, in Latin. 'I do whatever my mentor asks. In whichever language is necessary.'

Narses smiled fully now, 'Good answer. They said you were brighter than the average actress.'

'I was never an average actress,' Theodora snapped back, too soon.

Narses' smile went as quickly as it had come. 'Apparently not. Still, that life is behind you now. What other languages do you have?'

She bit back her pride, furious with herself for letting it show, and more furious for feeling it at all. 'I also have stage Greek, the older form – if you don't attend theatre you might think of it as classic Greek.'

He didn't bite and she wished she'd answered more plainly. 'What else?'

'Some Syriac, a very little Coptic, words and phrases I found useful in Alexandria and when travelling, and some Hebrew.'

'Hebrew?'

'Timothy believes there is much to be learned from the old teachers.'

'Timothy is the Alexandrian Patriarch to you.'

Theodora apologised, but she was pleased to have finally learned a little about her interlocutor. If he were truly the Emperor Justin's man he would not have acknowledged the status of the anti-Chalcedonian Patriarch so forcefully, no matter how important a man of God. So now she knew two things about Narses, who clearly knew a great deal more about her. Three, perhaps: she thought she could locate his first accent, although it was mostly hidden in years of City and Palace overtones. She risked another rebuke.

'I don't speak Armenian though, I'm sorry.'

Narses didn't answer, but the laugh lines around his eyes tightened just a very little. Then he stood up and walked to her, walked round her. Theodora held her place. Whatever was coming, a slap, the rant of one who had waited a day for her arrival, maybe a revelation from her mentor's letter, she would take it. She'd had her indulgences of flesh and spirit, she was ready now.

His next question was unexpected. 'Do you spin?'

Theodora laughed, 'God, no – oh, well, actually, I did play Arachne once, I had to spin then. But I was hopeless. Why?'

Narses walked back to his chair, but didn't sit. He stood looking out into the now dark evening, explaining his plan. 'I work primarily for Justinian, the Emperor's favourite nephew, his adopted son. Justinian is soon to be appointed Consul and the Patriarch thinks you would be ideal to advise him on the best form of celebration. You understand theatre, language – you are of the people, that much is obvious. The Patriarch and Severus, advised by Macedonia, believe you'll be able to counsel Justinian well.'

'On how to organise a party for the City?'

225

'Initially, yes. You've been away, you will not be aware that there have been certain . . .' Narses paused, reaching for the right words '. . . suggestions, about the deposition of Vitalian, the previous Consul.'

Theodora smiled. 'Away yes, but I did spend my first night home in a bar. Once I said I'd been in the desert with Severus, everyone was dying to tell me how Justinian and the Emperor had Vitalian executed. I'm glad they got rid of him.'

Narses winced. 'It is true that Vitalian did demand Severus' head some years ago; the disturbance was instrumental in the preacher's relocation to the desert.'

'So Justin and Justinian can't be that estranged from Severus and the Patriarch if they got rid of Vitalian, can they?'

'None of it is that easy –' Narses held up his hand to silence her – 'and please lower your voice, these matters are not easily resolved, and may never be, no matter how much Justinian wants to see a reunion between those divided in faith. It is too simple to say there are those who agree with the Council of Chalcedon on the nature of the Christ . . .'

'And those who don't?'

'Indeed.'

'But it is simple, isn't it, for most people? The Christ is solely divine, or He is not.'

'You are very reductive. And anyway, matters of faith, where they affect law, the governance of the people, can never be simple.'

'A pity,' Theodora said.

'Perhaps. And that is where you come in. The Patriarch believes, and I agree with him, that it could be valuable to his cause if Justinian were to find you . . . useful. Trustworthy.'

'To find one of an opposing belief useful and trustworthy?'

'Yes. Justinian is, though, very proper.'

'Prudish?'

226

'No, that role is reserved for his aunt Euphemia, the Emperor's wife. Now there's a reformed slut if ever there was one.' Narses had spoken under his breath, but he had intended Theodora to hear. 'For you to get close to Justinian we'll need to introduce you as a reformed woman.'

'I am reformed. I experienced—'

Narses cut her off, 'Truly I have no interest in your apparent conversion, real or imagined. I simply need to make sure that you are introduced to Justinian, and that he finds you pleasing. It is up to you to make him like you, trust you. And as soon as possible, so you can be taken on as an adviser for his own consular celebrations. Spinning is a good occupation for a woman who has converted and seen the error of her ways.'

Theodora's heart sank and her temper rose as she finally understood. 'Oh. Right. So the point of this letter, the only reason for me coming home, was for you all to set me up for this princeling of yours. Dear God,' she shook her head, 'I said as much to Macedonia, and I had thought more of the Patriarch, but apparently Timothy is just another pimp like the rest of you.'

And then she did feel Menander's slap across her face. Narses had his hand at her throat and there was nothing effeminate about his grip, he was spitting in his attempt to hold back his anger, and to keep his voice down in a place where anyone might be listening at any door.

'The Patriarch is your teacher, and he is mine. You've been away, so I'll forgive your utter ignorance, but Justinian is the most abstemious man this city has ever known. He has never paid any attention to a woman until now and I doubt, stage star though you were, that you are going to make a difference. He simply doesn't care for anything beyond his papers and his studies and anything else that can sooner fulfil his personal ambition which is, apparently, nothing less than the reformation of the

Empire, a full restoration to the glory days of old Rome, one people, one faith. He is one of the best minds ever to enter the Palace and, whatever his eventual rank in life, he will do well. The Patriarch seemed to think that in meeting you Justinian might be encouraged to see another side to those faithful to his own and Severus' teachings, something different to the current beliefs in the Palace, maybe lessen the excesses of his uncle's reactions. No one wants you to use your brothel ways with him, least of all the Patriarch, who apparently believes you a reformed woman, though judging by your assumption, your mind heading straight for the gutter, I'm sorry to say, he must be mistaken. Which is an enormous pity. Because until now, I had thought him exemplary in his decisions.'

When Narses eventually loosened his grip on Theodora's neck, all she could hear was her own blood pounding in her ears and the choking of her hoarse throat. Then, when a screaming, wheeling gull outside the window broke the silence, she was suddenly aware of where she was. That the quiet of the room indicated the depth of the walls, the strength of the Imperial Palace's defences, the enormous distance, in attitude and hierarchy, separating the teeming city outside, from this silent room down a long corridor manned by no one but the Emperor's own guards, men who were commanded by Narses. Timothy's letter had brought her into the belly of an unknown beast and, destiny or not, what she said next would determine all her future.

She said yes because there was no other answer. And Narses, who had evidently expected a yes all along, then handed over a bag containing all she'd need to get started. The address of her new home and tutor, a very little money, two plain gowns of plainer cloth. She had to get herself up to speed in the craft they had chosen for her, and in her new life, as soon as possible. Justinian would become Consul in ten weeks; the celebration would follow. That meant they had to arrange a meeting with Justinian in little more than a month. She'd need to make him trust her, offer a perfect plan for the celebration, something spectacular that could be arranged in less than six weeks, and do so while maintaining the mask of an ex-whore who now lived a life of pure simplicity and faith.

Despite his dismissal of the theatre, Narses knew of Theodora's skill. He had no qualms about giving her the job if the Patriarch trusted her to play the role well. The only thing that worried him was her big mouth and uncertain temper; sending her to a family of weavers would keep her quiet for now, and would confirm her status as a penitent while he studied her for himself. She took the bag he offered, tucked it into her own, and prepared to leave, assuring Narses she would do her best, meanwhile promising herself this was the last time she would take any role that was not her own truth, no matter who asked it of her.

Narses waved a hand, dismissing her to her new life.

'And Theodora?'

'Yes?'

'If you are late for me again, I will be harder on you than Menander ever knew how to be.'

'You knew him?'

'I loved him.'

Theodora stared, awareness dawning. 'You're the Armenian boyfriend?'

Narses smiled, a genuine smile this time, full and sad. 'I loved him.'

Twenty-Seven

Theodora's new home was in the Chalkoprateia, an entirely different neighbourhood to the warren of slum streets she'd grown up in, further still from the elegant houses and apartments where Comito now lived. Despite the cramped conditions of the overcrowded city, the copper and bronze artisans who gave the area its name still worked here, just down the hill from the Mese, as they had done since the founder's time. The goods that came from these few streets of homes that were also workshops were highly valued, and the sweat that went into producing them well paid, but the aroma of success here was vastly different to that enjoyed by the wealthy in their sea-aired houses on the hills. These streets smelt of fire and molten metal and the singed flesh of a young apprentice learning a valuable lesson at the forge. Beneath the acrid stink of cooking metal, Theodora quickly learned to discern the stench of dyes, the ammonia of urine, the sickly sweet of tallow, the acid of tannin and lye. These were the streets where wool and linen and that most precious of all commodities, silk, underwent the alchemy from simple thread to Imperial Purple, shot through with the finest gold and silver, Church and state woven together in each perfect bolt of new-made cloth.

Theodora spent both days and nights in a single back room large enough to house her own wheel and loom – her new teacher explained she might as well live with them, there would be no time off – with a narrow bed against one wall and a small table for her few goods in the corner. The room itself opened directly on to a back alley where she shared a well with a dozen other families, including the people of the house itself, the Jewish family who worked in the larger front rooms and lived upstairs. Originally from Aleppo, the patriarch of this family, like many Jews, had made his start in the City working in copper, but he soon realised that the constantly rising price of silk, and more importantly his connections among the silk traders, meant that if he could buy the thread when it first arrived from China there was a good living to be made and, invaluably, a reliable income in an unreliable world. It took him several years to turn his connections into serious business bonds, but by the time Theodora was first experiencing the rigours of stage training, the old man was dying happy in the knowledge that his family was well established in their trade, safe for the foreseeable future.

When Narses sent Theodora to them, they were doing as well as any Jew could in the City, and things felt easy, if not absolutely safe. The family lived with both acceptance and dis-trust, often in the same moment, as did all their people: permission to renovate the synagogue had been granted by the Palace last spring, though a request to consider a new build was summarily rejected. Certainly no one was talking of expulsion as had happened in other parts of the Empire, but there'd been a violent attack on the son of a copper worker by several Green youths just six months ago. The Greens said it was a matter of boy against boy, but the Jews felt differently, they'd heard the whispers behind the fists. More obviously, it was as apparent to the Jews as to the Christians that the Church was changing around them, and a Church that was fighting itself might instead be happier looking outside for argument. For now they were safe, in future they might not be. Copper and bronze workers needed heavy raw materials, the heat of a furnace, water to cool and set. A silk weaver, however, needed only a loom, which a smart man could make himself, while the raw material, that precious thread, was easily bundled away in a hurry and light to carry. With their relative stability and quiet faith, the old man's family were as good as any to double as Theodora's teacher and landlord. Moreover, as Jews, they had probably never entered a theatre in their lives, it was likely they had no real idea who she had once been, and Narses believed that was all to the good. Even for someone used to hard work, just a month to learn a new craft, one that most were born into, would be a challenge. The less that was known about Theodora, the faster she could get on with the new life.

A new life of spinning and weaving. Of calluses on her hands, cuts on her fingers, nails turned yellow and red from tannin and betel stains, the stench of dye and fixer deep in her hair and skin, no matter how fully she used the quiet hours of the Jews' Sabbath to wash in sea water or lemon juice. A life of learning daily from the granddaughter Esther, minding Esther's baby while she was shown the method and then trying herself, and failing, the baby given back as she was shown again.

It was hardly the homecoming she'd hoped for. Theodora went to bed aching from bending over the loom, dreamed of the stomp and shuffle through the night, and woke again to try to get it right, Esther's quiet and patient smile when she regularly failed infinitely more irritating than Menander's fury had ever been. Theodora was used to teachers who stood over her shouting, beating understanding into her flesh, compliance into her bones. Esther, three years younger than Theodora, a placid mother of one with another on the way, just shook her head, smiled with a grandmother's patience, added the wasted thread to the pile ready to re-use later, and began again. Theodora moaned she'd never get it, and Esther would simply take the baby back to her hip, hand over the shuttle and tell her to get on with it.

'Talk to me while we work.'

'What about?' Esther asked.

'Tell me things I don't know, things I've missed while I've been away. What do you think of this Emperor? Of his nephew? Is he really as boring as they all say?'

Esther shook her head. 'What do you think I know of the great and the good? There were all sorts of rumours a few years ago, that Justinian had tricked or cheated his way into the Emperor's favour, but nothing ever came of it, he stayed the golden boy. Some say he encourages his uncle to come down harder on the Greens than the Blues, but they used to say the opposite of the old Emperor. We never saw any difference down here, Blues or Greens – both sides will be friendly to us if it suits them, attack us if it doesn't.'

'Of course, there isn't one of them who got position without doing something, good or bad to gain it, but what about him as a person?'

'Theodora, I don't know. Or really care. We're not being harassed right now, that's good, that's all I need to know. Now get on with some work and stop trying to distract me from the fact that your weft is too tight, you've managed to weave two great long strands of your own hair into this seam, and if you were making that piece with real silk instead of rough-spun wool, you'd have thrown away the equivalent of one poor soldier's annual income on a wasted lot of thread.'

There came a day, three weeks in, and with a lot more solid concentration, when Theodora knew what she was doing, without thinking about it. The cloth grew beneath her hands, and she was simply making, as Esther had promised would happen eventually, with intent but without actual thought. Theodora's attention was on the whole, not the specific, and so, as in the best of dances, the most successful of shows, the specific was part of the whole and held perfectly within it.

'Oh my God, Esther. Look. Look!'

Esther sighed at the blasphemy, raised her eyes from the tiny hand-loom where she was weaving an intricate pattern, vastly more difficult than the simple fabric Theodora was working, and smiled. Her pupil's hands were working in the syncopated cross-rhythm she'd taught, her back was bent lightly over the work, allowing her arms to be neither too close nor too far, keeping the tension perfect in both warp and weft, and cloth was growing from thread. It was plain cloth, simply made, but it was cloth, and it would work, it would wear. It might even last.

'I've made it, I'm making it. This is incredible. Don't you think? I'm actually making a thing.'

And Theodora, who had received standing ovations for every possible performance, who had brought the Hippodrome to its knees with laughter and leaping up again in her praise, who had seduced the Governor of the Pentapolis, surviving his passion and his disdain, who had undergone trial by sadness and sickness and inner demons in the desert, and then had come home, brave enough to start again – and who was rightly proud of all these things – now understood the simple pleasure of making.

As a dancer, as an acrobat, and especially as a whore, Theodora had long ago learned to look forward to the moment when the mind relaxed and the body took over. She now realised that weaving cloth was no different, and that – exactly as with any new physical skill – once she'd mastered the basics, the rest was a matter of building. Taking the form and adding to it. From cotton, Esther promoted her to fine and then finer wool. Then, on the third day of frenzied making, Esther tried her out on her first silk. This was not the famous silk, more costly than gold, that the family specialised in. It was a lesser thread, sold by their Chinese contacts to traders who didn't really care about quality, or – in this case – sold cheaply to someone with Esther's skill to make into a perfect item, recreating the imperfections as a feature of the design. For Theodora's task though, the cheap silk, still costly compared to any other thread, was used as it was, with no pattern to incorporate the knobbly slubs which would otherwise spoil a perfect finished piece. The resulting fabric would not be dyed in the purple, or even the far cheaper reds and deep ochres of which the Imperial household were currently so fond, but it was silk and, like every other silk thread in the City, had travelled all the way from the East, keeping the secret of its provenance, to be remade here, in this workshop. It was precious.

Theodora gave herself over to this new dance, she relaxed into the cloth that did not yet exist, allowing the piece to use her to create itself. The first half-hour was sticky, stalling, slow, but the rhythm of the new material found itself in her body and the thread began to run smoothly through her hands, she in the trance of making and Esther sewing proudly nearby. By the end of the day there was a single piece of cloth, half an arm-length long and three fingers wide. The seams frayed a little, the tension was slightly too tight at one point, but Esther took the piece and, circling her forefinger to her thumb, leaving a hole the width of a child's fingernail, pulled the piece through.

'You see?' she said, 'Only silk – even poor silk, with these slubs and imperfections – can do this. My grandmother would take a stretch of fabric large enough to make robes for two full-grown men, and if she couldn't pull it through her wedding ring, then she would say it was not good enough and my grandfather would have to sell it more cheaply.'

'So how did your family make a living?'

'People come to us for the best. Once won, that trust remains.'

'You think that's why we value silk? Because it can be run through a grandmother's narrow ring?'

'And the secret of its origins, the distance it travels, the borders crossed. But no, that's not why I value it.' Esther leaned across to Theodora, pulled up the sleeve of her student's plain robe, and stroked the silk across Theodora's skin: 'This is.'

The fabric brushed her skin, barely touching, there and not there, light and warm as a kiss given to a sleeping lover. It was the closest Theodora had come to a caress since she'd said goodbye to Macedonia and Esther quickly moved the cloth before it caught the stain of Theodora's tears.

Theodora had just three days to enjoy the pleasure of her new skill. On the fourth day a messenger came from Narses, telling her to present herself at the Chalke. Adding, as plainly as only a Palace messenger sent to the Jewish industrial quarter to meet an ex-actress could, that Narses recommended she wear her sober best. Theodora spat after the insolent youth and then walked upstairs to enlist her landladies' help in the dressing. Mother and daughter were both well skilled in elegantly understated clothing. Their business meant they could have worn the finest fabrics, could have fashioned those fabrics into the most exquisite robes, but the fluctuating fortunes of their faith had proved that dressing down was always safer than dressing to attract interest. Theodora did not explain why she had been summoned to the Chalke, and neither woman asked. They had accepted Narses' payment for teaching and housing their student, they understood the fee also purchased a certain lack of interest. For now, Theodora was showing only nervous excitement; if she later came home showing another emotion, she

236

would probably share it. In the few weeks she'd lived with them it had become obvious that Theodora was not one to keep her feelings to herself.

Putting on Esther's dark blue gown, allowing Naomi to run tiny, invisible tacking stitches across the bodice so it fitted perfectly, and then to cover her shoulders and arms with a barely lighter blue shawl, fixing it so it covered her right up to her collarbones, bending to Esther's pressure to tie her hair back simply, with no tendrils to distract, to attract, Theodora submitted to the ministrations of mother and daughter as if she were allowing her dressers to costume her before a show. Whatever was to come this evening, it would be something of a performance. She would take herself to Narses as a penitent, a woman who was now a simple weaver, and he would then show her to Justinian, his boss who would be Consul. After that it was up to her to find a way to befriend, or at least interest, the man they said was interested in none of the things she usually had to offer – charm, elegance, humour, flesh. Narses had said Timothy wanted her to become useful to Justinian. There might be more to come, but for now, this was all. Theodora had been many things to many men: useful was new. As was covering her body in several layers just in case she might prove too tempting to the one man everyone said was more interested in books than flesh. If he was that staid, then surely one less shawl couldn't hurt. She thanked Naomi and Esther, handed back the final veil of dark silk they'd been trying to get her to wear over her hair, and stepped out into the street.

Twenty-Eight

Despite its high walls and self-sufficiency in almost every part of its daily business, the Palace was very much at the centre of City life. An army of domestic and civil servants was needed to run the buildings and offices, and not all of them lived in the Palace complex itself. Most people knew someone who had a sister in the kitchens or a brother in the Empress' retinue or an uncle who was a valued member of the library staff, and even those who did not have a direct family connection to the Palace could not help but be aware of its presence, at the physical head of the City, central to its functioning and the business of the Empire. The coming and going of Imperial processions to churches and Senate meant that most citizens felt some kind of physical as well as emotional connection to the Emperor and those who worked for him, maintained by a lively interest in the stories of what went on behind closed doors, drawn curtains. This interest was enthusiasm, concern, engagement, disappointment, mistrust, hope – and it was gossip.

Any number of these rumours centred on Justinian and, even in her short time back in the City, Theodora had heard most of them. He barely ate and slept even less, he roamed the Palace hallways at night, on occasion with his own head tucked beneath his arm. He hated politics, he loved politics. He and his uncle had been so perturbed by the former Consul Vitalian's offences against the old Emperor Anastasius that it was inevitable they would have Vitalian deposed, and then executed, once they came to power. Alternatively, he and his uncle had, as good supporters of the Council of Chalcedon, pretended to agree with Vitalian's stance against the old Emperor Anastasius' anti-Chalcedonian beliefs, and at the last moment turned against their ally, engineering his downfall for their own good. Justinian had entirely orchestrated his uncle's rise to prominence, over the heads of Anastasius' own family members, Probus, Hypatius and Pompeius; or perhaps he had simply been trying to secure a good situation for his uncle, and was horrified when Anastasius chose Justin as successor, not least because it forced him into the limelight of state. He was a virgin, he preferred eunuchs, he had been secretly promised to the Goth Princess Amalasuntha in an Imperial alliance that would one day unite East and West once and for all – all that was needed was for Amalasuntha's husband to die. He believed the second flood was on its way, he knew which of the many relics in the City's churches were true and which fakes, he planned to rewrite the findings of the Council of Chalcedon to patch up the growing schism, or he had no faith at all. He was true, he was false, he was really Justin's son, he was Justin's sister's bastard, his dream of one new Rome was the only way forward for the City and the Empire, he would bring the Empire to its knees. For a reputedly quiet academic, Justinian was a much-imagined man, and Theodora dreamed every possibility in her brief walk to the Chalke.

In reality he was shorter than she had expected, solid, serious-looking. Eighteen years her senior, he was certainly a man, not a boy, definitely a statesman rather than a soldier. While his uncle had the bearing of his many years in the military, Justinian already showed signs of the stoop and the heavy eye-lids of a book-bound lawyer, with ink-splattered fingers to match. Long, lovely fingers, Theodora was surprised to find herself noticing. He held out a hand to both welcome her in

239

and send his servant to wait for his next call, and she bowed low in honour of his status, which was soon to become even higher. The low bow allowed her to let slip the veil that covered her shoulders and collarbones. She wasn't entirely sure about Timothy's reasons for sending her to this man, but she knew that if the Patriarch's aims were to be met she needed to make Justinian like her, want to use her. So she presented herself in the way she knew any man of the Palace would appreciate.

Any man except Justinian, apparently. Instead of studying Theodora's charms, he took the fallen veil and rubbed it between his fingers.

'Not silk?'

'No, sir.'

'It's good, though?'

'Yes. It's a fake silk, made of wool, in an extremely fine weave.'

'As a deception?'

'Not at all. To offer something when the buyer wants good work but can't afford the best.'

Justinian nodded his approval. 'I have a dream that we might one day manufacture silk here, in the City. The amount we're paying these traders, it's beyond reason. Especially when other fabrics might do as well. There's no accounting for taste, is there, the choice of one fabric over another? Once something is a commodity, all we can do is try to make sure our people aren't being cheated too badly. Yes?'

'I suppose so.'

'Good. Now then, Narses tells me you were a performer? In the Hippodrome.'

'Yes, sir.'

'And successful? Famous, he says?'

'I had a certain following.'

'You were a dancer?'

'Yes,' Theodora answered more slowly this time, wondering where he was going with this, hoping she wouldn't be kicked out before she'd even tried to do the Patriarch's will, 'But not for a long time . . . I have been away.'

'Narses said.' Justinian stared at her, then shook his head. 'Well, I trust him, if he thinks you'll do, then you will. So, I know you've been away, but you can hardly have failed to hear the stories – the Emperor's strange nephew who doesn't eat and doesn't sleep and wouldn't know one end of the rank and file from the other, what's the old man doing making him Consul? Am I right? Yes?'

Theodora decided honesty was the better option in the presence of this strangely enthusiastic dark-eyed man with the heavy brows and the solid figure, and the surprisingly lovely hands, hands he now beckoned with, urging an answer, 'Well?'

'I have.'

Justinian nodded at her bravery. 'Good. As have I. So, we'll give them a story they do like, something good about me instead. We'll make a show. Yes? They like that, don't they? The people?'

'I think they do, sir.'

'Fine, fine. Let's get to work.'

They worked all that afternoon and into the early evening on plans for the Consul's ceremonials. Theodora talked him through every available option and some she imagined might be available for the right fee. She explained her view of the difference between a ceremonial for a figure of state, like Justinian, and that for a member of the military – someone the public, for perfectly understandable reasons, felt was one of them. She explained that Justinian himself fitted into neither category. She was not coy about the rumours, he had brought them up after all, nor did she fail to mention that both he and his uncle were, despite their grand status, still Slav foreigners to the many who were born and bred in the City. Even when Justinian launched into a rant about the nature of the Empire and his desire to bring all together, so that no Roman could ever feel a foreigner, no matter what part of the Empire they were born in, she brought him back to reality by reminding him that the accent he used in speaking to his servant was entirely different to the one that came out of his mouth now, in his excitement. In the five hours they were together Justinian neither ate nor drank, though he was solicitous in requesting food and drink for Theodora – which she, despite her own appetite, refused. He noted her refusal and nodded his approval; she was clearly working at it and he liked that. He paced the room, threw his arms around to make his points, constantly returned to the windows that looked out over the wall and into the City. He was never still except when he was saying yes or no to an idea. Then, once it was decided, he was off again on a new thought.

By the time she left that evening Theodora was convinced of two things. One, that almost all of the rumours about Justinian were probably right – he was both calm and crazy, wise and foolhardy, incredibly learned and almost childish in his enthusiasms. And two, that she really wanted this job. Working in the Palace, working with and somehow influencing Justinian – though she wasn't sure how much she could possibly influence that force of energy contained in such an oddly stolid, serious body – was what Timothy wanted from her. Now that she had met the man herself, it was definitely what she wanted as well. She hadn't had such an entertaining day in years. Fortunately, Justinian thought the same.

Two weeks later, Justinian had given her a small suite of rooms in the Palace; within the month she was producing the theatrical elements of his consular celebrations with a team of her own friends creating the entertainment, and even Sophia had managed to hold her tongue long enough to simply say thank you and get on with the work. With no interest whatsoever in the military component of the celebration, Theodora passed that section of the planning on to Narses who knew far more than she did about men in uniform – a fact she couldn't deny, given how unattractive soldiers had always seemed to her, even those of the higher ranks.

A month after her rise in fortune, she was so swamped with work that she was given two ladies to attend her. Narses had decided that Theodora needed help and she agreed, but stipulated that whoever was sent to help was as plain as possible. She'd been caught out once by Chrysomallo, it wasn't going to happen again. She put the society girls who arrived – too plain to marry money, too silly to marry well – to work sewing costumes for the private show Justinian would give his staff on the night of the celebration, a generous gesture from his own purse to thank them for their support. Theodora had no intention of letting the giggling girls dress her, no matter that Narses clearly felt she'd fit in better in the pretty pinks and warm reds they wore themselves. She was here as Timothy's envoy, not to party: she'd stay with sober grey and black. Besides, even if Justinian and those she was working with in the Palace guessed at the full truth of her past before her present incarnation as weaver and celebration adviser, it was important that the Emperor and Empress believed her cover story for a while at least, and they'd be more likely to do so if she didn't draw attention to her dress. Narses shrugged when he saw that his gift of virtual ladies-in-waiting was rejected; privately, though, he was impressed. Perhaps the Patriarch did know what he was doing after all, sending this girl to Justinian. At the very least, she worked hard – but then she would,

Menander had trained her well. Menander trained them all well.

On her forty-third day in the Palace, the consular celebrations took place. If no one truly believed the title meant a great deal any longer – certainly it was not the commanding role it had been in the glory days of the first Rome – it did at least indicate even more clearly to the people, and to the Palace, where Justin intended the succession to fall. Like any big royal event, it was a cause for public celebration, a chance for ordinary people to join in the festivities. Early in the morning there was a simple procession to Hagia Sophia, where Justinian was blessed, then everyone slowly marched back to the state rooms where Justin conferred the title of Consul on his nephew – while those four who had directly missed out, despite having their own familial claims on status – Germanus, Probus, Pompeius and Hypatius – did their best to smile on the scene, each one playing the role of less-favoured heir with varying degrees of success.

The City was a choreographed mess of joy and colour, song, dance and plenty of food. Theodora had insisted Justinian give pivotal roles to people from both Blue and Green factions, whatever the preferences of the Emperor and Empress, and whatever her own allegiances, this was the best way to ensure that no part of the celebrations, from the games in the Hippodrome to the street fair in the Mese, to the new performance on the Kynegion stage, would be interrupted by drunken youths from one faction provoking or attacking the other. Comito sang a new solo written for the occasion; Sophia sang another, decidedly less elegant version, and Constantinople partied for an entire day and night, praising the new Consul, appreciative of the Emperor's role in choosing him and, if anyone outside the Palace was aware of Theodora's role in the

244

proceedings, it was merely with a grateful nod in the haze of hangover. The new regime of Justin and Justinian had created a whole army of advisers for this and that under the eunuch in charge; appointing the reformed Theodora to advise on today's show had been one of his smarter decisions. Justinian would do well to hold on to that one, as a worker if not the lover most people assumed she already was.

'No, really, we're not.'

'Bollocks.' Sophia was leaning over the windowsill, looking down to the Palace gardens, the lawns laid out in symmetrical patterns, the raised beds and deep fountains sloping gently down to the wall, the sea beyond. 'Is it just because he's so boring you don't want to say?'

'I'm not. And he's not.'

'What?'

'Boring.'

'If you say so. Can we go out? That fountain's enormous. I could do with a swim, I'm shattered after last night.'

'You shouldn't have got quite so drunk after your performance, should you? Then you wouldn't have spent most of the night dancing with young men half your age.'

'And twice my size,' Sophia laughed. 'So go on, come for a swim?'

'Sophia, of course you can't dive into the fountain, we can't even go out there, that's the Empress' private garden, and she's angry enough that they've given me a room with a view of her lawn as it is, without you making it worse.'

'Yeah, but that's not the main reason she hates you, is it? Ex-tart comes knocking at the door of the would-be ruler? You really thought they'd buy that weaver story?'

'They did for a while – long enough for me to organise the celebration anyway.'

'Yeah, and long enough for Lupicina to feel even more duped when someone told her your real history.'

'I was introduced as a penitent, that is no lie. And she's the Empress Euphemia to you. The woman was a slave, you could show her some pity.'

'I would if she wasn't such an arrogant cow. I heard she was his concubine.'

'Justin's? Some say. But she was never a—'

'Dancer?'

'Actress.'

'Hah, not with a face like that, no.'

Both women laughed then, Theodora more carefully than Sophia, uncomfortably aware that these walls had far too many ways to siphon secrets.

'Really though, I'm not sleeping with the Consul.'

Sophia sat back down on the couch, picking through the bowl of nuts for the sugared almonds she preferred. 'What's stopping you?'

Theodora shook her head. 'I don't know . . . he likes me.'

'Plenty of men have liked you before.'

'He likes me for who I am, what I can do.'

'You made a nice job of the celebration, I'll give you that.'

'Thank you. And I enjoy talking to him.'

'He likes men?'

'No.'

'You sure? That Narses is his best boy, isn't he?'

Theodora winced. 'I don't think you'd call Narses his boy if you'd met him. And no, he's not sexual in that way, the way of men when they are lovers. Justinian listens to me, he thinks I have good ideas.'

'You do. When they involve giving me work. Though I'd have been happier with a paid job.'

'It's a prestigious appointment to sing for the Consul.'

246

'So you said. Go on.'

Theodora shook her head. She'd been trying to analyse it herself in the long nights when she'd been working out routes for street entertainers, and staying up with Narses to plot how best to keep both Blues and Greens mollified; in the few moments she'd had between work and exhausted sleep, she'd thought about little else other than what was growing between her and Justinian, what it was she felt.

'He acts as if he believes I know what I'm talking about.'

'You do as far as theatre is concerned. Less successful at picking your men, though.'

'I'm not picking this one, he's my friend, we talk.'

'About what?'

'About . . . everything, nothing.'

'Oh good, nice he's so specific.'

The call for evening mass rang out then, Sophia's cue to leave for her late rehearsal, and Theodora was glad to be spared explaining exactly what she and Justinian talked about when they sat together, as both the candle and his officials acting as unofficial chaperones burned out and the two of them continued on late into the night. In their discussions – first about the form of the celebration, then about how best to please the people, leading neatly into celebrations they both remembered, times they'd been happy to be party to big events – Theodora and Justinian had talked about memories, fleeting images caught as children and now recalled in this planning. Talking around past pleasures, remembered celebrations, meant they spoke more often in Greek. Even for Justinian, born into a Latin-speaking part of the Empire, Greek was an easier language for the nuance of nostalgia and remembrance. The Greek led them to discover their joint passion for language, for languages, a shared interest in the muscularity of Latin, the

247

poetry of Greek, the faith of Aramaic and Hebrew and Syriac, the secrets of Egyptian and the other African tongues Theodora had heard; Justinian's passion for his homeland's native languages, long superseded by the Latin of the conquerors, had never quite been lost. They taught each other new words from languages they barely knew, shared stories based on the foreign phrases they understood together, played word games around false translations. Between them they fed a desire to share words, play in words.

Theodora didn't have the words to help Sophia understand. She wasn't having sex with Justinian, not yet: maybe never. His role in the Imperial and government hierarchies meant it was impossible to think of him as anything but a potentially dangerous friend. If he ever did become her lover, it could only be difficult. She was well aware of an undercurrent of opposition to her presence in the Palace, an undercurrent that became more blatant the closer she found herself to the Empress, especially once the full extent of her past had been revealed and the Empress realised Theodora had taken the work of weaver as a penitent. Unlike the religious, Euphemia didn't fully believe in the possibility of total absolution. Even beyond the displeasure at their growing friendship, there was the simple fact that it was legally impossible for Theodora and Justinian to have anything more than an affair. The legal barriers that prevented an actress, indeed any woman of no status, from marrying a man of rank were no different than they had been when she was with Hecebolus.

Mindful of her duty to the Patriarch, who no doubt had his own plans for her future, as well as her precarious position as staff and yet not staff, Theodora left every step up to Justinian. It had been Justinian's idea for her to move into the Palace, the better to be able to work with him at all hours, Justinian's idea –

with Narses' prompting – to give her the small staff of her own, to help her feel more comfortable in the vast warren of buildings that could just as easily resemble a prison, Justinian's idea to speak in Greek when Latin did not offer them enough scope. Whatever came next, it would be Justinian's move. Theodora's job was to wait and see what that might be.

Twenty-Nine

During her work on the consular celebration, Theodora became friendly with Antonina, an older woman, the wife of Belisarius, one of the few men Justinian truly trusted. Belisarius was everything the new Consul was not: strong, brave, respected in the ranks and, as Theodora told his wife, he was really very lovely. According to Justinian, Belisarius was a fine specimen of the old Empire, the kind of Roman he kept in mind when he talked to Theodora, at length, about his plans for the new forms of government, law and architecture that might renew the Empire's pride. It was clear that Justinian was not merely interested in the law; no matter how bookish he was perceived to be, his ambition extended far beyond the borders of his library and office. Unlike most men though, as well as dreams, he now had the power to bring them to fruition.

Belisarius was indeed beautiful and his wife Antonina, ten years his senior at least, was one of the toughest women Theodora had ever met, herself and Sophia included. Like both of them, Antonina had once been a dancer. She had, however, only ever worked privately, and so had never gained the kind of reputation — for skill either on stage or in the bedroom — that provided Sophia with her hungry audience and made Theodora the target of snide Palace gossip. Antonina maintained she had remained virginal throughout her few years as a dancer, and had been a good wife to her first husband. Belisarius backed up her claim that she was a chaste widow when they first met, and though the priest was not a little disapproving, there was no legal reason that a young, very hopeful soldier and a widow could not be married. Had their union come later, when Belisarius had been promoted through the ranks, it would have been a different matter, but with Justin so heavily reliant on Justinian's judgement, and Justinian so fond of Belisarius, any censure Antonina might have experienced in the Palace could not readily show itself; not without seeming small-minded at least, or incurring the anger of the Emperor. This did not stop the Empress Euphemia or her friends from sneering at Antonina, but it did stop them doing so when either Justinian or his uncle was present.

The most vindictive of Euphemia's friends was the dowager Juliana Anicia. She of the bald spot Theodora had first spied from the aqueduct as a child. Now an even wealthier widow, Juliana had provided herself with an array of methods to hide her problem, creating something of a fashion for wigs and hairpieces among the older women at court. When the old lady spoke rudely to her, or condescendingly to Antonina – or not at all, which was more usual – it helped Theodora to remember that the wigs weren't merely for fun. As Theodora had been quick to learn and use in the consular celebration, the people liked shows of wealth, displays of grandeur, status symbols that included them, and for many years now Juliana had been endowing city buildings with her own personal wealth. A new church here, a monastery there, she gave the people what they wanted – not the bread and circuses provided by the state-supported games, but elegant, longer-lasting and determinedly Christian marble and stone. Further, the older woman understood perfectly that neither name nor money counted for long without power and so, while she mocked the once-concubine Empress in the privacy of her own home, in public she was happy to be seen as Euphemia's good friend. It did Euphemia no harm to have the aristocratic Juliana of the Anicii as her confidante either. Wealth met power, prestige met name in the friendship between these women. They made a successful and formidable pair. If Juliana Anicia had had her way, and she'd certainly tried, she would have married her own granddaughters into Justin's family, but although Germanus had married her niece Pasara, Justinian had never paid any attention to the girls of her dynasty. Which made it all the more galling when people began to say that the one woman he was interested in was that slut Theodora – not that Juliana Anicia had ever been to the theatre, but she'd certainly heard stories.

In one part of the Palace then, Juliana Anicia was regarded as the wealthy endower of grand new buildings, useful to the Emperor who needed someone to put gold into the walls and the streets, as he certainly wasn't interested in spending the Empire's wealth to do so. Justinian would have spent more on building and state occasions – for a man supposedly obsessed with his books, he had a passion for building that rivalled Juliana Anicia's – but Justinian was not Emperor, and while he and his uncle agreed on many things, finances weren't one of them. Which was why Theodora was applauded by the businessmen of the Palace: she'd not only brought the consular celebrations in under budget, she had somehow fooled the people into thinking more money had been spent on them than ever before. Theodora believed any good actor should be able to make something out of nothing, light from shade, rich cake from dry bread, but the Palace was not used to such impressively lavish economy. It was the reason the Emperor Justin warmed to the girl. That and her delicious breasts, though he didn't say so to Justinian, or to his own wife.

Justinian didn't enjoy Juliana Anicia's company any more

than Theodora did, but he did agree with the dowager on one thing: like her, he didn't much trust Antonina. He did not fear Antonina's ambition, Justinian had no problem with ambition that accorded with his own, and he trusted Belisarius implicitly for both his heart and his skills; he'd happily promote the younger man when the time came. It was more that Antonina seemed to enjoy too many secrets, and while Justinian was very keen to keep his own secrets, he didn't like other people to have them. Theodora noticed this early on and made sure she told him hers directly – those she wanted him to know. Once Narses had explained about her theatrical past, Justinian felt he knew more than enough anyway. It wasn't all, but it sounded like plenty, and helped him trust her. Most of the time.

'But why not? It's a very useful proposal.'

Theodora, always polite, certainly deferential in front of Justinian's servants, chose not to bite back the sharp tone in her voice. She'd been trying to get Justinian to agree to a dinner between City officials and several key military figures for a few days now. In her self-assumed mission to make the Consul more popular with the people, Theodora thought it an ideal opportunity for him to show that he could converse as well with soldiers and generals as with librarians and lawyers.

Justinian sighed, motioning for his servants to leave them. The small entourage backed out of the room as silently as possible and when the door was closed with a soft shush, he answered, 'Because I don't want a dinner. I can talk to any general or soldier any time I want in the baths, that's where half the conferences go on anyway.'

'Yes, and then the men keep it between themselves.'

'Isn't that the point?'

'It would be, sir,' she added, 'if you wanted a secret meeting

253

about kicking the Goths out of Italy or something equally irrelevant to our own City . . .'

Justinian winced, all too aware of Theodora's raised voice
and that this kind of talk kicked off wildfire rumours, especially
in Palace state rooms where no one was ever truly alone.
'Luckily I don't have to think about that right now, what with
merely being Consul?'

His heavy eyebrows were raised as high as they would go and
she lowered her tone, took a step closer. 'But you don't want,
always, to be just Consul . . .'

'Just?'

'You know what I mean, sir. As does the August himself.
And you also know that when talks happen purely between
men, they tend to stay that way. But when wives are present,
there is more chance of . . .'

'Gossip?'

Theodora smiled. 'Dissemination.'

'And you'd like to disseminate the idea that I'm capable of
talking intelligently to a couple of soldiers?'

'Frankly sir, I'd like to disseminate the idea that you're capable of talking at all.'

'We are not talking?' Justinian shifted to Latin to emphasise
his disappointment that this woman, with whom he enjoyed all
manner of conversation, seemed to be dismissing their relationship.

'What we do doesn't count,' she answered in Latin herself
now, before reverting to Greek, the better to make her point.
'It's what the people think that matters. And Narses is the one
who's keen on you talking to soldiers . . .'

'So you've dreamed this up between you?'

Theodora went on, 'Antonina would welcome a chance for
Belisarius to be seen more at the Palace.'

'I'm sure she would, she's an extremely ambitious woman.'

'Married to an extremely capable young man. Narses says—'

'Again? You two have become very close?'

'We have an understanding, sir. And we both have your best interests in mind.'

Justinian sat down heavily, causing the thick leather of the stool to creak. 'Go on.'

'Narses maintains that ambitious soldiers can be dangerous. I believe he feels it is best to encourage loyalty.'

'And he thinks I can best encourage loyalty in this boy-wonder, who is already a friend, by the way, by inviting him and his hard-faced wife and God knows how many others to a dinner? By making a show of a friendship that is already real?'

'Sir, the dinner is my idea. Yes, Antonina suggested it, but I'm sure she's right, she knows the City wives better than I do these days. She assures me it will do you good, as well as Belisarius, of course – it will show that the two of you have a working relationship.'

'We do.'

'Yes, but it needs to be shown. A meal is easy, it need not be lavish, we can keep it simple.'

'And brief?'

'If you like. But it is a statement, and the message will get out.'

'What message is that, Theodora?'

There was a pause. A moment for the gulls to scream out-side, for the sounds of the City to drift in over the wall, for Theodora to note the hurrying of feet down a distant corridor, to catch a brief scent of sweet spices, perhaps from the Palace kitchens, where cakes were being prepared for Euphemia's ladies. Justinian was waiting for an answer and she needed to pick her words well. She liked this job, loved having her own rooms in the Palace, but there was no need for Justinian to keep her if she had nothing to do and, mindful also of Timothy's

255

desire for her to stay put, Theodora didn't want to screw it up. She knew as well as Justinian that while the Emperor himself often spoke of his nephew following him in the purple, it could be dangerous for anyone else to suggest the possibility.

'The message that you can converse with anyone, sir.' She smiled, the distant feet came closer, ran past the door and away, quieter again. 'That you can tear yourself from your books every now and then to dine with friends, just as the ordinary people do.'

'I'm a farmer's son from Illyricum, what could be more ordinary?'

'And it doesn't hurt to show that the stars of our military find it easy to trust the farmer's son who has become a man of books and letters.'

Justinian shook his head, giving in. 'A simple meal, Theodora. And keep Antonina at the other end of the table. You and she might want to pass on all the comings and goings of the Palace to the eminent wives of the City. I'd rather everyone didn't know that I prefer meat to fish.'

'It's the abundance, sir. Proximity to the water. The fish are so easily caught, and fresh, our chefs get lazy. I'll make sure there is flesh on the menu.'

Theodora bowed, and left the room smiling. Even a small dinner needed a couple of weeks to plan properly. She was staying for now.

Justinian watched the door close behind her, waiting for his servants, idly dropping a heavy glass paperweight from one hand to the other. The weight was locally made, stamped with a bust of his uncle, the dark green of the laurel in late summer, he liked its smoothed edges, ran his thumb over the Imperial inscription. He would order a pile of papers to be brought from the library, there were several old folios he was keen to read. He liked the outlook of this room, not over the gardens or down to the water, but close to the wall; the noise and scents from the City assured him that the Palace wasn't entirely cut off from the people. He also liked that Theodora had been sitting here with him all morning, would come back later with plans and ideas, returning with the street passion she could not contain no matter how hard she tried – and he did enjoy watching her try. Justinian didn't want Theodora to leave the Palace any more than she did, there was something about her, a zeal he'd missed since he'd been under his uncle's protection, she was much more like the assertive women he'd grown up with back home in his town of Tauresium than the tamer delights he'd been offered since he'd come to the Palace.

He asked a servant to bring him the folios he required, and to send Narses to him later in the day: there were disturbing reports from his spies among the Goths in Italy, and Narses would be able to advise him so he would be fully informed when he presented the matter to his uncle. There was also an annoying Green leader in the east of the City who, a more local source reported, had been suggesting a little too forcefully that Germanus, not Justinian, might make a better successor to the purple one day. Narses could help him deal with that problem too.

Thirty

The silver platters were cleared, wine goblets removed, cushions stacked in the store room, wooden mixing bowls and copper pans washed and piled in cool dark cupboards, in careful rows. In the corner of a side galley, off the main kitchen, a young man from Damascus and a girl from Bithynia were kissing among the leftovers, their kitchen duties finally completed, they had crept into the little room to pick over an unfinished leg of mutton, sticky with cinnamon and wine, sweet with slow roasting on a low fire. The carcass finished, they found their hands touching, the slip of animal grease, the rich stink of roasted meat, a sliver of succulent marrow still to be sucked from the bone, and their mouths moved from the famine of food to the feasting of flesh.

There was no such pleasure upstairs in Justinian's study.

'She's an ill-bred slave.'

'I hardly think it's your place to criticise the upbringing of the Emperor's wife.'

Theodora would not be swayed. 'She wasn't invited.'

'She didn't need to be invited, this is her home.'

'And yours.'

'Yes, but I am here at the sufferance of my uncle – and my aunt.'

'Not so. Justin needs you. He knows how old he is, and he knows what they all say about her, they both do.'

Justinian's eyes could not have been wider. 'And what do you think they all say about you, Theodora?'

'I don't care what they say about me. That's the point. I have never – unlike the Empress – pretended to be anything but what I am. I know what I am, what I have been, and so does everyone else. She, though, she behaves like she was born into this life, when she started out as his concubine.'

'And became his wife. That isn't unusual.'

'Yes, I know it's normal, but I tell you, the next time she dares to look down on me or Antonina or any other woman I know – "dancing girls" for fuck's sake – she'll get a mouthful from me.'

'Because that would show her how well bred you are?'

'Because that would show her what I think about women like her. Euphemia never worked a day in her life.'

Justinian's voice was quiet. 'The Empress was born into slavery.'

'Fine, a day in her adult life – maybe she worked as child, but now she takes her name from him, her role from him, everything from him.'

'As do all women, I don't know what your problem is. Yes, my aunt can be abrasive, but she does have position, she has status. The role deserves recognition, if not the person occupying it. Don't you have respect for her place?'

Theodora shook her head, she wanted to scream in fury, instead lowered her voice still further, 'Most women I know have been working since we were girls, earning our own way, taking care of ourselves. Those wives of the great and the good, daughters of the great and the good, they do nothing but lie in the bed of their husbands – their masters – and treat providing an heir as if it were their vocation. Then they dare to look down on me, when I've worked my entire life, made my penance, done it all on my own – how can I not be angry?

259

That woman is no better than me. At least I gave up work as a whore.'

There was silence. Theodora stood, waiting for the thunderbolt of Justinian's anger, for the doors to fly open, guards to grab her, a hand to stifle the breath in her throat. She wanted to stifle the breath in her own throat. It was too late, though. As always, she'd said too much, too loud. Too late her teeth clamped shut, her jaw set, she could not have spoken now if Justinian had begged her to. He didn't.

Justinian turned away, speaking quietly. 'I think you should leave.'

Theodora didn't wait for a second command. She bowed and left the room.

Less than an hour later her old bag was packed and she was again wearing a simple dark shift; the soft, clean clothes she had acquired since she'd come to the Palace were neatly folded in a small pile at the end of her bed, the red slippers she'd worn in the quiet corridors were by the door and her own dusty sandals were back on her feet, one ankle tie looking as if it would snap within the week, she'd have to be careful as she walked away. The emerald, her sole possession of value, was strapped back in place beneath her breast, strapped a little too tightly, digging into her ribs, no doubt marking her skin. If this was the least punishment Theodora earned she thought she would be lucky.

It was late, only a few servants were awake at this time of night, some to attend on Justinian who slept so little, and lightly when he did, a few others to stay alert in case the Emperor or Empress needed them, a couple to make sure the fires were kept stoked through the night for the early baking that would begin soon enough. It was time to go.

Theodora was grateful that no one had yet arrived to throw her out, that she'd been allowed time to gather her things, time to work out a plan. She would go immediately to Comito, ask for money and clothes, and then down to the docks to see who could take her with them. If she were not stopped on her way, if the silence that came from Justinian's rooms meant he intended to let her escape punishment, then she might get away from Constantinople by midday. She would return to Antioch perhaps, or Alexandria even, if there was a ship going so far, she could beg Timothy's forgiveness, ask to be taken in, give herself over to a nunnery, to prayer and peace and the blessed silence of once and for all shutting her treacherous mouth. There wasn't time now for self-accusation, but Theodora was well past the accusing stage anyway. She had tried and judged herself the minute the damning words were said. Not that she didn't believe them, just that she didn't believe she'd been so stupid as to say them. She didn't deserve Timothy's trust or Justinian's work – she wouldn't have employed a chorus girl who didn't know when to shut her mouth and, more than anything, she hated the fact that all those years since Menander last told her that her mouth would get her hanged she still hadn't learned when to shut up.

When Narses walked into her room, without knocking, it was as though she had conjured up her dead teacher's presence – even more so when the living lover of the dead eunuch slapped her across the face. Clearly not trusting himself to say anything beyond the absolute minimum, Narses dragged her out of the room with him, spitting, 'Justinian wants you. Now.'

He stopped as they turned the corner to the covered pathway leading to Justinian's rooms: evidently she was going on alone. It was still before dawn, she could hear market traders setting up their stalls in the street beyond the walls; they were the fruit and vegetable and flower sellers, many of whom had harvested their goods yesterday and travelled all night to bring them into the City. In an hour or so the meats would arrive, live chickens ready to kill at home, fresh carcasses of sheep and goats and even cows, slaughtered and bled, hung for inspection by calculating housewives and tougher household servants. Down at the harbour the fishing boats were long gone, out on the last of the night tide, ready to make their day's first catch with the breaking sun. Theodora felt as if everyone was beginning a new day but her. Her day was still firmly stuck in the consequences of last night. She really should have packed sooner, run faster. Now it was too late. Another lesson to learn. Theodora was sick of learning lessons.

A servant let her into Justinian's study, backed out and left them alone. Justinian's desk was piled even higher with papers than usual, there were half-rolled scrolls everywhere, slivers of paper marking places in larger piles squashed between folios that were larger still, threatening to topple any moment.

Theodora took four steps to the centre of the small room, put down her bag, and immediately prostrated herself. Even now it was killing her pride to do so, but whether Justinian had asked her here to give her a last chance, or called her to gloat over whatever punishment he had in store, either way, it was worth a try. She lay on the floor for a moment, and then another, then more, waiting for a reaction. When it came, the reaction was not what she'd expected.

Justinian's voice was quiet and softer than she'd heard before, exasperated and almost laughing. 'Get up, you stupid girl.'

Theodora looked up. He gestured, she stood, slowly

Justinian was smiling, grinning. She hadn't seen him smile like this before, wide and open. He sighed, shook his head, lifted his hands and then let them fall again to his lap. Opened and closed his mouth. She didn't understand the look on his face, it didn't make sense. It was in the wrong place, on the wrong face, at the wrong time. He looked as if he were pleased to see her.

'Sir?'

Theodora had no idea what was going on, but whatever it was, it didn't feel as if she was about to discover the truth of those stories Menander always used to frighten them with as little girls, stories about the Palace dungeons and secret torture chambers, and the long passageways deep underground with steps leading only down, where the tide came in to slowly drown badly behaved little girls.

Justinian waved his hand over the papers on his desk, still grinning. 'I've been working.'

She waited.

'And I think I've worked it out.'

'Worked what out . . . sir?'

'How we can fix it.'

The day was brighter now, reflecting white off the old stone walls opposite, a man in the market was shouting at his son to get the damn oranges out, the housewives would be arriving soon. The room smelt of dry parchment, and Justinian. It smelt of the sweat of a man who had been thinking hard for many hours.

'Fix what?'

'Oh for God's sake, Theodora, don't be so dense. You. Me. I want to marry you.'

She looked from Justinian to the gardeners below. They were cutting back miniature lemon trees. She was listening and not understanding.

Justinian was speaking. 'Which would be fine if you weren't – as Euphemia so aptly put it and managed to upset you so much, when after all, she was only speaking the truth – well, if you weren't one of those brothel girls, but you are. An actress. Your father's daughter. Bear-keeper, wasn't he?'

Theodora was five, wearing white, flowers in her hair, standing in the Hippodrome begging the Greens to take them on, rejected. She nodded.

He nodded back. 'Yes, right, and so I can't marry you, not yet, according to the law, because of the theatre, you having worked in the theatre. But look, I think we can fix it. We've been talking for a while now – I have, with some of the advisers – about a few legal changes, things I'd like to do, if . . . when . . . you know,' he waved his hand again, the impossibility of mentioning the possibility of purple. 'Anyway, there's a lot to do, but this would be a start. It's a small law change really, it wouldn't affect all that many people, and it looks generous, kind. The people like a kind law, I think? We can see how they take it, if there's not too much fuss, then it's a good tester, you see? I can move on with bigger things later. Of course, if they're not happy, we'll just sit tight for a bit, keep quiet. You can do that, do you think? Keep quiet?'

Theodora nodded.

'Yes. Narses says you can. He seems to think you can do anything you set your mind to. Very fond of you, Narses is.'

'Odd way of showing it.' Theodora's hand went to her cheek as she found her voice. 'Sir, I know you understand the law better than I, but we can't – I can't marry, it's illegal.'

'Yes, it is at the moment. You'll be my case in point. I'll change the law for you.'

Theodora didn't answer, looking at Justinian as if he were mad. Perhaps he was. Perhaps that's why he barely slept and spent night after night with his books instead. Perhaps he really was the farmer's son from God knows where with too many ideas and plans above his station that his cousin believed him to be, a words and ideas man, no action beyond the inane, the insane.

Only mildly disturbed by her lack of response – even in his

fervour he did realise this must all come as a bit of a shock – Justinian explained, 'I have been looking into it for a while.' And then, when she still looked confused, he tried another tack, 'Timothy thinks it's a good idea.'

'The Patriarch?'

'Of Alexandria, yes. Haven't mentioned it to the Constantinople one, not yet. Or Rome, well, who knows what's going on over there. Anyway, Timothy thinks it'll help.'

'Help what?'

Justinian explained. That Theodora's coming to the Palace was Timothy's idea – as she knew. What she hadn't known was that Justinian had always known she was there as Timothy's agent and advocate. Did Theodora really think Narses would have agreed to anything without getting Justinian's permission first? Narses had been playing the Patriarch as much as the Patriarch thought he was playing Justinian. The threat of schism was quite evident to all of them, and Justinian agreed it was a good idea to stop a split in its tracks. One Church, one Empire, one people – admittedly, not necessarily in that order. He understood it was impossible to change the mind of either the Church or the faithful simply by force of will. And, whatever Timothy's take on Chalcedon, the man was still a churchman of great power, great influence, it had been useful to let his group think they had the upper hand. More recently, once Justinian had realised how useful Theodora might be – and that he enjoyed her company, of course – there had been an exchange of letters, a coming clean all round. Timothy would be delighted with this marriage idea: if they could force it, he might even shut up some of his complaining about the treatment of his followers.

'Right. So the Patriarch sent me to befriend you, and you already knew that was his plan, and you've been keeping me around to keep him happy, and now you want to marry me because that will make a liaison between both sides?'

'On the divinity question, yes,' Justinian agreed. 'Naturally we can't be seen to be condoning their beliefs outright. On the other hand, if they feel we are privately finding a way . . . well then, all might be well. We really do have enough to worry about with the Goths in the west without taking on the Church in the east too.'

'So I marry you and we let it be known, quietly, that I am sympathetic to the Alexandrian Patriarch's views?'

'I thought you were more than sympathetic?'

'I am.'

'There you are then. First, though, we need to change the law. Actually, having put some effort into the preparation, I don't think it'll be too hard. I've been working on the phrasing for some time; "Taking into account proper renunciation, forgiveness, redemption, blah blah blah, a woman, once an actress, might – with correct teaching, penance, guidance etcetera – be deemed renewed, take up a fresh life . . ." and so on. You get the gist.'

'Yes.'

'And you're a Constantinopolitan. That will go down very well with the people . . . if, when . . .' and here Justinian waved his hand again, indicating what neither of them could comfortably say within these walls. 'You understand the people in a way I don't. And we get on well enough, don't we?'

'Yes. I think so.'

'Good. And when you speak, when you don't let your temper get the better of you as last night – you're brilliant. Far more clever in speech than I could ever hope to be. Better even than Macedonia suggested in that letter she sent Narses in the first place. I should show it to you some time, Macedonia's letter, very impressive.'

Theodora was trying to take it all in, all that had been plotted while she'd been blind to it.

Justinian went on, giving her time to catch up as he spoke. 'I have to take a wife eventually, there'll need to be an heir, you already have a child, so we know that you can bear children . . . and, you know . . .' He was speaking softly, more quietly, looking over towards the market, to the City, not sure how to say this to her, saying it to the air instead, 'I do . . . I enjoy your company. So we might work, as a couple, but first we need to change the law. And before that . . .' He looked back from the window, looked at Theodora, 'You need, of course, to agree?'

Theodora did not say she doubted she could ever conceive again, not after what she'd been through in the cave in the desert. She did not say that she felt both betrayed and blessed by Timothy, that she felt managed and handled by all these men and was sick of being sent to do their bidding without knowing all the facts. She did not say that she'd like to see that ageing fucking eunuch Narses raise a finger to her once she was Justinian's wife or that she was hurt Macedonia hadn't told her the full story. She did not even say that she suspected Justinian was a bigger fool than his cousin's people took him for if he thought he could get a law change like that past the Empress Euphemia without a fight. Theodora knew a good offer when she saw one. At the very least, even if the law, as was likely, was rejected out of hand, she might manage a position as Justinian's mistress when he found he had to put up with one of the boring Anicii virgins for his bride after all. Nor did she question if love or passion were to be part of the equation. Hecebolus had been about love. Theodora had never been offered such good terms in her life.

She knelt and accepted Justinian's offer.

She thought he might kiss her when he took her hand and

267

raised her to him; instead he held her with both hands on her shoulders and thanked her. He was happy, and keen to get back to his papers. He'd send someone to unpack her bag and bring her a few new dresses. That penitent look would do well for the law change he was proposing, good to show herself like that to his counsellors, but she probably didn't need to go around looking quite so sorry. The black and grey shifts were all very well, but he was sure they could find a dark green silk that would do nicely. She had lovely eyes, no point pretending otherwise.

Thirty-One

Theodora thought she had heard every nasty epithet that could be applied to a woman of her rank and profession, she'd used most of them herself, either talking about her own work or slagging off other actress-whores while drunk with Sophia. But the vicious phrases that Euphemia now directed at Theodora were different. They were loaded, barbed, often more blatant than anything she'd ever heard whispered and, unlike the sniggers whispered in a bar, or even the outright taunts from the Hippodrome's cheap seats, there was nothing she could do about them.

Whenever Theodora was in the presence of the Empress – and Euphemia made sure it was often, inviting her for pastries in the afternoon, to walk with her ladies in the gardens, to stand with them in church – Theodora simply had to smile and take it. Take being called the Bear-Girl, while ladies-in-waiting covered their delicate noses. Take being offered the largest cake, the fattest sweetmeat: after all, so much physical work must sap her energy, she had to be hungry. Take being offered longer time in church: with so many sins to expiate, Euphemia and her entourage didn't mind waiting a few more minutes, hours, days. Then the laughter from the women, the rustle of silk robes pulled a little closer that they might not touch Theodora as they swept out of the room, leaving her alone. And every day she went back for more.

*

269

Justinian said she should simply turn down the invitations from the Empress' household, but Theodora knew better than that.

'No, that's what she wants me to do, to run away. I won't give her the opportunity to say I refused her friendship. Her women will tire of it eventually, even if she doesn't. Already one or two of them have started looking sympathetically at me when she's not around. You have no reason to know this, but most concubines are a bit stupid.'

'How so?'

'They've never done anything else but please their men . . .'

'Not like you?' Justinian asked, looking up from his papers, mock-frowning.

'Not like me. My work has been to give and to pleasure – that is not entirely the same as to please.'

'Interesting distinction,' Justinian put down his pen. 'Go on.'

'Thank you, sir. I appreciate your interest.'

Theodora smiled. For the first time in her life she was enjoying a relationship with a man as her friend. She was not fighting him for control of her body or her spirit, and though his status was so much higher than hers, he was not interested in being in charge. There had been a few times in the past weeks when she'd tried to manufacture an argument with him, simply because it was what she was used to. Justinian very quickly made it clear that he had no intention of playing those games, he did not want to subdue her or to shut her up, he was not interested in training her. If Theodora was to be his wife, she would need to train herself, he was a busy man and he simply needed his partner to step up – as his equal.

She went on, 'When a girl is raised to be a concubine, that's all she ever thinks about – she spends all her time working out how to please her "master". It makes them stupid. Euphemia . . .'

'My aunt?' Justinian asked, reminding her of the closeness of their tie, if not their relationship.

'If you'll excuse me speaking openly about the August's wife?'

Justinian nodded.

'The Empress is behaving like a sixteen-year-old concubine who's just discovered her master has brought home a new woman. Her nastiness makes her ugly – she's already old.'

'And not very well, I hear.'

'No, but, you know, her women are not all as stupid as she is, only impressed by appearance.' Theodora was warming to her speech, balanced on the balls of her feet, ready to explain more. Her dark features were animated, not pretty, certainly not traditionally beautiful, but more interesting to Justinian than most of the women he'd been introduced to in his life in the Palace, the daughters of the gentry. 'It does her no favours to make herself look unkind in the eyes of those who serve her.'

Justinian leaned forward. 'I agree. But is it good for you to be hurt, so often?'

Theodora shrugged. 'It's not like I've spent my life with people only being kind to me.'

Justinian held her gaze. 'That's not what I asked.'

Theodora laughed, shrugged again. Justinian waited for an answer. And waited. Eventually she gave in. 'Must all the men in my life want to know everything?'

Justinian liked this. 'All the men?'

'You, Timothy, Severus, Menander. Hecebolus.'

'The Governor?'

'Yes. And Narses now, to a degree.'

'Really?'

Theodora picked at the skirt of her dress. 'For a man more interested in the military, he's pretty good at second-guessing my clothing requirements.'

271

'Wonderful. So that's me, the priests, the eunuchs, and the oaf. Now that you've lumped us all in together, perhaps you'd like to actually answer the question? I'm concerned about you, I don't want my grand plan to mean you have to suffer.'

Justinian pointed at a stool against the far wall and a silent servant ran to fetch it so that Theodora might, with Justinian's permission, sit closer.

She spoke quietly, not wanting this dissection of her feelings to get around the Palace. She'd begun making friends of her own among the servants, this boy who worked for Justinian was one of those she trusted, but Euphemia was the Empress, her affiliations were legendary. 'Yes, it does hurt, more than I would have expected. Partly because I know she has the right to say what she wants, but also because what she says here, within these walls, must be soft compared to whatever they're saying out there, beyond the Palace. You think Juliana Anicia isn't furious?'

'She can know nothing other than that we have requested that you are made patrician, prior to the law change going through.'

'That's all you've said publicly, but unlike the Empress, the dowager is not stupid.'

'She's arrogant, with too much money and appalling taste in architecture.'

Theodora agreed. 'But not stupid, and neither, sir, are the people.' She leaned in, closer still: 'You really do need to understand this. The people hear things and it runs through them as one body, they feel as one body. The Greens are one half and the Blues another, but between them they are one, they learn as one. What's repeated in the market at first light, a trader telling another a secret he heard from his wife in the dark of their bed, is carved into stone as truth by the evening. According to Comito, everyone out there knows about your plan for me, for us. Some people will like it, they love a good rags-to-riches story. Those who were my fans in the theatre will be

272

delighted, this sounds like just another role to them, becoming patrician, maybe marrying the Consul.'

'Definitely marrying the Consul.'

Justinian was serious: since first suggesting the plan to Theodora, he'd become even more keen on the idea, precisely because of what she was showing him now. She knew the City, and the people, far better than he ever could, and he needed this knowledge close at hand, would need it even more if his ambitions were fulfilled.

'You have to get the law changed first,' Theodora reminded him. 'And so yes, those who were fond of me on stage, they'll be excited for me. As you hoped, it makes you look good too, they like you for it, for making an effort to make the lives of their favourite actresses better.'

'Even if it means their most favourite actress can never perform again?'

Theodora laughed. 'You don't know much about audiences, do you?'

'Very little.'

'They've already got another most favourite actress, many more. They replaced me with someone else the day I left the stage, but they enjoy their memory of me. They like the idea of their little Theodora bettering herself – but only the fans. The others, those who thought I was a slut back then, will not have changed their minds, and unlike the fans, they do like to pick a scapegoat and hang on to her for as long as they can.'

Justinian sat for a long time. Theodora waited. It was a nice room, his study. Even without a sea view, she liked being here.

Eventually he spoke. 'I'm sorry that my idea to help both of us causes you pain. I would not want that. I thought, simply it now seems, that we would be good together, useful to each other.'

Theodora stood to leave, touched by his care. 'We are, sir,

273

we will be, in time.' She leaned in closer, whispering against the servant's attentive pose, 'And anyway, Narses said her servants say she's been unwell for weeks now, they excuse her nastiness because she's in pain.'

'My uncle suggested something similar.'

'So maybe the old cow won't hang on much longer.'

She offered a low bow and left the room, leaving Justinian to his work, to his creation of the law that would change her life. She waited until she was back in the privacy of her room before punching the air with delight. She had a friend in a very high place.

Four weeks later Euphemia was dead. Narses brought Theodora the news with appropriate ceremony and regard. Aware that far too many people in the Palace knew about the discord between herself and the Empress, Theodora didn't betray the tiniest hint of a smile. Nodding at the information, she then dressed in appropriate mourning and hurried to Justinian, to comfort the man that everyone but Narses now believed to be her paramour. They had still not kissed.

Later that week, after the body had lain in state, and Justin had prayed with the corpse of his purple-shrouded wife, prayed with and for the woman who had risen with him to the highest office of the secular world, the ceremonies of her funeral began. Incense and chanting, several masses, both for Euphemia's soul and for the strength Justin now required to continue without his helpmeet. Finally there was the long procession through the streets, as always, bringing the Palace to the people, the outer form of Justin's personal grief taking shape in customs as old, and as new, as the City. Euphemia was laid out with full ceremony, wearing not only her own precious jewellery but also one of Justin's intaglio rings, his name scored into the green

274

jasper, held in place with a filigree setting from a solid gold band. She was buried with the full ceremony as her husband's wife and with his mark.

Theodora stayed away from most of the funeral fuss, partly out of respect for the old woman, more out of respect for the Emperor. On the day of Euphemia's interment, she sat with Narses when he came back from the church and listened to his story of the day's events. She was listening patiently, but it was obvious she was simply waiting to speak.

'So, enough of Juliana Anicia's mourning display – though the silk was quite impressive, she certainly couldn't have got closer to the purple without being accused of treason – what are you worrying about?' Narses asked.

Theodora took a breath, she had a question, and no idea how to phrase it. Eventually she managed, 'One of the girls who comes to tidy my room has become quite fond of me.'

'Oh yes?' Narses raised an eyebrow.

'Not in that way, she's practically a child. I mean she likes me. Respects me.'

'How nice.'

'Yes, it is. But she told me something today, something she'd heard other servants discussing. She thought I ought to know.'

Narses waited for her to go on.

'Apparently some people think I killed her. Euphemia.'

'I see.' Narses sat quite still.

'I didn't.'

'No, of course not, but you're new in the Palace, and you have travelled – you might well have picked up any number of tricks in your time away. There are plenty of stories about you hypnotising your audiences in the past, charming men to do all sorts of insane things for your love.'

'Those stories were made up by the publicists, that's how a theatre gets an audience.'

275

'Quite, but the servants aren't to know that. Then there are those who knew that Euphemia did not approve of your promotion to patrician, let alone this law change, or the proposal that you marry Justinian.'

'That's not public.'

'It's not private either Theodora, not in the Palace. What is? You must understand, there will always be rumours, this is a small and intense world of its own, it takes itself very seriously. You are an interloper and, in truth, you're not the most beautiful girl Justinian has ever met. Not the prettiest, tallest, fairest, or even the youngest, not any more.'

'Yes, thank you.' Theodora had had quite enough of Narses enjoying himself.

'So . . . they see you here, they hear he wants to marry you, they assume you've bewitched him somehow. They know Euphemia wants you out of the Palace, they believe Justin will do anything for his namesake, she is the only threat to your promotion – and then she becomes ill. And she dies.'

'She was old. She was never very well, not even when I first arrived.'

'No, but these are truths we keep from the people, they don't know who of their leaders is sick or well, mad or sane, that would do them no good at all. The first they knew of Euphemia even being unwell was the week she died. And they're a superstitious lot, your City fellows.'

Theodora was a little surprised by his calm. 'Narses, why don't you think this is a problem? People are saying I killed her!'

Narses stood, a call was echoing from the end of a corridor, someone needed his advice or his attention.

'As time goes on, Theodora, as your status rises, you will find it does you no harm to have the people a little frightened of you. Euphemia never quite managed it, she was always too aware of her own rise in status, too grateful and too guarded about her position, she angered people rather than made them respect or fear her. I suspect you'll be better at it than she was. Should things work out well for the Consul, in the way we would all hope, you'll probably find you enjoy being linked to his elevation. Being feared by the people is not so different to being loved by the masses. They can be a little afraid of you for many reasons. Your power will be obvious one day, if you – if he – rises that high, but beyond that, if there is something in you they believe they see, some hint of darkness perhaps, then all well and good. You have been loved for your body and your mind – and your mouth,' he added, raising a hand to stop her interrupting. 'Now perhaps it's time to become a little less known, a little less obvious. Sometimes a shadow can be useful.'

Narses was at the door before Theodora had the chance to reply.

'Narses—'

'Yes?' he answered without turning back to her.

'You do know I didn't kill her?'

Narses spoke quietly, his hand on the door, his face turned away. 'I know for a fact that you didn't kill her.'

Theodora sat alone then, looking out of the high window across the gardens and the wall to Justinian's grand new build-ing works on the waterfront, the scaffolding and stonemasonry that was building the City out, further into the water, into the east. She looked across the Bosphorus to where the old city of Chalcedon shimmered in the distance, wondering how well Menander had known his lover. Wondering how much Justinian really knew about Narses. Wishing now that she didn't know him quite so well herself.

Thirty-Two

The period of mourning for Euphemia came to an end. The Emperor continued to privately grieve his wife, and took up his public duties again. Among the first of his tasks was to pass the law Euphemia had so opposed. He had never agreed with her, but nor had he wanted to anger her – there had not been many issues in their life that Euphemia had taken a stance on; the propriety of women had been one of the very few. She had always felt her own background too keenly, no matter that Justin had been clear where his concerns lay. Now she was gone, he was free to do what he felt was right. In their new world it made sense that, with a priest's blessing, an actress might prove that she had renounced her past and could be redeemed, the law On Marriage would make that possible: what better sign could there be of the strength of true faith? This law suited the possibilities both for the new Empire and the new Church, it would do well. However, Justin wasn't prepared to accept any old priest's recommendation, and he wasn't prepared to accept Timothy's recommendation either, Patriarch of Alexandria or not. He sent his own priest to question Theodora; he was ready to accede to his nephew's new law, as aware as Justinian that Theodora could be a valuable ally in his nephew's future – but only when his priest had proved her repentant, only when Theodora had set the precedent for actress repentance.

Theodora sighed, pulled on another plain shift, and

prepared to act the sorry sinner one more time. One last time.

Thomas had seen a lot of theatre in the past, he couldn't tell his own leaders in faith, but he'd seen Theodora often when he was younger and he knew she was a good actress, a great one when she chose, when she wasn't giving the scene away for the sake of a laugh. So he was prepared for a show when he came to her rooms in the Palace, and he set out his terms very clearly. Yes, she could certainly be forgiven – but not without true penitence. As he said at their first meeting, and then again at their second, third, fourth and was now saying, yet again, at their fifth. Theodora was doing her best to remain patient, but it wasn't easy. Partly because his tone was more condescending than she had expected from a priest barely three years older than herself, partly because this priest barely three years older than herself was even better looking than the lovely Belisarius.

'I have suffered, I am repentant, believe me.'

Theodora kept her eyes downcast, waited for him to speak before she spoke again.

'So you say, and while I don't doubt you believe you're sorry – for your sins, for the pain that your soul has been through for them and, understandably, fearful of death and being cast out – I have to wonder if you are actually penitent. Penitence and remorse are not at all the same things.'

'How stupid do you think I am? Do you think I haven't listened to a word you've said?' The anger was out of Theodora's mouth before she could stop it and she kicked herself. She'd been working this priest for days now, sure he was almost about to make the leap, grant his permission, and here he was, causing her to shout like a child. She closed her eyes, and forced herself to kneel at his side in apology. 'I should not have shouted.'

'No.'

'And I know you understand the intricacies of penitence better than I.'

'I do.'

There was silence. Thomas was waiting. Theodora hated this. The show of shame, forcing herself to fit the image of the penitent. From Menander to Hecebolus, Severus and even Timothy, all these men, always wanting her to bow down. Justinian was the only one who ever seemed content to have her stand beside him. Thomas was right, she wasn't sorry, not in the way the new law would have her be. She wasn't penitent in the way he required either – open about her faults, ashamed of her past, of the things she had been through – but she was doing what she had to, because the Emperor asked it of her and because it would make all the difference. She was on her knees, going through the tedious motions, to finally have the priest agree she was good enough now, that her past was forgiven, that she could move on.

It should all have been easy, really, Theodora should have been able to summon up a flood of tears, a chaste and embarrassed smile, a look of sincere regret: she'd learned those skills well enough from Menander. The problem was, she'd never fancied Menander, or Timothy – not beyond his lovely voice anyway. While she could absolutely see herself as Justinian's wife, and of course she knew everything she was now going through would be worth it in the end, there was the unfortunate matter of her attraction to this priest. And it was hard to expose herself, her true feelings, her real soul to a man she felt for. Harder still because he, quite obviously, was also attracted to Theodora.

Unlike many of his brothers in the clergy, Thomas not only publicly espoused celibacy but had also chosen to live the celibate life in truth. He knew exactly what he was dealing with in taking on this job, the temptation he was placing in his own path as well

280

as hers. In some ways that was why he'd agreed to take her on: to test himself as much as her. So far, though, Thomas was winning. In Theodora he recognised a wilful spirit and a daring ambition. He recognised it because he had both himself and, while he admitted he had not yet fully tamed his own vaulting ambition, he was now in control of the spirit. Which was why he also saw that Theodora was not in control of her spirit. Why he understood her to be remorseful, not penitent. Sorry, but not yet ready to sacrifice. Why he didn't believe her for a moment when she said the lusts of her past were not only entirely behind her, but also abhorrent to her. And why, having suffered the enormous privations he himself had undergone in order to renounce his own past life, and then again to enter the priesthood, he had absolutely no intention of letting her off easily.

The priest maintained his silence and eventually Theodora cracked, as he knew she would, as she knew she had to. Thomas after all, held all the power in this room.

She groaned, rubbed her face.

He said nothing.

'Come on, Thomas, you know how hard this is.'

'And I know how much it matters.'

'Of course it matters, Justinian cares enormously . . .'

'No, not for your potential marriage, if you get that far. For you, Theodora, for your soul.'

'Yes,' she nodded, 'yes, my soul. As you keep saying. But please . . . can't you just . . . I don't know, trust me? I've told you enough of what happened in Antioch, in the desert – you know I have faith. And I'll make a great Palace wife. I'll be good. I'll do everything they expect of me and more. You know I'll be good at it.'

'Pride again?'

She wanted to scream, spoke softly instead. 'Would it be so wrong to be proud of being a good wife?'

Thomas shook his head. 'It would be better to simply be a good wife and leave pride out of it entirely.'

Theodora started to get up and Thomas stopped her with a single gesture, one raised finger sending her back down on her knees. She complied. Her years of training meant that she felt the sharp sting of the stone floor digging into her kneecaps, but was perfectly capable of refusing to let him see it.

Kneeling, she tried again. 'Look, it's just show you want from me. Show of sorrow and show of penitence and show of remorse. I tell you the words, the truth, but that's not enough. You want me on my knees, in tears, wailing.'

Thomas waited. He considered her words, this strong woman at his feet. He weighed his own feelings, questioned himself as to why he kept her there: was it truly for her own redemption or was there something else here, too much, that he enjoyed himself? He waited until that sensation had passed, until he was more priest than man, and then he waited longer still, to make sure that when he spoke his words got through.

Fifty minutes later, when still she knelt beside him, with not even the slightest sign of giving in, Thomas began to speak, very softly, choosing his words with great deliberation. He needed to say this perfectly.

'You complain that true penitence requires show, and yet you are not willing to show me the physical pain you must be in right now.' She nodded, started to speak, he stopped her. 'No. You speak too well. I think maybe you do it all too well for your own good. Theodora, we all have a sin to which we return time after time. Your sin is pride. It shines from you.' He omitted to say that this particular shine was one of her loveliest attributes. Theodora's pride in what she had come through, in

282

her own strength, was perfectly understandable, yet it was still a sin, and it was his job to help her change. He went on, 'Any other penitent would have been begging me to allow them off their knees by now, confessing countless sins, real and imagined, simply so I would allow them to stretch their aching muscles and ease the pain that must now be shooting through you, but you stay here and you bear it. You endure physical pain, as I imagine some of the martyrs must have done, taking it into themselves, absorbing it. But those martyrs were already penitent, they had already bowed down. You are too fond of your own strength, just as you have been too fond of your skills, your abilities on stage and off. I know your faith is strong, and who am I to discount the blessing given you in the desert? What is vital, though, is that you allow yourself to be less strong than your faith. You are the first sinner I have ever met not to cry, not really, and until you are prepared to show me the deepest part of your soul, then I cannot deem you worthy of Justinian. There is every chance he may rise higher still, I will not provide him with a less than perfect partner. There is no point in false penitence. God is not fooled.'

Theodora nodded. She understood exactly what he was asking for. She looked up at the priest, revealed. 'You want me to show you my pain, Thomas?'

'I want you to give in.'

Theodora gave in. She told him of Menander and Hecebolus and the dreams of her father's death, of her regrets about her daughter, how she had still not created the relationship she had promised to try to achieve, she told him of her fear and her sorrow. She cried. When she was done, he was satisfied. He told the Emperor she was a good woman, and their test case with the new law was a true penitent. And Theodora told Narses that if and when Justinian ever became Emperor, he had better get that young priest out of the City before the purple was on her back, or Thomas would be the one in pain. A week later Thomas was on a ship to the Holy Land.

Theodora was preparing to marry Justinian, a man she felt no passion for though she was very fond of him, but still a good man who, through Timothy and Narses and his own connivance, was about to change her life beyond imagining. The priest Thomas knew her well now, but Theodora knew herself better. She didn't want Thomas's lovely face – or his knowledge of her past – getting in the way.

Thirty-Three

Permission was granted for Justinian to marry Theodora, the wedding date was set, the City was thrilled with the news, theatregoers were delighted, street traders praised the equality of hope in the City and therefore the Empire, Greens were disgruntled, Blues gloated, and in the newest wing of her mansion that was palatial in appearance if not in fact, Juliana Anicia seethed in well-bred rage. This particular news thrilled Theodora more than she had expected, not least because it was Justinian who shared the information with her, and their slightly shamed, largely gleeful complicity at Juliana's chagrin was a new step forward for the couple. While Theodora was as aware as the next woman that marriage was a business transaction, she knew they would work better as a team if they were also friends. Sharing pleasure in Juliana Anicia's pain was something they could easily do together: both felt slighted by the old woman, and – unlike the elaborate wedding plans Theodora was now creating with Narses, all designed to present a coupled and successful Justinian to the City – this joy was consciously present, not some time in the future. Better still, it was theirs, not part of a strategy drawn up by Narses or Timothy or the leader of the Blues, come to ask for another favour. With all too much of her life feeling as if it were part of someone else's greater plan, Theodora was keen to enjoy the moments that existed solely in themselves. She and her betrothed giggled like nasty children at their own impressions of Juliana's face when she heard their happy announcement, felt guilty, straightened their faces, and then giggled again.

Elsewhere in the City other friends were expressing their pleasure for the couple. Comito said she was delighted for her little sister. She said so in meetings at the theatre when Theodora's name – and newly patrician status – came up, she said so in post-show parties when other singers and actors were happily getting drunk and Comito was holding back, ever careful of the voice. She said so when strangers in the street asked her when she was going to marry a senator herself, and she hurried off to rehearsals not bothering to answer, not answering because she simply didn't know what to say. Comito now made a very good living from her voice, she had not had to trade in her own body for long, and mostly she preferred to behave as if that part of her youth had simply not existed. Theodora's public renunciation of her theatrical past, becoming patrician – even this new law that was being passed in order to allow her to marry the Consul – it was wonderful for Theodora, but all it did for Comito was bring up her own past, while simultaneously denying the value of her present. The elder sister had worked hard to craft the respect she'd been granted – a singer not an actress, a lady if not by birth then by demeanour, welcome in many of the most respectable homes. Now Theodora had come home and, as so often in their childhood, had taken both the attention and the glory in one swift move, and what was especially galling was that she had also managed to gain respect. In private, Comito did not say she was happy for her little sister.

Sophia thought it was hilarious. The idea that her old friend, stage companion, and occasional lover – though perhaps she'd have to shut her mouth about that now – was headed for marriage with Justinian made her snort with laughter. Even more insanely funny that, according to the last senator she'd shagged,

286

and also the general before him, Justinian was now certain to reach the highest office possible. Having seen him at a distance, Sophia thought Justinian seemed far too staid to please Theodora for long, even if he intended to try, and that definitely wasn't the way of most rulers. But, as she said to anyone who'd listen, usually when she'd had an extra jug of wine, Theodora wasn't blind to the possibilities of Justinian's future, even if she was blind to the heavy jowls and portly frame of the Slav – purple was an astonishing colour, it could hide any number of physical failings.

Antonina was delighted. She had become still closer to Theodora recently, and now the word from the Senate was that all the right voices were speaking in praise of Justinian, in closed as well as open rooms. She knew a deeper friendship with Theodora would do her husband the world of good. Belisarius was too honourable for his own career, Antonina would take charge where she had to.

Three pretty voices, each singing a different song of pleasure at Theodora's unheard-of advance, each crowing horror and laughter when Theodora told them she was preparing to marry a man she had not yet slept with.

'Fair enough. He's hardly in your usual league.' Sophia helped herself to another glass of wine, pushing aside the hovering servant, preferring to serve herself, not through any altruistic concerns, more because the skinny girl was so sparing in her pouring.

'It's probably right, isn't it? You've been recreated as a patrician, now they can recreate you as a virgin bride.' Comito couldn't quite keep the bitterness from her voice, but she almost managed to make it sound as if she thought it was amusing rather than really very irritating.

It was Antonina who made the most salient point. 'I don't

mean to be rude, but there's a way to go yet. I know everyone's agreed and all the plans are under way, but really, anything could still happen. Wouldn't it be safer to get pregnant between now and the wedding? It's only six weeks away and whatever happens, you do want to be sure to keep his patronage.'

The other two women fell about laughing at this, though Sophia agreed Antonina had a point.

'I might not become pregnant.' Theodora did not elaborate. She shared a great deal with her friends, with her sister – though Comito was usually less interested than the others – but she did not want to share this. What she knew about her time in the desert was far too dangerous to reveal. Justinian might believe she was everything he needed in a wife, someone who would please the masses in a way he never could, who could help him create the semblance of, if not a real, union between warring Church factions, who truly understood his belief in the potential of a new, restored Empire, one Church, one state – but no one would allow him to marry a barren woman, and Theodora knew they would be right to take such a stand. Germanus made no secret of his hopes for the purple, no matter that everyone knew Justin himself preferred Justinian for the succession. It would be an entirely different matter if Justinian's wife were unable to conceive. Theodora had no intention of letting this particular secret become even whispered knowledge. If it were true that she could no longer bear a child, then it would show itself plainly enough with time, there was no need to ruin everything with honesty now.

Antonina continued, 'You might not become pregnant immediately, none of us are as young as we used to be—'

'Speak for yourself.' Sophia sat up, looking every inch the child-woman temptress.

'How well we paint ourselves is another matter,' Antonina was not fazed, 'but you do need to ensure you get him through the ceremony . . .' She smiled now, more coyly than Theodora would have expected. 'I did not, unlike our sisters here,' indicating the two women on the divans, 'have the pleasure of seeing your finest work in the theatre, or elsewhere. But I have heard the stories . . .' She leaned in, away from the hungry eyes and ears of the servant. 'Isn't there a trick or two you learned back then? Something to make sure he's yours now and into the future? It's not as if the Consul has a reputation himself, it wouldn't take much, would it, to convince him that your marriage can be more than just a strategic move? Maybe you can do some business of your own? You are, you were, after all, highly celebrated in that arena, weren't you?'

The sister, the old friend, and the new friend were agreed. The celibacy between Theodora and Justinian must end. If she wanted to hold on to him, at least until the wedding, then she was going to have to hold him with more than just her suitability as a regal consort. A world-shattering bedding for the man who seemed to prefer paperwork to people was needed. And soon.

Theodora broached the subject the next day. Sitting with Justinian, quietly together, the two of them on her now-favourite balcony, in a room high on the southern edge of the Palace, away from the bustle of the Imperial buildings, the noise of the City behind them as they looked out to the Sea of Marmara, the eastern world turning yellow then orange then dark red as the sun set behind them. Her speech was shy at first, totally unlike the Theodora he was used to, and Justinian thought something was wrong, that he had failed in some way, behaved badly.

'I'm sorry, is there a problem?'

'No. No, not at all . . . I just, we should . . . maybe we should . . .'

Theodora shy and Justinian questioning, it was a first for both of them. Eventually he understood. Eventually, she did too.

As with so many things between Theodora and Justinian, his reaction wasn't what she'd expected when she carefully rehearsed her words in her own rooms. Justinian was kind, and appreciative, slightly dismissive at first of her suggestion that they should, perhaps, consider spending some more time together, some more time alone together and then, once she clarified what exactly she was offering, he understood her meaning completely and agreed that she should come to his room that night. He would send his servants away. She was right, he said, it was about time.

Theodora dressed carefully, took care to choose the perfect robe that would elegantly acknowledge her past as well as emphasise her present, and her future with him. She did not want to look like a wife yet, nor could she risk reminding him too much of her previous careers. Then again, anything that smacked too much of the reformed Theodora might make it impossible for her to deliver the sexual promise that was meant to tie the quiet, serious Consul to his wedding day promises, at least for a couple of years. Theodora was used to the concept of men straying – before Hecebolus she had often been the woman they strayed to; she agreed with Comito and Sophia that it would be wise to let Justinian know exactly what he was getting with their marriage. An insurance policy of sorts. She chose a green dress to reflect the colour of her eyes, opted for simple jewellery because it would be easier to remove – and because being unadorned now would offer a striking contrast with the highly decorated woman he would meet on their wedding day. She wore soft, thin slippers, her hair was barely tied, caught up with a fine ivory needle piercing a narrow band of plain leather. When the moment came, her hair would fall just as it should, covering her naked shoulders, reaching to her nearly naked breasts. Her own hair as prop, as symbol, as image. Menander had always dismissed the girls who preferred hair-acting to the real thing. Theodora knew it could come in handy on occasion.

They sat together on the divan for a few minutes, the room cool now the sun had fully set, the cushions soft. Justinian poured her a glass of wine and she noted his lovely hands, the fine long fingers of a scholar, not the farmer he might have been, more the Emperor he could be. He passed her drink, offered her food – tiny chunks of sweet chicken in an almond paste crust, shredded lamb ripped from the bone and wrapped in fine flatbread, a vine leaf stuffed with spiced grains, another with smoked fish, water, then more wine, then pastry dripping honey and scented with rose oil. He was attentive and she read-ily ate from his hand, ate what he offered, but Theodora was not thinking about the food, she was thinking about how best to place herself, how best to get this started.

She needn't have bothered. Justinian knew exactly what he was doing when he kissed her, knew what he was doing when he held her in the places she suddenly realised she wanted to be held, knew what he was doing when a touch across her back sent a tremor into her lower belly. He knew what he was doing when he stopped her letting her hair loose and said he didn't want her hair hiding her lovely face. In all the years that people and audiences, teachers and lovers had praised her, no one had ever told Theodora she had a lovely face. A brilliant mind cer-tainly, a wicked sense of humour, a disgusting laugh, a skilled body, a startling malleability of both heart and frame, but now, one of his hands on her neck, the other low on her back,

291

Justinian said she had a lovely face. And Theodora was amazed to find herself believing him, her inner cynic silenced for once, because he looked as if he really meant it – that she had a lovely face.

Then he was leaning over her and lifting her and holding her, and it was useful that she was so narrow, so small really, had always been so small, not Sophia small, but that she never quite had the height to be a real dancer, the frame to be a singer, what she did have, what she had always had, was the perfect body to do this. Her robe was removed and she could not work out how he did it, but he did, he opened the clasp holding the cloth together; the clasp she had meant to undo in two simple actions, Justinian removed in just one. He lifted her to the windowsill, there was soft night air and it was scented with a hundred different trees and the perfumes of the garden and the sea and the City, always the City, and then, close to her face, close to her mouth, to her nose, the air was scented with him. Justinian did not smell of old papers and tired scrolls and warm ink, he smelt like the man she would have him be, like the man she had no idea he could be, and then there was a reason, many reasons, for his hands working her, readying her, preparing her, and then they were fucking, not on the divan where the food was carefully laid out, not on the bed where the sheets were clean and fresh, not even against the far wall where it would be politic and careful, where it would be sensible just in case someone was outside, just in case someone could see beyond the walls to this window, but here they were fucking and rutting, laughing, both of them, in amazed joy at the union, framed in the window, lit by the candles all along the far wall, they were here together. And the part of Theodora's mind that was still watching, the piece of her that could not believe this was her Justinian, the same man she had chatted to and sat with and

292

whose sensible, knowledgeable, wise company she had calmly enjoyed for the past months – the part of her mind that was still above her own body, only just hovering above her own skin and bone and blood and flesh – was amazed by his strength, but more stunned by his brazen attitude, it was as if he did not care who might see them. Justinian did not care who might see them. And then there was none of Theodora floating above her own flesh, and then all of her was only her own flesh. His flesh and hers. And then he gave in. And then she gave in. Though perhaps not quite in the way the priest Thomas had intended.

'Definitely about time.' Justinian was smiling, they had found the bed, Theodora was staring at him. He had the grace to shrug as he said, 'There was a woman.'

Theodora could feel her body cooling now, gentle against the soft sheet, against his warmer body, her heartbeat approaching normal, she felt the room begin to pull them apart, he the nephew of the Emperor, she the woman who had been brought in to make the perfect consort. She didn't want that separation, not yet; right now she wanted the joining they'd had by the window, against the wall, in this bed, wanted the union to continue, for a few minutes at least before she was dismissed, before he sent her back to her own rooms, returned to his desk and his papers. Keeping the conversation going was a way to stay close, though it separated them, highlighted their different lives, even while it gave her a reason to stay.

She questioned, he talked, she stayed.

'Just one woman?'

'One who really mattered. Some time ago. I hadn't long been in the City, my uncle arranged for various tutors to take care of my education . . .'

She laughed, 'Your uncle was very generous in his provision of tutors.'

'Not like that. She was the daughter of a man who taught intellectual discourse.'

'People teach intellectual discourse?'

'Not well, according to my detractors.'

'Your discourse is fine, Justinian.'

'Yours is better.'

'I was better trained, and certainly not in intellectual discourse. Tell me about this girl.'

'She wasn't a girl.'

'No?'

'I was fifteen, she was nearing thirty.'

'Ah, the spinster daughter of your intellectual discourse teacher. What was wrong with her?'

'Nothing at all. She had never wanted to marry, and I loved her, and it was impossible.'

'Where is she now?'

'A convent. She didn't want any of the men her father could find for her. A teacher, he couldn't offer much in the way of dowry anyway. When she was young it might have been possible, but she said there were no good offers . . . she was a strong woman.'

'You like strong women?'

Justinian turned on his back, one arm behind his head. With the other he pulled Theodora closer. 'I do.' He could feel her smiling and added quietly, 'In their place.'

'Of course,' she replied, neither entirely sure if the other was serious or not. There would be time to find out.

'As she grew older it became impossible. Her father died, she had no skills, she was too old for a conventional marriage, even if she had wanted one. I had Narses find her a place. I believe she is happy.'

'You don't see her?'

'It's a convent, Theodora.'

'So?'

'I don't see her. She wouldn't see me anyway.'

'You tried?'

'I asked before she went in. She said if she was going to do it at all, she would do it well.'

'Not many do.'

'No. But she has always done what she wants, and done it wholeheartedly.'

Theodora shifted against him, toes on her left foot cramping as she did so. 'It would seem so.'

'How?'

'Teaching you. Wholeheartedly.'

Justinian was puzzled, 'Teaching me?'

'This, sex, love-making. Your skill.'

'Oh no, she didn't teach me that, she taught me passion. Love, certainly, but she didn't teach me that.'

'Then who did?'

'There was another girl. At home.'

'You left Illyricum at twelve!'

'Almost thirteen. We grow up fast in the West.'

When they laughed it was easy, when they slept it was quiet, and when the servant called to wake Justinian in the morning, Justinian did not pretend Theodora was not in his bed, but asked that washing water be brought for her too. He helped her dress, tidy her hair, fit her slippers before she walked from his rooms. He thanked her for spending the night with him. It was the first time any man had ever thanked her for sleeping with him, and it brought Theodora to tears – but only once she was safely in the privacy of her own room. Justinian might be willing to tell his secrets, and she was delighted to hear them, but Theodora needed to keep hers. She was marrying in a fortnight. Her stories, and the emerald, would be all she had left of her own. It would take more than a night of great sex and easy friendship to make her give them up.

Thirty-Four

Three years after her return to the City, fourteen months after Euphemia's death, six months after the law allowing her marriage was passed, Theodora entered the Church of Hagia Sophia a single woman, and emerged married to the man who would in time, Justin had promised, be Emperor. She went in through the heavy front doors, past dark wood and warm stone, was lit by sunshine through windows of translucent alabaster, while candlelight refracted from gold mosaic tiles, glinting off her own jewels and the cloth of gold that Esther had made for her. She followed the procession as they had rehearsed, and then, for the first time in her life she stood – with permission – in the body of the hundred and twenty year old church. Her church, the place she had felt safest as a child, the cool marble that had given solace to her aching flesh, the chanting and praying and liturgy that had provided the background for her dreams of escape, were now the foreground of her very real wedding ceremony.

Up in the gallery the women were watching. Her mother, aware that she was no closer to this Theodora than to any of her daughter's previous incarnations; Theodora's much-vaunted rise in status could only increase that discomfort. Ana, amazed that this creature in gold silk could be her mother, the woman she barely remembered from her childhood, the mother she had slowly, haltingly, come to know a little more since her return, the mother who had already begun making arrangements for her own betrothal in a few years. Comito watched too, a little envious, she could not deny this marriage was the greatest thing either of them had ever achieved, but much more relieved. She would use Theodora's rise in rank to help herself, the law change that had benefited Theodora would also be valuable to her as an ex-actress. Theodora had found a husband inside the Palace walls, there might be another man there for Comito; certainly she would be more attractive to those men now that her sister was Justinian's wife. At twenty-six, Comito had been earning her own living, and helping to provide for their extended family, for over fifteen years. She would not relinquish the title of elder sister, but she was very happy to let Theodora take on the responsibility. The middle sister had greater rank now, let her use it for all their good.

Beside the women of the family, stood Sophia, higher than usual on a raised box. Of all those watching, her joy was possibly the purest. Sophia could never have been there in Theodora's place, her body made it impossible, it was easy for her to feel simple joy for her friend's good fortune. As friend rather than family, her pleasure in the day was far less complicated than that experienced by the mother or the sister beside her, and so she held Ana's hand to make her feel safer. Sophia was sorry for the girl by her side. Theodora had done well to keep Ana out of the theatre, the girl was no performer, was shy in company, quieter still in public, but now as Justinian's step-daughter, they could no longer keep her in the shadows. It was time someone helped her find her voice, and if Theodora did not care to help the child, then Sophia would take it on herself. It was a while since she'd had a special project, and Ana would definitely be a challenge.

There was a brief pause in the ceremony below, in the droning voice of the Patriarch Epiphanius, and, infinitely briefly, Theodora looked up and back. It was barely a move, something

Menander had taught them long ago, a way to check what was going on at the side of the stage, or the highest tier of the audience, to move without moving, look without being seen to do so. She was looking for Sophia. Their eyes met for no time at all and then Theodora was back in the perfect placing for a nearly wed woman, eyes downcast, listening, waiting, not speaking, while the man she was marrying and the priests made the statements necessary on her behalf.

The presence of her women made all the difference to Theodora, Sophia in particular. A month earlier, when they were planning who would be present, where they would stand, in what order of precedence and priority, Theodora had fought solidly with Narses for more than a day, and, astonishingly, had won in the end. She thought it was because he had finally realised, despite so many years in the institution of the Palace, that it was right the women she cared for should be there to support her. The truth was that Justinian had eventually stepped in and told Narses to agree, he was bored with the argument and there were more important things to worry about, among them Justin's health and mutterings of Germanus' unhappiness. Justinian was a little surprised that his wife-to-be was behaving quite so much like a traditional bride, overly concerned with position and rank and clothes, things he thought irrelevant, but he also took her point that the wedding was an important opportunity for them to show themselves to the people as a couple. Theodora believed the people would expect to see her favouring her own family and friends, that it would look odd, and unkind, if she did not. Justinian was persuaded, Narses was commanded, Theodora had her way.

So now Hypatia, Comito, Ana, Indaro and Sophia stood at the front of the gallery, even if Juliana Anicia and her old cronies, five places along, had glared from the moment they

299

began to climb the women's stairs, and glared still from behind hands composed in pious prayer. The women of Theodora's family could, with her help, make themselves look just like all the other wealthy women of the City arranged around the gallery, all the women who were now craning their necks – and trying to look as if they weren't – to get a look at the theatre slut who had taken the place they'd wanted for their own daughters or granddaughters. Her family could dress just like the women who so despised them, they could, mostly, pass as ladies; Hypatia and Comito in particular were doing a very good job of it today, but Sophia never would, and that delighted Theodora. Sophia looked beautiful in the dark red silk Esther had made for her, slippers to match, and Theodora's gift of the pearls she now wore, tiny black pearls at her ears and throat, perfectly formed in miniature. Theodora had no doubt that same dress would be flung to the floor before the day was out, the new slippers would certainly rip on whatever uneven floor or table Sophia found herself dancing upon, but she knew, too, that the pearls would be kept safe, in case they were needed to keep Sophia safe. She had left her friend behind once before, she would not do so again.

There was someone else she would not leave again. He stood slightly apart, downstairs, in the place of the men, but not. Armeneus had arrived at the Chalke Gate three days earlier, demanding entry: he had a precious gift from the Governor of the Pentapolis, a wedding tribute for the blessed couple. Theodora would probably never have been told he'd even arrived if he hadn't somehow managed to convince the guards to at least let him speak to Narses. Apparently the older eunuch found the younger one very persuasive and Armeneus, exhausted from his long journey and with a smile as wide as the Bosphorus, was finally shown into Theodora's rooms.

'Took you long enough, I thought you'd be waiting for me

when I got off the boat,' Theodora said, dismissing her servants with a nod and wrapping her arms around the young man.

Armeneus hugged her back and then stepped away, looking around the room at the hangings, the mosaic floor, the sparkling glass and gold, more sumptuous than anything he'd ever seen in Africa or on his journey to the City.

'They said you'd done well for yourself.'

'They?'

'People on the ship.'

'Ah, bitter gossip.'

'No, not at all. They like you, and they like that you've done well. You're them.'

'Yes, I am.'

They smiled at each other again then, both very aware of all that had passed since Theodora had run out into the night five years earlier, the enormous difference in their status.

'Should I have bowed?' Armeneus asked.

'Not yet. After the wedding maybe, and certainly in front of the servants. You are staying for the wedding?'

'If I may. That's why I'm here. They sent me.'

'You're the envoy from the Pentapolis?'

'You thought I was going to remain a houseboy all my life?'

'Not at all. I'm just a little surprised you stayed working for that bastard for quite so long.'

'It wasn't as easy to get away as I thought. She . . .'

'Chrysomallo?'

Armeneus nodded. 'Yes, things weren't easy for her.'

'Oh. Good.'

'She had a hard time in the birth.'

'Wonderful.'

'And he . . .'

'Treated her badly?'

'Eventually, yes.'

301

'So you stayed to be her friend? I thought you had more ambition.'

'So did I.'

Theodora frowned. 'She doesn't need your friendship now? What changed?'

'The Governor has a new woman.'

'A wife?'

'No.'

'Just another slut then. So where has she gone? Did he keep the child?'

'He threw them both out, six months ago. We had heard about you and the Consul.'

'News travels slowly across the sea.'

'Good news, yes.'

'I told her to come and ask for your mercy, that you might help. But she said she didn't want to trouble you more, she took the child to Alexandria.'

'There's plenty of work for whores in Egypt, she'll be fine.' Theodora had no intention of talking further about Chrysomallo. 'So what about you? I assume you have a gift for us or a tribute from the Five Cities?'

'I do.'

'Good. I'll get someone to destroy it.'

Armeneus shook his head. 'You don't even want to know what it is?' Theodora shrugged and he produced a small ivory pyxis, beautifully carved, barely the size of his hand. 'A jewellery box.'

'How appropriate. Seeing as he wouldn't give me a ring.'

'I think she chose it.'

'Yes, she would.'

'It has the Holy Menas on it, see?'

'To remind me of the wonderful time I had in Africa and Egypt? Tasteful.'

302

'And there's an owl here, on the lid, she thought you might like it—'

Theodora stopped him. 'Armeneus, I don't care. Really. You keep it. Or sell it.'

'You don't want it?'

'No. And nor do I want you to ever mention either of them again. The Governor will be losing his job soon enough, it sounds as if she's already living her punishment, I don't need to think about them more. Now, let's get you a bath and some new clothes and then see what we can find for you to do. I assume you're not desperate to get back to the armpit of Africa? I'm sure Narses can find something useful for you to do – he seemed to approve of you.'

Armeneus grinned, 'I try. And yes, please, I would love a bath. And a job. And anything else you've got to offer.'

'Good. I like a willing man.'

'So you haven't changed that much.'

'Some would say I haven't changed at all, Armeneus.'

Theodora quietly acknowledged her friends in the church, the Patriarch chanted on, the chorus intoned, prayers were offered, a litany was sung, more prayers, then the liturgy, then the sacraments, the incense and the heat of the church pressing them all in – all those bodies close together, all the candles, the warm alabaster-filtered sunlight adding to the slow ceremonial of the occasion. Everyone in the building, as well as those outside, waiting in the Augusteum and out in the Forum of Constantine to see the newlywed couple, ready to raise a cheer for this union of state and people, everyone knew the form and the content of the service, any of them could have followed it without thought, and yet today, in the body of the church and in the squares of the City, there was a sense that something important was about to happen. Partly this feeling had been fanned by the leaders of the Blues, two of their own, from very different ends of the spectrum, who were about to stand together as man and wife; it was a good time to be a Blue. Partly it was the myth of Theodora that the theatre people were now pumping up. The brothel-to-bride story was too exciting for any of them to let pass without taking a piece for themselves: anyone who was anyone in theatre had now once danced with Theodora or sung with Theodora, held her arm in an acrobatic display, passed her a mask for her mime, inherited a cast-off cloak for a new show when Theodora was done with it. The number of men who recalled moment for moment her triumphs on stage, in particular the comedy of her farewell show with the geese, were at least double the audience who had actually attended that performance. There was a thrill to be had from just being in the City on the day, something to tell the grandchildren years later, the day that Theodora-from-the-Brothel married the Emperor's nephew. When Justinian took the throne, as was now so generally assumed as to have become an expectation, then there would be an even greater celebration, more exaggerated stories to tell. For now, this was the biggest party Constantinople had seen in a while. It would suffice and, for once, the nuptial mass would be given its due attention.

Rings were exchanged, blessings given, more prayers, more chants intoned, someone cried – not Theodora, she had cried enough in this church – someone else fainted, and finally the nuptial crowns were placed on their heads and the happy couple, the new couple, turned and walked hand in hand from the church. Now Theodora did look up, directly, intentionally, wanting to be seen blowing a kiss to her mother, her daughter, her sister, her friends, waving openly from the body of the church, nodding too, to Juliana Anicia who did not dare refuse to nod back. Then Justinian squeezed her other hand, and Theodora, the good wife, publicly good wife, returned her gaze to the priests and prelates waiting on them, to the men before her.

With Justinian she bowed to the Emperor, the man who was now also her uncle, the old man who was ill and sincere and kind to her and who had also driven thousands of people who believed as she did from the City, had put some of them to death, had exiled Severus. Theodora bowed and blessed both of her spiritual mentors and Macedonia as she did so. Then they walked out into the Augusteum and from there to the main streets in public procession. Theodora thought the man beside her, the husband beside her, did very well, nodding to the crowd, waving as she had taught him for the consular celebrations, looking directly at individuals and smiling as if each one mattered, not so briefly that the targeted individual realised it was part of the act, not so long they thought it meant something more, taking each one in for a moment and no longer, so that within five minutes he had seemingly greeted every second person ranged around them to his side, and she had done the same to hers. They made a good team.

The people were cheering and waving, Justinian's men were doing a fine job of handing out alms to the poor, nice and fast with no messy tears or gratitude holding up the giving. The early evening sky was a high, clear blue, the gentle wind from the sea a welcome change from the high heat inside, and Theodora breathed in the welcome rapture of the assembled crowd. Someone at the back started to clap and the applause quickly rippled forward through to the front rows; for one wild moment she thought she might just get away with a fast flick-flack, a swift cartwheel, really give them something to cheer about, and then she remembered where she was and who she now was and that she would never again be that performer. A different kind of performance might be needed, but never again one of leaping and flying from solid ground. She stilled herself, made her tense muscles ease, forced herself to walk slowly, breathe calmly. She did not need the spring in her step now, but it was hard to hold it down. Theodora had to admit, she had missed the theatre, but at least she wouldn't have to give this costume back at the end of the night, and while Justinian was, in many ways, in every way, now paying her to be his companion, she was happy for that to be the case. Theodora and the girls she had grown up with, trained with, worked with, had always understood marriage to be a sanctified prostitution. Despite her friendship with Justinian, her pleasure in their passion, this view had not changed: she knew herself now to be his.

That night, after she had been bathed again and her skin oiled with precious perfume, and she had been led through underground passages and hidden staircases to their new marriage chamber, dressed in even finer silks, and offered up to her husband as the virgin bride neither believed in, as she lay awake beside him and listened to the regular rhythm of her husband's breathing, in the few hours of sleep he allowed himself before starting work again, Theodora knew she belonged to her husband, not emotionally, but literally. She was pleasantly surprised at how content she felt about the trade-off. She hadn't stopped being a businesswoman and after all, it wasn't as if she'd just married some actor.

Thirty-Five

Justinian's life after the wedding went on very much as before. He still spent hours locked away in his study with his papers, working both alone and with his advisers on his grand new idea for the legal system, the project just in the planning stages and none of it especially interesting to Theodora. He still worked on budgets and ideas for new building schemes, made himself available to Justin several times a day as an adviser and, more often than not, though Justin did not make it obvious, their discussions were a way for Justin to educate Justinian in the intricacies of higher-echelon politics. In the first months after the wedding, much of their talk was about how best to deal with unrest between the two factions, the more often reported presence of knives in the fighting, as they questioned whether now was the time to be seen to be enforcing the law, or to sit back and trust the people. Justinian, supported by Narses and Belisarius, counselled taking their time, speaking to the Blue and Green elders, not making a fuss, not until it was really necessary. The Emperor, in almost constant pain now and understandably less patient was, along with Germanus and Hypatius, all for sending in the military to quell the excesses of the young men once and for all. The argument for restraint was won, though possibly this was less to do with the power of Justinian's reasoned thought, than with the fact that Germanus was as much in awe of Belisarius as every other military man. There were private and public audiences with the Patriarch of Constantinople, balanced against long missives from Timothy in Alexandria, and occasional more secret letters from Macedonia to Narses, shared with both his bosses. Justinian and Theodora both hoped that in time and with a further elevation in status, they might be able to effect greater communion between the two sides of the religious divide. In public though, Theodora could not admit her more Eastern leanings, and the old Emperor was still vehemently opposed to any suggestion that the Church might accommodate both views, no matter how keenly Justinian feared the possibility of schism. With Justin openly readying himself, and his advisers, for his death, it was business as usual, and Justinian working even longer hours than before.

Theodora's daily life was more obviously changed. The more blatant Justin became about his desire to have Justinian succeed him – and the rumours that the old man was ready to name her husband as Caesar were becoming more pronounced – the more there was for Theodora to learn. Narses, though busy with his own work for both Justin and Justinian, undertook to arrange a series of master-classes for Theodora. While she was very happy to support her husband, she was slightly less keen to find that her mornings were now to be given over to tutorials in everything from international geography to Imperial history.

'Narses, I know the shape of the world. I can't go into Justinian's study without seeing the maps he has pinned up all over.'

'Good, then those tutors will be dispensed with quickly and we can spend more time on your knowledge of history, both state and Church.'

'I'm his wife, not his adviser. I don't need to know these things.'

Narses let out a snort that turned into a cough. Since their marriage and Theodora's elevation in status, he'd been trying to be more polite to the young woman, but it was clear he found it hard.

'What?' she asked.

'Theodora – Madam – you and I both know very well that no matter what protocol demands, the Consul will speak to you of his work. He will engage you in discussions about territories and dominions, there is every chance that he will do so even more in future. He already asks your opinion . . .'

'And I give it.'

'It has been noted. So you will understand, therefore, that both the Emperor himself and the Patriarch—'

'Which one?'

'Timothy, Madam, of Alexandria, though I would not say so outside this room.'

'Go on.'

'Both learned men are concerned that you should be able to offer the best advice. Not simply now, but in the future. They would have you—'

'Trained? So I can best force their own views on my husband?'

Narses shrugged. 'Both wise gentlemen, they disagree on several important points of theology, as you well know. I don't imagine they are of one voice on all matters. They would, however, have you as well informed as possible, the better to be . . . useful.'

'Oh yes, I only want to be useful.'

Narses tried again. 'It is clear the Consul respects your views.'

'Shame everyone else doesn't.'

His smile was closer to a grimace now but he didn't bite. Clearly the effort of maintaining a polite demeanour when he wanted to shake her was wearing him down – wearing his teeth down too, Theodora guessed from the set of his jaw – and she was rather enjoying forcing him to dispense with the strained politeness he'd taken on since her marriage and get back to his old self, the one Menander would no doubt have preferred, the one she'd heard Armeneus now preferred – if Palace rumour was to be trusted, and it usually was.

'For God's sake, Narses, spit it out. I have no actual learning. Other than Menander and the relatively brief time with Severus and Timothy, I never had a real teacher, not one I listened to anyway. What little I do know I gained from my own life, from my travels. We both know that. You civil servants and military would have me know what you know, believe what you believe, so you can use me to influence my husband when he is beyond your reach and yet still within mine. Am I right?' Narses did not reply, so she went on, 'I'll take that as a yes. You've all finally realised that Justinian takes me seriously, and you're also only too aware of what will come when the old man, when the Emperor, well . . . so now you want me to think what you think so that I can make Justinian also think what you think. That is how power works, isn't it?'

Narses looked at her, long and hard. He rubbed his face and went to the window. From his office he could see down to the Hippodrome, catch a glimpse of the markets and the Mese beyond. He called Theodora to the window and waited while she crossed the floor, her reluctance to come too close shown by the drag of her feet, by the way she stood slightly behind him. He was not Menander but, having pushed him this far, Theodora was not sure he might not lash out at her in the way his old lover all too often had.

'Power has very little to do with how the people behave towards you, Theodora, and everything to do with what you know. You can't understand that yet, not fully, but you will.' Narses spoke quietly and forced her to come to him. When she was beside him, he asked, 'What do you see out there?'

'The City.'

'Specifically?'

'The Hippodrome, obelisk, church roofs, buildings. The people. My people, I know these people, I know what they're like, I don't think there's anything you can tell me about them, Narses.'

'You know what it's like to be in them, to be of them.'

'And that is useful to my husband.'

'It certainly is, but you have no idea what it is like to lead them, to stand in front of them.'

'I stood in front of them on stage.'

'Yes, because they let you. If they had not wanted you there, they'd have made it clear soon enough.'

'They did, on occasion, until I persuaded them to want me.'

'Good. And do you think you can persuade them to want you as Empress?'

'I don't . . . we shouldn't . . .'

Narses shook his head, 'No, we shouldn't, but we will. There's only you and I here. Tell me, do you think you can persuade them to accept you as Empress? As you are now? This Theodora? The one they still remember from the stage, the one some of them believe has bewitched the Consul with her sex, others are sure has bewitched him with Egyptian drugs and Coptic magic, while some even think that he is a lover of men – why else would he have me so close after all? – and you are just here to make him look a better Christian.'

'They really think that?'

'That's my point. You have no idea what they think any more. Even your own sister can't tell you exactly what's going on out there, because people are different around her too, now that she is the sister of Theodora first, Comito second.'

'And how that angers her.'

Narses ignored her; sibling rivalry was the least of his

concerns right now. 'You were of these people, you did know them, you played them and they were happy for you to play them. It was a pact created between you, as performer, and audience, you made them love you, laugh with you, and because of that you can be useful to Justinian, who will never be of them. But I assure you, you have no idea who they are now, any more than they know who you are since you have travelled, since you have found faith, since you have become a wife. I have people out there who report to me every day, from both Green and Blue camps, from every faithful sect and none, men and women, locals and refugees, rich and poor. Yes, we wanted you for Justinian, and when it became apparent that might work, we were delighted.'

'We?'

'Some of us in the Palace, others in the Church. You complete him in some ways that were sadly lacking. You are of the City, as he is a foreigner. You are of the people, as he was raised in the Palace. You are—'

'Common?'

'As he is, through his uncle, royal. Despite the obvious problems in getting you beside him, it is a good match, but don't kid yourself it will suffice. You found it hard enough to cope with the animosity of the likes of the old Empress and Juliana Anicia, how will you cope when sitting with the Persian ambassador and he asks you about his country's policies regarding the Nestorians, asks you because he knows you don't know and he wants to take home a story about how the brothel girl could not compete with his Sassanid sophistry? How will you support Justinian to deal with warring bishops and patriarchs – and believe me, it may well come to that – if you only know your own beliefs, and then only from personal experience, and have not read the lessons and treatises that would give you greater understanding, more measured sympathies, wise counsel to share with this man who will come to need you even more than he does now, this man you have married, who has given you so much in the transaction?'

'I've given back to him.'

'What? Sex? He could have got that anywhere. And with less aggravation from the likes of his aunt and the City dowagers.'

'It's more than that.'

'Is it?'

Theodora's voice was quieter now. Thinking as she was speaking, opening her mouth and surprising herself, she said the words, 'I love him.'

She had not said this before, had not knowingly thought it of the man who had become her friend before he was her lover, but understood it to be true as the words were formed and spoken.

Narses paused, took it in. 'Then act as if you do. You've been married for six months, you should be used to it by now. This really isn't about you any more.'

His point made, Narses left the room, his own room, and Theodora could not have felt more like the eight-year-old bludgeoned into Menander's idea of trained elegance if she had been made to stand on one leg, in perfect attitude for half an hour, before kissing her master's left foot in penance for being insolent yet again.

Later that day she called Narses to her and agreed to his offer of lessons. He smiled and accepted her request as if it had all been her own idea, congratulating her on her good sense.

'I do want a favour from you though, in return.'

'Madam?' Narses was irritated, he'd made his point perfectly well, was not expecting an exchange.

'I have heard, from Leon, the uncle of my friend Sophia . . .'

'Sophia the dwarf?'

313

'Yes, that's the one.'

'Nice voice.'

'She thinks so. Anyway, there was a man, a trader, on the ship from Antioch.'

'When you came back?'

'Yes. I have heard from my friend's uncle that this trader has been dealing in young girls. There was a pilgrim family on the ship and Leon now thinks he saw one of the two daughters, Mariam, in the slave market. She was bought by a dance master, apparently.'

Narses simply looked at Theodora, waiting for her to continue. When she did not, he asked, 'Yes?'

'She was a sweet child, innocent. I would not wish for her . . .'

'It may be too late, Madam.'

Theodora was tired of the coyness. 'Yes, it may be too late for her virginity. But you know as well as I do that most of these dance masters are little more than whore traders. Even your beloved Menander sold us when we were girls, both as dancers and as women.'

'And you would like to save just one?'

Narses couldn't keep the cynicism from his voice, or he wasn't trying. Theodora couldn't be sure, but she wasn't going to fight with him.

'Narses, do I have any power with you at all?'

'Madam, you are my master's wife. Of course you do.'

'Right. Then send someone to Leon, get a description of the dance master, find the girl and bring her to me. And find out where the trader is while you're at it. The one who sold her to him in the first place.'

'Madam, this is impracticable, it was four years ago—'

'I don't care,' Theodora hissed, furious. 'Yes, it's quite probably too late. But I saw that trader spot her on the ship and

314

there was nothing I could do to stop him then. There is something I can do now. Or rather, there is something you can do now. I'm sure, Narses, you have the ability to make something happen? You seem to have made such a lot happen already. Lessons and tutors and . . . well, there was Euphemia's opposition to my marriage . . .'

Theodora stared at Narses and he glared back. He understood she knew him better than his other masters had, knew him as well as he knew her.

'I'll see what I can do.'

'Thank you.'

'Your first tutor will be here in half an hour. You should be ready.'

'I will.'

'Good. I'll get back to you.'

With Leon's help and Sophia's connections, Narses found the girl within the week. He was right, it was too late to stop her being used for sex, but Theodora was sure it was not too late to give her some new hope. The family had long ago given up on finding their child and moved away, she had no one. Theodora arranged for Mariam to have a place in her own retinue, plenty of time to play with the children of other staff, and with Ana who now lived in the Palace with Comito and Indaro. Mariam barely spoke, and smiled less, she was a very different child to the one who had played so openly on the ship, but Theodora once heard her humming almost happily as she and Ana played in a corner of a warm courtyard; the girls were obviously company for each other. Having grown up closer to her sisters and her fellow dancers than to Hypatia, Theodora relaxed a little seeing the girls together – she might never be the best mother for Ana, maybe it was too late now to become any more than an interested adult – but with a friend of her own, Ana might

315

do well enough. She would certainly never want for food or clothing or money, never have to work with her body as Mariam had already been forced to.

The trader himself was found several weeks later, his mutilated corpse dumped well outside the City walls. When Narses passed on the news to Theodora she congratulated him. He told her he had no idea what she was talking about, and reminded her that her afternoon lesson would begin soon, she'd do better to spend more time in preparation than in imagining extravagant scenarios: apparently her grasp of early philosophy was really quite poor.

Thirty-Six

There were those in the City who saw Justinian and Theodora's marriage as a great new start for the Empire, exactly as Narses maintained; they believed the two were a perfect coming together of rich and poor, East and West. Those who knew about Theodora's links with Timothy and Severus – and it was not something that had been widely promoted – saw hope for the Church in their union. These were the citizens who entirely approved Justinian's waterfront building works, loved the City's renewed ports and walkways, heard talk of the new cathedral being planned so far away in Ravenna, that last stronghold of true Roman Imperialism in Italy and loudly applauded the couple's work, who were quietly keen to see Justinian named Caesar, before or after the old Emperor's death, they didn't mind which. There were others, though, perhaps less outspoken, who were not concerned about the works of man, but who saw the earthquakes in Antioch, the floods in Ephesus, and the drought in Palestine, as part of a divine warning. A warning of what in particular they would not say, but a warning nonetheless.

In the two years following Justinian and Theodora's wedding it became increasingly obvious that age had suddenly caught up with the soldier Emperor. Already an old man when he came to the throne, Justin had given his best years and much of his strength to the military. Most of the young men now commanding his army were masters of rote-learned strategy; the Emperor's knowledge had been won on the battlefield, as his body was now reminding him. Suddenly Justin looked, and felt himself to be, the seventy-five-year-old that he was. Unlike his nephew, Justin had always been an intensely active man, which made it all the harder when ill health forced him to bed. He'd been barely content to allow the constraints of ruling to confine him to the Palace and the City, missing the freedom to ride out with his men whenever he wanted, and he now found it terribly frustrating that it was his weakness forcing him to keep to his rooms. There were still times when he felt better, occasions when he showed himself to the City and the Senate, as much for the happiness of the people as his own, but by late winter, when he could no longer walk ten steps unaided, when lying down brought on racking coughing fits, and sitting up the same, it was obvious the Emperor was preparing to die.

On the advice of his doctors and, eventually, by his own inclination, Justin began to further limit his public appearances. Soon after, with very little preamble, almost as a matter of simply stating what had come to be expected anyway, Justinian was proclaimed co-Emperor, anointed Caesar. The coronation was quiet by earlier standards, there was no big celebratory mass and meal as there had been for the wedding: the kind of money spent on the consular celebrations was happily saved for the City, and the citizens approved the economy.

Justinian's coronation was a serious, solemn occasion, performed on Holy Thursday, allowing a clear comparison between the Christ's passion and His sacrifice with the exaltation and similar sacrifice of rank. Purple-robed, in the chlamys of the August, and with the Imperial crown on his head, Justinian was now Justin's equal, in the sight of both God and the state – and he was more than thirty years younger. The Empire had had old men in charge for so long; Justinian was young and healthy and hopeful. His bride, at her own coronation three days later on Easter Sunday, was younger still.

318

Again the solemnity, again a quiet occasion by City standards. Where Justinian's coronation had taken place in Hagia Sophia, Theodora's was a more private event within the Palace, with a very few dignitaries present. The Patriarch of Constantinople stood with Justinian to represent God and law. Justin, still tired from Justinian's ceremony three days earlier, sat close by, watching carefully, pleased to see his plans for his nephew coming to fruition. Yes, his own wife had been against this marriage, but Euphemia had understood as well as he did that it was easier to govern with a partner, easier to rule with someone compassionate by one's side. Justinian had chosen Theodora from any number of women he had been offered over many years. The lad – the lad who was now a man – was no soldier, but he was bright and well read. His nephew had made his choice, Justin respected it. Anyway, he liked the girl, she had fire, and Justinian could do with some fire.

The night before the coronation, alone in her rooms, more nervous than she had ever been, worrying about what was to take place the next day, worrying that all the machinations and planning and organising by so many different people and factions to get her to this place were somehow forcing a position upon her that she did not have the right to take, Theodora found herself on her knees in prayer. After a time, in the kind of semi-trance she had not experienced since she'd been in the desert, she recalled her dream of the huge domed church, and the words promising that Mary was the star of Bethlehem. And then, not entirely sure if she was making this connection herself because she wanted to see it or because it was truly there, Theodora decided she did have the right to assume the crown. If a fourteen-year-old Jewess in Nazareth could be Theotokos, then a twenty-six-year-old ex-dancer could probably become Augusta. It was the kind of comparison that might also have her damned as a heretic, so she thought it best to keep it in her heart, and went quietly to bed, where she slept easily and well, waking smiling.

Later that day, Justinian raised the Imperial crown and lowered it on to his wife's head. The dutiful shout came up from the men in the hall, both blessing and acclamation. Theodora's resurrection in the purple was complete.

The immediate sign of the couple's new status was the move to the Daphne Palace, the Emperor's wing in the complex of buildings that made up the larger Palace. Bigger rooms, more light, better views of the City, an easier walk to the Kathisma, the Emperor's box in the Hippodrome where, when Justin eventually died, they would present themselves to the people. They had the right to do so now, but Justinian was wary of seeming too triumphant, and Theodora was surprised to find she was nervous about showing herself in the Hippodrome after all this time. The doctors thought Justin had some months yet; until then, the business of getting on with the Empire, the day-to-day life in the Palace would help both Justinian and Theodora prepare.

The City and the state went on, no matter who was in charge, and Justinian needed to take on his uncle's role more fully, to order his staff, get on with the job. The Emperor's rooms were a better place from which to do the Emperor's work. The civil servants who had spent Holy Week carefully and almost silently packing and transferring things from one place to another knew this only too well. Many of them had been around for the passing from Anastasius to Justin just over a decade ago, and a few thought they might well be here for the next changeover too. Some rulers were better than others, some leaders had skill in battle, others in business: each of them needed assistance and good guidance, with the minimum of fuss. There would be a funeral before the end of the year, and then there would be a single Caesar, one August and one Augusta, and both would be judged on their merits. Meanwhile, the business of the state went on no matter whose head was on the coins. For the Palace functionaries, it was always business as usual. Justin was carefully moved to a quiet wing where he could more easily rest, and Justinian was placed more firmly at the centre of their days.

That first night after both coronations, after the endless prayers, both for the celebration of Easter Sunday and the celebration of the August couple, Justinian and Theodora went together to their new rooms. Many of their things had simply been moved, but others had been entirely replaced – there was no need, for instance, for Theodora to keep a gown of red for ceremony, when now her only ceremonial wear was purple. Yet neither of them had so much as glimpsed the work that went into making the change happen. Justinian was used to this, had moved from City to Palace with Justin and Euphemia and then lived in different palaces inside these walls as his uncle climbed the ranks, so he understood the careful, quiet ways of servants and slaves. Theodora, even after five years in the complex, two of them as Justinian's wife, was still amazed.

'How did they do all this? All my things moved in three hours!'

Justinian walked to her room through the connecting offices and corridors between, not entirely grateful that her voice was so well trained he could hear her perfectly well despite their rooms now being so much further apart.

'Well, you don't have that much really, do you? When Euphemia used to take her staff away in summer, up to the hills, she needed a retinue of several hundred. It's not as if they had to shift a lot for you, you haven't had long to accumulate the stuff of an Empress.'

Theodora shook her head. 'You're too used to staff, Justinian. I promise you, this was a lot of work.'

'Then thank them, it's always good to show gratitude. They like that.'

Theodora nodded, suddenly unable to speak.

'What is it?' Justinian asked.

'Gratitude. I am grateful. Dear God, I am so grateful.'

She sank to the ground in front of him, the purple of her robe softer and smoother against the infinitesimally darker purple of his; she was laughing and crying at the same time, big racking sobs and gasps of hysterical laughter. Justinian looked around the unfamiliar room for a jug of water or wine to offer her, not knowing how to help his wife, who had collapsed in the centre of a deep and soft carpet he only now realised he had never seen before. It must have been brand new, made for her perhaps, a pattern of reds and swirling blues spiked through with gold flecks, clashing gorgeously with the robes she was wearing.

'Take this —' he found a glass and thrust it at her. 'It's been a long day, a long week. We're both tired. Come on, we'll be fine. I promise.'

He was kissing her and holding her, not sure what to say, repeating the only words he knew of comfort over and over, first in the Latin of his childhood, then more forcefully in the Greek of hers, hoping to get through the tears and the tremor that appeared to have overtaken her.

From inside the hysteria Theodora could see she was frightening him but it was all, just now, too much, and she truly couldn't stop herself. It was hilarious and awful and incredible, all at the same time. She was Theodora and a whore and a redeemed woman and the Empress. She had her emerald for safety still strapped beneath her breast and she was staining her purple robe with tears for all she had been and the woman she now needed to be. Everything had been organised and orchestrated by these men, by Justin and Justinian and Timothy and Narses, and now it was sinking in that none of this had ever been her ambition, her desire. She had gone along with it, and for the first time in her life she had accepted other people's plans for her without question. Finally it had come to fruition and only now was she becoming aware of what it really meant. She was the highest woman in the Empire and she was exactly the same. Everything had changed and nothing, and that she was still the same woman who had seen those revelations in the desert cave astonished her. The robes and the crown and the purple, even the anointing, she was still the same Theodora and she was Empress. The duality was impossible to comprehend.

Mariam appeared at the door, scared that her mistress needed her, or worse, that Justinian was harming her. Justinian waved the child away: if he didn't know how to make this better, he doubted very much that the damaged girl could. Theodora went on sobbing and laughing, and eventually, when his kisses and the wine and his holding her still seemed to have made no difference, when Justinian was ready to send for Antonina or Comito or Sophia, his wife abruptly pulled herself together, wiped her eyes, drank the glass of wine and sat up.

'I'm sorry.'

'It's all right.' Justinian wasn't sure it was, but he didn't know what else to say.

'No, it's not. I apologise. It's been a long day, a long time. I needed . . . a release. Or something. But I shouldn't have shown you that.'

'Why not?'

'You're my husband – Antonina would have slapped me, and been right to do so.'

'She damn well would not.'

'Antonina says we should never show ourselves as anything

323

but perfect to our husbands. Perfectly made up, perfectly poised, always composed, always ready to care for them. She's been married longer than I have, I expect she's right.'

'She's been married longer to a man fifteen years younger than her, I think that explains a great deal. Anyway, I'm not sure there is anyone else you can allow to see this. There is no one else I can show my fears or my joy to either. Other than Justin, and I wouldn't want to concern him now, he is too easily tired.'

'Yes.'

'So we are just the two of us. Here. And right now, we are not really husband and wife . . .'

'No?'

'We are August and Augusta. And while I am happy to see you as my honest Theodora, and have always been content to show you my failings, I agree with Antonina that no one else should see August and Augusta as anything less than perfectly controlled. There is no one who can see this but me, no one I can show myself to but you.'

Theodora sat back, her legs beneath her, twisted in her robes so that one thigh was almost completely exposed. Her arms were crossed in front of her and she hugged herself tight, feeling – as always – the press of the emerald bound beneath her left breast. She could feel the makeup her servant had applied this morning smudged down her cheeks, curls from the hair carefully arranged to hold the crown were stroking her back and one bare shoulder, there were tear stains on the perfect silk of her robe. Justinian sat in front of her, looking exhausted from his three-night Easter and coronation vigil: he was frowning hard and stroking her free leg with one hand, while pulling at his hair with the other, the most obvious sign he ever gave of his concern.

She laughed, 'No, I don't suppose there is anyone else we

can allow to see August and Augusta on the floor, in a mess of purple.'

She kissed him then, and the mess of purple and the soft new carpet were a soft new bed for two people making love on the floor of the Augusta's meeting room, two people who were higher than any other, taking joy in each other's body, Theodora the shield for Justinian's worries, he the shield for her fears. No one else would ever see them like this, their concerns about authority and governing, their elation at the elevation, the pleasure and terror of power as private as the bed.

Thirty-Seven

In the morning Armeneus, in charge of Theodora's new personal staff, let them both sleep a little later in the new rooms. Their privacy was not disturbed, but the scattered robes told their own story. Justinian was woken, late for him, at six, with honeyed water and the papers he needed to study – permits to allow or deny, petitions to analyse. Theodora slept on in her own bed until ten, the latest she had slept since coming to the Palace. When she woke she called for hot water and two maids. She wanted a long bath and breakfast of fruit, with fresh juices and perhaps some music if they could find a girl with a sweet voice. She was only joking when she said it, repeating the demands that, according to rumour, Juliana Anicia made every morning of her wizened old life, but she was delighted when she went to the bathing room and found it all laid on, little girl with lovely voice included. Theodora sank into the warm, scented water, looking at the exquisitely carved ivory of the new triptych that had been placed on her dressing table, another of her wedding gifts from Justinian, thinking she could possibly get used to this.

As Justin faded from bad to worse health, Justinian needed to immediately step up in every area of governing the Empire. There was both Ostrogoth and Visigoth aggression in the west, problems closer to home with the interminable small disputes between Green and Blue, the ongoing problem of potential schism with new claims from the Arian and Coptic branches of the Church and, as always, Persian demands for border negotiations. Justinian was also not entirely well himself. It was a far lesser complaint than the disease that had infested his uncle's lungs and was killing him, and therefore one he took some time to bring before the doctor, not least because he was shy about the ailment. What had started out as the lightly bruised testicle any healthy man in possession of an even healthier young wife might expect, was now a more intense problem, with swelling and pain and a discomfort that was not easily attributable to Theodora's kindness. The problem resolved itself after a while. The jokes that Theodora had battered her husband's privates with her excessive demands took a little longer to go away, but the rumour that perhaps Justinian would not now be able to father a child persisted – and Theodora did nothing to dispel the suggestion. She'd certainly seen him in great pain; the twisted testicle had swollen and reddened, and it had taken careful work on the part of a skilled Syrian physician to bring Justinian back to the role of a still-generous lover who was just a little less ready to spend the night on the floor with her. For all she knew, the passing problem truly had damaged his ability to make her a mother again. At the very least, it took the pressure off Theodora, stopped the City's high-born women from looking quite so intently at her belly whenever she was in public.

Once her husband was perfectly well and constantly busy again, Theodora was thrown back on the company of her old friends and new Palace acquaintances. Old friends like Sophia and Leon were around, of course, but they were getting used to Theodora's change of role, having to ask her staff if they could meet up. It didn't sit easily with Sophia to have to time an appointment that didn't clash with a lesson in Persian etiquette or a discussion on Vandal history. No matter that she knew Theodora hungrily welcomed her company, Sophia herself needed time to adjust. Theodora knew her old friend would accustom herself to the new regime eventually, hoped for sooner rather than later. Antonina too was a welcome distraction, and her knowledge of court and military form came in very handy, but while she was keen to become better friends with Theodora, Antonina was far less interested in Palace life than most women of her age and class. She was an army wife, had been on tours of duty with her husband, would happily go away with him again, but while they were here in the City she saw it as her job to do her best for her husband and his men. Just at the point when Theodora could have done with a good new friend, Antonina was working daily on a military match-making task, and one that Theodora could not but approve, much as she wanted Antonina's company for herself. Antonina was endeavouring to bring Comito together with Sittas, one of Justinian's most favoured generals. Theodora's rise in station had not made Comito any less arrogant about her own work, it just meant she confined her performances to even more exclusive and better-paid events. Sittas was famously uninterested in anything or anyone but war, horses and his men, more or less in that order. If it could be arranged, their union would be a good move for her sister and her family – Theodora was finding marriage so much to her own liking, she did not want Comito to miss out on similar happiness. Antonina got on with the match-making and Theodora turned even closer to home for companionship.

Narses still looked in on her every now and then, but primarily to check on the reports from Theodora's tutors. According to most of them, she was doing as well as could be expected, and better than many had hoped. The eunuch offered a gentle nod of approval, but no more than that. Much as he'd encouraged her to get on with the work in the first place, she was the Augusta now, and as Justinian was so new to his job and there was so much to do getting him up to speed, it wouldn't do Theodora any harm to learn to be her own mentor.

More bored than lonely, Theodora tried making friends with some of the new servants she had been assigned, chatting to the woman who did her hair, trying to encourage Esther – who now came once a fortnight to discuss clothing requirements – to talk about her own life, but it quickly became obvious that while Theodora might be able to disregard her status, they certainly couldn't, and her overtures of friendship simply made them feel uncomfortable. The people attending her were pleased with their work. Most of them had jostled hard to get positions in the Augusta's household and none were prepared to risk losing the Empress' favour and losing their place. Friendship and secrets were fine between people who already knew each other, and Theodora might prove a friend in time, let her prove herself a good Empress first.

Finally, Theodora realised she would have to look elsewhere for companionship, and then the call came for her to visit Justin. The old Emperor had always been kind to her, especially surprising given his commitment to his wife, even more surprising given his disapproval of Theodora's religious mentor. He'd had time for the girl while Euphemia was alive, and these days he had even more. Justin realised he now had all the permission in the world to do exactly, and only, what he wanted; he also had very little time left to enjoy that freedom. As the old man became more frail, he took to asking Theodora to visit him more often.

Theodora had been trained from her youth to be a good listener and, with the classes Narses had arranged for her, she had become a better conversationalist. Both her husband and his uncle had been supportive of the idea of her new lessons, not that either man dared tell Theodora directly that they had been party to a discussion about her intellect and education – they happily left those delicate matters to the eunuch. Now she was developing an interest in matters Justin had himself learned to care about a great deal, the questions his own wife had been too frightened to discuss once he had become Emperor. Nervous of making the kind of mistake that would remind people of her past, Euphemia had been happy to offer her views to all and sundry, and regularly did, but never to her own husband. Theodora, though, had learned in Menander's training that mistakes were simply steps from which to move forward. Euphemia had been scared that her accent or her phrasing or a misinterpretation of foreign protocol would point up her slave origins, betray her as a product of her past, Theodora had no doubt that everyone knew her history, and the very few who hadn't known about her before were hearing it now.

She was the talk of the town. There were those in the taverns who railed against her promotion, who spat at her name in the bars, blessed themselves against catching her corruption when they stood in the same church, cited her husband's passing illness as another example of her dangerous ways. These detractors were few, but very loud. In some ways worse though, were her fellow performers who, so proud of her elevation, thought nothing of embellishing her story to give themselves roles in her past, more often than not as sexual partners. The whore-Empress had a known history: how simple then for a young man making a name for himself on the stage to cite himself as one of her early conquests and gain the kind of notoriety that went down very well indeed with the Hippodrome crowd – even better when his routine was about how well she herself went down.

Theodora had nothing to hide and everything to learn, and

to gain. Justin's militarily biased views on the history of the Empire, the various uses of the Latin she was coming to know better and the formal old Greek she was perfecting were all very useful, but far more interesting were his opinions on the elegant and intensely rigid court manners of the Sassanids compared to the rough Huns, the singing Celts in favour of the passionate Vandals. He knew them all, as often as not because he had spent time with these people, had met them when discussing treaties or borders, had faced them both in battle and in troubled peace. Now, childlessly facing his own death, Justin was anxious to pass on what he knew, he had shared this knowledge with Justinian over time but he wanted to make sure his opinions did not stay solely with Justinian. Especially knowing how eager Justinian was to empty the coffers Justin himself had filled all these years, he was keen to encourage Theodora to understand his thinking, for later, when he was no longer here.

Gratifyingly, Theodora did not just want to listen, she also asked questions. Where other people – analysts and students of military strategy – asked Justin what he and other soldiers had done, Theodora asked how he felt. Facts were all very well, but there were plenty of scholars both in the present and the future who would be able to provide Justinian with any number of facts for any number of scenarios. What really mattered in the moment, when pressing and difficult choices needed to be made, was the heart. How it felt to deal with this huge problem or that private joy, how it felt to know that every action, however small, would eventually be made public, be seen by all. Soon, Justin would die, and then the one man who had been in Justinian's position, who knew how it actually felt to command, to lead, would be gone, no longer able to offer his counsel.

And so Theodora dutifully spent hours by Justin's bedside. Even the most censorious of Palace staff had to admit they were impressed by the little whore's behaviour with the old man. It was good of her to humour him, especially now that she didn't have to, now that she and Justinian had the crown. What they didn't know was that now his censorious wife was out of the way, Justin was more relaxed than he had been in years. The old Emperor had a wicked sense of humour and, when he was detailing some of his less salubrious exploits in the army, admitting in a painful but animated croak that he, not his nephew, had been behind the deposition and execution of Vitalian, or whispering through pain and exhaustion his favourite story of the Greek whore and the dolphin – not a story he'd ever shared with Justinian – he also had a really very dirty laugh.

Thirty-Eight

The old man lay on the narrow bed. Those who had begun readying the body for the lying in state, for the funeral, hurried from the room. Justinian and Theodora, who had come to see their uncle, wanted an empty space and quiet. They did not want the bustle of funeral preparations, they did not need to see Justin in the clothes of his coffin, they simply wanted to spend some time, to say their prayers, in the presence of the old man's body. Both believed that his spirit had already departed.

Theodora was sure, contrary to all teachings, that Justin's spirit had probably gone some days before. She had been sitting with him when the pain became too great, when it was obvious he would not return this time, and he had whispered to her, as she held his hand, the papery skin dry and thin, the words gurgling in his throat against the fluid that was drowning him, 'I am worried to see Euphemia.'

She knew exactly what he meant, they had been talking more often of what was to come, what might be waiting for him, the truth of his wife as she was now: would her soul include all her temporal emotions and feelings, or would he merely find a form of her? Theodora had promised Justin that Euphemia would be gentle, though she was sure the old man knew she was offering the kind of soft truths given to the dying by anyone other than the most honest of priests.

She held his hand and spoke quietly. 'You are the Emperor, your choices were bigger than mere family allegiances, your

333

decisions have been for the City and more, for Rome. Justinian will do well, I promise. You trained him, and he has me as his support.'

In kindness to the old man who was in such extreme pain, fighting his own drowning on dry land, she deflected his fears from his dead wife's ire to the genuinely capable nephew. Euphemia had been fond of Germanus, had a certain respect for the Emperor Anastasius' relatives, but she'd loved Justinian. Justin knew it too, and he understood that Theodora was making it safe for him, easing his concerns with her quiet avoidance. He smiled and closed his eyes, his bony fingers moving restlessly in her hand. Even as she reassured him, Theodora was sure she could feel him leaving, his spirit moving away. Justin fell asleep that evening, and did not wake again.

Beside the thin corpse, Justinian prayed for the repose of his uncle's soul and for the strength to take on his work, to be the good son, to live up to the trust Justin had shown in him. He prayed to be a good Emperor.

Theodora knelt beside her husband and prayed, yet again, to be a good wife, to support Justinian, to be the perfect consort. She did not pray to be a good Empress. Empress was just another job, many people had been involved in getting her that appointment: her choice now was to be Justinian's partner, and it was for that role that she prayed.

They were quiet with the body, and quiet when they left, walking slowly back to the rooms that had not truly felt theirs while Justin was alive, rooms that would still take time to become theirs, now he had really gone.

Later, after the funeral, Justinian lay on his bed, Theodora stroking his forehead with a cloth infused in camomile and lavender.

Eventually, he spoke aloud, 'It's over.'

'Yes.'

'I'm old to consider myself an orphan, I know, but I feel it now, I feel them gone.'

'They were your family, it makes sense.'

Justinian cried a little, and Theodora continued to stroke his forehead. After a while they both slept for a short time and when she woke, Justinian was staring at her in the gloom of the semi-dark room, the sun nearly set, no candles yet lit.

'What is it?'

'It is just me now, isn't it?'

'In the purple?'

'With you beside me.'

'Yes,' she answered. 'With me beside you.'

He smiled then, and she smiled back, and a thrill of fear and excitement, astonishment and joy ran from one to the other. Grief was still present, grief for his uncle-father and for her friend, but it was not the only emotion, not at all.

A week later Justinian and Theodora, August and Augusta, walked the short distance from their state rooms, through the private tunnel to emerge into the Kathisma, the royal box of the Hippodrome, the box now draped in purple and gold and fresh greenery for their first presentation to the public. The capacity crowd of a hundred thousand were already in their seats. Most of them had been there since the early morning, many more stood crammed together on the top tiers, by the gates, outside the stands. The Imperial couple were in the heavy purple silk of Emperor and Empress, a small retinue behind them. Narses was already seated with Belisarius and Antonina, Comito and Sittas close by. Hypatia was keeping an eye on Ana and Mariam. Germanus was there, of course, as were Hypatius, Pompeius, Probus, and the ranks of senators, citizens and soldiers. Sophia was not seated, she was part of the troupe picked to entertain the crowd while they waited for the August to arrive.

The performances had begun two hours earlier. Coming closer to the doors of the Kathisma, Theodora knew exactly the temperature of the Hippodrome, could smell the heat in the arena, the sweet-acid perfume of the people's keen anticipation. She held Justinian's hand, feeling the new Imperial ring on her finger, with her own regal inscription, saw herself lifted on to her father's shoulders, carried out into the centre of the performance space, saw three little girls with flowers in their hair begging for kindness, saw the owl on her obelisk bringing her home.

Just before the doors were opened for them and Justinian walked out on to the Kathisma, he turned to her and whispered, 'I saw you once, years ago, at a dinner. You were a child and you stopped your little sister from being punished, you were the keeper and she the bear. You were magnificent. As you are now.'

She thought she might weep at the enormity of it all, and she heard Menander reminding her to take her time, to make them wait, to make them want her.

Justinian walked forward, a step ahead, the cry went up from the crowd, calling Emperor, calling August, and then he turned, holding out his hand for his partner, and the people called Theodora.

Bibliography

Bridge, Antony, *Theodora – Portrait in a Byzantine Landscape* (Academy Chicago Publishers, 1993; first published Academy Chicago, 1984)

Browning, Robert, *Justinian & Theodora* (Thames and Hudson, 1987)

Cesaretti, Paolo (trans Rosanna M. Giammanco), *Theodora Empress of Byzantium* (Magowan Publishing and Vendome Press, 2004)

Cormack, Robin and Vassilaki, Maria (eds), *Byzantium 330–1453* (Royal Academy of Arts, 2008)

Evans, James Allen, *The Empress Theodora, Partner of Justinian* (University of Texas Press, 2002)

Freely, John, *Istanbul: The Imperial City* (Penguin, 1998; first published Viking, 1996)

Graves, Robert, *Count Belisarius* (Penguin, 2006; first published Cassells, 1938)

Herrin, Judith, *Byzantium – The Surprising Life of a Medieval Empire* (Allen Lane, 2007)

——, *Women in Purple – Rulers of Medieval Byzantium* (Phoenix Press, 2002; first published in Great Britain Weidenfeld & Nicolson, 2001)

Maas, Michael (ed.), *The Cambridge Companion to the Age of Justinian* (Cambridge University Press, 2005)

Norwich, John Julius, *Byzantium: The Early Centuries* (Penguin, 1990; first published Viking, 1988)

O'Donnell, James J., *The Ruin of the Roman Empire* (Profile Books, 2009)

Procopius (trans G. A. Williamson), *The Secret History* (Penguin, 1981; first published 1966)

Rosen, William, *Justinian's Flea* (Jonathan Cape, 2007)

Salti, Stefania and Venturini, Renata, *The Life of Theodora* (Edizioni Tipolito Stear, 2001)

Author's Note and Acknowledgements

It goes without saying that this is a work of fiction – but I'll say it anyway. While Theodora was a very real person, like most women of history, her story has been hidden, watered down and in some cases (Procopius!) certainly exaggerated; all of which makes her ripe for fiction. And while I've done my best to offer a real setting – historically, geographically, politically – what personally excites me is the story and so there are inevitably moments where historical accuracy has been sacrificed for plot or pace or character. I'm a novelist, not a historian, and this book makes no claims to be the one true story – just a story.

There are many people who have helped with this new leap in my work, from those in Ravenna who proudly showed off their Eighth Wonder of the World, to those in London who made all the right noises when I first gave them my Theodora précis. Specifically, I also owe great thanks to: Antonia Hodgson, Zoe Gullen, Beth Humphries and everyone at Virago and Little, Brown, along with my agents Stephanie Cabot and Lucinda Prain, all wonderfully enthusiastic Theodorans. Chiara de Stefani and Nevio Galeati, Paolo Pingani, Giancarlo Daissè, Federica Angelini, Mariacristina Savioli of the Gialla Luno Nero Notte, Ravenna, who gave me the mosaics and a great time. Rehan Kularatne, who would make a splendid RA guide. Manda Scott, who made 'writing history' a little less scary. Shelley Silas, who has had to live with Theodora for far too long now. And the Board, as ever. A special thank you to Brooks of SE24 who showed me the magic garden and then said of the Theodora on his mantelpiece, 'Ask her questions, she will give you answers.' Maybe some of those answers are here.